No Man's Dog

Also by Jon A. Jackson

The Diehard
The Blind Pig
Grootka
Hit on the House
Deadman
Dead Folks
Man with an Axe
La Donna Detroit
Badger Games

No Man's Dog

A Detective Sergeant Mulheisen Mystery

Jon A. Jackson

ATLANTIC MONTHLY PRESS
NEW YORK

Published simultaneously in Canada
Printed in the United States of America

FIRST EDITION

Library of Congress Cataloging-in-Publication Data
Jackson, Jon A.
    No man's dog : a Detective Sergeant Mulheisen mystery / Jon A. Jackson.
        p. cm.
    ISBN 0-87113-920-0
    1. Mulheisen, Detective Sergeant (Fictitious character)—Fiction.   2. Police—Michigan—Detroit—Fiction.   3. Government investigators—Fiction. 4. Detroit (Mich.)—Fiction.   5. Drug traffic—Fiction.   6. Terrorism—Fiction.   I. Title.
    PS3560.A216N6 2004   2003069500

Atlantic Monthly Press
841 Broadway
New York, NY 10003

04 05 06 07 08   10 9 8 7 6 5 4 3 2 1

For Fritz, a man of inspiring character

No Man's Dog

Save the Sparrow

Cora Mulheisen was much older than she looked, a birdlike woman. It was the tightness of the deeply tanned skin on her face, which hardly seemed wrinkled, until you looked closely. Then you could see a very fine network of tiny cross-hatchings, as if drawn with a superfine nib using a faint sepia-tone ink.

She was eighty if she was a day, but she was very agile, with hardly a trace of creakiness in her gait, and she dressed as if she were a younger woman, in well-tailored slacks, an oxford cloth shirt, and a navy blue cashmere blazer. She wore cordovan walking shoes, the kind of oddly formal shoes that one might see at English hunt weekends—waxed and brushed to a dull sheen.

The hands always give it away. Hers looked too large and knotty, mottled with pale blotches and bony, the nails too thick. She fumbled for her reading glasses, which reposed in the breast pocket of the blazer.

Interestingly, her eyesight had improved remarkably with age. When she was sixteen she had begun to have trouble in school because of her eyes. Her mother had been reluctant to send her to the optometrist. In those days, a girl wearing spectacles was considered doomed to spinsterhood. But Cora laughed at her mother's fears. She loved her new glasses. She thought the tortoiseshell frames made her look sophisticated and intelligent. And the doctor had told her that, if nothing else went wrong with her eyesight, when she got older her myopia would be countered by a natural astigmatism. "You'll trade in your specs for reading glasses," he said. And so it proved.

She had largely given up regular glasses nearly thirty years ago, not long after she had belatedly discovered the joys of bird-watching. She had struggled with binoculars initially. They were clumsy and she couldn't focus fast enough to spot the bird. It was the glasses—they got in the way and one was too conscious of them. But as her distance vision improved she found that she could dispense with the glasses and now she was able to see birds and their distinguishing features even without binoculars, except of course at great distances. And, naturally, as one becomes more and more familiar with the birds, one learns to recognize them by a whole host of signs, such as shape or form, size, posture, general behavior, and so on; one "knows" instinctively what species a bird is, to a degree. In fact, she was the one to whom her fellow birders invariably looked for verification of a bird's identity. They would peer at a bird and say, tentatively, "Marsh wren . . . I think?" Then wait for her to say, "I think you'll find it's a sedge wren."

But the other part of the doctor's prediction also proved true: her close vision declined. Now, she held the reading glasses up to the light to see if the lenses were too murky, then perched them on her beaky nose. She looked around her seat for the bag in which she carried her papers.

Before her was a low dais on which several men sat, behind microphones. One of them was reading from a sheaf of papers. An American flag stood off to one side. Cora ignored what the man was saying, searching for her bag. After a moment, however, it was obvious that it was not with her. She leaned over to her neighbor, a middle-aged man in a tweed jacket, and whispered, "I've forgotten my questions."

He frowned. "Oh, dear," he said. "Are you sure? Perhaps you left them in the bus."

"That's what I mean," she said, nodding. "I left them in the bus. I'll just run out and get them. Won't be a minute."

The man nodded and Cora eased out of her row, one of several rows of folding chairs in this public room, most of them occupied by people who were listening to the droning speaker, or themselves rummaging through papers.

When Cora exited the room she realized right away that the first thing she ought to do was go to the bathroom. A policeman was standing in the hallway, evidently assigned to this municipal building, the site of the mayor's office, the council chambers, as well as courtrooms and hearing rooms. Cora asked the policeman where the public toilets were and he escorted her down the hallway a few feet and pointed toward the sign for LADIES.

She turned to thank him and, at the same time, noticed a young man being brought along the corridor, evidently a prisoner, dressed in an orange coverall, his hands behind him as if in restraints. He was guided by two uniformed policemen, accompanied by a couple of men in sport coats who she was sure were detectives. Cora's son was a detective, though not in this suburb of Detroit. The group stopped outside a door, before which was a sign on a stand describing it as the courtroom of a Judge Ed DePeau.

The policeman who had assisted her also watched the men outside the courtroom and lifted his hand to acknowledge the other officers, who nodded at him. Cora smiled at this but paid no further attention and turned back toward the restroom.

She was abruptly confronted with a man who issued from the MEN.

"Oops, pardon me, ma'am," he said. He held her by the arms to avoid crashing into her. "Are you all right?"

"Oh, I'm fine, thank you," Cora said.

The man looked over her shoulder intently, staring down the corridor toward the courtroom. He was a tall, nice-looking man wearing a Filson hat, one of those rakish waterproof canvas affairs that were popular with outdoorsmen. He seemed to her to be a youthful sixty, with the weathered face of a bird-watcher. She supposed he was with her group, or some related group, protesting the proposed draining of the Wards Lake marsh, but she had never seen him before.

He glanced down at her, still holding her stick-thin upper arms, in fact gripping them more tightly, as he suddenly blurted, in a low but intense voice, "Get out of this! Now!" Then he released her and hurried away with long strides.

Cora stared after his back, astonished, then called after him, indignantly, "But what about *Ammodramus nelsoni?*"

But the man was gone, around a corner. Cora took a deep breath, recovered her composure, and strolled on to the LADIES. Whatever this agitated gentleman was about, she refused to hurry. She knew the men on the dais would be talking for many more minutes before they allowed questions from the floor. She had plenty of time. She would protest the destruction of the habitat of Nelson's sharp-tailed sparrow, and no snippy antienvironmentalist could stop her.

Still, the encounter had startled her. She retained a vivid impression of the man's face, his dark eyebrows, the strong nose and firm chin, the glow of his eyes.

What was his problem? she wondered. Well, she'd no doubt hear from him when she got back. She attended to her needs quickly and then went out. The group by the courtroom had evidently gone in.

She walked out the front door of the municipal building and down the broad walkway toward the street. There was a drive that ran closely along the front of the building, separated from the not very busy street by a broad grassy median that was bounded by curbs. This drive was no longer accessible to the automobiles of the general public, being blocked at either end by heavy steel barriers, manned by police, a consequence of the new and heightened security that the public now endured, ostensibly because of terrorism.

Cora thought: This is the world we have to live in now.

The municipal building, a rather modern structure with tall expanses of tinted glass and immense wooden posts and beams, stood at the end of a broad avenue. A cross street passed in front of the building. As a further safety measure, a series of heavy precast concrete traffic dividers, tapered from broad bases to narrow tops, about four feet high and six feet long, had been arranged along the median between the drive and the cross street. This was not part of the original design to protect pedestrians from errant drivers—some iron posts had been sunk into the concrete of the walk to accomplish this purpose—but was supposed to prevent a motorized attack from the avenue. Cora, like most of the citizenry in this area, thought it was ridiculous and unnecessary. This suburban government building was hardly a terrorist target. This was just public officials going through the motions of being security conscious or, perhaps, taking themselves rather too seriously.

She spent no time on this thought, instead looking about for the bus. It had been granted a special permit to enter the drive, for the convenience of debarking passengers, and it had been allowed to park and wait there. It stood close by the entry to the building, at the head of a line of other vehicles, which appeared to be police vehicles, including the van from the county jail, which she noticed. Presumably, that was how the prisoner she'd seen had been transported.

Usually, her group traveled to these meetings in a yellow school bus that they rented from a company in her town, which was a different suburb of Detroit, miles away on the eastern edge of the vast Detroit metropolitan region. But for some reason, this morning the bus company had provided them with a much larger and fancier bus, which was welcomed because it was a warm day and this bus was air-conditioned. It was more of an inter-city bus, suitable for the highway, with comfortable seats.

There was another line of the waist-high precast concrete dividers between the drive and sidewalk that ran along the front of the building, but the bus had been drawn up next to the barriers. The old woman went up to the very front of the bus and rapped on the glass to get the attention of the driver, who was watching the activity of a large industrial machine, a noisy piece of heavy equipment. It was a front-end loader, she thought, and it nosed around the segments of concrete barriers next to the street like a monstrous yellow elephant, shoving them this way and that. It wasn't clear just what the operator was up to, and she supposed that was what was occupying the attention of the bus driver.

The driver turned at last, saw her, and opened the door with a hiss of hydraulics. He was a pleasant, heavyset black man wearing a nice black suit with a white shirt and red tie that could almost be a uniform, but wasn't, quite. He had introduced himself to the group when they had boarded as John Larribee. He had a neatly trimmed black mustache, which the old woman liked, and he wore dark aviator glasses. He was bald, which she also liked.

"Mr. Larribee," Cora said, speaking up to where he sat at the wheel of the bus. Cool air wafted out to her. He had arisen from his seat and taken a step down to help her up. "Thank you. I just need to find my bag. I'm afraid I left it in my seat."

"Yes, ma'am," Larribee said. "Can I help you look for it?"

"No thanks. I'm sure I can find it." She went past him toward the back of the bus. She found her bag, checked it quickly, finding her papers within, and returned to the front.

"Now what the devil is he up to?" Larribee said, looking out at the street.

"What is it?" Cora asked, peering around him.

"That guy's flattened all them posts and he's shifting them barriers," Larribee said. "And he ain't doing a very neat job of it. They must be gonna put some permanent barrier in there."

Then, as they both watched, the loader roared and lunged forward, shoving the barriers completely aside, one of them actually tumbling sideways into the street. The machine ran on down the sidewalk at an unusually fast pace.

"Holy shit!" Larribee yelled. He turned to the old woman and shouted, "Get off! Get off! Get away!" He actually pushed at her.

The old woman stumbled down the steps of the bus, missed her footing, and fell to one side, actually tumbling over and behind the barrier. She landed in an awkward and painful bump on her shoulder. In her amazement, the only thing she noticed was that the bus suddenly lurched ahead, blocking the entrance to the municipal building. A moment later, the bus was struck with a tremendous crash by something heavy and it leaned precipitously over toward the fallen woman. It hung there for a moment, then toppled sideways, crashing against the concrete barriers behind which the old woman was sprawled. Then there was a brilliant flash and a roaring noise even louder than the smashing and breaking tumult of the bus. She lost consciousness.

1

Wunney

You always remember the guy who brings bad news. In this case it was a detective from the Detroit Police Department's special operations. Mulheisen knew the guy, L. E. Wunney. They had worked together in Homicide. That was a long time ago now. Mulheisen had long since returned to the Ninth Precinct, his old stomping grounds. But he remembered L. E. Wunney, the guy now standing at Mulheisen's door with his raincoat open and his hands hanging at his side, seemingly at ease.

Mulheisen didn't recognize Wunney immediately . . . or, rather, he recognized him first for what he was, not who he was.

This is a cop. That's what was written all over Wunney. And even for Mulheisen recognition was followed by, *What did I do wrong?*

Wunney could affect one like that, even an old cop like Mulheisen (older than Wunney, for sure, and one of the city's ranking detectives, in terms of seniority, anyway. If he was still just a sergeant, it was only because he had managed to wriggle out of taking the test for lieutenant).

It was Wunney's face, Mulheisen thought. The face and the general beefy build. He was a man about Mulheisen's height, pushing six feet, but Wunney had much more beef on his frame, well-marbled beef, no doubt. Wunney's face had that implacable look . . . that flat, give-nothing-away, neither-joy-nor-sorrow look. The eyes were hazel and on the small side. They betrayed no special interest in what they observed, but it was certain that they observed it, shifting slightly to one side or another, up, down, taking it all in. As with any well-trained, experienced policeman, the hands hung free and ready to act. The raincoat was unbuttoned and so was the sport coat. Wunney also stood slightly to the side of the door, not directly in the line of fire. He was alone on the porch, although Mulheisen thought there might be another man in the nondescript gray car parked in his landlady's driveway.

The raincoat distracted Mulheisen. What was the significance of the raincoat in police work, he wondered? He wore one himself, often when there was no apparent need for a raincoat, as today, a day with a high, milky overcast. He supposed it was something to do with formality, a sense that one needed more than a sport coat to establish one's dignity and authority. An overcoat would be too much. It was also too expensive. Though, come to think of it, Mulheisen recalled that his Aquascutum had cost two hundred dollars, some time back. Wunney's raincoat was identical to Mulheisen's, but for some reason Mulheisen doubted that it was anything more than an inexpensive domestic version.

Annoyed at himself for these irrelevant (and snobbish) observations, Mulheisen opened the door. "Hello, Wunney," he said.

"Hi, Mul. Can I come in?" Wunney moved forward, knowing that Mulheisen didn't object. When they stood in the little foyer, Wunney glanced into the den to the left. A television, some easy chairs, and bookshelves declared its normal usage. Wunney made a questioning gesture.

"Let's go upstairs," Mulheisen said. They clumped up the stairs to Mulheisen's quarters, and all the way Mulheisen was still speculating on raincoats: was there some psychological significance, having to do perhaps with a detective's instinctive need for cover, for obscurity? But another vein of thought intruded: was he trying to ignore the warning signs of Wunney's visit? Had he violated some departmental rule? He didn't think so; he wasn't a rule-breaking guy. Still, there were rules he didn't even know about.

Mulheisen led Wunney to a room like the den below, except that this was all books and CDs, a stereo system, and no television. "Would you like a beer?" Mulheisen said.

"Ah . . . ," Wunney hesitated, then replied, ". . . got anything, you know . . . stronger?" He wiggled his big, thick fingers in a kind of gesture that was meant to suggest hoisting a shot glass.

"Sure," Mulheisen said. He opened a nearby cabinet and extracted a bottle of Irish whiskey—the good stuff, to privately atone for his snobbishness about Wunney's coat. He poured two inches of the whiskey into two glasses, handed one glass to Wunney, and lifted his own in a kind of toast. They sipped, sighed, and Mulheisen waited.

"Your mother's been hurt," Wunney said, weighing the empty glass in his hand.

"How bad?"

"Pretty bad. She's at Henry Ford. She's stable now, but you better go. I got the car, if you don't want to drive, but you might want your car there."

"Pretty bad . . . she's expected to live?" Mulheisen said. He felt unnaturally calm. When Wunney shrugged, he added, "What's the nature of her injuries? Bleeding? What?"

"Might be internal bleeding," Wunney said. "But no visible injuries except some scratches. She was in a vehicle, a bus, and a bomb went off nearby. Up at Wards Cove, the municipal building. They think it's Arabs. Terrorists. Five people killed, including the driver of the bus and apparently some people in the building. Your mother was the only one in the bus besides the driver. The other passengers had gone into a public meeting in the building. Your mother went back to the bus to get something. They think the bomb was in a car or a pickup that drove up just minutes before and pulled in front of the building, in front of the bus."

That was it. Things changed like that. One day you're sitting in your study, listening to old jazz records and perusing a manuscript sent to you by an amateur historian in Ohio, concerning a contemporary report on Pontiac's Rebellion. Then a man like Wunney comes to your door. Within a few days, Mulheisen wasn't a policeman any longer. He was a nurse, a son, a caretaker.

Cora Mulheisen lived. Spring and summer passed. Mulheisen no longer lived upstairs from a lively—possibly too lively—woman named Becky. He had moved back from that house to his childhood home in St. Clair Flats to look after his mother. She had not spoken a word in the interim. She was passive, sat when guided to a seat and gently pressed on the shoulder, capable at last of walking, shuffling rather absently along if held by the arm and directed.

This is what Mulheisen did now. He had assistance. A nurse came every day to help wash, dress, and feed Mrs. Mulheisen breakfast and lunch, but the nurse left at five. Mulheisen would feed his mother supper, then put her to bed. She would lie in the bed staring at the ceiling, but soon enough her eyelids would close and then it appeared that she slept. Mulheisen would sit with her for a while and then he would move to his old room nearby, where he could hear any noise that might issue from her room. None ever did. He couldn't even hear her breathing, and at first he had been like a new father, going into the baby's room at night and putting his head right down to those lips to detect a sign of breathing, or placing his hand on his mother's chest to feel the slight rise and fall.

Lately, acutely attuned to his mother's condition, Mulheisen thought he detected some rising viability, perhaps a minute increase in awareness. He might be imagining it, but he had taken to sitting her in a chair in his room in the evening. He would play music, mostly CDs of Bach's piano music or Haydn's string quartets. Nothing loud. And he would read to her. He read the paper, at first, but then bits of books—stories, essays, even history . . . inevitably, passages from Peckham's *Pontiac and the Indian Uprising*.

Through all of this Cora Mulheisen would sit with her hands in her lap, dressed in pajamas and a robe, socks and slippers, her eyes half-closed and anyway unfocused, gazing before her.

She was an old woman, looking her age, at last. She weighed only eighty or ninety pounds. According to the doctors, she was surprisingly fit. She had recovered readily from the trauma of the bombing. At first, she didn't seem to have her physical senses in order: she could see and hear, but she couldn't or wouldn't speak. She reacted to physical stimuli, like the familiar *tonk* on the knee with a mallet. MRIs, CAT scans, all the available tests had shown no damage to the brain or the rest of her system. But she wasn't functioning properly. Within a couple of weeks, however, her brain seemed to have sorted out what may have been some crossed wires and it was evident that she could see, smell, hear, and at least make noises in her sleep. Still, her aphasia persisted—she was unable to speak, or, to be precise, she showed no interest in speaking, which is another matter.

Because of her age, there was no intense program of rehabilitation. But the doctors strongly encouraged Mulheisen to see that she got regular and frequent exercise, just gentle walking about the house for a few minutes. Later, he began to take her on slow, easy walks around the yard, if the weather was fine. By now, they could walk as far as the old barn, sometimes a little ways along the path that led to the channel where the great ships came up from Lake St. Clair to enter the St. Clair River for their run to Lake Huron. As yet, they didn't go quite to the riverside. Mulheisen was curious to see if his mother, an enthusiastic bird-watcher, would react to the flying sparrows, gulls, and other birds, or hearken to their cries. She didn't seem to.

Immediately following the bombing, Mulheisen had taken a leave of absence from the department. He'd spent most of his time in the hospital room. When it became apparent that she would be discharged, he'd moved back to his old home and announced to the department that he was taking early retirement. Other than his friends, of whom he had many, including some in high places, the police department didn't seem to care if he left or not. His retirement was facilitated. He surrendered his badge, his gun, and his files.

The most amazing thing, as far as his associates were concerned, was his absolute lack of interest in the bombing incident that had so damaged his mother.

His erstwhile landlady, Becky, was of course properly concerned about his mother's disaster. Yet when the old lady was out of danger, and Mulheisen stayed on at home and announced he was leaving, Becky had gone a little sour. It wasn't something that Mulheisen could concern himself with, but he couldn't help noticing a veiled attitude of disapproval from Becky, almost jealousy, as if he was leaving her for another woman. But what could one do? It wasn't as if the relationship between them had progressed so very much during the few months Mulheisen had spent in her house. They'd been intimate a few times, always at Becky's choosing. Mulheisen had felt, in fact, a little baffled and frustrated by it all. He wasn't sure how he was supposed to act. He liked Becky very much and the sex was great, but beyond that he had no desire for marriage or even an extended partnership.

As a matter of fact, Mulheisen could not suppress a vaguely shameful sense of relief to be home, almost as if he were escaping from Becky and the slightly uneasy relationship. And within a few days after the move the "Becky episode" was so firmly behind him that it was almost as if it was ancient history.

He fell into the routine of being a caretaker with a certain pleasure; a calm and contemplative lassitude overtook him. When the nurse was present he would go out for long walks down to the channel—the river, as he'd always known it as a boy—ostensibly to smoke a cigar.

His favorite walk took him across the grassy field in the warm summer sun and he would turn toward the lake and walk to the very end of the path, from which he could see down the lake, toward Detroit. From here, he could easily see the Canadian side, of course, but looking to the southwest it all faded away in the haze off the lake.

One small problem, he found, was that it wasn't easy to have a cigar. His mother's general health not being all that good, he had quit smoking in the house. She'd never complained about it before, but he'd also not done it much when home. At Becky's, it was no problem. She loved the smell of cigars. She'd been in the business. And she'd fixed up his quarters with an excellent ventilating system that miraculously wafted away the odors. At home, when he found himself in residence, as it were, with his mother, it was a minor nuisance. A cigar takes too long to smoke and they cost too much to toss away after a few puffs. So the walks had been the main occasion for having a cigar.

Also, there was the matter of listening to music, once she'd gone to bed. He didn't like to disturb her. But he also didn't like having to keep the music so low. He'd hit upon the excellent idea of building himself a small study. They had plenty of land. He'd begun to think about where such a place would best be sited, and how big it should be. At present, of course, he needed to be in the house to attend to his mother. Later, if her condition continued to improve, he supposed the study would be an ideal place to repair for an evening. He could hook up an intercom system, perhaps, some way of monitoring what was going on in the house, some instant communication. Oh, there were lots of possibilities.

In the end, he decided that a small cottage might be the best idea. After all, the day would come, probably sooner than later, when he'd have the house to himself. What to do then with a small study? It would be a pointless expense. Of course, if it were small enough, inexpensive . . .

Out by the barn would be a good location. Finally, he decided to build a small house, which could be sold, or rented, at some future date. The project intrigued him. He began to sketch pictures of ideal houses and look at magazines that featured dream houses, studies. Shortly, he engaged a contractor and they began to plan. Soon enough, they were actually building. In the meantime, he could smoke his cigars on his walks.

One day he was standing on the river path as usual, watching a couple of freighters passing each other just beyond the entrance to the channel, when a man approached. That was unusual. Rarely did anyone use this path, only locals, sometimes boys fishing or exploring. This man was somewhat older than Mulheisen, who was now about fifty. He wore city clothes, a nicely tailored jacket of some kind of silk and linen blend, a white shirt, a tie, slacks, and low-cut shoes. Mulheisen was in his customary baggy khakis, a light nylon jacket over a short-sleeved checkered shirt, and his feet dry in green rubber half boots. Mulheisen was taking this opportunity to smoke one of his favorite cigars, a locally made brand called La Donna Detroit.

"Smells pretty good," the stranger said. "Cuban?"

"Oh, no," Mulheisen said. "I think the tobacco is probably Dominican. Care for one?" He offered a leather cigar holder.

The man declined. "I like the smell, but I never got the habit, somehow. You don't remember me, do you? We met . . . oh, maybe a year ago. Vern Tucker." The man offered his hand and Mulheisen shook it, warily.

"I remember," Mulheisen said. "You're with the FBI, aren't you? Or was it the DEA? Colonel Tucker?"

"That's right," the man said. "I think we share an air force past, if I'm not mistaken. You were in AACS, I think."

Mulheisen nodded, his interest moderately piqued. "You were a pilot, I think you said. F-105s. Wild Weasels."

"Very good," Tucker said, pleasantly. He clasped his hands behind his back and stood looking at the lake. He was not a large man, certainly a head shorter than Mulheisen. He nodded toward the ships and asked, "What ships are those?"

Mulheisen said, "Oceangoing. Probably foreign, trading to and from Chicago, or Milwaukee, Duluth maybe. I couldn't make out the logos or the names. I used to know all the lake boats. Cleveland Cliffs, Ford, but you don't see them anymore. There's an old guy comes out here once in a while, brings a chair and a notebook, binoculars. He used to keep track of all the names of the companies. That was a long time ago, come to think of it. I haven't seen him in ages. Maybe he's died, by now."

"Why would he keep track of the ships?" Tucker asked.

"Who knows? He was interested. Maybe it's like collecting stamps. He collected ships."

Tucker shook his head, as if dismissing the silliness of that. "What's that island, way down there?"

"You can see that?" Mulheisen asked. "You must still have pilot's vision. That's Peach Island. It's at the head of the Detroit River. That's what the locals call it, it's on the maps, but it's really Peche Island . . . the fish, not the fruit. There were never any peaches on that island, but they say that Pontiac, the Ottawa chief, used to hang out there in the summer. He had a fishing camp, probably. People still go out there and camp in the summer, I guess. I haven't been out there in a long time, since I gave up my boat."

They chatted about boats for a bit. Tucker wasn't too familiar with them. He was from a dry country, he said, a river country, where the idea of a boat was a canoe or a rubber fishing raft. "But imagine," he said, "Pontiac used to hang out there. A little bit of history."

"See that island over there?" Mulheisen pointed to a nearby island, across the channel, not more than a few hundred yards distant. "That's where the Chippewas ambushed Sir Robert Davers and Lieutenant Robertson and their party. They killed Davers and Robertson, and supposedly they ate Robertson."

"Ate him! My god!" Tucker stared across the narrow channel. "Cannibals! I had no idea that they practiced cannibalism."

"Well, who knows?" Mulheisen said. "His body was never found, although Davers's rifle and Robertson's powder horn were given to one of the French settlers in Detroit. This was in 1762, about two hundred and forty-some years ago."

"Who was this Davers, anyway?" the colonel asked.

Mulheisen shrugged. "A tourist," he said. "One of those odd Brits. He was just traveling around, apparently, learning the Indians' language, sightseeing."

Tucker gazed at Mulheisen, a good-sized man with thinning, sandy hair, almost homely but attractive in a way. When he smiled, which wasn't often, he bared rather long teeth. This was a feature that had given rise to his street cognomen, "Sergeant Fang."

"You seem to know quite a bit about this stuff," Tucker said, "but I suppose it's from living around here."

Mulheisen shrugged. "I'm interested in the history," he said. "Pontiac was a crucial figure in American history. Where are you from?"

"Me? I'm an American. Oh, you mean . . . I grew up in Montana, up near Great Falls."

"Great Falls? I've been there. Butte, too. Well, you're from Injun Country, as they used to say in the movies. I'm surprised you're not more interested."

"Who says I'm not interested?" Tucker sounded almost indignant. But, in fact, he wasn't interested. He'd seen plenty of Indians in his youth, been to school with some. There was a Blackfeet reservation not far from his folks' ranch. Several Blackfeet had worked on the ranch, from time to time. One of them in particular, Albert Sees Crow—or was it "Seize Crow"?—had been fairly important to him at one time. (It was funny, now that he thought about it, he'd never considered that Albert's name could have been Seize Crow.) Indians didn't seem exotic or especially fascinating to him, but he supposed that it might be different for someone like Mulheisen, growing up in industrial Michigan.

Mulheisen said, "Are you familiar with the period?" He gestured toward the channel, the lake, as if history were lying there. As a matter of fact, that was often the way it seemed to Mulheisen, like a not quite visible panorama or tableau.

"Not very," Tucker said, hesitantly. He wasn't prepared to hear a long presentation about an obscure episode. Mulheisen had the air of one of those enthusiasts, an amateur who had immersed himself in a subject and was not above bending one's ear with his theories. "I'm sure it's fascinating, but as it happens I came out to see you for a reason."

"I assumed you did," Mulheisen said. "Shall we?" He gestured toward the distant house and they turned to walk back.

"It's about the bombers," Tucker said. "The ones who almost killed your mother."

"I don't think she was the target," Mulheisen observed.

"Oh, no, of course not," Tucker hastened to agree. "An innocent bystander, fundamentally. But I thought you might be interested. We have begun to develop a different line on them."

"Really? I thought it was some Muslim group," Mulheisen said. "The terrorist was killed in the explosion. Isn't that right? Do you know who he was?"

"That's the point," Tucker said. "We thought we had an identification. This group that claimed responsibility—a Gulf group—
even provided the name of the so-called martyr. But now it looks
like that was just an attempt to make us believe one of their key
operatives was dead. It's a useful ploy, not uncommon. The man
whose name they put forth is still in action, in Germany, we think."

"Hah. That's clever, sort of," Mulheisen said. "So who did
do it?"

"We're not sure, but we suspect it wasn't a Muslim or even a
foreign group at all. We think it was homegrown."

"Locals?" Mulheisen asked. "You mean, Detroit people?
Arabs? Some other group?"

"Actually, more homegrown than that. A right-wing American group, radicals."

"Hah. Like the Oklahoma City bombing?"

"Something like that," Tucker said. "There was a Michigan
connection in Oklahoma City, you'll recall."

"Oh, yes." Mulheisen stopped. They were halfway back to the
house. He looked over at his study, now already closed in, although
the roof wasn't shingled. He started to point it out, then decided
the man wouldn't be interested in his domestic plans. Instead, he
shook his head with a rueful grimace, then looked up and around.
"I'll be damned."

Tucker stood by, watching him.

After a minute, Mulheisen snorted, then shrugged. "Well,
when you think about it," he said, "what difference does it make?"

Tucker looked shocked.

Mulheisen noticed and hastened to add, "I mean . . . well,
I'm glad you're on to them, of course, but it doesn't make much
difference to my mother, does it? It was in the nature of an accident. She was there, the bomb was there. The two aren't connected.
It's like that airplane that crashed in Brooklyn, a couple days after

the planes crashed into the World Trade Center towers. Everybody thought at first it was more terrorists, but it wasn't. But what difference did it make? To the people who were killed, I mean, and their families. And then . . . naturally, you thought about the ones in the towers. What did that mean? Wasn't it the same as the crash in Brooklyn? Those people weren't *involved* with the terrorists, either. It might as well have been a bolt of lightning that struck the bus. The bomb wasn't aimed at her, after all."

Tucker's amazement was very evident—eyes wide, mouth agape.

Mulheisen felt compelled to reassure the man, to explain himself. "It's a horrible thing," he said. "Madmen. But, you see, on a personal level . . . well, I suppose people in the Blitz, or in Vietnam, say, who were injured by bombs falling out of the sky . . . not meant for them, of course, but for a ball-bearing plant, or a railroad . . . they probably couldn't help feeling personally attacked, I suppose. Who could blame them, eh? You always hear about country people, mobs, attacking downed airmen . . ."

Mulheisen hesitated, catching a wince from Tucker. *Of course,* he thought, *the man had been a bomber himself, in Vietnam.* "Of course, it's not the same, is it?" he said.

"No, certainly not," Tucker responded. "That's a war, a declared war. There are bound to be civilian casualties, but the action was aimed at the enemy's resources, the industrial infrastructure."

Mulheisen was annoyed by this shameless defense. "Oh sure," he said, drily, "but you can't expect folks to appreciate the difference when they're being blown up. It doesn't matter if it's the Vietcong tossing a grenade into a beer hall full of American troops, or American airplanes tossing a few tons of bombs into the heart of a rail depot where there are civilians working, or a factory . . . or maybe just dumping their 'unused ordnance,' as they say, as they climb out of the bombing run, only it happens to fall on a hamlet. Wouldn't you say? Just from the vantage point of the civilians?"

Tucker was not to be drawn. "Perhaps you're right," he said. He seemed to have regained control of his anger. "In this case, however, there may have been more to it."

"How so?"

"Perhaps, if only obliquely, your mother was a target."

"Oh, come on," Mulheisen said. "A bird-watcher? So, who was this, some bird-hater? Are there such people?"

"An antienvironmentalist, perhaps," Tucker said. "Your mother was more than a bird-watcher. She was what some would call an activist. There are quite a few people who get upset at environmental activists. Out where I come from, it's common to refer to all environmentalists as extremists. Wasn't her group, in fact, at that city hall to present a protest at the draining of a marsh area?"

Mulheisen frowned. "I think they were objecting to the proposed building of a power plant, a not very clean plant, in an important drainage zone. There was a question of contamination of—what do they call it?—the aquifer. But I'm not all that sure about it. I was more concerned with my mother's injuries, so I didn't really pay that much attention. I suppose I should have."

"Oh, no, no, my dear fellow," Tucker said, quickly, "you were quite right to be focused on the problem at hand. I'm just saying . . . the possibility can't be ruled out that, in some weird, far-fetched way, these nuts were targeting your mother's group. There was also, you may recall, an Arab restaurant next door. It's possible that the restaurant was the target. It was a popular meeting place for some prominent Arab leaders in the community. There is a very large Arab population in these parts, as I'm sure you know. We can't rule out any of those possibilities. But my point is, it wasn't by any stretch a legitimate military target."

So, Mulheisen thought, he was back to that. The man must have been a bomber pilot. Rather than debate the issue, Mulheisen decided to let it go. "I take your point," he said. "So who were these guys?"

"We have a few leads," Tucker said, evidently relieved to put the ambiguous aspect of bombing aside. "But it occurred to me . . . you're free, aren't you? That is, you've left the police force? I thought so. I was thinking you might be interested in joining us, assisting us, in this investigation."

Mulheisen quickly shook his head. "No. I'm retired. I have plenty to do, just taking care of my mother. No, my detective days are behind me, Colonel. Nowadays, I spend my free time, in the evenings, reading about Pontiac, doing a little amateur research on the period."

"I understand, I understand," Tucker said, "but, you know, it's not good simply to subside into the woodwork. You have hired a nurse, possibly you could get a little more help, and that would free up some time. . . . We pay very well, you know."

"Who is 'we'? The DEA? CIA? Who are we talking about?" Mulheisen asked.

"It's actually a coalition of agencies," Tucker said. "In fact, it's a special task force, under the new Homeland Security aegis. I'm running it. You'd be answerable only to me. So you see, if you're concerned about joining some government agency, it wouldn't be like that. No training, no elaborate security clearance, no civil service exam or requirements. You would be simply a civilian contractor, for a set fee. Say, one hundred thousand dollars?"

Mulheisen stopped. "A hundred grand? For the duration? I mean, what if it gets wrapped up in a couple of weeks? Or in two years? What then?"

Tucker liked the way this was going. As long as Mulheisen was in negotiation, other issues could be shunted aside. "A hun-

dred grand for the duration of the investigation . . . that is, until we
have our perpetrators."

"Ah. Until you have them? Identified them? Arrested them?
Convicted them?"

"Identified them," Tucker said, "to our satisfaction, at least.
And, naturally, we'd want to know where they are, if they're still
alive, but that wouldn't necessarily involve tracking them down and
arresting them. But, that could be part of it, if you're interested. Let's
say the investigation runs longer than six months . . . we could
negotiate an additional fee. And so on . . . for the duration. Sound
okay?"

"Okay? It sounds too good. I never got anything like that on
the force."

"These are special times," Tucker said. "Congress is responding to the anxiety of the public. The funds are there. And you're a
man with special abilities, with a special interest. You're motivated."

"You mean, my mother? Well, to be honest, Colonel, I've
never quite bought into revenge as a motive."

Tucker was surprised. "Revenge is a very familiar motive,"
he asserted.

"So they say," Mulheisen agreed, "but I've always been a little
skeptical. In practice, I get the feeling that the desire for revenge is
intense immediately following the . . . ah, event. But it begins to
fade pretty quickly, I suspect. People begin to think about reality,
making a living, getting on with their lives. I felt a lot of anger, but
it soon got pushed aside in favor of my concern for my mother. Still,
I know that some cultures . . ."

He looked thoughtful, then added, "I can remember a couple
of cases. The murder of Big Sid Sedlacek, for instance. His daughter was certainly on fire about that. We figured she was behind the
subsequent murder of Carmine Busoni, the mob boss who ordered
the hit."

Tucker's eyes lit up. "I know about that case," he said. "We were interested in his successor, DiEbola. It's funny that you should mention it, because there is a kind of connection with the bombing."

"What!" It was Mulheisen's turn to be amazed. "What possible connection?"

"It's tenuous," Tucker said. "Just a name that keeps popping up. Service."

"You're kidding. Joe Service? What could Service possibly have to do with terrorists?"

Tucker was delighted with Mulheisen's kindled interest. "Who knows?" he said. "Maybe nothing. But it's one of the things we have to find out."

"What was the connection?"

"Just the name," Tucker said. "Maybe it was irrelevant, but there it was. Some of the people we were interested in, possible connections to the incident, had been in communication with Service. His name came up on some telephone intercepts. Possibly, he supplied some expertise, or some weapons . . . it isn't clear."

Mulheisen looked very interested. He stood there, thoughtfully chewing on a cigar that had gone out. Finally, he took the cigar from his mouth, looked at it carefully, prodded the dead end to see if it was still lit, then dropped it onto the path and ground it under his boot. "Joe Service," he said. "Imagine that." Abruptly, he raised his eyebrows as if clearing his mind and said, "Oh, well."

Tucker said, "Then you'll join us?"

"Nah. Sorry. I really can't. Thanks for the offer, though."

Tucker was astounded. He followed after as Mulheisen strode toward the house. "But, but . . . you're not interested?" he said. He really was amazed. "What about your mother?"

"I'm thinking of my mother," Mulheisen said. "She needs my help." He stopped at the door and thrust out his hand to shake. "Say, keep in touch, will you? I'm interested, naturally, in case you find out anything. Thanks for coming by. Bye."

He went in the back door and closed it, firmly. Tucker stood openmouthed, staring after him. Finally, he went to his car and drove away.

2

A Dog's Conscience

To say that Joe Service was a man with a dog's conscience is not to say that he was innocent. But in his heart he was innocent. It was true that he had killed a few men, and he had taken a few dollars to which, strictly speaking, he had no legitimate claim, but these things could be explained. To wit: self-defense and the money was owed him . . . more or less. There was that unlucky guy in Iowa City, a few years back, and there might be some who would regard his role in the assassination of Carmine Busoni as straining the limits of self-defense. Some would say he had been more than an enabler in that case, not just encouraging his lover, Helen Sedlacek, in avenging the murder of her father, but conceiving the hit plan, showing her how to do it, and even driving the getaway car. Carmine deserved it, to be sure. Joe was free of recriminations about any of these killings.

At the moment, Joe felt especially virtuous now that he was on the straight and narrow. He had lately become a home builder, a carpenter, a man who owned a dog, a man who bought license plates for his car and even a legitimate driver's license. It was true that his car and the plates and the license were acquired with the use of an alias, but that was a mere precaution. Joe Humann was his name now.

Joe also represented Helen as his wife, which in the eyes of the state of Montana meant that he was in fact married, although Joe wasn't aware of that. (One might pose a reasonable legal question as to whether the fact that they represented themselves as Mr. and Mrs. Humann rendered their common-law marriage moot, as well as unconscious.) Doubtless it didn't matter, but had Joe known that he was now legally married—theoretically—it would bolster his feelings of an innocent heart (although he might have other qualms).

It was remarkable how readily Joe fell in with his newfound probity. Helen had no such feelings. Until she'd met Joe she had been "straight," as it were—a square, a home guard. Her father had been a crook, a well-known gangster, but in the way of such things he had always denied that, claiming he was falsely accused, merely because he knew a few mobsters and he made his income in an unorthodox way—as a business adviser to men suspected of criminal activities. A child doesn't question these things too deeply. If a beloved parent insists that he's innocent, merely a friend of people who are unfairly suspected by the cops, why even an intelligent child like Helen is likely to accept that. A child could even play with that popular myth, at once relishing the special status that seemed to accrue to so-called gangsters, and at another moment, if the canard were seriously alleged, she might spiritedly defend her father's putative honesty. It was only in her late teens when she realized, with a frisson of wicked delight, that her beloved father, Big Sid Sedlacek, surely was a gangster. But by then she had already lived the life of innocence, so this new condition was not nearly so amusing or even interesting to her. Nowadays, she thought of herself as having made an irrevocable choice when she decided to avenge her father: a road that led one-way and not toward any conventional domain of virtue.

One of the things that both Helen and Joe equally enjoyed, however, was work. They had gotten very physically involved in the building of their new home in Montana. The contractor was an amiable man named Anders Ericsson, from Missoula, a city about a hundred miles as the eagle flies from their building site up in the mountains between Butte and Helena. This contractor had to drive over from his home on Mondays, at least a hundred and seventy-five miles. He had a camper on his old Chevy pickup. He camped out at the site, with his irritable dog, a border collie named Skippy.

Ericsson was about forty years old, a rangy, humorous fellow who, as a veteran of graduate studies in literature, was decidedly overeducated for his occupation. He had a thriving business in Missoula, but he enjoyed jobs like this, which were very lucrative and involved some unusual kinds of carpentry. He was also a man who liked to get away, from time to time, from a wife who was beautiful and talented but also critical about his taste for beer and an occasional toke of marijuana. It was this latter taste that had provided the point of contact, since Joe and Helen had purchased their remote property from a reclusive young fellow named Frank Oberavich, who owned about two thousand acres along a clear and cold and trouty stream called the French Forque, where he grew a strain of marijuana that was known in certain quarters as "righteous." While at the university in Missoula, Oberavich had met Ericsson in a creative writing class and had even worked for him from time to time. They had kept up the friendship and when Franko, as he was known, built his own elaborate solar-, wind-, and hydro-powered hideway, he had naturally called upon his buddy Anders for assistance. He had recommended Anders to Joe and Helen for their place and it had worked out quite well.

Anders was happy to take on Joe and Helen, not only as clients but as assistants in the building. It kept the number of strangers to a minimum, which pleased the couple, and they thoroughly enjoyed the labor. They were young, in their early thirties, and quite physically active and strong. They readily fell in with the regimen of hammering and sawing, nailing, learning new techniques like compressor-driven nailers, or by contrast the old traditions of framing or post-and-beam construction. Even the hauling and stacking of lumber and materials, which is so much of building, pleased them.

They loved poring over plans and blueprints with Anders and considering the strategies of design and structure. The weather was great, the company fine. The two young people relished the feeling of being tired at the end of the day, of getting something positive done, and the wonderful license it gave them to leap into the river in the heat of the day, to say nothing of soaking in the hot springs along the river.

So thoroughly had Joe immersed himself in his new straight life that he was surprised to get a phone call one day from Smokey Stover. This was the elderly owner of Smokey's Corner, a Butte beer garden. He was an old mob contact for this area, a man who had gotten his fingers dirty in untold varieties of activities and now was placidly living out his years in boring comfort. He'd had at least a passing acquaintance with Joe's old employer from Detroit, Humphrey DiEbola. Joe had almost forgotten that Smokey existed. But Smokey had intriguing news: someone had been asking about Joe.

A few months earlier, Joe would have instantly pricked up his ears at this news, but now he was merely baffled. Who could be looking for him? He was totally out of the mob, had been for a couple of years. The Carmine thing was old stuff and anyway, thanks to some fence-mending with Humphrey, now himself deceased, that connection was defunct.

It was true that Joe and Helen had since put in some time for a curious group of federal agents, who liked to style themselves "the Lucani," but Joe didn't consider himself employed by them; that was just a bit of contract work. In fact, he had no intention of working for them again, if he could help it. He believed they were a dangerous group of deluded men and women, tantamount to vigilantes, who themselves were operating on the edges of criminal behavior. If the Lucani were looking for Joe, they knew where to find him, not that it would do them much good.

Joe thought it over and decided that it must just be an old acquaintance from his mob days, some guy passing through who had stopped into Smokey's Corner, as one might do—somehow, old grifters always knew where to go when in a strange town. Perhaps this guy had heard on the grapevine that Joe was rumored to be in the Butte area and had idly asked Smokey about him, assuming naturally that Smokey would pass on the news to Joe that an old pal had been in town. Except that the asker hadn't given his name and Smokey seemed to be a little uneasy about this contact. But Joe, in his newfound innocence, couldn't take it seriously. He didn't even mention it to Helen, but he made a note to himself to ask Smokey for more details when next he was in town.

He didn't get the opportunity for a couple of days, but then he had to drive in to Butte to pick up some hardwood flooring they'd ordered for the living room. He dropped Helen at the supermarket, drove to the lumberyard, and got the flooring loaded into the bed of the new four-wheel-drive Dodge pickup truck they'd bought when they decided to become carpenters.

Smokey's Corner was a pleasant if none too clean tavern halfway up the hill in one of Butte's delapidated older neighborhoods. It was a long room with a pressed-tin ceiling, slowly rotating overhead fans, and a long, elegant bar, now somewhat scarred with carved initials and faded by many swipes of a bartender's rag to mop up spilled whiskey. The back bar was still beautiful, with beveled glass mirrors. The wooden floor was littered with peanut shells and cigarette butts at this time of the day, late afternoon. A couple of the coin-operated pool tables were in play by tough-looking fellows in sleeveless sweatshirts, their hairy arms well decorated with tattoos.

Smokey slouched in his regular place down at the end of the bar, which was presided over by the usual young, handsome muscle guy. The regulars were hunched over their shots and beers, mostly watching a sports news broadcast on TV. Smokey, a man past seventy, watched Joe approach. He had a long, sad face with baby blue irises painted onto hardboiled eyeballs hooded by heavy dark lids. He smoked a corncob pipe. He smiled at Joe's approach.

"So, I drug you out of the woods," Smokey said. "Ain't seen much of you since last fall. How you gettin' along out there?"

Joe assured him everything was fine. Life was good. The weather was a little dry. Fish were biting—mostly at pale morning duns and #12 hoppers.

"Jeez, I didn't know you was a fisherman," Smokey said.

"I had to take it up," Joe said. "It comes with the territory— you live out here, you have to fish. Otherwise, what can you talk about?"

They moved to a table and Joe accepted a cold draft beer. "So tell me about this guy," Joe said.

"Jeez, Joe, I'm gettin' to be your social seckaterry," Smokey said. "Well, he didn't give a name, except Sidney. I don't know if that's a last or first name." To Joe's further questions he described a small, rather dark man, middle-aged, maybe forty. Smokey thought he was Italian. "Not long outside," he threw in.

"Hunh," Joe grunted. "This guy connected?"

"Seemed likely," Smokey said. "He'd been away for a while. Not quite comfortable in his new clothes. Stands to one side, looking at things without looking, you know?"

Joe knew. But the name Sidney didn't mean anything to him and he wondered if it should.

"He dropped the name kind of odd, mumbled or something," Smokey said. "I didn't quite catch it. Ray!" He called to the young bartender and beckoned. When the man came over he asked, "That guy who was in here? Aksed about Joe, here." Smokey nodded toward Joe. "Did he say his name was Sidney? Or what was that?"

Ray nodded to Joe. "I thought he asked *about* Sidney. You know, first about Mr. Service. I said I never heard of him. Then he said something about Sidney someone. I thought he meant another guy. I said I never heard of Sidney." Ray shot his eyebrows upward in an expression of incomprehension. "Of course, he could of been asking about Sid Kiprovica, but I didn't think of that. I doubt he was asking about him. Sid never comes in here anymore, not since you eighty-sixed him last winter."

They chatted about Kiprovica for a minute or two. Joe didn't know him, had never known him. A man of no consequence, it seemed. Nobody was interested in Kip, a shiftless drunk on disability from the mines.

The trouble with this was that the only Sid that Joe could think of was Helen's late father, whom Joe had met a couple of times but could hardly claim as an acquaintance, even if by now he knew rather more about the man than he wanted to. In some way, Big Sid Sedlacek had been a key figure in Joe's history, since it was Carmine's ill-advised hit on him that had led to Joe's involvement with Helen, and, subsequently, his difficulties with his old employers, the mob. Those issues were long resolved, Joe felt. But . . . he had to face it, with the mob some things are never over until they're over. Still, damn, that was years ago. He'd known that, once Humphrey died, he'd never be employed by the mob again. So he'd let that phase of his life expire, without much thought about it. It was over. On to whatever was next.

What was next was now so different. He was finding it difficult to get his mind back into the old track, the Life. He was no longer involved in the Life, the Inside. He felt an unfamiliar pang, and realized for the first time how completely he'd left that old life behind. He wondered if he could ever find his way back, if he wanted to. He didn't miss it, but he had to admit that he felt disconnected.

This must be one of those watershed moments, he thought. His life had changed and he hadn't even noticed how much, until now.

He assured Smokey that it was of no consequence. Unless, of course, the guy reappeared, asking more questions. They passed on to other chitchat. They even discussed fishing. Smokey was a devotee of the Big Hole, a good fishing river south of Butte. They discussed the salmonfly hatch, always a topic of conversation for fly-fishing enthusiasts. The hatch had been good, but it was history. Smokey didn't get out much anymore, but he'd be glad to take Joe fishing on the Big Hole. He had a good boat. The Big Hole could only really be fished by drift boat.

Then Smokey made a mistake. He seemed eager to be friendly, but he started talking about the explosion and fire that had wrecked Joe's old place, down in the Ruby Valley. "I didn't have nothin' to do with that, you know, Joe," he said.

"It's all right, Smoke," Joe said, for what he thought must be the tenth time. "Forget it."

But Smokey wouldn't let it drop. "It was The Fat Man," he said, meaning Humphrey. "He borrowed a couple of my guys to go down there. What could I do? One of 'em was killed, you know. I had to take care of his wife, his kids . . ."

This was too much, Joe thought. The notion flashed through his head how it was often like this: a guy does you an injury, first he wants forgiveness and absolution, and before you know it he ends with demanding that you apologize to *him*! Now it looked like he wanted compensation!

Joe leaned a little closer and said, quietly but with an edge to his voice, "If I hear one more word about this, Smoke, I won't like it."

Smokey was instantly contrite. "Sure, Joe." He held his hands up, palms out. "I was just say—"

"One word," Joe said.

Smokey dropped it. "Hey, we're pals . . . right?"

Joe didn't even nod. He pushed his beer away and got up.

Smokey called after him, "What should I say if the guy comes back?"

"Tell him to call me. You know the number," Joe said over his shoulder.

Before he picked up Helen, Joe did something he hadn't planned to do. He called the Colonel. He'd hoped never to talk to the Colonel again, but the stranger had made it necessary.

Lieutenant Colonel Tucker wasn't in, according to his assistant, Edna. But she was sure that he'd want to talk to Joe. He'd call him back. Was there something she could help with? Joe said, No, it was nothing. He just wondered if the Colonel had sent somebody around. Some guy had been asking, in Butte. He gave the particulars, as he'd gotten them from Smokey. But Edna hadn't heard anything. The Colonel would call him.

Joe didn't mention any of this to Helen. The more he thought of it the less it seemed that it concerned her. The guy asking questions didn't sound like someone involved with the Lucani, the Colonel's little group of disaffected agents. Joe trusted Smokey's instincts: the guy was a mob guy. But Joe couldn't believe that anyone from the mob was still pursuing the issue of Carmine's death. It made no sense. And, after all, Joe had no direct connection to Big Sid—well, he did, through Helen, but Joe was determined to believe that it was a dead issue with the mob. And, finally, he didn't want to think about all this stuff. He had other things on his mind, like electrical wiring, insulation, whether to build a little cabin up in the woods, a place to retire to when he needed to think, or putter with his stuff—guns and the new fishing rods he'd bought. It was an attractive notion, a kind of retreat from Helen.

He discovered in himself, just thinking about it as they drove back from Butte, a kind of disloyalty toward Helen. They were inseparable. But was that the way it would always be? Shouldn't a man and a woman have some relief from each other's company? Did Helen ever feel that? He glanced at her. She was gazing out at the countryside, the beautiful mountains.

"What?" she said, catching his look.

"Nothing," Joe said. "I was just wondering . . . ?"

"What?"

"Are you . . . happy?"

"Am I happy? Sure. I'm happy. You mean, this?" She gestured at the mountains. They were descending from the pass, spinning along a grand highway that swept around curves, along a wooded canyon, past rugged cliffs.

Joe nodded. "You miss Detroit?"

"Well, I'd like to see Mama," she said. "She's getting old, you know. I suppose she's happy. She has her old ladies, of course. Lunch, and dinner after church. She'd never appreciate this, I think, but maybe we could have her out for a week . . . once we get the house done."

"Oh sure," Joe said. "We'll have her out. We could take her up to the lake, near Helena. Rent a boat. She'd like that."

Helen had purchased a ton of food, including an enormous bag of dog food. They were now in the habit of feeding Anders Ericsson's dog as well as their own. Their dog was a small, white bundle of energy that had been foisted on them by their neighbor Franko. It had belonged to Franko's late uncle and aunt, a couple who had been murdered by a madman named Bazok, who had also terrorized Franko and Joe and Helen. This little dog got along famously with Anders's Skippy, which the carpenter was delighted to see.

"Skip," he told them, "likes nobody, including other dogs. You really ought to keep him. My wife hates him. To tell you the truth, I don't think he likes me. But he seems to like you, Joe. And Homes." That was the name they had given the orphaned dog, shortened from "Home, boy!," which is what they had found themselves yelling at the little dog every time they tried to leave. He would follow them halfway to the gate, which was more than a mile from the house. They didn't know the dog's original name, so they decided on Homeboy, which soon became just Homes.

The idea of owning a dog was repellent to Joe. Just another attachment, another bother when you had to go somewhere. Owning a dog was so . . . so "straight." It was yet another indication of the couple's growing ordinariness. Franko owned dogs. They were handsome rottweilers and invaluable to him, as he never tired of pointing out. They had ultimately defended Franko and the Humanns against the madman Bazok. The obvious point of their usefulness could not be denied. People who lived as they did needed all the warning devices they could muster, it seemed, and dogs were invaluable. Joe was surprised that the dogs took to him so readily, especially Anders's cranky Skippy. But he found himself oddly attached to Homes.

When they entered the gate, where was Homes? Usually, he'd be leaping with ecstasy, in company with Skippy. But no Homes or Skippy today. The couple soon found out why. He had besieged a strange car, parked in the driveway of Franko's house. Skippy lounged nearby, in the shade, watching with interest. Franko's wife, a slender Kosovar woman named Fedima, came out to explain.

"He will not let this man leave his car," she said. "I am sorry, Joe, but I didn't know what to do. Franko is fishing. The man wishes to speak with you."

"That's all right, Fedima," Joe said. "I'll take care of it."

Joe called the dog to him and put him in the truck, where he continued to yap. The stranger got out of the car, warily. This, Joe instantly realized, was the man who had been asking about him in Butte. He also recognized him. Caspar Darnay.

The two men greeted each other effusively. Joe had known Darnay since childhood, in Philadelphia. He hadn't seen him in years. But he was the same old Caspar. He was a short man, not much taller than Joe, with the same old quiet, watchful look, doubt-less reinforced by several years in the penitentiary. Joe was glad to see him, sort of. He represented the past, which was past.

Joe and Helen were living in their new house, even though it wasn't finished yet—and it was uncertain when it would be. They called it camping out, but in fact it was merely an inconvenience, what with having to periodically empty a room to put down a floor, which they would soon have to do in the kitchen, with the hardwood Joe had just picked up. They had lots of room. Joe insisted on putting up Caspar.

While Helen started dinner, Joe went for a walk with Caspar . . . and Homes, of course, who was now docilely accepting of the newcomer, with Skippy trailing along as usual. They walked down from the house toward the river. They stood on a bluff and watched as, in the distance, they could see Franko casting to a pool where the stream ran along a cliff.

"Man, it's beautiful," Caspar said, fervently. "I can't get used to all this open space. You've got a fabulous house, Joe, and your wife is gorgeous. You got it made, man."

Joe accepted these praises without a remark, merely smiling. He understood that it was heartfelt, and that the enthusiasm was due in part to the man's long incarceration. But it was beautiful. Very quiet. Deer were visible picking their way along the banks of the stream, among some aspen. A hawk was circling in the sky. The mountains seemed to guard their privacy.

They talked a bit about the expanse, the relative privacy—the only neighbors being the Oberaviches. It was a paradise, clearly, the ideal hole-in-the-wall.

Joe asked how Caspar had found him. It was fairly simple. Caspar had continued to ask around, after being rebuffed by Smokey. "I could tell he knew you," Caspar said, "he just wasn't saying. Which is all right." He shrugged, to indicate he understood the circumstance. "But I kept looking, and finally I found this real estate babe, Carmen or something. She gave me a lead. So I came out here."

Joe could see it. It made him a little anxious to realize that he was so locatable. He didn't much like that. But he let it pass.

"So what brings you out this way?" he asked, finally.

"I finished up my time at Deer Lodge," Caspar said. "They transferred me, sixteen months ago. I had a little difficulty in Illinoise. I had to testify against some guys. The deal was, I got a few months knocked off and they moved me." He shrugged. It wasn't an issue for discussion, obviously.

"Anyways," he went on, "I always knew you was out this way. I'd heard from some guys who knew you. But when I went to the place they said, it was burned down, no one around."

That was another story, Joe's story, also not worth discussing. Joe didn't offer any explanation, except, "I moved up here about a year ago."

"I just wanted to come by and tell you thanks, for Charles," Caspar said.

"Ah, yes. Charles." That was Caspar's kid brother, dead in a shoot-out with cops, in Detroit. Joe had been very close to Charles, more than with Caspar. They had both gone to work for the mob, back in Philadelphia, and before that had been pals on the street. Joe had claimed Charles's body and sent it home. This was Caspar's big deal: making a trek to thank Joe.

"I know Ma really appreciated what you done," Caspar said. "And paying for the funeral, too. I wanted to repay you for that. But I'm not exactly flush, you understand."

"Oh, jeez, Caz, don't even think about it. You would have done it, but you weren't there." Caspar had been in prison, of course. "Anyone would have done it," Joe said.

"Sure," Caspar said, "but it wasn't . . . there wasn't anyone there to do it, but you. They'd a buried him in the potter's field. We'd a never known what happened."

"I just happened to be there, in Detroit, at the time," Joe said. "I mean, I wasn't into anything with Charles, you know. I wouldn't have known about it, but I happened to be in town and I realized who the papers were talking about. That's all. I can't tell you much about what happened to him. It didn't have anything to do with me, see?"

"Oh, I know that, I know that," Caspar reassured him. "I didn't mean anything. I guess he just . . . well, I guess he was just in the wrong place at the wrong time."

"Something like that," Joe said. "I don't even remember what the situation was, you know? I just read about it, heard about it from some other guys. So I thought, well, this is an old pal, I thought I could take the time to see that he got home. How is your Ma?"

"Oh, she's fine, fine. She's getting on. Anyways, thanks for doing that, for Charles. And Ma."

They stood there, not looking at each other, just taking in the view. "Man, this is really something," Caspar said. "I got to hand it to you, Joe. You done good. You doin' all right?" He glanced at Joe, a little concerned. "I mean . . . I can see you're doin' all right . . . but everything going okay?"

"Yeah, sure. I'm retired now, you know."

"Ah. That's good. Me, I got to be looking for work. You get out, after all this time. . . . I tell you, Joe, the world is so different now. Everything is changed. I guess I'll look up some guys, but . . . hell, I'm not even sure where to start."

"Hey, what am I thinking?" Joe said. "Look, I got plenty. You need something to tide you over? No, really, I mean it. I got too much. I can help you out. You'll pay me back later. When you get back on your feet."

Caspar looked almost embarrassed, but he didn't show much emotion. "Thanks, I appreciate that," he said. "I'll pay you back. You know that."

"We'll figure something out," Joe said. "Would a couple grand do you? You think so? I could spring for more, if you need it."

"No. A couple grand is terrific, Joe. I'd appreciate it. Everything's so much more expensive now. But, listen," he turned away from the river and leaned a bit closer, as if to avoid being overheard, although only the dogs could have heard him, and the wind rippling across the grass. "I don't want you to think I just come by to borrow money, Joe. I wanted to thank you for Charles, and I done that. And I'll pay you back for that . . . and the two grand. You know that."

"I know that," Joe said. "What is it?" He could tell that something was bothering Caspar, something else. "Tell me."

"I heard something that you ought to know," Caspar said. "I couldn't go home without finding you and telling you. That's why I stuck around so long. I been out for a week. I was beginning to wonder if I would find you."

"Something you learned inside?"

"Yeah." Caspar looked around, then leaned closer. "There's some heavy guys looking for you, Joe. If I found you, they'll find you. You need to keep your eyes open. They ain't looking to give you the lottery winnings, or nothing."

"Who are they?"

"Some kind of heat. Foreign heat. I got a couple of names. One of 'em's some kind of Spanish guy—Echeverria."

3

Sniff

For a change,
Mulheisen played some jazz while he read one of Robert Louis
Stevenson's stories to his mother. He had an idea that she would
like Stevenson because the story was not so modern. Her situation
was a peculiarly modern, contemporary one, it seemed to him, and
so an old story of the nineteenth century, about people cast away
on South Sea islands might be better, somehow, less threatening,
perhaps more soothing . . . balmy islands . . . balm . . . healing. Of
course, it was true that he had, himself, a kind of nostalgic taste for
Stevenson.

The music he chose was a collection of Gershwin tunes,
played by the cornetist Ruby Braff, accompanied by the guitarist
George Barnes. Very mellow, lightly swinging stuff. When he noticed that his mother was nodding, he stopped and helped her to
her bed. She was quite docile. But as he tucked her in he was suddenly electrified to see that she was looking at him intently. He
started to say something, but stopped when he saw her lips move.

He lowered his head to hear her. She seemed to be singing!
It was just a very, very faint sound, with no more than a hint of
musicality, a whisper with a lilt.

"It's very clear," she sang, "our love is here . . . to stay."

It was one of the tunes from the CD he'd been playing.

"Not . . . for . . . a year," he sang along with her, slowly, patiently, whispering too, "but . . . ever . . . and a day . . ."

She stopped, evidently out of breath, and her eyes closed. A very faint but definite smile stretched her withered lips. And then she seemed to fall asleep, her mouth still slightly open. Mulheisen sat by her, on the bed, and held her hand. When he was sure that she was asleep, he got up and went back to his room. His eyes were a little glassy, almost moist.

He called his old friend Jimmy Marshall, now a precinct commander. "Say, Jimbo, how's it going?" They chatted for a few moments and Mulheisen told him his mother seemed to be improving. He described the singing. Marshall was excited.

"Ruby Braff? I'll be damned," Marshall said. "Well, you know Braff, he was one of the last of the real swinging cornets. Very infectious, that kind of what-do-you-call it, *joie de vivre*. You should play her some Louis." Marshall was a fellow devotee.

"'Struttin' With Some Barbecue,'" Mulheisen suggested, "or, 'Potato Head Blues'?"

"How about 'I'm Comin' Virginia'?"

They went on in this vein, discussing music, but finally Mulheisen said, "Who's investigating the bombing? You know?"

Marshall told him it was the new agency, the Homeland Security people, but there were other groups involved. The Wards Cove police, for instance. And some of the Detroit cops were involved, drafted into it by the Homeland group. Wunney was one of them.

Mulheisen called Wunney. He was willing to discuss the investigation in the most general sort of way, as a courtesy to Mulheisen, because of his mother and because he had been a colleague. But it was clear after a minute or two that he didn't feel free to provide any details. The case seemed to have stalled.

"I talked to Tucker," Mulheisen said. "He came out to see me."

"What for?" Wunney said.

"He seemed to be recruiting," Mulheisen said. "He suggested you guys needed help."

"What guys? He's the liaison with the Homeland Security people, running this Special Task Force, they call it," Wunney said. "I probably shouldn't even be discussing him with you, not on the phone, anyway."

"Oh. Okay," Mulheisen said. "Well, I turned him down, anyway. It didn't sound like my kind of thing. I'm retired, you know."

"Yeah, I know. Well, if you're out and about, stop in and see us sometime, for old times. We're downtown." He mentioned an address in an office building just off Cadillac Square.

Mulheisen took a drive downtown the next day. He'd arranged for another nurse to be on hand, in case he was late getting back. His mother seemed livelier, but if he'd expected her to wake up talking he was disappointed. He hadn't exactly expected that, but she seemed more aware of her surroundings, at least. He wasn't sure he wanted to leave her alone at this critical juncture, but he was intrigued about the task force. He thought he could get away for a few hours.

The task force had taken a number of offices in one of those old buildings that Detroit seemed overstocked with these days. They looked pretty busy, with lots of computers, copiers, telephones, and secretaries. Wunney wasn't surprised to see him.

"Let's go for a walk, Mul," he said.

They strolled a block to a small bar on the square. Mulheisen remembered it as being called Johnny's, but now it belonged to some chain. Franchise bars—what a concept, Mulheisen thought. It seemed a little bright and clean for a Detroit tavern, but he wasn't interested in booze these days. He opted for coffee, as did Wunney. The coffee was very good, as it should be, costing what one used to pay for a shot of Jack Daniels.

"What do you know about Colonel Tucker?" Wunney asked.

Mulheisen smiled. "I was going to ask you that. I don't know anything about him."

"I don't know much," Wunney said. "Seems like a capable guy, in a way. Except I can never figure out what the fuck he does. Mysterious, you know? These spooks cultivate that style. They must think it adds to their image. They're into very deep stuff, doncha know? And on a very high level, the highest. But are they? Maybe they don't know shit—how could you tell? I guess he was CIA at one time."

Mulheisen said that when he'd first met the man, out in Salt Lake City, on a case involving money laundering, Tucker had been running an agency, or at least an operation, that was fronted by the Immigration and Naturalization Service.

"The INS is very big these days," Wunney said. "It's all under the umbrella of the Homeland guys. I'm detached to Homeland, for this task force. The pay is great! I think I'm supposed to be their link to the DPD. I provide them with Detroit info."

"Tucker mentioned Joe Service," Mulheisen said. "The name mean anything to you?"

"Not offhand," Wunney said. Then he added, "Oh, wasn't he a mob guy? He had something to do with Carmine and the Fat Man, but that's a few years back. You remember Andy Deane, Rackets and Conspiracy? Andy got it in his head that Service whacked Carmine."

"Yeah, Andy ran it down to me," Mulheisen said. "I couldn't quite see it. I thought it was the daughter, Helen, Big Sid's kid. The angle was that Carmine had Sid zipped, for skimming on some dope deal. There was a connection between the daughter and Service, which I guess is why Andy figured it must have been Service who did the job. The funny thing is, the reason I was in Salt Lake in the first place—when I met Tucker—was because I had a lead on the daughter. She was smurfing cash there, or that was the lead. You know, laundering dope money. I figured that would be Sid's money, the skim from Carmine. The word was the Fat Man, as Carmine's successor, was after her."

Wunney snorted. "Humphrey wasn't exactly the revenge type."

Mulheisen nodded. "More likely he just wanted to recover the skim. Anyway, the short of it is Helen winds up back in Humphrey's good graces. So much for revenge. It looked like Joe Service had engineered all this—recovered the money, made amends with Humphrey. That's the kind of stuff Service did. He made a career out of finding things for the mob, like who took their money, and where they were now. That doesn't mean he didn't pop Carmine, it just seems unlikely."

Wunney was interested. He knew pieces and bits of this tale, picked up here and there. "Okay, I think I see it," he said, "kinda." He didn't seem convinced.

Mulheisen shrugged. "Who knows? My impression is that Joe Service is perfectly capable of yanking the plug on anyone, but that was evidently not his real function in the mob. I never heard that he had any beef with Carmine, but he was pretty tight with Humphrey. Who knows? Maybe Humphrey had him hit Carmine. I had him in my hands once. But he was that close"— he snapped his fingers—"to being popped by that little weasel Itchy. Remember him?"

Wunney remembered Ezio "Itchy" Spinodi. A gunman who had taken a fall for Carmine or one of the other big boys many years ago. "Why would Itchy be after Service, if he was so tight with the Fat Man?" he wanted to know.

Mulheisen shook his head. "These guys live complicated lives. It looked to me like the national mob wanted Service dead. They must have figured he had to be at least too deep into Carmine's death to walk, even if he didn't actually pull the trigger. Humphrey either couldn't protect him, or didn't want to, at the time. There was an earlier hit attempt that almost succeeded. Service was recovering from that when I found him and headed off Itchy, but he had a serious relapse, a kind of stroke. I stashed him in a hospital, in Denver, thinking when he came out of his coma we could get together, maybe iron out some of the wrinkles. But they let the guy walk on me."

The two old detectives chewed on this one for a while, decrying the laxity of hospital security, sheriff's deputies. Finally Mulheisen said, "Tucker mentioned Service to me when he visited. In connection with the bombing. Joe Service the mad bomber? I don't think so, even if some kind of connection could be made out. Maybe it goes back to the deal in Salt Lake. Tucker and his guys were about to grab Helen. Service waltzed in and sprang her. He left Tucker handcuffed to a water pipe in the kitchen. A guy like Tucker isn't going to forget that insult to his dignity. Somewhere down the line he's going to find a jacket for Joe Service, don't you know?"

Wunney grunted, his version of a laugh. "Oh, yeah. Well, we were passed a thing about Service. An intercept, a phone call to some guy in Florida. This guy talked to Service about some Muslim group. It didn't make much sense to me. I didn't see a connection, except that someone else said the group might have a tie-in with the bombing, possibly."

"Might have a tie-in? That's the level you're working on?" Mulheisen shook his head. "Tucker kind of waved the Muslim angle off. He hinted at some local militia-type group."

"Well, if there's no Muslim angle," Wunney pointed out, "what's the connection with Service?" He almost managed to convey an expression of derisory disbelief, but he wasn't capable of that kind of facial mobility.

Mulheisen managed a complementary expression, suggesting that it was all nonsense. But he asked, "Isn't that the way they

do it? One Muslim is the same as any other, any connection becomes a universal coupling—it'll work in any context. So who was
the guy in Florida?"

"Ah, I don't know . . ." Wunney gazed at Mulheisen for a long
moment through slightly narrowed eyes. Then he said, "You know
him. Big Sid's old hench, the Yak."

"Yakovich?" Mulheisen smiled, his long teeth bared in the
expression that had given rise to his street nickname, Fang. "One
thing I know about the Yak, he's no Muslim."

"No, he's no Muslim, but he was in conversation with Service and Helen Sid, the daughter, about some Muslim group in
Brooklyn. The conversation was so vague, it was hard to get a take
on it. It sounded like the Muslims had something that Helen Sid
wanted. Maybe it was just info. I couldn't get anywhere with it. The
FBI was in on it. They thought it was a dope deal, but evidently
that didn't turn out."

"Who are these Muslims?" Mulheisen asked.

Wunney offered a nominal grin. "Albanians. They seemed
to have some connection with Kosovar refugees."

Mulheisen was baffled. The idea of Helen Sedlacek, Joe Service, and Roman Yakovich involved in a dope deal with Muslims
was too much for him.

"Where does the bombing come in?" he asked.

Wunney shrugged. "Muslims, Detroit mobsters. That's about
it. Like you say, it's a universal joint, turns in any direction."

"Makes my head spin," Mulheisen said. "So, what about this
militia group?"

"Mul? You in or out?"

"I don't know," Mulheisen said. "I have an interest, that's all.
Don't tell me anything that'll get you in trouble. Not that I'd say
anything, of course."

Wunney sighed. "Okay. All's it is's a joker named Luck, lives upstate, he's got visions of black helicopters, New World Order, ZOG—that's the Zionist Occupational Government—hates environmentalists, liberals, cops, any kind of government it looks like, dogcatchers, game wardens, you name it. Rumored to have been in Wards Cove at the wrong time. Access to explosives. Blah, blah, blah."

Mulheisen nodded. "You talk to him?"

"Oh, yeah. Nothing. He was off fishing, he says. He's got alibis . . . from guys who need alibis."

"What about the vehicle that was used? The explosive?"

"Vehicle was stolen in Detroit, no connection with Luck. Explosive was military, U.S., stolen. No Luck." He almost chuckled, a kind of choking sound. "That's what some of the boys call the case: No Luck."

"Ah, well." Mulheisen grimaced. "And if I go talk to him it won't go over too well—if I'm not in. Hmmmm. Any connection to Service?"

"The only connection that I know of is Service's name turned up on this guy's Web site," Wunney said.

"Terrorists have Web sites?"

"Of course they do, Mul. Where have you been? Anyway, all's he said about Service was that Service was a fed, an agent. It was supposed to be a word to the faithful to avoid him. But, as Tucker said, they say that about anyone, sometimes it's just a cover, disinformation." He paused, then asked, "So? You in?"

"I'll let you know," Mulheisen said. "What's this guy's full name?"

"Martin Parvis Luck," Wunney said, "but he goes by just the initials, M.P. He lives upstate, a little town called Queensleap."

It was such a muddle, Mulheisen thought, as he drove home along Lake St. Clair. Too many different services and factions, running around like the Keystone Kops, waving billy clubs and tumbling all over one another. And anyway, he was not a man obsessed with justice, not a revenger; he was with the late Humphrey DiEbola on that issue. So what, he asked himself, was he? An old dog, addicted to old tricks? Why had he ever gotten into this game? He had an orderly mind. He liked to know as much as he could. Puzzles attracted him; he liked to see a pattern. He was also patient. He felt that many puzzles, over time, simply resolved themselves.

He sometimes thought that up close, in the turbulence of the present, things were clouded. But with the passage of time, as in a river, the silt fell away. The opaque became translucent, if not transparent. One came to understand, more or less, how something happened, or could have happened, who was involved, what was behind the issue once so mysterious and later so evident.

There was no denying that there was a personal element here, but he refused to feel compulsive about this. It would resolve itself without him, he was sure.

His mother was old. She would die soon. He felt fairly cold-blooded about it. It made him sad, but beyond that he couldn't see that there was anything compelling about this mystery. He would die too. Perhaps before his mother. If it could be avoided, of course, one would avoid it. But death would come, willy-nilly.

In the long run the great trivial purpose of maximum entropy will prevail, he said to himself, quoting Norbert Wiener, the great mathematician, a statement that had sometimes soothed his mind, got him through the night. It didn't particularly soothe him at the moment.

Did that mean he didn't love his mother? Oh, no. All he wanted to do at the moment was take care of her, see her returned to at least a semblance of her old self. He'd like to go on a bird walk with her, have her point out the rose-breasted grosbeak. That wasn't much to ask, he thought. That, and build his little study.

The sun was very bright on the lake. Unconsciously, he whistled that Gershwin tune under his breath, "Love Is Here to Stay."

For the next few days he was busy taking his mother to the doctor for new tests. They were thrilled with her progress. She wasn't just singing, she was clearly becoming aware. This wasn't unmitigated joy. She was alarmed. Mulheisen could only imagine what was racing through her mind: What has happened to me? Am I all right? Why is Mul here? Am I dying?

It was too much for her. She lapsed into long periods of sleep. The doctors said that was good. They were excited that she had not experienced the classic symptoms of a stroke, of permanent aphasia. She wasn't incapable of speech. Of course, she hadn't had a stroke. She'd had a tremendous shock. As they explained it, her systems had not shut down, thankfully, but they had provided something like buffers, or filters, an inner sanctum where she could recover without further input. Now these buffers were dissolving, allowing her more sensory input . . . and output. No doubt, there was more to it, medically speaking, but as an explanation it sufficed for Mulheisen.

Unfortunately, as he saw it, this recovery prompted the renewed attention of Colonel Tucker and his minions. They were eager to talk to Cora Mulheisen, to learn what she might have observed just prior to the explosion. At present she wasn't up to that. She couldn't recall the explosion at all. She didn't even remember going to Wards Cove. Indeed, it was difficult to know what she did remember or think, because although she could now speak hesitantly, inquire about a few simple things, she was not capable of anything like an extended conversation on topics more complex than what was for lunch, how soon would it be ready, whether it was a nice day, warm out or cold. But just in the course of a day it seemed that her perceptions and her ability to converse improved.

She was much stronger. She could walk unaided, even with a degree of energy. She ate very well and put on weight. She dressed every day, could take a sitting-down shower with only a nurse to keep an eye on her and assist with a few of the more complicated tasks. Very soon she asked Mulheisen what he was doing home.

He said he'd taken a leave of absence. He was looking after her. He didn't know why he did not say he'd retired. Perhaps he hadn't wanted to complicate the discussion. She was quite aware that she'd suffered an injury, that she needed assistance. She wasn't ill, though, she knew that and said as much.

"You're back in your room," she said. He nodded. "What happened with"—she paused and looked at a loss, then finished with—"her? The woman. Ah! Becky!" She seemed pleased to recall the name.

Mulheisen shrugged. "It didn't work out," he said.

"Good," she said, and dropped the subject.

She enjoyed his readings, and the music. She was intrigued about his building project. She thought it was a good idea. "You'll have a place to smoke those old cigars," she said.

She also enjoyed the walks. A great day was the one on which they saw a green heron, crouching among the reeds along the river. She had noticed it first, even though it was in its camouflage posture of extending its long striped neck to emulate the reeds among which it stood. She pointed it out to Mul but he couldn't see it.

"Some detective," she muttered slyly. "Watch. There he is. He flattens his body, somehow. He's just beyond that old buoy. *Butorides virescens!*"

Mulheisen saw the bird. With its long neck outstretched, its beak pointing directly into the sky, the stripes on its throat looked very much like the reeds among which it was standing—it even swayed when the breeze ruffled the reeds. He was amazed. How had she noticed it? The creature seemed to be another reed. But as they stealthily approached it slowly withdrew its head and neck into its now expanded body until, finally, only the tip of its beak was visible. Now it looked like nothing more than a darkish lump among the reeds, perhaps a large rock. They took a few more steps, closer, and abruptly the bird launched itself into the air with a hoarse croaking cry and spread its surprisingly large wings, flapping powerfully. It emitted a great stream of chalky white liquid as it fled across the water.

The pair of them fell back, laughing. "My god, did you see that!" she cried. As they walked home, elated, she recited: "I saw a bird up in the sky. He dropped some whitewash in my eye. Aren't you glad that cows don't fly?"

That evening, as they prepared to read Stevenson's *The Beach of Falesá*, Cora suddenly said, "Shouldn't you be going back to work, Feddy?"

Mulheisen didn't know if he was more shocked at her inquiry or at her use of his childhood nickname. He stammered something like, "Ma! I've got plenty to do. I'm building a house. Maybe later, when you're feeling better . . . I might go back." It seemed to satisfy her, for the moment. He knew better than to suggest that she needed him to look after her. As it was, she just scoffed at his protests.

"Oh, you and your study! Well, I suppose you'll go back when curiosity gets the better of you."

A few days later she volunteered that she'd remembered a couple of things. She wondered if the police shouldn't know. Mulheisen sighed and called Tucker.

4

Home Guard

Joe Service was on his way to kill his neighbor's wife. He hadn't killed anybody in so long that he had begun to feel innocent . . . not that Joe's conscience had ever plagued him on this score. He never thought of these targets as victims, only as . . . targets, some more deserving of Joe's dispensation than others. The last person he'd chilled had richly deserved it. The guy had, in fact, been on the verge of killing Joe. Several men had been on that verge, over the years. It wasn't a comfortable verge: all of them had tumbled into the abyss of Hell, to use a convenient name for the trash bin of homicidal incompetence.

This dispensation of Fedima Oberavich was different: not, strictly speaking, a matter of self-defense. Although, as Joe saw it, in the long run it was totally defensive, in the manner of a pre-emptive strike. Fedima was bound to bring him into mortal danger, he felt. She was threatening his well-being, at present, and his life, ultimately.

Fedima Oberavich had given birth to her first child four months after she was married. It was a bit of a surprise, since she hadn't appeared to be pregnant at the time of the wedding. Anyone acquainted with her history immediately did a little mental math and then sighed at least inwardly with relief. It couldn't have been the child of the monster, Bozi Bazok, who had murdered her family, kidnapped her and raped her innumerable times during their trek out of Kosovo, too many months earlier.

No one alive knew that her lover in Kosovo had been her husband Frank's late cousin, Paulie. But obviously, he was not the father of the child. Nor could it have been her husband, whom she'd met only a few weeks before the marriage took place. It had to have been some unknown fellow along the route that brought her to America. Fedima wasn't talking. After all, it was of no consequence. The significant thing was that she was now a mother. It was a transforming event.

There was no one in the world who could now testify to the character of Fedima, at least in the sense of knowing her past. Her entire family had been wiped out by the paramilitary beast Bozi Bazok, who had all by himself slaughtered her mother and younger siblings and her extended family in a cave in the hills behind the farm where her people had tilled the land and piled the rocks of the fields for more than a hundred years. Fedima, and now her son— inevitably named Paul—were the sole living descendants of the family Daliljaj . . . at least, as far as Fedima knew. There may have been some cousins, but she didn't know of them.

This horrendous situation was shockingly not rare among the peasants of Kosovo. But for Fedima it was no less devastating. Who knew that she had been a heroine of sorts? Who saw that in the demure, seemingly complacent young girl who had somehow made her way to America and been, finally, offered as a bride to a young man of remote Serbian heritage in faraway Montana, here was a young woman of unusual courage and determination?

Among those living about her now it soon became apparent that she was not a shrinking violet. She was no pushover, no complaisant wife for Frank Oberavich. An early indication was her adamant insistence that something must be done about the two dogs,

Sylvie and Bruno. These two dogs were the faithful servants of Frank, an important component of his security system. But they had demonstrated that they would attack a human being: they had torn to pieces the villainous woman Jamala Sanders, who had murdered their favorite human, Paul, and then threatened the lives of Frank and Joe. Fedima had not witnessed this incident; it didn't sway her. She insisted that the dogs were a threat to her child.

Others were concerned. Dogs that would attack a human, albeit one who represented a danger to their master, were considered by many to be irrevocably damaged. Frank was devoted to them, however. He offered to have them retrained. But that was not acceptable to Fedima. The dogs must be put down. Joe and Helen were drawn into the discussion. They were grateful to the dogs, which were always complaisant toward them. But they soon saw that Fedima would not be swayed. The only compromise was that they would be "gotten rid of," which meant they would be sent away, presumably to be retrained and given into the possession of someone else, far away. Colonel Tucker saw to it. The dogs were "reassigned" to a K-9 program in another state, to be used by law enforcement.

The incident pained Frank considerably, but he was learning that his lovely young wife was not to be swayed in matters where she felt strongly. In addition, he found that she would brook no replacement with similar dogs of such a nature. The dog of Anders Ericsson was viewed with suspicion, but it was not really a resident dog and it was not in Fedima's power to banish it. Anyway, it was tame enough, and the little dog of Joe and Helen, Homes, was deemed safe.

The next issue encountered was Fedima's argument that all this open space belonging to her husband, two thousand acres, should be converted to some useful agricultural purpose. For a young woman raised in Kosovo it was unconscionable that so much open land was allowed to be "idle." If Frank refused to cultivate the land, perhaps to raise a good crop of wheat, at least it must be put to use as grazing land. Perhaps a small herd of cattle could be introduced. The land was well fenced, there was ample water, corrals could be built, barns. The idea appalled Frank. Who would tend the cattle? He wasn't a cowboy. He was a talented gardener, of sorts, dedicated to his small crop of marijuana, which he grew in the house, essentially a greenhouse, complete with an elaborate irrigation system. He had no notion of raising cattle, seeing to their health, feeding them in winter, buying hay, marketing them. Given his avocation, if you could call it that, he was not about to hire hands, more or less strangers who might expose him to legal problems.

Again, Fedima was insistent. Soon, some fifty head of cross-bred red Angus were wandering the hills, placidly chomping on grass, trampling in the hot springs, leaving their abominable splatter everywhere. Fences had to be erected around Joe and Helen's property, along the river, around the hot springs. A gate was installed on the road to Joe and Helen's place. It was annoying. It took up far too much of Frank's time and energy. What next?

Joe was angry. This was an altogether unacceptable imposition on his Eden. Life had been fine until this idiot woman and her baby had come into the picture. First the dogs, then the cows. Now, with the disquieting information provided by Caspar, Joe felt insecure without the dogs. Franko was supposed to keep an eye on security—he had an elaborate alarm system and even remote TV cameras at the gate—but now he was so busy that Joe knew he wasn't monitoring the system. Well, who could? The remoteness made you feel secure, at first, and the openness of the approaches, but it was impossible to really be secure without guards. Who wanted that? Strangers couldn't really protect you. But Joe and Helen had fallen into that square, Home Guard mode. They were no longer Inside, no longer part of the Life. Caspar was just a residue of that life. They were outside, now, out in the free world, and yet not really of that life. Joe marveled at how readily he had fallen in with it. He felt exposed.

He considered the situation calmly as he drove from his unfinished house, where he had left Helen sprawled and spent on their bed. It was no more than a half mile to Frank's house, down a dusty two-track road. Joe drove slowly. He had ample time to weigh his thoughts on this fateful act. He had been more shocked than he realized by the implications of Caspar's warning. His life was changing again. He didn't feel angry, just resolved.

He had a feeling that he'd not be coming back this way afterward. He'd very likely never see Helen again. It wouldn't even be wise for him to visit Montana again, which made him sad. At present, he wasn't sure where he would go; he didn't have time for these thoughts but he was sure it would be somewhere nice.

He wasn't angry. Joe avoided anger. It was a waste of time. Very early in life he had given a great deal of thought to the problem of anger. His analysis was that typically anger arose as a result of an injury. Anger made it difficult to act. It clouded one's mind, blinded one to further danger. If one needed to retaliate, or otherwise compensate for the injury, especially quickly, anger was something one couldn't afford. If the injury was not sufficient to require action, then one ought to shrug off the injury. He'd practiced this, over the years, and he'd become proficient at it.

Yet he'd ponder anger in idle moments. It seemed to him that most people indulged their anger, nourished it. Apparently, they did this because they were afraid to act. They didn't want to disturb things. They were content to live with their anger, he felt. Presumably, they eventually forgot about the source of it, although he supposed there was always some bitter residue stuffed away in the back of the mind, likely to surface at odd moments.

Jon A. Jackson

That was probably the case with most anger-inducing situations. There were also, of course, those situations where one simply couldn't react, daren't react, because the source of the injury was too powerful. In that case, one was forced to swallow one's anger, which became a corrosive acid in one's stomach. Perhaps, in some uncharted future, one could react, savagely no doubt, but it would likely be too late.

Joe didn't want any of that. When an occasion for anger arose, he felt he should recognize it, decide as quickly as possible if it was an actionable offense, and, if it wasn't, wave it away. That didn't mean he would forget that an injury had been done to him, although he supposed he had forgotten most if not all of the minor injuries done. But if it didn't require a response, then admit as much to himself, promptly, and let that be enough.

Case in point: it was bad enough that Fedima had successfully convinced Frank to get rid of the two watchdogs Bruno and Sylvie. Joe had conceded that these dogs, having demonstrated that they would attack human beings, must have seemed to Fedima too great a threat to the life of her child, Paulie, to ignore. When Joe looked at it from her point of view, he felt that her fears were, if far-fetched, simply too intense to be overcome. So he'd shrugged off Frank's decision to send the dogs away.

But the cows were too much. Farming might be in Fedima's blood, but that blood could be let. It was ridiculous. Frank was not a farmer, or a rancher. He raised marijuana. That might be considered gardening, but it wasn't farming, and definitely not ranching. Beyond that, they had plenty of money. They didn't need to do anything but fish and hunt and dawdle in the hot springs. Most important, Joe and Helen depended on Frank to provide a kind of buffer between them and the rest of the world, which couldn't otherwise reach Joe's place without going through Frank's. It was a security issue. Joe was very keen on security. Now, with Caspar's revelations, he didn't have that anymore.

And he hated cows—miserable, slab-sided, shit-smeared, stupid beasts that wandered everywhere as if in a daze, treading down the banks of the stream, dirtying the hot springs, leaving their splattered crap everywhere, bringing flies. If Frank had cows, Joe necessarily had cows. He didn't like looking out of his window and seeing cows. Well, he wouldn't have cows anymore, but he couldn't leave without doing something about it.

"Why do cows get out?" he'd asked Anders Ericsson.

"A cow is about the stupidest creature on earth," Anders had explained to Joe. "It grazes along a fence line—for no good reason, there's plenty of grass all around—but it's grazed over to the fence, so now the fence is like a guide. Then, the cow comes to a hole in the fence. Maybe a tree fell on it, or a deer tripped jumping over. Anyway, the cow immediately ducks through the hole. Why? There's no better grass on the other side, usually. But the guide line has been disrupted, so the cow goes through, looking for the next barrier. It could walk two steps and find where the barrier resumed, but it doesn't want to do that. The cow goes through every time. Cows will not walk past a hole in a fence. They're either committed opportunists, or mindless hammerheads."

Joe hated that kind of mindlessness. He was leaving, but he couldn't let the cows win. Frank, he knew, didn't give a damn about the cows. He'd like to get rid of them himself. They took up too much of his time. It was just Fedima. You had pastureland, you had to have cows. It was bullshit . . . or, rather, cowshit.

Luckily, the issue had come to a head at a good time. It was fall, time to market the cows. Otherwise, you had to feed them through the winter. Fedima didn't want to market them, not all of them. The bigger, healthier cows should be bred. They'd calve in the spring. They would build their herd. They could artificially inseminate or they could buy a bull. Fedima leaned toward buying a bull. She also wanted some milk cows, a couple of goats, some sheep. Even pigs.

"Pigs?" Frank was surprised. Fedima was a Muslim woman. Why would she want a pig? But it seemed that even Muslims raised pigs where she was from. In Kosovo, as in Serbia proper, pigs were traditional market animals—the Serbs, the Croats and Slovenes, and beyond them the Hungarians and the Germans had a seemingly insatiable appetite for pork. The Kosovars ate pork too, although perhaps not these days. One of the reasons, in fact, that the Kosovars had not gotten much aid from other Muslims in their struggle for independence, at least initially, was that they had become so like their Serbian neighbors that traditional Muslims tended to shake their heads and say, These are not Believers. They eat pork.

Frank was bound to side with Fedima if it came to a dispute with Joe, but not over a pig. He was having no pigs. Fedima relented. No pigs. But having relented on that she held firm for sheep, goats, and building up the cattle stock. She had convinced Frank, in July, that there was so much ungrazed native grass it could be mowed and picked up for fodder. He had an old barn, in which there was already some very old hay, moldering away. That hay had been in there for years. Some of it had been used to hide a rented vehicle that the ogre Bazok had abandoned near their fence line. The idea had been to conceal it in the event that cops came around looking for Bazok. Frank had dug a hole in the field with a backhoe and they'd buried the car. They cleaned out the hay and stored the fresh. So now they had hay. They could keep, say, a third of the cattle, the best ones. Fedima consented to artificial insemination, for now.

Joe wasn't having it. As a concerned neighbor, not a tenant, he felt compelled to insist on the primacy of security. All this agriculture and husbandry had given him a headache. At his old place, down on the Ruby, some sixty miles south, he had owned a hundred acres or so of a mountain, with his land backing onto thousands of acres of national forest and BLM land. He still owned this property, but for complicated reasons he had no intention of living on it. A rancher owned all the land between him and the highway. That rancher had left him alone, tended the fences, and took good care of the cattle, providing a de facto barrier between Joe and the outside world. This was a different situation. Frank was not a rancher. Joe explained this to him, patiently.

"I'm thinking of going into it more," Frank said. "Fedima's right, it's time I gave up this marijuana stuff. We got a kid now. It's not good. That was okay when I was batching it, you know? The kid'll be going to school before you know it. What's he gonna do, tell the teacher his daddy's a dope dealer? Nah, Fedima's right. We could put in a couple hundred acres of good hay, timothy, maybe. We'd have enough to sell, even."

Joe listened, dispiritedly. Frank was into a rave about the irrigation system he'd build. That appealed to him, Joe knew. Just the idea of building a new, elaborate irrigation system was enough to excite Frank. Joe had let it ride, but now he thought he'd do something about it.

A couple of days after Caspar's visit and Joe's call to the Colonel, Tucker had called back. "I think I found something, about the guys who were supposed to be interested in you," he said.

"Who are they?" Joe asked.

The Colonel told him about a bombing in Detroit. Joe hadn't heard anything about it. He never followed the news. Tucker said it was believed at first to have been the work of Arab terrorists. But now the feeling was that it was another, unrelated group. "Anyway, your name came up," the Colonel said.

Joe was shocked. "Me? I'm no bomber. What's this?"

"Did you sell any explosives, any arms, in the last couple of years?"

"No," Joe said.

"Think, Joe. Your house down in the Ruby. It blew up. How did that happen?"

"That's my business," Joe said. He had rigged the house when he'd built it. It was rigged to be totally destroyed in case he was raided. He had wanted no telltale evidence left behind in the event that he had to leave in a hurry. The system was rigged to involve a large propane tank. The house would burn to fine ashes and it would seem to be simply a propane explosion, not so unusual in rural Montana. And, as it happened, he'd had to trigger the system. Echeverria had been all but killed in that blast.

Joe's recent visitor, Caspar, of course, had mentioned Echeverria as one of the names of the men involved in the search for him. Echeverria had actually escaped from that inferno, though badly burned. Joe had been employed by the Colonel to finish the job, months later. So Echeverria was dead, but he would have friends.

"So now you're telling me that Echeverria's pals are involved in bombing, in Detroit?" Joe said. "They've gone into the terrorist business?"

"Not exactly," the Colonel said. "It's complicated. We should talk, but not on the phone. I think it's the lead you wanted."

Joe agreed to meet. They didn't make a date. Both men were too careful for that. Joe would call him in a few days, from some unspecified location, and set a rendezvous.

Joe told Helen he had to go and meet Colonel Tucker. The way he explained it, this would close out their contact with the Colonel and his group, the Lucani. Neither of them wanted anything further to do with these rogue agents. They were too unstable, and too likely to both betray and be betrayed. But it had to be resolved. He might be gone for a week or so. He was sorry he had to leave her with so much work. Helen didn't mind. It was what mainly occupied her, working on the place. She wanted to get the house ready so her mother could visit for Christmas.

"Don't get into trouble with Anders," Joe said, joking.

Helen bridled. "You must be kidding. He's over forty."

"He's got the hots for you," Joe said. "I've seen the way he looks at you in the hot springs. But I'm not worried about him. It's you. You might get lonely."

They sparred over that for a while, but as always it ended in wrestling and then making love. An hour later, having packed up the Durango, Joe was driving out, already engaged in road thoughts. He had taken everything he needed to take. He was glad that he and Helen had parted as they had. If he never came back, well, at least they'd had that.

He believed that he was making a clean break. He had regrets, but basically he felt all right. He'd gotten too into this straight life, he knew. The visit from Caspar had been the jolt he'd needed. He'd gotten so complacent with domestic concerns that he'd forgotten who he was. He was crazy about Helen, but he'd have had to leave her eventually anyway, he supposed. Even if they'd grown old together, he thought, one of them would die. And there had been the nagging feeling about the Colonel and the Lucani. That relationship wouldn't have gone on much longer, he was sure. Well, now he'd take of that, too, after he dealt with this problem with Echeverria's men. And Fedima.

It was the irritation with Fedima that had precipitated all this, he saw. Those damned cows. What to do about Fedima? This woman had a different agenda. This kind of thing would only go on, build to greater and greater issues. Next, she'd feel lonely. She would start thinking about the value of this hidden paradise, the money it would bring if they sold some river frontage for vacation homes. The lovely neighbors they would have.

It was inevitable: paradise was threatened. Joe had no long-range plans. He hadn't considered this, but if asked he would have supposed that very likely he would eventually live somewhere else. But that was some purely putative future. For now, he could be satisfied that he'd left a safe, beautiful place, a hole-in-the-wall, for Helen.

It was odd, he thought, but he had never considered the consequences of Frank marrying Fedima, having a family. A family! He was sure, now that he thought of it, that Fedima was bound to have many more kids, dozens. Good god! She had to be stopped.

He drove slowly over the ridge and saw Fedima outside the house. She was hanging clothes on the line. She wore a housedress with a floral print and a babushka. When she saw the Durango, she waved to him. Joe pulled into the drive and sat in the car, waiting. He reached down between the front seats to make sure his automatic was handy. He swiftly racked a shell into the chamber as she walked down the drive, barefoot. He settled the .38 into the crevice between the seat and the center console.

Joe looked around. Was this the last time he'd see this country? It was very beautiful, the long, sweeping meadows rising to the ridge, and far beyond them the dark crags of the continental divide.

Fedima looked rather fetching, a slim, dark beauty in her early twenties, with large dark eyes. The light was behind her as she approached and Joe realized that she was clearly wearing nothing more than the housedress. She smiled as she came up to the Durango. Joe did not get out. He liked her, almost against his will. A pretty girl can do that to a man.

She leaned with both hands on the door, her fingers curled over the window opening, peering in. She saw his bags. "Joe, where you going?"

"Ah, business," Joe said. "Where's the baby?"

"He is taking a nap," she said, glancing back at the house. "Frank is fishing, again."

"Where?" Joe said. It occurred to him that he would have to kill Frank, too. Frank would never harm a soul, intentionally, but he could tell investigators far too much about Joe. He felt a bitter regret—it was Fedima's fault. But what about the baby? Joe hadn't considered that. He dismissed the thought; it wouldn't be necessary to kill the baby. Perhaps Helen would take the baby. But he realized, almost in the act of thinking it, that Helen would never get that baby. Some state agency or, perhaps, one of Frank's relatives, in Butte.

"Up that way, I think," Fedima said, stepping back from the car and waving a bare arm over toward the river. The gesture exposed her to the backlight of the sun, the thin cotton of the dress not much more than a chiffon veil. Joe could see the shadow of her pubic hair, the actual shape and thrust of those youthful breasts, the dark nipples. Then she leaned close again. "He won't be back for hours." Her voice was husky.

Joe stared at her. Was she coming on to him? She was leaning on the door of the car, her face very near. He could feel her breath. A mere nod would bring their lips into contact. Her smile was tentative, almost mocking, and it made his blood quicken. He couldn't help but notice that the buttons of her dress were undone, revealing a deep cleavage.

Joe looked away from her close face, out the windshield. It was one of those splendid Montana fall days, a deep blue sky without a cloud. The wind drifted quietly across the hills, stirring the grass gently, lifting the sheets on the line languorously. They'd be dry in minutes in this air.

He thought, Why not? He visualized the quiet midmorning house, the baby asleep, the usual drowsy heaviness of the marijuana plants and the flowers on the air. He imagined unbuttoning that dress, her warm tanned skin, her breath hot and fast, the wet tongue. She would be supple to his touch, silky dry here, then gluily moist there . . .

But he had just made love to Helen. The idea vanished, replaced by annoyance. He let his hand slip to the crevice, feeling the cool metal of the automatic.

Then she said, "Joe, you are not angry with me? About the dogs? You must understand how a mother feels. I am scared of every little thing. I have been thinking, we need to be good neighbors. I don't want this feeling I have, that we are not easy. Is it the cows?"

She stepped back, her hands on her hips. She looked very sensible, thoughtful.

"Perhaps you are right about the cows," she conceded. "I am thinking . . . you are upset about the fence. Security is important. I feel that also. You can imagine, after what I went through, in Kosovo. We could fence the cows, away someplace, over the ridge. A double fence. There is so much room. What do you think?"

"Over the ridge?" Joe said.

"You know, the far meadow," she said. She pointed up beyond the house. Joe was bemused by the all-but-perfect outline of her left breast, full and rounded. Helen was a woman with the breasts of a boy, a feature that had a kind of negative attraction for Joe. He hadn't really contemplated a full figure in some time.

"Would there be enough grazing?" he managed to ask.

"Oh, yes, very much grass, I think," she said. "And, now I think . . . we do not need so many cows. A few beefs . . . is it 'beefs'? That don't sound izzack. And a couple of milking cows. I miss the milking cows, when they come home in the evening . . . *ding, ding* . . . the bells, when they walk. When I was a little girl, my father sends me to bring home the cows to milk. I am a farm girl, you see? I do not, I cannot forget it. Everything else . . . they are all gone now, but perhaps I can hear the ding, ding of the milking cows again."

She smiled and stood, hands on hips, legs spread, and bare feet planted on the solid earth. She looked around, her eyes taking in the distance.

"Is so beautiful here," she said. "So peaceful. That I like very much. That is the most important thing. I think you agree, Joe? We must first be sure of that."

Joe's hand crept back into his lap.

"But I would like a few chickens," she said. "Maybe the chickens will be enough—no sheep, or goats. We will keep them in the barn. Enough so that we can have fresh eggs. There will be enough eggs for you, Joe. And Helen."

"If you have chickens," Joe said, "you must be careful of the hawks." He nodded toward the large red-tailed hawk that was soaring beyond the ridge. "And there are bobcats, too. I've heard them. Frank should build a regular coop."

"A coop? A house for chickens? Yes, maybe." Fedima shrugged. "But you cannot protect every chicken," she said. "My father said that. The fox used to come and take a chicken, sometimes. He would not shoot the fox."

"No? Why not?"

Fedima shrugged. "The fox was too beautiful, I think. A wild thing. But my father says only,'The fox has to live. I have many chickens. If the fox will not be greedy, I am not greedy.'"

"A few chickens would be all right," Joe said. "Yes, that would work, I think."

She stood back, smiling frankly, pleased to have solved an annoying problem. But then she frowned. "Joe, you will not be gone long?"

"Not too long, I hope," Joe said. "Why?"

"I wanted to speak with you. About that woman. Frank showed me a picture of her, that Paul had sketched. I have seen her before, in Tsamet."

She was speaking of Jamala Sanders, an agent of the Colonel's, who had turned out to be a double agent. Frank's cousin Paul had met her in Kosovo and sketched her. He had also met Bazok, which was how tragedy had come from the Balkans to Montana. Bazok and Jamala were both dead and, tragically, so was Paul. But in their wake had come Fedima, looking for Paul but finding Frank.

"I understood that Paul had seen her there," Joe said. "Tsamet must be just a small town."

"But I saw her with a man," Fedima said. "They were in a car. Later, I saw this man in America, when I was living in the house in Brooklyn. He came to the house where I was staying. I thought I should tell you. Frank says that you and the Colonel would want to know this."

"I suppose it would interest the Colonel," Joe said. "Who was he?"

"The people I stay with, they did not trust him, but they had to . . ." She hesitated, searching for a word. "They must tolerate him. He is important man in Kosovo, with the KLA."

"The KLA? The Kosovo Liberation Army? Was he a Kosovar?"

"Oh, no. He was an Arab. Muhammad al-Huq. In Tsamet, he also came to my father's house, to talk to my father and some of the other farmers. He was Saudi, they said."

Joe had nothing to say about it. He supposed the Colonel would be interested. He promised Fedima he would mention it to him the next time they spoke.

"Will it be soon?" Fedima pressed him. "This man was very . . ." she hesitated, frowning as she tried to find a word.

"Very what?" Joe said.

"Very dark," she said, lamely. "A very dark heart. They called him 'al-Qaeda.' After he left. It was a . . . what do you say? . . . a nix-name."

"A nickname. Al-Qaeda? That, I'm sure, the Colonel will like to know. Especially the fact that he knew Jammie Sanders."

A half hour later, as he pulled up to to the stop sign at the highway, Joe thought for a second or two—left or right? The right led to Butte, the left to Helena. For no reason that he could think of, he took the left turn.

A few minutes later when the car was up to highway speed, his road thoughts resumed. How can you kill someone if you start imagining what they think, if you see things with their eyes? He was glad he hadn't killed her. Things would work out, they were on the same page. And—he couldn't repress the thought—he would see her again. Who knows, they might even be lovers. Anyway, if he'd killed her the Colonel would be pissed. Perhaps, he thought, I'll kill this Hook.

5

A Dog's Luck

"More is less" was not a byword with Mulheisen, especially when it came to information. But sometimes, he thought, what you already know can influence what you think about what you don't yet know. Still, he felt light on information about this case. On the other hand, he'd been out of the loop long enough that he felt quite refreshed. It had been a mistake to poke around in the task force, he thought, although it was important to have heard a little from Wunney. The name M. P. Luck, for instance, that was good to know.

Mul had no intention of rejoining anybody's force, at least not yet, despite his mother's suggestion. At this point, his lack of official status served him as well as being on the payroll. He looked in the various telephone books he'd kept when he left the DPD and quickly found Luck. Queensleap was a little town more than two hundred miles from Detroit, up near Kalkaska, between Traverse City and Cadillac. He had some familiarity with that north woods country, from when he'd belatedly investigated the death of Jimmy Hoffa.

From what Mulheisen could find out from atlases and guides now somewhat out of date, the town had a population of five hundred or so. It had apparently been a part of the potato boom early in the twentieth century, after the great stands of white pine had been logged off. Now it was little more than a bedroom community for larger towns like Traverse City, about fifteen miles north.

He drove up there on a cool autumn day, listening to CDs of Coleman Hawkins and Benny Carter while he drove, smoking cigars. The fall foliage was spectacular, especially north of Midland, the last outpost of industrialism in the lower Michigan peninsula. This was rolling country, more pronounced as one drove north. He'd left the freeway for the blue highways, two-lane roads that led through one small town after another. It was farm country, but the corn was harvested, the vegetable stands closed and shuttered for the winter. It was orchard country too, however, and here and there were farm trucks parked at crossroads, offering fresh McIntosh for sale, with occasional bushels of rarer apples like Sweet Sixteen, Jonathan, Winesap, and Northern Spy. Mulheisen stopped to buy a peck of incredibly crisp and juicy hybrids called Jonamacs.

Deer were abundant; he had to keep his eye out for them. There were also orchards that offered something called "deer apples, all you can pick, $5." Apparently, it was legal to bait deer with apples, an idea that struck Mul as goofy, considering that there were plenty of apples in the older orchards, just lying on the ground or still hanging, for the deer to eat. But he wasn't a hunter. Perhaps there was an angle he didn't know about.

An old-timer with "Charlie" embroidered on his greasy overalls pumped gas at a Sinclair station in Queensleap and wiped the windshield. He admired Mul's old Checker. "I thought they quit making these," he said. "What year is it? Seventy-two?"

Mulheisen informed Charlie that Checker had gone out of business in 1982, mostly because the plant was so outmoded that it would have cost millions to bring it up to a competitive state. But there were still mechanics who worked on Checkers and kept them running. This one had a sturdy old Chevrolet V-8 engine.

"I worked on a million of 'em," Charlie said. "The Chevy engines, anyways."

Mul asked how the town had gotten its name. Charlie said that he'd heard it was named after some Indian woman, sort of a wise woman, or maybe even the chief—who knew? These were farmer Indians, Potawatomie, maybe. They were pretty well off, not dependent on hunting so much, or the fur trade. They'd naturally been at odds with some other tribes, or bands, who were hunters and in need of food in the winter. These hunting Indians had attacked the village. The queen, or whatever she was, had escaped being murdered by leaping across the little creek that ran through the town, Fox Creek.

"The creek must of been bigger in them days," Charlie said. "It wouldn't be an Olympic leap, nowadays. Anyways, the later settlers must of heard the story and liked it. They named it after her instead of old man Luckenbach, which is why it wasn't called— thank god—Luckenbach."

"Who is Luckenbach?" Mulheisen asked.

"Oh, he was in the timber business," Charlie said. "He made a lot of money logging off the country and then he got into the bank racket, and a bunch of other things."

Mulheisen asked if there were any Luckenbachs still around.

"No," Charlie said. "They went the way of the Indians. But there's some Lucks. They're half-ass Luckenbachs, just shortened the name."

"I'm looking for a Luck," Mul said. "M. P. Luck. You know him?"

Charlie's eyes narrowed. "Yeah, I know Imp. Known him all my life, so far. You a friend of his?"

"Not really," Mul said. "I just want to talk to him."

"He lives out quite a ways. Not so easy to find the place. Does he know you're comin'?"

Mul admitted that he didn't. Was that a problem?

"Could be," Charlie said. "Imp's gotten to be a solitary cuss. Since his old lady died, a couple years back. You a cop? Or one of these patriot fellows?"

Mulheisen replied rather cautiously that he wasn't a cop, but while he'd always thought of himself as a patriot, that wasn't why he wanted to talk to Luck.

That seemed to be the right answer. Charlie observed, "Seems like Imp don't care for unannounced visitors these days. He's got some signs and stuff, warning folks not to trespass. You might better call him."

This wasn't good news. Mulheisen had hoped that he could just drop in. But he went to the pay phone and called the number in the book. There was no answer.

Charlie said that he was pretty sure Luck was around, although he was often in and out of the area, traveling. He might be hunting, or maybe just out in the yard. He gave complicated instructions on how to find the place. It involved driving several miles west, past various farms that would have signs indicating who lived there or had barns one could recognize.

"Go on out past the old Grange hall," Charlie explained, "to where the blacktop ends. The cross road is gravel. Hang a left and go about a quarter mile—you'll see Imp's mailbox—take that two-track that runs back into the woods. There's a locked gate down there a ways." He cautioned Mulheisen about wandering around in the woods out there. Luck didn't like strangers wandering around. He had a tendency to shoot.

"Has he ever shot anyone?" Mulheisen asked.

"Not that I know of, but he's threatened to. He's had some problems with the law. The law don't go in there without they tell him they're coming."

Mulheisen said he'd be careful and took off. He had a cell phone, just in case, but he wasn't confident about using it. He wasn't that familiar with it. As he drove he was surprised by the number of new houses that had been built back in these hills. They were amazingly large houses—some of them with absurd pillars, in some kind of faux neo-Greek or antebellum mode—but all with huge lawns well mowed, long drives, fancy cars or SUVs parked in the drives. This was side by side with dilapidated farmhouses, some of them occupied, with numerous dogs in elaborate kennels, pickup trucks and abandoned farm machinery standing about, enormous stacks of firewood. There were also the more prosperous old farms that Charlie had mentioned, with big barns and signs advertising various enterprises like hay or grain, apples or maple syrup.

Mulheisen followed the directions scrupulously and soon came to the graveled county road. A short way along this he spotted the large mailbox with the name M. P. LUCK painted on it. Despite a prominent sign warning that this was a private road and NO TRESPASSING, he turned onto the narrow two-track that led back in the brush toward the woods. It was at least a half mile down this road to a gate that had some kind of electric or electronic lock. That was as far as he could drive. He was surrounded by thick sumac and a mixture of mature hardwoods and dense scrub pine.

Mulheisen got out the phone and, with the aid of the instruction booklet he'd wisely remembered to bring along, he managed to dial the right number. It rang and rang. No answering machine and no one picked up the phone.

Mulheisen got out of the car and walked along the fence that ran into the woods. The fence posts were steel, sunk in concrete with frequent bracing, the four strands of barbed wire very taut. No good place to get over. He returned to the car and sat there, eating one of his apples, which was so juicy that he had to dig out some paper toweling and wipe his sticky hands. He'd left Detroit that morning but it had been a long drive. It was getting late. He had seen school buses on the road on his way out from town. It had been a sunny day but now that the sun was going down it was cool. He tried the phone again. No answer. He decided to go back to Queensleap, find a motel, and try to contact Luck later.

There was no place to turn around. He began to back up the car, an awkward process, the road twisty and hemmed in by the brush. He looked for a little clearing, or at least a wide spot, but none offered. He was halfway back to the county road when a large, four-wheel-drive pickup truck with a massive steel brush guard came hustling up in his rear and stopped just in time. Mulheisen slammed on his brakes. The two men he could see in the cab of the pickup were bearded and wore dark baseball caps. They just sat in the vehicle and waited.

"Well, now what?" Mulheisen thought. He started to get out, but when he turned back to the wheel he realized that, unheard, another truck had come up from the other direction. It had stopped barely a couple of feet from his bumper. He was trapped, with heavy brush on either side, barely enough room to open a door. But he managed, squeezing out and deciding that the later arrival was more likely to be Luck, still sitting behind the wheel of the pickup in front of him.

It was a peculiar impasse, he thought. It appeared that the custom in these parts was to just sit in one's vehicle and wait for the stranger to make a move. Like the other vehicle, the new arrival was one of those high-riding, monster pickups with four-wheel drive and a sturdy brush guard. It was a fairly new Dodge Ram, he noticed, a little smaller than a B-17 and covered with mud and dirt.

Mulheisen approached the truck. The window rolled down electrically and the driver peered down. He was a mild-looking fellow, clean-shaven, wearing photo-sensitive glasses that just retained a shadow of tint. He had steel-gray hair under a canvas waterproof field hat.

Mulheisen's cop mind registered this as: *handsome man, and conscious of it . . . strong, straight nose, firm mouth, prominent chin . . . late middle age but could pass for much younger . . . could be a businessman, more likely an executive in a large corporation rather than an entrepreneur.*

"Having trouble reading?" the man said. He didn't smile, but he didn't frown either.

"Are you M. P. Luck?"

"I am, and you're on my land. Who might you be?"

"The name is Mulheisen. I'm from Detroit. I came up here to see you."

"Mulheisen?" The man's calm gaze turned to a speculative frown. "Are you a cop?" he asked, not suspiciously so much as mildly curious.

"No," Mulheisen said.

"Funny, you look like a cop," Luck said. From his tone, he might have been teasing.

"Well, the truth is, I used to be. But I quit."

"How come?"

"Personal problems," Mulheisen said. "My mother was . . . injured. She needed my help."

Luck nodded, thoughtfully. "Was? She's better now?"

Mulheisen nodded. "She's much improved."

"What happened to her?"

Mulheisen glanced around. It seemed inappropriate to be having this kind of conversation out here in the woods, in this odd situation. Perhaps it didn't seem odd to country people, although he didn't have the impression that Luck was any kind of bucolic character. "She got blown up," he said.

"Blown up? Your mother was blown up? What the—? You mean she was in an explosion? Was she hurt bad?"

"Pretty bad," Mulheisen said. "She's pretty much recovered now, after six months. But she was dazed and confused . . . it was more like a walking coma. She didn't say anything for quite a while."

"But now she's all right?"

"Pretty much," Mulheisen said. "She doesn't remember what happened, but she appears to be okay physically."

"Well that's good," Luck said. "I'm glad to hear it. And you're Mulheisen? Where did this happen?"

"The explosion? It was in a suburb, outside of Detroit, a little town called Wards Cove."

"I heard about that. It was a city hall, or something?"

"That's right," Mulheisen said, nodding. Luck seemed genuinely interested, looking at him more keenly.

"Mulheisen," Luck said, appearing to savor the name. "That's German. I'm from German stock myself."

"You are? Luck—," Mulheisen started to say.

Luck interrupted him. "It doesn't sound German. It was originally Luckenbach—*loukenbock*, they pronounce it in the old country. The brook at Lucken. That's where my people are from."

"Is that so?" Mulheisen said. "I've heard of Luckenwalde. In fact, I was there once. It's near Berlin."

"That's right," Luck said. "I've never been to Germany myself. What's it like?"

"Luckenwalde? Oh, I don't recall much about it. It's kind of flat country, I think." Mulheisen was just guessing. His memory of Luckenwalde was dim. Was it the village with the ancient stone church? He wasn't sure. Was there a brook? He seemed to recall an old stone bridge, but he wasn't positive and didn't mention it to Luck.

Mulheisen glanced about him. Evening was upon them, the darkness seemingly welling up out of the woods. He could no longer see the two men in the other truck, who in any case had not gotten out or made any sign of impatience.

"And you," Luck said, "you're *Ironmill*. Am I right?"

"Hunh? Oh, yeah. Mulheisen. I guess that's what it means."

"Two Germans meet in a dark woods," Luck said. "One German says, 'Wie gehts.' What does the other say?"

Mulheisen struggled to recall his nato-Deutsche, from thirty years back. "Uh, I guess he says, 'Wohin das biergarten?'"

Luck laughed. "I don't have any beer, and I'm not about to drive into Queen to get some, but let me speak to these boys and we can go on back to the house. You can tell me about your exploded mother. Oh, I'm sorry . . . I shouldn't have said that."

"Not at all," Mulheisen said. He stepped away so that Luck could dismount from the cab. The man turned out to be about Mulheisen's height, six feet or so. He was a trim fellow, from what Mulheisen could see, wearing a loose, heavy duck barn coat, twill trousers, and heavy-soled shoes, the brim of his canvas hat rakishly tilted. He had an athletic grace, an easy movement. The coat pocket was bulging, Mulheisen noted, and caused the coat to swing heavily. Luck was armed.

"I don't like to ask this, Mul," Luck said, when they stood between the two vehicles, "but are you packing?"

Mulheisen shook his head. "Packing? A gun? Nah, I had to turn it in when I left the force." He held his arms out.

Luck smiled apologetically and waved his hand. "I'll take your word. All right. I'll just be a minute." Luck made his way around Mulheisen's car to the other truck. He talked quietly to the men. They turned on their headlights and began to back out the way they had come, but shortly they merely backed into the brush, with a loud crackle of breaking branches, then turned and drove on out.

Luck returned and said, "Just a couple of neighbors. I was on my way to get my mail. If you can wait here a minute, I'll be back in a second."

He hopped up into the cab and with a roar drove into the brush, breaking limbs and crushing sumac as he steered around Mulheisen's car.

Mulheisen stood in the gathering darkness. The truck had disappeared. He could hear an owl hooting from the woods. He wondered if he should light up a cigar but decided not to. He went to stand by the car. Presently, Luck's vehicle came roaring back and pulled around the Checker, back onto the two-track, and stopped. He rolled down his window and called to Mulheisen to follow him.

Once through the gate, which Luck stopped to lock closed behind them, Mulheisen followed the truck another quarter of a mile or so, the woods getting deeper, until suddenly they broke out into a broad clearing. The house was ahead. It was a low, single-story house with a shallow-pitched roof and large stone chimney. It had a broad porch along the front, over which the roof extended.

Luck parked his truck next to another vehicle, an older-model Buick sedan. He motioned Mulheisen to park to one side of the truck.

"Kind of lonely, back in these woods," Mulheisen ventured as he got out. "Smells good though, those pines." There were a couple of large white pines soaring up on either side of the house, easily eighty feet tall. There was a long stack of firewood to one side, with more stacked on the porch. Beyond the house a ways were two buildings, one of them an equipment shed, the other a small barn.

"I had more of those pines once," Luck said. "One of the last stands of virgin white pine in these parts. I don't know how it got missed by the timber company. I had to cut them down."

"Why is that?"

"Field of fire, Mul. Before I cut them you could have walked right up to the house without me knowing you were there. If you were careful."

Mulheisen nodded as if he understood. He drew in a deep, hearty breath. "I wonder if there's a word for that pine smell?" he said. "Resiny? Maybe, 'resinance'?"

"'Resinance'? I like that," Luck said. "Poetic, although one would inevitably have to explain that it wasn't 'resonance,' like the sound."

Mulheisen glanced at the AK-47 that Luck had taken from the rack on the rear window of the pickup. He was carrying the gun casually in one hand, a large bundle of mail under his other arm. When they went into the house he set the gun to one side, leaning against the wall. He hung his hat on a peg set in a rail alongside the door and set the mail on the kitchen counter.

It was a pleasant, ordinary-looking house. The kitchen to one side, with standard cupboards, a work counter with stools around it. A large archway led to the living room, furnished with couches and chairs. An enameled green woodstove sat on a brick hearth, vented into what had been an attractive fireplace made of faced fieldstone. It was putting out quite a bit of heat. Luck opened the door of the stove and poked at the logs within, then made some sort of adjustment to the draft device in the chimney pipe. He turned around to face Mulheisen.

"Take your coat?" he asked. He hung Mul's jacket and his own coat side by side on pegs by the kitchen door, where other coats hung. He looked very rustic in his wool plaid shirt and red suspenders.

"Hungry, Mul? I made a stew before I set out to get the mail. Venison. Shot it myself, a young buck."

When Mulheisen accepted, Luck promptly said, "Great! How about a little whiskey to celebrate the end of the day, while I get the dinner together? Better than beer, eh?" He rubbed his hands together briskly and poured them each a hefty shot of George Dickel Sour Mash from a bottle that stood on the counter.

Mulheisen happily sipped the whiskey and stood about while his host tossed down his drink. The place looked like a hunting lodge, Mulheisen thought. Very masculine, but very orderly. No sign of a woman's touch, no flowers, no polka dot curtains, just adjustable blinds. No doilies or place mats.

Luck set out the plain sturdy plates on the bare kitchen table. He hoisted a heavy iron pot off the range to set on a trivet on the table. Then he dished out very large portions of the steaming stew, full of chunks of meat and potatoes, a carrot or a rutabaga here and there, along with what looked like some parsnip and the odd mushroom. He got bread out of the bread box and sawed off large chunks on a bread board. "Baked it myself," Luck said. "Good bread, if I say so."

Mulheisen sat and was on the verge of digging in when Luck stopped him. "Just a minute, Mul, if you don't mind." He clasped his hands and bowed his head, eyes closed, to say grace. "Dear Lord, bless this simple meal which you have provided. We humbly thank thee for all your gifts and pray that you will guide us in everything we do. In Jesus' name, amen." He looked up and said, "All right! Let's eat. Oops! Forgot the wine."

He jumped up and darted into a nearby room, returning with a bottle, which was already open, and poured some out for both of them in plain, everyday wineglasses.

The stew was hot and good. The wine was Californian, quite appropriate, a dark and spicy red. "I like that Oregon pinot noir," Luck said, "but I'd already opened this Napa cab. Hope you don't mind."

Mulheisen didn't mind. It tasted fine. He ate hungrily. They didn't speak much and were soon finished. "I usually have some pie, but I'm all out," Luck said apologetically. "A neighbor lady makes

great cherry pie. When you're up in cherry country, that's the spe-
cialty. But I've got some ice cream. No?"

Luck pushed back from the table. "I'll clear those dishes up,
just leave them for now. How about a little more of that Dickel with
our coffee?"

Mulheisen was agreeable. Luck poured them each a generous amount in the glasses they'd used before. "Go on in and relax,"
Luck said, waving a hand toward the living room, "while I get the
coffee going. Smoke if you got 'em," he said grandly.

"You don't mind cigars?" Mulheisen inquired.

"Not at all," Luck said. "I'll join you in a minute."

Mulheisen lingered in the kitchen, politely, while Luck
ground the coffee and put it to drip in the automatic maker. The
two of them stood and sipped the whiskey and Mulheisen offered
him a La Donna Detroit. Luck accepted it graciously. "I was going
to offer you a Cuban," he said. "Maybe later, eh? I've never seen
this brand."

"An outfit in Detroit makes them," Mulheisen said. "I know
the people. Supposedly they're made with Cuban tobacco, but I
suspect it's Dominican. Rolled by Cuban émigrés. They're not bad."
He clipped them and they lit up.

"Not bad," Luck agreed. "All right." They both puffed. "Ain't
this the life?" Luck said. "All my own provender, except for the wine
and the coffee . . . and your cigars, of course. Now what's this about
your mother? What does it have to do with me, Mul? Hey, let's go
in the living room and get comfortable."

He turned on a couple of standing reading lamps and settled
into a chair near the stove. Mulheisen sat across from him on a
couch. Mulheisen glanced out the window and realized that the yard
was bathed in light.

"Comes on automatically," Luck remarked. "Now, you were
saying, about your mother."

Mulheisen didn't really know how to proceed. "Well, she was going to a meeting of the county commissioners. I don't know what it was about, exactly, a public hearing, I think, about some kind of development project. She's a bird-watcher, you see . . ."

"Ah. One of those radical environmentalists," Luck said jokingly.

"Something like that," Mulheisen said. "Anyway, she left something in the bus and went back to get it and a bomb went off. It killed the driver, but it just stunned her. Stunned her pretty badly. A few bruises, a few cuts. That healed up." He went on, describing the situation briefly.

Luck sipped at his whiskey. "You ready for some coffee, Mul?" When Mulheisen nodded he got up and went into the kitchen, returning with a couple of mugs full of coffee. "Black all right?" he asked. "More Dickel?" He poured their whiskey glasses full.

When he was seated again, he said, "I'm glad your mother's okay. It must have been quite an ordeal for her. Tell me, does she remember much of the, uh, event?"

Mulheisen said that so far she didn't. She remembered going to the meeting, but as for the rest, how she got out to the bus, and so on, he'd reconstructed it from talking to the investigators.

Luck nodded sympathetically. "Maybe she'll remember more, later on," he said. "But where do I come in? Oh, don't bother. I know all about it, Mul. I don't mean to act dumb. You'll have to forgive me. The feds came to see me. They tried to lay it on me. It was all bullshit, of course. Nothing came of it. I haven't heard a word about it since. But how did you hear about me? I'd have thought they'd given up on that angle."

Mulheisen sipped the coffee. "Your name came up," he said. "Along with several others, of course. I just thought . . . well, I don't know what I thought. None of the other suspects were available to me, but you were in Michigan . . ."

"So you thought you'd drive up here and see what I was like, what was going on? Something like that?" Luck sat back, at ease, and puffed his cigar. He looked at it. "Not bad." Then he leaned forward and looked at Mulheisen carefully. "But tell me, Mul, you say you quit the force to look after your mother. So am I to understand that this is strictly a personal thing, unofficial?"

Mulheisen lifted his eyebrows, a gesture of apology. "I was a cop, Mr. Luck—"

"Call me Imp, Mul. Everyone always has."

"Anyway, I quit, true. But naturally, I know some of the people who are investigating."

Luck sat back then. "Thanks for being open about it, Mul. But let me confess . . . I recognized your name. I've seen your name in the papers. I was being a little paranoid, forgive me. I just wondered how far you'd take the undercover routine."

"I'm not undercover, Imp. I'm just—as you say—up here to see what you were like, see if I couldn't get a sense of what this is all about, as far as it involves you."

"Well, it doesn't involve me, at all," Luck said, firmly. "I hope you believe that. It's true. I don't know anything about what happened down there. But the way it is, something like that happens anywhere I'm near and the cops come calling." He shrugged. "I don't like it—who would? But there doesn't seem to be much I can do about it."

"'Anywhere near,'" Mulheisen said. "How near were you?"

"I was in Michigan. That's near enough for the federales. As a matter of fact, I was probably, oh, about a hundred and fifty miles away. Fishing. Caught some good walleyes. Well, I guess you've seen my file. My dossier. You'd know all that."

"No, I haven't. I'm not on the force. My old associates might talk a bit, but they're not sharing their files with me. All I know is your name. I can't say I'd ever heard anything substantive about you, before or since."

There was a brief silence. Luck seemed to digest this information, such as it was. Then he said, "So where are we? That it? Satisfied?"

Mulheisen just looked at him and drew on the cigar. "What's your take on this, Luck?"

"You mean, who did it? I don't know. Arabs, maybe. Though why they'd bomb a bunch of environmentalists, I don't know. Maybe they were after somebody else, some other agenda."

"Arabs doesn't make any sense to me, either," Mulheisen said. "But what about bombing? What do you feel about that?"

"Unofficially? I'm agin it," Luck said. "Oh, to be frank, I'm not philosophically opposed to violent actions, not categorically. When something of importance is at stake. I don't know what could have been at stake here. Like I say, it may not have been aimed at your mother and her group at all."

"What about those fellows at the World Trade Center, or at Oklahoma City?" Mulheisen inquired.

"Two different things," Luck said. "The 9-11 thing, that was an Arab thing. My understanding of this al-Qaeda group is that they're radical Muslims, terrorists with a complicated religious and political ax to grind. They don't like the U.S. We're too powerful, too secular. They want us out of their world and their governments aren't doing anything about it. Oklahoma City, now, that's a little different. I knew some of the boys who were involved in that. If you'd read my dossier, which you say you haven't, you'd know that I got questioned pretty thoroughly on that one, too. Pretty thoroughly." He looked grim.

"What's your take on it?" Mulheisen asked.

"You'll laugh," Luck said, "but I do believe it was the U.S. government. Clinton needed an incident, to take the heat off the Waco mess. It was supposed to be a right-wing conspiracy that the FBI would miraculously intercept at the last minute. Oh, there would be a small explosion, maybe. The trouble was, they hired the wrong guys, got it all screwed up. It was a sting, in a sense. They set up a phony front that promoted the whole thing to these guys. But the feds set up something like this and then they forget that the people who bought into the plan are in it for real, they want to do it. To them, it's not a scheme, you see? The feds slip into the habit of regarding it as an operation, while their dupes don't think that way."

Mulheisen nodded. He'd had some similar problems with federal agencies, a conflict of purpose. "But were the bombers aware that it was a federal project?" he wondered aloud.

"Well, we can't be sure, can we?" Luck said. "The other problem was that the feds didn't realize that these guys were really capable. They knew how to build a bomb—a couple of tons of nitrates in a rental truck. McVeigh knew how to do that. I'd guess that at least one of the other guys was on to the real nature of the project. Not Terry Nichols, but the so-called Mr. X. He was an undercover agent."

"Did you know any of these people?"

"I knew Nichols. I'd met him at some meetings of patriotic groups. The man is a patriot. I truly believe he intended to pull the plug at the last minute, only Mr. X and McVeigh jumped the gun. I can see you're skeptical."

"It sounds kind of complicated," Mulheisen offered.

"These things get complicated, inevitably," Luck said. "McVeigh wasn't too complicated. The key is Mr. X. You start down a road, an enterprise based on deception, people working at cross purposes. It's like Watergate: a simple little break-in that gets complicated, because of a janitor who notices some tape over the latch of a door that's supposed to be locked. In this case, you have a guy like Mr. X, who starts out as part of a double cross, but somewhere down the line maybe he starts thinking like the others, gets caught up in their enthusiasm, or maybe he's even converted to the cause."

Luck laughed lightly. "If you're a cynic, you might believe he got to thinking he'd be the star of this show, be the hero who takes down the bombers. Only, McVeigh is a little too sharp for him and he ends up getting blown to bits."

"It's an interesting theory," Mulheisen said.

Luck, who had gotten more intense as he explained it, suddenly sat back and smiled. "Well, it's just a theory. Totally speculative. Nobody can know for certain now. Mr. X got blown to pieces. Only his leg was found. Which, of course, the FBI passed off as the leg of one of the innocent victims."

"What about McVeigh? Was he just a nut, or what?"

"McVeigh wasn't a nut," Luck said, sweeping that suggestion away with a contemptuous gesture of his hand. "McVeigh was a soldier. He knew what he was doing. The way he saw it, our government had taken to attacking innocent civilians, at Ruby Ridge, Waco. And not just some rogue elements in the government, but the very highest officials—the attorney general, the president. And what was the result? The Anti-terrorist Act, which directly impacts on everyone's civil liberties. So, was he crazy? Is it okay to blow up innocent people in the pursuit of a noble cause? I don't know. Are there innocent people?"

"There were children there," Mulheisen said.

"Half a million children have died in Iraq because of our pursuit of oil, so Americans can drive SUVs. And that was before the war, just from the embargo. Is that a noble cause? I don't think McVeigh thought that there would be children at the Murrah building. I'm not saying it would have deterred him if he'd known, just that he didn't seem to have known it. But, hey! You're running low. Let me get you another George Dickel."

When he'd poured them another large jolt of whiskey and had sat down again, Mulheisen said, "You seem to respect these guys, McVeigh and Nichols, or their philosophy. What's your philosophy?"

"I am . . . ," Luck started to say, but hesitated, seemingly to gather his thoughts, ". . . let's say I'm a libertarian anarchist." He smiled disarmingly. "I'm a realist. I figure folks will act in what they think is their best interests. It doesn't always seem logical to the outsider, looking on. McVeigh believed in what he was doing. He was bound to do it as well as he could, and he was quite competent. He was a patriot. He believed in America. I'm a patriot, too."

"Would you have done that?" Mulheisen asked. "I mean, if you'd been invited in?"

"No. I'm more of a realist than McVeigh. I'm sure it would have seemed too . . . too far-fetched. I don't think the federal government is going to be changed by blowing up the odd building. I don't think they would get the intended message. I think you have to work in more fundamental, political ways, get people thinking your way. The public wasn't positively influenced by that act."

"But you said that you believed that violence was sometimes a legitimate act," Mulheisen said.

"Well, the Boston Tea Party seemed to have an effect," Luck said. "It wasn't all that violent, perhaps, but a lot of valuable property was destroyed. Unions believe in strikes, and they sometimes result in pretty brutal actions."

Mulheisen was piqued. He almost blurted out that the violence was usually enacted upon the strikers. But he didn't respond. It wasn't his purpose to provoke Luck. Instead, he remarked, almost offhandedly, "Quite often people don't act in their own best interest. Don't you agree? They do things that they know damn well they shouldn't do, that will harm *them*. It's as if they can't help themselves."

Luck stared at him. He seemed stunned. "You mean . . . like compulsive behavior?" Then he seemed relieved. "Well, that's just psychology," he said. "I was talking about something else entirely, not about abnormal states."

"No, I didn't mean 'abnormal states,'" Mulheisen said mildly. "I was just thinking of the guy who, let's say, suddenly does something erratic. He hardly knows why he did it, but it wasn't to his advantage, maybe it even was obviously to his disadvantage, but he does it anyway. And when you confront him with it, later, he often starts by outrageously denying it, although it was well observed, but then he quickly subsides, saying 'I don't know why I did that. I knew it was wrong. I could have stopped, but I went straight on and did it.' I've run into that phenomenon in my work fairly often."

Luck leaned forward, obviously interested. "For instance?" he demanded.

"Oh, I don't know. I was just musing," Mulheisen said. "It's difficult to think of an example, right offhand. It typically comes up in confessions."

"Ah, it's a kind of alibi," Luck said, sitting back. "A way of exonerating yourself—'I don't know what came over me. I must have been out of my head.'"

"No, it's not that," Mulheisen said. "Okay, here's a classic example. Let's say a guy steals, he embezzles from his company. But he gets away with it. Nobody knows, the lost money is accounted for in some other plausible fashion and everyone forgets about it. Five years later, he's chatting with his boss, and all of a sudden he blurts out, 'I stole that money.' I'm called in, I talk to him, and after he's given me all the details, I ask him: 'Why did you confess?' First he says he doesn't know, but when pressed he'll often say he couldn't help himself. It suddenly occurred to him that the only way anyone would ever know is if he told. And from the moment he thought that, he felt compelled to tell. He might give hints, allusions. People don't pay attention. Finally, he just blurts it out. 'I did it.'"

Luck said, "That's just compulsive behavior. If you're

suggesting that about McVeigh, he wasn't a compulsive person. He knew what he was doing."

Mulheisen nodded, as if conceding that point, and said, "Well, it's not uncommon. Anyway, you've given me something to think about. I appreciate it. But let me ask you: what kind of thing would motivate you to act in . . . oh, let's say, a violent way?"

"Whoa! That's a leading question." Luck grinned broadly. "Well, as you're no longer a cop, I suppose it's innocent enough. Oh, I'd say what would motivate me is about what would motivate most folks—say, the government, or someone, tried to take my land, and I found I had no legal recourse. Then, well, it's purely hypothetical, but I might be driven to take action."

Mulheisen nodded.

"How about another drink?" Luck said.

"No, no, I'm fine. I've had enough." Mulheisen stood up. "I've got to drive. I'm not so sure I can find my way back to town."

"Hey, you can stay here," Luck said. "I've been enjoying this. I don't often get interesting folks out here, not that I'm lonely, or some kind of hermit. But I've got a great little guest room fixed up, out in the barn. It's not like being in a barn, believe me. All the comforts of home, running water, bath. I make a hell of a breakfast."

"No, that's nice of you to offer," Mulheisen said, "but I really have to get going. I've taken up enough of your time. I'm sure you have stuff to take care of. I'd like to talk again, though, maybe in a day or two."

"Oh? Still not satisfied? I'm sure you'll find I'm pretty much what I said I am."

"You didn't exactly say what you were," Mulheisen noted. "Other than an anarchist libertarian."

"That's just philosophically," Luck said, "in theory, or by disposition. In reality, in practice, that is, I've been a carpenter, a pilot, a federal employee. I worked for one of Lyndon Johnson's War on Poverty programs, teaching adult literacy . . . hell, I've done everything. I'm also a student of history, of politics, economics, you name it."

"A pilot? Were you in the service?"

"Not really, not the regular service. I flew for a private outfit, contracts in Southeast Asia, later in Central America. You won't find it in the dossier but it was government work."

"Sounds important," Mulheisen said.

"It was important for me," Luck said. "Kind of opened my eyes, gave me some insight into how our government really works. But it's not something I can discuss. Yeah, I've done a lot of things. Worked for the Forest Service at one time. Heck, I'm even an environmentalist."

Mulheisen smiled. He didn't show his fangs much. "You are?"

"Well, a naturalist, of sorts, anyway. I don't go along with most of these radical environmental groups, naturally. But, hey, I'm a bird-watcher, if not a tree hugger, exactly."

"A bird-watcher!" Mulheisen was surprised.

"Heck, yeah," Luck said. "I know all these birds around here, practically by their first names. Hey, you know the weirdest thing I ever saw? I was in the woods one day, out back of here, and I heard this buzzing in the ground. Really! It was amazing! Just like a giant beehive or something, a regular dynamo. I was standing on a little hill, sort of like a mound, in a clearing. So I'm looking around, trying to figure out what's going on, and I notice all these birds flying around, silver martins. It's a kind of swallow we have. And I'll be damned if I don't see one of 'em dive right into the ground!"

"I'll be darned," Mulheisen said, intrigued.

"Yeah! It was crazy. So now I look a little closer and, by gosh, I see a bird fly *out* of the ground! It turns out there's millions of 'em down there, in the ground! You could put your ear next to the ground and it's absolutely humming, like a giant dynamo, right under the ground. It's amazing! You think of these birds as being, you know, aerial things, creatures of the air. Right? And here they are, living in the earth. It doesn't seem right. It was toward the end of the summer, see? They're getting ready to hibernate!"

"Birds hibernate? I thought they migrated," Mulheisen said.

"Well, they do, most of 'em," Luck said. "But I looked it up and they say that some swallows hibernate. They must stock up that cave, or their burrows, or whatever they got there. I didn't excavate, or anything, didn't want to disturb them, see? And then they spend the winter there, feeding on what they've stored up, and in the spring they come out. There must have been . . . well, maybe not a million, but probably a thousand or more. Most amazing thing I've ever seen."

"Did you see them come out in the spring?" Mulheisen asked.

"I meant to," Luck said, "but I'd go out there, once in a while, and then one day they'd all be out, flying around. They evidently don't use the hive, or whatever you'd call it, during the summer, because I didn't see them flying in and out. I watched the next fall but I couldn't find the hive. I figure they must only use the hive one winter, find a new one the next winter. Well, it'd be quite a mess, wouldn't it? All that bird shit in there. And maybe they don't want to raise the chicks in there. Or who knows? Maybe a skunk or a weasel got in there, or a coyote. There's a lot of coyotes around here. They ought to be exterminated, but the government's against it."

"Well, that is amazing," Mulheisen said. "I'll have to tell my mother about that."

"You do that," Luck said. "I'm sure she knows about silver martins hibernating. If she's a real bird-watcher."

"Oh, she's pretty keen on it," Mulheisen said. "Always has been."

Luck was standing now. "Well, I wish you'd stay. But you're right, I've got stuff to do. These days, I spend my nights on the Internet. I've got my own Web site, www.hillmartin.net. I'll have a ton of e-mails to answer. I'm one of those guys who has trouble sleeping. The Net has been a comfort, since my wife died."

"Hillmartin?" Mulheisen said.

Luck smiled shyly and shrugged.

"How long ago did your wife die?"

"It'll be three years next spring," Luck said.

"I'm very sorry. You must miss her a lot, especially living out here by yourself. I suppose it gets kind of lonely."

Luck nodded. "It was a loss," he said.

"I suppose she was a fairly young woman," Mulheisen offered.

"She was, she was. But . . . these things happen. You have to buck up and go on. It doesn't help to mope."

"Was it an accident, or . . . ?" Mulheisen let the question hang.

Luck eyed him quietly, showing no emotion. "An illness," he said. "Congenital. A little glitch ticking away, waiting to emerge. She didn't suffer, thank God. Maybe," he said, brightening, "that's the best way. You're healthy and happy and then one day . . . *click!*" He snapped his fingers. "You're gone."

They had moved toward the door and Mulheisen picked up his coat and pulled it on. They went out onto the porch. The night was cool. Luck took a deep breath, then sniffed the air.

"Hint of frost," he said. "Winter is icumen in. Hey, I'll have to go out there and unlock that gate. Wait a minute, I'll be right with you."

He ran back into the house, leaving the door wide open. Mulheisen wandered over to his car. He could hear the owl hooting again, not distant. He got out another cigar and clipped it, then got into the car and started it. When several minutes passed and

Luck didn't reappear, he lit the cigar and backed out, waiting in the yard.

Finally, Luck came running out, pulling on his coat, his hat on his head. To Mulheisen's surprise, he came around and got into the passenger seat of the Checker.

"This'll be more convenient," he explained. "I can walk back. I enjoy the night air. You got another one of those stogies, Mul?"

6

Offisa Pup

Here was a
night so black that Mulheisen had an irrational feeling that the
headlights were piercing it only with difficulty. He drove at a creeping pace through the long wooded stretch. An enormous owl
swooped in front of his headlights, startling the owl into a panicky
pull-up, wings as white and broad as an angel's. Mulheisen braked,
not realizing at first what it was. Luck laughed. "That's my hoot owl,"
he said. "He hangs out around here. I tried to shoot him a couple of
times, but he's too crafty."

"Tried to shoot him? Why?"

"Well, these owls, they eat all my pheasants. There aren't
hardly any pheasants around here anymore. I tried to introduce
some, had them in pens, till they got big enough to release, and you'll
never guess what happened. I'd find them in the pen with their heads
missing!"

Mulheisen was startled. "What happened?"

"They'd roost on this shed I had. I'd put chicken wire over
the whole business. But that shed was so high they could stick their
heads out through the wire. The owl would swoop down and tear
the heads right off!"

Just at that moment they arrived at the gate. Luck hopped out to open it. He held the gate as Mulheisen drove through. "Thanks for coming by, Mulheisen. It was a treat. I don't get so many visitors, especially not ones who are willing to talk philosophy. Drive safe."

Mulheisen waved and drove off, but slowly. Twice, between the gate and the county road, he had to stop because deer were standing directly in the track—once a couple of does or yearlings, then a young spikehorn buck that merely glanced back over its shoulder before taking a few steps and disappearing into the brush.

Perhaps it was the pace, but the drive seemed much longer than he'd remembered it. When he finally reached the graveled county road the cool night air seemed a little less densely black. The headlights traveled much farther and he picked up speed. He was no more than a mile along the paved road when he was surprised to see the rotating, oscillating blue-and-red lights of an approaching police vehicle. Mulheisen slowed, although he was going no more than forty-five. The other vehicle, which bore the markings of the county sheriff, slowed as well then immediately swung around behind him. Mulheisen drew the Checker over to the shoulder; the police car hauled up behind him.

Mulheisen could not ignore the impression that the sheriff's patrol had been waiting for him. This was hardly a highway, but he supposed it wasn't too unusual for the sheriff to patrol. At this hour—Mulheisen never carried a watch, but there was a clock on the dash that read 11:23—he reckoned the sheriff's deputy was hoping to nab some yokels careening home from the Queensleap tavern. So he wasn't surprised when the deputy, after looking over his driver's license and registration, asked him to step out of the car. Mulheisen stuffed his cigar into the ashtray and got out.

"What's up, Corporal Dean?" Mulheisen said, purposely citing the officer's name as engraved on the metal plate under his badge. "I was only going forty-five."

"Just step over here, Mr. Mulheisen," the deputy said, indicating the white line that marked the edge of the pavement. There were no farms within view, but Mulheisen could hear a distant dog barking.

He noticed that Corporal Dean was alone. He'd also been drinking, judging by his breath, but then so had Mulheisen, although he'd been careful not to finish his drinks as Luck had. Dean didn't appear to be drunk, but he seemed a trifle unsure of himself. He kept touching the handle of the gun in his holster. His tie was slightly askew.

Mulheisen didn't protest. He proceeded to perform the usual field test, touching his nose with a finger, walking along the line. The deputy asked him to lean against the car, with his back to him, his legs spread and hands outstretched. Mulheisen felt a little nervous about this request but, after looking sharply at the deputy, he complied. The officer made a fumbling attempt at patting him down. It occurred to Mulheisen that he could probably get the best of this officer, who seemed a little clumsy, not quite focused.

When the pat down was finished, the deputy said he wanted Mulheisen to get into the back of the police car. He said this with his hand resting on the holstered gun.

"What for?" Mulheisen asked. "I did the field test."

"Just get in the car," the deputy said. His voice showed an edge of anger, or it might have been nervousness.

Mulheisen shrugged and got into the backseat of the squad car. As he'd expected, Dean went to his car and began to search it. While the man was at it, Mulheisen pulled out a piece of paper, wrote his name on it, the name of the officer, the approximate time—by now, he reckoned it at 11:35—and the notation that he'd been stopped on county road H20 (he thought that was the number) for no obvious reason, and that the officer had searched his car without permission. He stuffed the piece of paper down on the edge of the seat, where the backrest met it. He barely finished this before Dean returned.

"Go back to your car," the deputy said.

"Am I free to go? No ticket?"

"Just go back to your car," Dean said. "I'll be with you in a moment."

Mulheisen went to his car and immediately began to search it himself, leaning into the backseat, as he'd seen the deputy do, and then look in the trunk.

"Hey! What the hell do you think you're doing?" Dean yelled, coming toward him. "Get in that car!"

Mulheisen looked at him calmly and finished looking through his bags in the trunk, lifting the rubber mat, and then, satisfied, slammed the lid shut. He walked around the car with the deputy following and opened the other side of the backseat, again as he'd noticed the deputy had done.

The deputy grabbed Mulheisen's shoulder and wrenched him away from the door, against the side of the car. Mulheisen offered no resistance. He looked down at the gun that the deputy had drawn. "You sure you want to do that, Dean?" he asked.

"What the hell do you think you're up to?" Dean demanded.

"Just checking," Mulheisen said.

"Checking?" Dean sounded stupid.

"Just making sure everything is there that should be there . . . and nothing more."

"Get in the car and sit still," Dean said. His voice was hoarse.

Mulheisen got in the car and immediately opened the glove compartment. He took out the cell phone.

"Give me that," Dean said, reaching through the window.

Mulheisen did not resist. But he continued to look through the papers in the glove compartment and feel about in the interstices of the seat cushion beside him. He kept a sidelong view of Dean, who watched him for a minute then stalked away toward his vehicle.

Mulheisen sat patiently, then slipped a Coleman Hawkins CD into the player. He fished out a fresh cigar and lit it up. He puffed it, calmly.

The deputy took a little longer than Mulheisen expected. Eventually, he returned with a packet in his hand, which Mulheisen recognized as an alcohol testing device, the balloon test. When the deputy asked him to inflate the balloon, Mulheisen, who knew how erratic these devices were, declined.

Corporal Dean almost smiled. "You refuse?" the deputy asked.

"I'd prefer a blood test," Mulheisen said. He figured that he'd had half a glass of wine and about an ounce and a half of George Dickel in the past four hours. That wouldn't register as intoxication in a blood test, but he wasn't confident of what the balloon test might show. "I'll pay for it, of course," Mulheisen said. "You can drive me, or follow me to the nearest hospital or clinic." That would surely be another half hour, further diminishing the alcohol in his system.

"Just inflate the balloon," the deputy insisted.

"I'll tell you what," Mulheisen suggested. "I'll take it if you also take it. We'll turn them both in for analysis."

Dean flushed. "I'm the officer here!" he snapped. "You just do what I say!"

"I'd rather not, Corporal Dean. I'm happy to take the blood test, though."

The deputy stared down at him for a long moment, then he said, "You wait here." He returned to his car. A few moments later he came back and tossed Mulheisen's phone and his license and registration onto his lap without a word, then returned to the car, flicked off the overhead lights, and departed.

Mulheisen watched him go, then drove after him. The sheriff's vehicle sped away. Mulheisen followed until the speed began to creep over sixty-five, then dropped back. The car was soon lost to sight, down a hill and over another one. Mulheisen didn't see him again.

In the town, he was relieved to see that the Queensleap Inn Motel had not turned off its VACANCY light. He stopped and checked in. The room was clean and pleasant enough. He drank a glass of water and watched *NHL Tonight* on cable. The Red Wings had won, he was glad to see, and he regretted not having been there in time to catch the game. Zetterberg had scored two goals against Montreal. Mulheisen switched off the television and went outside to light up a cigar. He could see that the Queensleap tavern was still open. It was just a short walk.

Hardly anyone was there, just four sodden men sitting at the bar, regulars he supposed. The only one of them who bothered to look up when he entered was the old guy from the Sinclair station. Charlie, now in a gray uniform shirt that also had his name embroidered on the breast pocket flap, greeted him. "Hi, Mul. You find ol' Imp all right?"

"Oh, yeah," Mulheisen said. "He was real friendly, even gave me dinner. Pretty tasty, too. But I got stopped by that deputy, Dean, on my way back."

"Frog?" Charlie said. "What the hell's he out and about for? Frog'd be drunk by now. By damn, I bet ol' Imp sicced him onta you."

"You think?"

"Be just like him," Charlie said. "Bet he was pouring that George Dickel, wa'n't he? Tha's our Imp. Pour the Dickel'n call the law." He laughed, a low, damp chortle. Charlie was far from sober himself.

Mulheisen bought them both a shot of Dickel with beer chasers. "Luck told me some interesting stories," he said. "He ever tell you about the silver martins, the ones he saw nesting in the ground?"

"Why that sumbitch," Charlie said. "He wouldn't know a silver martin from a hoot owl."

"He told me a story about a hoot owl, too," Mulheisen said.

Charlie snorted. "I tol' him 'bout silver martins, only they wasn't nesting in the ground. Say, thanks for the drink." He hoisted the shot glass, in a toast, then downed it. "It was a lard bucket they was nestin' in. Only, the lard bucket had been knocked down. Them martins was swoopin' around the pole where I useta had the lard bucket up—one a them ol' Farmer Peet's buckets? I been away and when I come home one a the neighbor boys, I guess, had blasted that bucket with a shotgun—blew it right off'n the pole. I just let it lay. But when the martins came back, in the spring? Why they just circled roun' and roun' that pole, like they knew there was s'posed to be a bucket there, like before. Damnedest thing I ever saw. I tol' Imp that story. Now he's fucked it up."

"Maybe he was just trying to improve it," Mulheisen said. "But you know, he's a pretty good cook. Wonder where he learned that. Was his wife a good cook?"

"Connie? Oh, she was a great cook," Charlie said. "Great loss, Connie."

"What did she die of? Some kind of stroke or something?"

"Where'd you hear that? I never heard that. We didn't see much of her there, for a while. And then she was just gone." Charlie sighed and shook his head. He sipped at his beer.

Mulheisen looked at him, waiting for some further explication, but when none came he said, "She was 'just gone'?"

Charlie merely nodded his head, over and over, staring at his beer. Mulheisen couldn't tell if he was drunk or thinking. After a moment, he said, again, "'Just gone'?"

Charlie looked up. "Yeah. One day you're here"—he held his

hand out, palm upward—"next thing you know . . . you're gone." He turned his palm down abruptly, then performed the hand gesture again for effect.

Mulheisen smiled slightly, baring his teeth just a bit. "Is that right? Well, somebody must know how she died. People die, and if the doctor isn't present, the coroner has to come in."

Charlie looked at him. "Is that right? I didn't know that."

"It's the law," Mulheisen said. "When was it?"

"Two, maybe two and a half years ago. In the spring."

"Big funeral?" Mulheisen said. "It sounds like she was well liked."

"Connie? Naw. She wa'n't from 'round here. Oh, I knew her. I all's liked Connie. Good-lookin' woman. Hell of a cook."

"Really?" Mulheisen said. He signaled for another drink for himself and Charlie. "What did she cook that you liked so much?"

"Sweetbreads," Charlie said.

"Sweetbreads?" Mulheisen was surprised. It seemed a bit upscale for a country cook. His mother used to make sweetbreads, perhaps once a year. It was a favorite dish.

"When did you have sweetbreads at Luck's?" Mulheisen asked.

"I was out there working on Imp's tractor. To tell the truth, me and Imp don't get along all that good, but he ditten't have much choice—timin' belt went out. Imp must of been feeling grateful, he invited me to stay for dinner. Man, she could cook."

"I love sweetbreads," Mulheisen said. "How did she prepare them?"

"Some kinda cream sauce. I ain't had a lotta sweetbreads in my life, but now if I go to a restrunt in Traverse and they got sweetbreads on the board, I order 'em. I never had any better'n Connie's."

"So when was this?"

"Why, it was a couple of weeks before Christmas, the winter before she died. Imp'd been using that tractor to push snow." He went on to explain at length the cold, the amount of snow, the long driveway to be plowed.

"Connie Luck was all right then, I guess," Mulheisen said. "Not ill?"

"Oh, yeah. She was fine. But come to think of it, that was the last time I seen her."

"She wasn't from around here," Mulheisen said. "Where was she from?"

"Down below, I heard. Seems like they must of took the body down there, I guess, for the funeral."

"You know," Mulheisen said, "I never saw any sign of her out at the house. No pictures, no sign that a woman had ever lived there. Kind of a bachelor existence Luck lives."

Charlie contemplated his beer. "A woman like that, a man'd have to be made of stone not to be just killed by the loss. She was a good bit younger'n ol' Imp. Damn fine-lookin' woman. He prob'ly decided it was best to just clear all her gear away, try to put it behind him. Be a hard thing. Not like my old lady," he added, almost under his breath.

Mulheisen was intrigued. "A woman like that, I imagine she had a lot of friends."

"I don't think so," Charlie said. "She wa'n't around all that long, just a couple of years. And they kind of kept to themselves, out there. Came and went, just like that." He tried to snap his fingers but he didn't succeed. Charlie had put down a couple more shots while they were talking.

"I wonder how they met?" Mulheisen said.

"Don' know," Charlie said. "It was like Imp to find a woman like that, from away. He was all's a kind of outsider kind of guy, though you wouldn't expect it. Some folks admire him. Him and me are the same age, went to school here in the same room, first grade through senior. He was the smartest kid in school, best athlete, All-State in basketball, you know. But he never really fit in."

"You don't say," Mulheisen said. "I wonder why?"

"It was his Ma, I think. She was an outsider. His Pa married her 'gainst the old man's wishes. Oh, they had a big foofaraw about it, seems like. Imp's Pa never spoke to Old Man Luckenbach again. They was cut off. Eb, Imp's Pa, even changed his name, cut it to Luck. I don't know what that was all about. It was before my time. Nowadays, a course, Imp has quite a following 'round here. New folks, mostly. But some of the old backwoods trash, too," Charlie conceded.

"What kind of following?"

"Oh, it's that patriotic bullshit," Charlie said. "Militia, and all that bull. Buncha Nazis, if you ask me. Say, how about another shot?"

Mulheisen said, "Charlie, you're going to have a little trouble driving home. You want me to drive you?"

But Charlie wasn't driving. He had a little apartment behind the garage. He was staying there tonight. He muttered some rough comments about " . . . my War Department. She wou'n't open the door if I came home now."

Mulheisen decided that was about it for Charlie. He got up and said good night and walked back to the motel.

It was too late to reach his mother. She'd be in bed by now. But he felt obliged to call. The night nurse would be on duty. She was. His mother had gone to bed at eight, according to the nurse she'd relieved. Mrs. Mulheisen was fine, sleeping peacefully.

"Well, tell her I called," Mulheisen said. "I'll call in the morning. Tell her I heard an interesting story about silver martins."

Mulheisen went to bed. The motel was next to the highway, but there was no traffic. He slept like a baby. In the morning, he went out for coffee and a copy of the *Traverse City Record-Eagle* at a restaurant next door called the Queen's Table. He was tempted by the massive "Hunter's Special" breakfast on the menu—a steak, eggs, hash browns with gravy, biscuits. He decided that he could never get half of it down. He settled for pancakes with local maple syrup, then smoked a cigar as he walked back to the motel. He called his mother.

Cora Mulheisen was quite perky. He told her about the apples he'd bought. She asked about the silver martins. The story made her chuckle.

"There are no such things as 'silver martins,'" she assured him. "It must be some local name for a swallow, or maybe that's what they call swifts up there. The only martins we have in these parts are purple martins, and they are dark birds. The story about the lard bucket sounds authentic. Very likely, if they'd been used to nesting at that site they'd return there. That's all there is to that. They're very social birds, nest in large houses that people used to put up. We had a martin house, don't you remember? I can't remember what happened to it. Probably something like what happened to your friend Charlie's martin house. Oh, I remember. Your father took it down. It was so ramshackle. He was going to build a new one, but . . . just another of those things that didn't get done. Martins are purple. Actually, dark blue, with that kind of iridescence that makes them seem to change tones in certain kinds of light. They're a kind of swallow, you know."

"What about the hibernation thing?" Mulheisen asked. "That didn't sound quite right."

An old folk tale, she assured him. Birds didn't hibernate. "But you know," she said, "thinking about it, I would guess that the story arose from the fact that a related species, like the bank swallow, excavates tunnels in cliffs and sandbanks next to water. The swallows make hundreds of these holes for nests. And then, of course, one day they're gone. If the local people don't notice, I suppose someone might jump to the conclusion that they've gone into hibernation. Then one day, they're back, en masse. People don't often see them return, but suddenly they're here, flying in and out of their holes in the sandbank. Yes, I would imagine that's it."

Mulheisen was pleased that she sounded so normal. He told her he'd be back soon, possibly that evening. Otherwise, the next day for sure.

"You know," she said suddenly, obviously having been thinking about the hibernation problem, "it occurs to me that I have read, somewhere, that a few birds do sometimes become rather torpid, if there has been a sudden change of temperature. They're able to reduce their metabolism, it seems. Then it might seem that they're in a state similar to hibernation. You can see how beneficial that might be, since in a cold snap the number of airborne insects they live on would obviously diminish as well. I think swifts might be one of the species. They're sort of like swallows. Laymen might confuse them with swallows. Then, you see, country folks are used to the idea of hibernation, from bears, and so on. They might naturally extrapolate from that to include birds."

When they finally said good-bye, Mulheisen turned his attention to other information he'd picked up. He called his old friend Jimmy Marshall at the Ninth Precinct in Detroit.

"I need a favor," he said. "What can you find out for me about M. P. Luck? Military service, criminal record, that kind of thing?"

"Mul, Mul, Mul," Jimmy said. "I thought you retired."

"I did retire," Mulheisen said. "I just need a little information."

"You know what you are?" Jimmy said. "I was thinking about it the other night. I was wondering how you were getting on with this retirement. Since I didn't hear anything from you, I decided retirement must agree with you. But I guess I was wrong. You sound like you got that old fever."

"What fever is that?" Mulheisen asked.

"You want to know things. Something catches your interest, so you want to know. But I was saying, it occurred to me that retirement might be right for you, even if you're too young for that. You're one of those outcats."

"What's an outcat?"

"You know, like the Hawk."

"The Hawk? You mean, Coleman Hawkins?"

"What other Hawk is there?" Jimmy said. "I know you were always partial to the Hawk. Great player, but he was one of those people, you know. He played in lots of bands, but he was always special. He was someone separate. Seems like he kept himself apart, somehow. I mean, he was in the scene, sure, but he was the cat who walked by himself, you know? That's you. The department wasn't really your gig."

Mulheisen couldn't help but feel gratified by this comparison. Coleman Hawkins! But "outcat"! He wasn't so sure if this was wholly complimentary. "I've never been a cat person," he remarked.

"Well, maybe you're an odd duck, then," Jimmy said. "That better?"

"Oh, there's another thing," Mulheisen said, letting this discussion slide. "Luck was supposedly married, but his wife died. Can you find out something about that? Oh, and maybe you could check out these license plates for me."

Marshall sighed. "You're still in it, outcat or odd duck." He put him on hold and told him when he returned that the plates belonged to a Dodge pickup, owned by an Earl Huley, of Beckley, a town Mulheisen recognized as being not far from Queensleap. The rest of the information he'd requested would take a little while to gather. Mulheisen thanked him and said he'd check back later.

A little while later he drove to Traverse City, the county seat. He looked up the plat maps. The property owned by Luck consisted of some three hundred acres. It bordered an immense swamp on one side, and extended almost, but not quite, to the Manistee River. The land had been registered to one Constance Malachi, subsequently transferred to one Martin Parvis Luckenbach. For some reason, the two parcels of land that blocked the access to the river were registered to Ms. Malachi and a Thomas Adams, respectively. They were just strips of riverfront property, extending back approximately a few hundred feet from the river and running for several acres. The Adams property had devolved to a Charles McVey, upon the decease of Adams. There was no similar disposition of the Malachi property. Mulheisen presumed it had been inherited by Luck.

When he looked in the civil records, there was no record of a marriage certificate for Martin Parvis Luckenbach, or for Constance Malachi. No death certificate, either. Idly, he looked up a birth certificate for Luck. Nothing. And nothing for M. P. Luckenbach.

He went by the sheriff's office. He identified himself as a retired police officer from Detroit. He chatted up the sergeant at the desk, a young woman named Candace, very pretty and quite intelligent and voluble. Things didn't seem too busy at the office that morning. Candace was mildly flirtatious with this older, retired cop. He suggested that he was possibly interested in relocating up that way. What were land prices like? Candace said they were, or had been, pretty low for land that was marginally useful for agriculture, but in recent years they'd been creeping up.

"Why is that?" Mulheisen wanted to know.

"Inflation, I guess," Candace said. "But there's been quite a few people moving up from down below. Retirees, some of them. Building big houses. Queensleap's a good area for them. And folks moving out from town. Lot of building. Or was, until the slowdown."

Mulheisen agreed he'd seen the houses they were building. Way too big for a bachelor like him. He supposed the sheriff's department had a little more work, break-ins, and so forth. Probably a lot of these folks are just summer folks, he opined. Candace agreed.

"That reminds me," Mulheisen said. "I was stopped last night, by a Corporal Dean, out west of Queensleap. About eleven-thirty or so. I couldn't figure out what for. Did he give any indication in his report? He didn't issue a ticket or anything."

Candace looked it up in the log. There wasn't any report from Dean. He wasn't on duty last night. Was he sure it was Dean? Mulheisen wasn't absolutely sure. He thought that was the name, but he could be wrong. But no, there wasn't any report.

Mulheisen thanked her and left. He called Jimmy Marshall on the cell phone. As he'd feared, there was no information on M. P. Luck, militarily. Mulheisen suggested he try the name Luckenbach, and also to check on Constance Malachi. He gave the number of the cell phone and drove back to Queensleap. He'd decided to take the motel unit for another night, so he called home to let his mother know. There was no answer. He assumed she had gone out for a walk, accompanied by the nurse. He left a message on the answering machine. As Jimmy had not called back, Mulheisen called him.

"I called you," Jimmy said, "but evidently you had the phone turned off."

"Well, of course I had it turned off," Mulheisen said. "This thing runs down if you leave it on."

"Well, you can't get calls if it's off," Jimmy pointed out. "Sure, it runs down, but you just charge it up again. Don't you have one of those gewgaws that you plug it in with?"

"Oh, yeah. It's in the box. I think I left it at home."

"Well, it'll help a lot there," Jimmy said. "Anyway, Luckenbach worked a little better, except that there's a hold on his military record. The Homeland Security people have it. You'd have to contact them. I'd guess it means that either he's on their list or maybe he works for them."

Mulheisen was intrigued. Evidently, the hold also applied to any other public record of Luckenbach, including legal affairs. That apparently included Constance Malachi. Thinking about the plat map, he recalled that it had simply showed a name crossed off and another name, a successor, added. Whoever had been blocking files hadn't thought of that. But still, it seemed remarkable to Mulheisen that an agency could remove files at all.

"Can they do that?" Mulheisen asked.

"Well, there's something called the Patriot Act," Jimmy said. "I'm not sure this kind of secrecy would stand up to an official request, but they're saying that. You know, if it was something official . . ."

"Ah, well, thanks, Jimmy. I appreciate your help. Maybe we can get together one of these days and play some Ellington or something."

"That would be nice. Come on by, Mul. So," Jimmy spoke casually, "what are you gonna do?"

"I think I'll hang around up here for a couple of days," Mulheisen said. "Nice weather."

"Enjoy your retirement, Mul," Jimmy said.

7

Run Spot

Joe was well into North Dakota when he saw a man by the side of the road, far ahead. At first he didn't pay much attention. He had been thinking about other things. He had begun with thinking about Fedima and their encounter, followed by just thinking about Fedima, about what it might be like to be in bed with her. Would they wrestle? Probably not. Would it be interesting? Oh yeah, he was sure it would be. What would be the consequences, for him, for Helen, for Frank, if he and Fedima began to disturb the domestic tranquillity? Was he, after all, just looking for some excuse to bail out of a life that was beginning to bore him? He didn't feel bored. He felt rather excited right now.

But these were road ramblings, that was all . . . the dreamy wanderings of the mind that come when you've been driving for a while, with a long road ahead, no traffic, and especially when driving through a slightly surreal landscape like the one flowing by. . . . Long rising runs, with distant ridges, maybe an occasional barn or a silo, a radio tower in the distance . . . And now, he had gotten to that place where the land began to break up into weird eroded outcroppings, twisted canyons, scrub brush, sage, and tumbleweeds.

It reminded Joe of something out of an old cartoon strip he had seen—Krazy Kat. The weird formations, the great space. Sometimes he could see a distant donkey engine, pumping oil or gas, or whatever, dipping its birdlike head again and again, like one of those gag devices one used to see perched on a cocktail glass. The Roadrunner was in it too, except that out here in the Dakotas there weren't any road-runners, just hawks hunched on the occasional fence post.

He wondered how Fedima would take to a life with him, if he got her to leave. Would she leave? No, he was sure that she wouldn't. He was confident that he could seduce her—hell, it was she who had initiated the business. Or had she? Was that just her open, frank style, which he had misread as an interest in seduction? It may have been that. Was he tired of Helen? No, but he was . . . what? He had to admit that he was a little alarmed at the kind of life into which he had so easily and comfortably slipped. He hadn't even noticed it happening until he was deeply into it. It was like some trite joke . . . the Tender Trap. This whole attraction to Fedima could be nothing more than an attempt to jar himself out of the trap of the straight life. He was just restless.

These thoughts seemed idle, but they hurtled through his mind. And all the time, the car was hurtling toward the figure on the road, which wasn't distant anymore. He saw that the man by the side of the road was not walking. He wasn't a hitchhiker, either—not that Joe was going to stop. Once he might have stopped, just out of curiosity, to find out why a man might be way out here in the badlands, with no sign of a car broken down, no other road from which the man might have been dropped off. But Joe didn't stop anymore. The last time he'd stopped, one of the two hitch-hikers had already been dead and shortly thereafter Joe bid fair to join him. Joe had taken a bullet in the head for his generosity that time. He had still not fully recovered; maybe one never recovered from being shot in the head.

Maybe that's how I got into this straight life, Joe thought. *My head tried to get me into a safer place*. And then, as he flashed by the man at eighty miles per hour, he realized it was the Colonel.

Joe almost hit the brakes. It was a close thing. Instead, in the mirror he watched. The Colonel did not turn around, he continued to gaze down the road, hands clasped behind his back. Evidently, the Colonel had not recognized Joe. As far as Joe could tell, he hadn't even turned his head to glance at Joe as he'd passed.

One reason the Colonel hadn't looked was that Joe was no longer driving the green Dodge Durango in which he'd left the place on French Forque. He was driving a Ford Taurus, a light brown one with tinted windows. Unless a hitchhiker is very intent upon the face of the driver of a vehicle approaching him at eighty miles per hour there is a good chance that he will be able to determine little more than that the driver is male or female, and perhaps not even that. And if the windows are tinted, it's even less likely that he'll be able to identify the driver, especially if he's not expecting to see the person he's looking for in that kind of car.

The Durango was not Joe's car. It belonged to Helen. He'd left with the Durango because it seemed more useful for the driving he anticipated, leaving his pickup truck for Helen to use. But by the time he'd gotten to the end of the road his mind had changed, and by the time he reached Helena he knew he didn't want the Durango. He wanted something more nondescript. He'd found the vehicle he wanted in a used-car lot.

Joe wasn't in the least concerned about the Colonel, standing out on the lonely highway. In the mirror Joe could see a couple of vehicles far back, perhaps two miles behind him. The figure of the Colonel had almost dwindled from sight. Whatever the Colonel was up to out there, Joe was sure he was in no need of help.

It struck Joe now with renewed clarity: he was making one of those turns on the road. Something new was in the offing. He didn't know what it was, but it was bound to be interesting. A quiet wave of relief swept over him. He'd wanted to do this for a long time, he realized. It was gratifying that it felt so . . . right.

He scanned the skies as he sped on. Sure enough, he saw a helicopter, way off to the south, skimming along the horizon. That would be the Colonel's ride. It irritated him. Ever since he had first encountered the Colonel, a couple of years ago in Salt Lake City, Joe had felt observed, manipulated. Joe didn't like that. He was a lone wolf, he felt . . . well, no, that sounded pretentious. He'd heard another person described, once, as "a cat who walked by himself." Joe liked the sound of that. He was an outside cat . . . or maybe an outside dog; he wasn't a cat person. He'd never been an inside guy. He didn't want to be part of anyone's network, someone else's program. Well, cats, he thought, were said to be like that. Dogs . . . well, he wasn't against dogs, but he was no man's dog.

The thing to do, he thought, was to take the next road south . . . or north . . . or back to the west. Get off this interstate—it was a trap—and get on with his own life. He took the next exit north. It was a two-lane highway, a perfectly good, empty road, running north through the badlands, headed toward the Missouri River. No more sign of the chopper skimming the horizon.

He breathed a little freer, but he had no illusions. There was still that nagging business of Echeverria. What to do about that? The trouble was, he had no idea what it was all about. Echeverria was dead. Joe had killed him with a missile from an RPG launcher at the airport in Salt Lake City. Or had he?

He'd certainly launched the rocket at the airplane. The ambulance that was carrying Echeverria had drawn up under the wing of the plane, almost instantly engulfed in flames. The attendants had fled. The newspapers had reported the death. But he had never seen Echeverria, who was presumably trapped inside, incapacitated on a gurney. To be honest, he had little idea what Echeverria even looked like. He'd never seen the man.

"I'll be damned," he said aloud. Maybe that was the moment when he'd begun to slip into this dependent role, believing what he'd been told. He thought there was a good chance that Echeverria had never been in that ambulance.

And what was all this stuff about him being connected with a bombing in Detroit? As he drove on, quite alert now, keeping his eye out for choppers, Joe ran back over his contacts with people in Detroit, or people with Detroit connections. He'd known a few, almost all of them people involved in the mob. He couldn't think of a one who fiddled about with bombs.

Mile after lonely mile ticked off. He saw no further sign of the chopper, nor of the Colonel. No connection came to mind, however remote, with bombers, especially bombers who seemed political rather than criminal.

The highway came to a tee at a small town. Watford City. Just another western town. You could head west or east. Joe turned right. A little while later he crossed over the broad Missouri River, climbed up out of the river valley, and drove on, out into the plains of the Dakotas. Another long, straight stretch of highway, across gently rising and falling plains, with distant silos, barns. Minot was coming up, a large town. Joe considered his next step.

By now, of course, the Colonel knew that Joe wasn't on the interstate. Some time back Joe had concluded that the Colonel must have had a reason to intercept him before he reached Bismarck, the state capital now some 115 miles south. It might have been a good reason, but Joe didn't care. He wanted nothing to do with the Colonel.

The Colonel would be aware that there were not a lot of route options. Doubtless back in the chopper by now, he may have decided to check out that brown Ford that had passed him. Joe bought a used pickup truck in Minot, a four-year-old Toyota with the extended cab and with a canopy over the bed, in which he could stow the gear he'd taken with him, mostly guns, but also a box or two of important papers and money. At a sporting goods store he picked up an air mattress and a sleeping bag and some interesting camping gear, including a cooler. At a supermarket he bought ice and groceries.

It was time to make some phone calls. Joe had several safe phone systems, telephone exchanges that would pass on messages. He requested the operators to pass on messages to three different numbers, asking that if possible he should be called back at the number of this pay phone in Minot. On one of the exchanges— this one located in Fort Smith, Arkansas—he also recorded a message that would be passed on to Helen. The message didn't reveal his location but it warned her to beware of visitors. "Don't talk to the Colonel," he'd said. "Your Durango is in the parking lot behind the Holiday Inn Hotel, on Last Chance Gulch, in downtown Helena." He did not say anything about missing her, or coming back.

By the time he'd finished with that message and hung up it was just a short wait until one of his contacts called back. He spent the time sitting in his newly acquired pickup truck, next to the phone, with the truck door open, eating a sandwich. The caller was an old pal from Philadelphia. Joe asked him to check out a few things for him. One was the whereabouts of Caspar Darnay. Also, whatever information could be gathered about this bombing in Detroit, and if his name was really associated with it. And finally, what was Mulheisen's address and phone number? The caller said he'd do his best. Joe thanked him and said he'd call him again, in a few hours, using a different network.

Minot did not interest Joe. He wasn't staying. He finished his meal and, when he didn't hear from his other contacts, he took off. He drove north again for a while, then resumed his eastward movement, sticking to small roads. It was slower than traveling the interstate, or the main trunk lines, but as there was no traffic, few towns, it wasn't much slower. The main thing slowing him was that he continued to take alternate routes rather than direct routes. The little Toyota pleased him. It drove comfortably, was compact, and got very good gas mileage.

It was quite dark when he stopped at a crossroads service station near the Minnesota border. He fueled up and called his contacts. This time he had only a short time to wait before they called back. The Philadelphia guy informed him of what he already knew, that Caspar was out of the pen. Apparently, he was in Chicago, but the Philly connection didn't have a contact for him. He'd keep working on it. He informed Joe that Mulheisen had retired from the Detroit police force. He also filled him in on the fact of Mulheisen's mother having been injured in the bombing, the same one Joe had asked about. As for that, so far he hadn't come up with any mention on the grapevine of Joe's name in connection. He'd keep on that too. He provided Mulheisen's phone number and address.

Joe thanked him and turned to his other sources. One of them, in Los Angeles, had heard that Echeverria was, indeed, still alive. He was said to be looking for Joe. If Joe liked, L.A. would make further inquiries. Joe liked.

Where was Caspar? L.A. had heard he was still in the pen, in Illinois. Joe asked about a few other old friends, chatted a bit, and said he'd call back . . . tomorrow, possibly.

The third contact was a deep mob insider, now living in Miami. Joe's message had been passed on from his old contact number in Brooklyn. "How do you like Miami?" Joe asked. The guy said he liked it, but it wasn't Brooklyn. You had a feeling, he said, that you weren't in the middle of things, you were in some place that didn't matter. Joe knew the feeling, he said, and asked: "You ever run into the Yak?"

"Oh, yeah," Miami said, "Alla time. I din't know you knew the Yak."

Joe said he knew *of* him, mostly. "What do you know about this bombing in Detroit, a while back?"

Miami didn't know much. It was nothing to do with the mob, the old mob, as far as he knew—maybe the Colombians, or one of them. He'd never heard Joe's name mentioned in that context. He knew nothing about the investigation. He was retired. He said he'd say hi to the Yak when he saw him. Joe told him not to bother; the Yak wouldn't remember him.

Joe could hardly wait for the guy to hang up so he could call Roman Yakovich, onetime back watcher, gun bearer, and all-around henchman to the late Big Sid Sedlacek, Helen's father. The Yak, too, was retired, but he and Joe had collaborated successfully on a few occasions of late. Joe couldn't think why he hadn't called the Yak in the first place.

"Roman," he said, when he got through, "I'm kind of in a jam. Can you meet me in Detroit?"

The Yak could. He said he'd leave Miami that evening. But Joe calmed him. There was no great hurry. And no, this had nothing to do with Helen. It was a problem strictly relating to Joe. Better not to mention it to Helen. They agreed to meet in three days, at a bar in Grosse Pointe, Cupid's.

Joe was pleased with his day's work. He'd planned to find a state park, or maybe just a lonely country road, and sack out under the stars. But he didn't feel in the least tired. He'd spent the previous night in a motel in Glendive, near the Montana line. It was from there that he'd called the Colonel and arranged to meet him in Bismarck. Clearly, the Colonel had attempted to jump the gun and had calculated about when Joe would be in western North Dakota. Joe was glad that the Colonel had gotten a little too cute; it had jarred Joe awake.

He decided to drive on through the night. It had been years since he'd done anything like this. He used to love driving through the night when he was a kid. This would be enjoyable, he felt.

It was a quiet night of small towns, few and far between at first, under the huge black sky. Usually, drifting through on the main street, his was the only vehicle. A gas station might be open, but little else. The one traffic light was a blinker. Joe liked, for some reason, the lighted clocks in the windows of closed gas stations— they looked nice and lonely, archaic.

Toward dawn, when he found himself edging down through the Minnesota north country, the towns began to pop up more frequently. Still, the rare traffic was usually a lone pickup dragging a fishing boat on a trailer, eager to be first on one of the many lakes— whether fishing or getting out to set the decoys for duck hunting, Joe didn't know. The sun came bobbling over the pines and not long after he saw the first yellow school bus. Joe stopped for coffee and gas and studied his road maps.

Did he really want to go down to Chicago to look up Caspar? He didn't feel like it. Caspar could wait. So now the choice was to either drive to Manitowoc, on Lake Michigan, and take the ferry across to Michigan, or head across the Upper Peninsula. Either way, he was sure, would be safe. If the Colonel was still looking for him he'd need a lot of resources to cover all the possible routes.

Another possibility occurred to him. He had a contact in Green Bay, a strange guy who spent a lot of time on the Internet. Brooker Moos was a conspiracy junkie, a poop dump, a place where information went to die. Joe had met him in a tavern, in Chicago, and they'd hit it off for some reason. They had played bumper pool, then some other machine games. Brooker was a whiz at games. But most of all he liked to get his teeth into a story, a myth, particularly a conspiracy theory, and run it down to the last shred of credibility.

Moos (he pronounced it "Mooz," and said the unusual first name was an old family name—"generations of Brookers . . . we're Dutch") was a slender, handsome young man who wore photo-sensitive lenses mounted in genuine tortoiseshell frames. He was always meticulously shaven, with a fresh haircut, given to wearing neat slacks and a tattersall shirt, with a knit tie and a corduroy sport coat. He would have been an ordinary, nice-looking fellow, but there was something amiss, some vagueness in his expression, a shadow of weakness, or it might have been a half-obscured cruelty. It was that ambiguous face that had attracted Joe's attention: the man could be your friendly dentist or a mass murderer . . . perhaps both. At first, he'd wondered if Brooker was gay, but he had yet to find any real sign of it. Still, something was a bit wrong. Joe liked him, though. He was bright, amusing, and even charming, in a way.

Brooker had moved from Chicago to Green Bay a while back. Joe wasn't sure why, but Brooker had said that it was because there was "too much to do" in Chicago. It was distracting. It was much quieter in Green Bay, presumably. There may have been other reasons, Joe reckoned, possibly legal reasons.

Brooker didn't seem to have a regular source of income, or if he did it wasn't enough. And yet he kept up appearances. "People respect a man who is dressed nicely. They answer your questions, tell you just about anything, really, at least if you're not too pressing or trying to throw your weight around. Why wouldn't I wear a tie? Should I go out in baggy, dirty jeans and an old shirt with a sports logo on it?" Joe saw his point.

Moos had won a nice chunk of cash from Joe playing the games. That didn't bother Joe, but he noticed that Brooker seemed truly delighted. Obviously, the money was sorely needed. Joe also noticed that Brooker was a guy who possessed unusual information, of a vaguely suspect nature, about people who didn't care for information about them being made public.

They were watching a fellow on the television news being arraigned. The man had posted a bond for $250,000. "He can afford it," Brooker had said. "He lives out in Briarwood, a million-dollar house. His income just from the limo companies runs a couple of hundred thou a year, and that's only one of his businesses."

Brooker had tossed this off with confidence. He'd noticed that Joe was interested. He smiled. "His wife is an ex-airline hostess. She runs the hair parlor biz. That's worth a couple of million. You know how many hair parlors there are in Chicago? Close to two thousand. They all have to pay to stay in business."

"How do you know?" Joe said skeptically.

"It's based on their income," Brooker said. "That runs to something like fifty million. It's a matter of record." He went on to outline it in terms of number of clients, the cost of a perm, a tint, a whole host of other services. Anyone could figure it out. "Plus, of course, I know a few people, who tell me things."

Joe was impressed. Later, Brooker had provided him with some interesting information on a client. After that, Joe sent him money, from time to time, just to keep the connection alive.

Joe was still in Minnesota. He had just crossed the Mississippi River. It wasn't far to the Wisconsin border. He figured he could make it to Green Bay in a few more hours. It was more or less on his way, regardless of what route he took from there to Detroit. He could go north, to the U.P., or take the ferry across the lake, or even go down to Chicago.

It was now full morning. Joe called Brooker. The phone rang four times and then Brooker's recorded voice said, "I gotta sleep some time. Leave a message." Joe left a message: he'd be in Green Bay around noon, he thought. In the meantime, Brooker might want to investigate what was available on the Net concerning the bombing in Detroit. Especially, Joe suggested, he should look for any connection with Joe, any mention of his name. Joe would call when he got there.

"Don't call here," a voice broke in.

"I thought you were sleeping," Joe said.

"I never actually sleep," Brooker said. "But don't call here. I'm pretty sure this line is bugged."

"So where do I call?"

"I don't know. I'll think of something. And don't come here. We'll figure something out. I'll get going on this stuff." He hung up.

Now what? Joe shrugged and got into the truck. Wisconsin was a different place, all rolling hills, farms, trees still in their autumn colors. Very beautiful, but too crowded for a guy who had gotten used to Montana—you couldn't even see to the next hill because the trees were in the way. Small towns, one after another, with odd new industries in the middle of nowhere, all with grandly landscaped grounds—the electronics industry, insurance companies. It was a strange countryside; silicon valley among the cheesemakers.

By the time he got to Green Bay Joe had a plan. He didn't feel tired, but he knew he should rest. Brooker lived in a small house on the edge of the city, all but surrounded by industrial works of a generally maritime nature, structures for loading lake boats, huge parking lots for semitrailers, small manufacturers of maritime gear. There were only a couple of houses on the block. The paving of the street was broken up by the passage of heavy equipment. Joe cruised past.

The house was a little square clapboard affair with a four-sided roof, probably four rooms, at the most. It had a stout, industrial-strength mesh wire fence around it. The yard was bare of all but tufts of grass and weeds. An old Pontiac was parked in front, the tires a little low. Joe noticed a couple of satellite dishes mounted on the roof. He didn't see any other vehicles around.

Joe drove out on a county road toward the lake. It was only a mile or so to the shore road. He turned south. From this road he could occasionally glimpse the lake through trees, cottages, and the sparsely grassed dunes, a narrow view, gray-blue and cold as the North Sea, but without significant surf. Eventually, he came to a small town and found a Bide-A-Wee motel with worn and shabby cottage units. He went to bed and slept for several hours, until well after dark.

After he'd showered and shaved he dressed in dark clothes and went out to eat. An hour later he slipped into the back door of Brooker's house and found him hunched over one of his computers in the living room. There were three other computers, all displaying either Web sites or screen savers.

The house was as clean and spare as a barracks. In the kitchen, where Joe had entered, the linoleum floor was waxed, the empty chairs propped against an old Formica-topped red table with chrome legs. The counter was also red Formica and bare, the glass-fronted cabinets containing a few colorful Fiestaware plates, with matching cups and bowls, a collection of colored plastic glasses. One cupboard seemed filled with packages of food and cans of chili. There was an enameled white tin bread box next to the gleaming toaster, and a Mr. Coffee with an empty carafe nestled on the warmer. A microwave oven sat on the counter near the sink, which was an old-fashioned affair with a high, swivel faucet, everything scoured and smelling of Bon Ami. The kitchen exhaust fan was on, doing battle against a haze of cigarette smoke.

"Dr. Moos, I presume," Joe said, leaning on the doorjamb. The reference was to Brooker's clean white lab coat, in the pocket of which was a plastic "nerd pack" filled with pens.

Brooker looked up and jumped. "How did you get in? I thought I said—"

"I figured it was better to just come on," Joe interrupted. "We could spend days screwing around. I didn't see any sign of surveillance. So what's up?"

"No, I mean it . . . how did you get in? I've got electronics . . . the gate, the porch . . ."

"Professional secret," Joe quipped. "Sorry, I can't tell you. Maybe later, if you're good. So, what did you find out?"

"I think I'm tapped," Brooker said. He pushed his castered chair back from the console. He was smoking a cigarette. A large ashtray was already overflowing with butts. Next to it was a can of Faygo orange soda.

"Why?" Joe asked.

Brooker shrugged. "It started a few weeks ago. Strange clicking noises, a kind of . . . hollow sound? Not that I use the phone that much, anyway, but I thought . . . just to be on the safe side."

"You in any kind of trouble?"

"No. I'm clean. A few bills in arrears, that's all."

Joe took out a wad of money and tossed it on the table that Brooker used for a workplace. The table was actually an old door, resting on two small filing cabinets. There were two large-screen terminals, their accompanying computer towers next to them, but with gray or black boxes in between and other boxes under the table. Joe supposed they were copiers, or scanners, or something. The other computers were similarly disposed about the room on card tables. Cables ran everywhere, with cords plugged into heavy-duty multiple-jack connectors that had glowing red lights.

"You evidently pay your power bill," Joe said.

"Got to," Brooker said. He mashed out the cigarette and picked up the wad of money, fanned through it, and smiled. His teeth were a dull yellow. "Thanks, Joe. This will keep me online for a while."

"Gotta keep the data flowing," Joe said. "Well, did you . . . ?"

"Oh, yeah. All kinds of stuff. Care for a pop?"

"Sure." Joe went out to the kitchen and looked in the old round-shouldered reefer. It was full of Faygo and little else—a package of hot dogs, a jar of mustard, some relish, a block of cheese wrapped in a ziplock plastic bag, and the inevitable jar of peanut butter. He plucked a can of Faygo ginger ale from a plastic-ringed collar and opened it as he returned to the living room.

"Don't you eat any veggies?" Joe asked. He was always interested in people like Brooker, how they lived, what they ate, how they kept it all together.

"Don't have to," Brooker said. "I take vitamins, and supplements. That's all you really need, Joe. Doesn't your wife make sure you take your vitamins?"

"My wife? What makes you think I'm married?"

"It's all over the Internet, Joe. You're married to Helen Sedlacek, the daughter of the late Sid. You live near Butte, Montana, under the name of Joe Humann.

"Here," Brooker said. He pulled up to one of the computers and typed rapidly on an orthopedic-looking keyboard. A Web site soon appeared on the screen. The home page was a lovely photograph of a bucolic scene, with drooping willow trees, a red barn, an elegant old farmhouse. Bright letters welcomed the viewer to Lynn Park and out of the speakers on either side of the console poured the melodious strains of "My Old Kentucky Home," played on banjo and mandolin.

"What the—" Joe said. He leaned over Brooker's back, looking.

"Wait," Brooker said. He typed some more, then manipulated his roller mouse, clicking away. A series of pages flickered past until the display stopped with a screenful of text. Brooker scanned down the screen, which rolled up quickly, until he paused and highlighted the name "Joe Service."

"A good man to know," the text read. "Now goes by Joe Humann. Retired. Married to Helen, nee Sedlacek . . ." A blue Web link referred the viewer to another site, or perhaps just another place on this site, Joe couldn't tell. "Retired with a difference," the commentary went on. "Joe is now employed by the U.S. government! Who'd have thought?"

"There's a lot of other info scattered around, on this site and others," Brooker said. He pushed back and looked triumphantly at Joe.

Joe did not attempt to conceal his shock. "What the hell is this? How can they do this? Where do they get their information?"

"It's just gossip, Joe. The Internet is all about gossip. There are a million Web sites, maybe more. A lot of them are like this one. Family sites. This guy is John Lynn. Do you know him?"

"John Lynn?" Joe thought. "Big John Lynn? The Peter Man?"

"Peter Man?"

"Safecracker. The explosives guy," Joe said.

"That's him," Brooker said. "He's lamed up now. Maybe he blew himself up. Spent some time in the pen, which may be where he got onto the Web. Now he runs this site. There are several like this, but this is one of the better ones. He keeps track of all his old pals, passes on messages, et cetera."

"But how can they do this? It's crazy," Joe said. He was not over his shock.

Brooker explained how it worked. The criminal world had gotten online, inevitably. It was the new grapevine. But in order to access the grapevine you had to be in the Life. It was very much an inside thing. Elaborate codes, which one knew if one were in the Life, opened it up. This site, for instance, appeared to be just one of the thousands of family sites spread all across the country, around the world. There were sites for Stewarts, complete with the plaid background; for Smiths, in their hundreds of different families and first names; for Jacksons and Millers and Purdys and Pritchards and Baums. But if you knew the code you could find access to the "back pages." Other kinds of sites existed, of course, as fronts for the "inside poop."

"But it's all right out there," Joe said, pointing at the screen in horror. "The cops . . . anyone can crack in there. Can't they?"

"Well, they can," Moos conceded, "but it isn't so easy. For that matter, the cops already know how to crack into the street grapevine. They have funds built into their budgets for paying for that kind of info. Actually, this is a lot more secure. There are so many of these sites, and new ones coming online all the time . . . I don't think the cops could keep up. Besides, if they do crack into it, what do they learn? Just a bunch of gossip. Who knows if any of it is true? Even if you were a cop and knew what you were looking for, could you trust something like this, even if you found it in the first place?"

"Well, Big John got one thing wrong," Joe said, calming down. "I'm not married."

"Oh, yes, you are," Brooker said. "You live in Montana and there, if you represent yourself as married, you're married. Even if you and Helen say you're Mr. and Mrs. Humann. You're married."

"Good lord! Is it true?" Joe was aghast. "Can't I do something about this? Do I have to get divorced?"

"Do you want to be divorced?"

"Well, I sure as hell don't want to be married," Joe said. "I mean, that wasn't the point."

"Relax," Brooker said. "It probably won't make any difference, as long as Helen doesn't contest it in court."

"She wouldn't do that," Joe said.

"So, what's the prob?"

"Well, it's right there, on the Internet."

"Oh, that. I can take care of that. In fact, I was going to discuss that with you. I've decided to start a service. I'll be your private little eraser and go through the Internet, constantly, and remove or change any data that mention you. For a fee, of course."

Joe was relieved. "That's a great service. Can you actually do that? I mean, that there . . ."—he pointed at the screen—"that's Big John's site. How can you change stuff on his site?"

"I haff mein vays," Brooker said, mimicking a movie SS man. He bent to the keyboard and began to type in instructions. Soon he was presented with a series of technical-looking sites, with numbers and odd code figures. He typed some more, hit a final key with a flourish, and sat back. Shortly, they were presented with the page they had been looking at. It now reported that Jim Sarris was living in Crested Butte, Colorado, married to Hallie Bury, under the name of Jim Sarkisian.

"Big John will see that," Joe said. "He'll change it back."

"You know what?" Brooker said. "I'll bet he won't see it. These guys put up tons of stuff every day. They rarely, if ever, go back to read what's on there. But if he does change it, I've left a little invisible code. It'll notify me that 'Joe Service' has been mentioned. I'll change it again, or even delete it, make it impossible for the page to function, to be called up. If John notices that, he'll fiddle with it for a while, then go on to something else. He'll think something has gone haywire with the formatting on that page and it isn't worth his time to fix it. Don't forget, he isn't that interested in these 'items.' In the meantime, I have a search device out, constantly scanning the network, looking for your name. I get messages all the time. I've got some waiting on those computers over there. I'll get to them in a bit."

"That's great," Joe said. "Uh, what do you charge?"

"Well, you know, Joe, I'm going to make you a deal. I only thought of this after I started looking for your name, this morning. When your name started popping up, I have to admit, I was a little surprised. My first thought was, Joe ain't gonna like this. And then it occurred to me, How can I remove this stuff? I figured it out in about twenty minutes, maybe an hour. It's a great gambit, eh? I can market this. I'm always looking for something to pay the rent. You know? There's got to be a lot of guys like you out there who'd pay for this service."

"How much?" Joe said, tiring of Brooker's gleeful prating.

"Well, you've been very generous, over the years," Brooker said, "and you just laid a bundle on me. This first time is free. How's that? That would include the stuff I already gleaned, that's waiting for me to work on. All subsequent 'hits,' how about a hundred a hit?"

"Hey, sure," Joe said. "It sounds like a deal. Only . . . ," he hesitated.

"How many are there likely to be? Over a week? I don't know," Brooker admitted. "I'll tell you what, though. I'm not a guy to skin you. How about we put a cap on it? Say, a grand a month, max."

"That's quite a nut," Joe said.

"Well, you think about it," Brooker said. "I'm excited about this prospect. It may turn out to be lucrative. Right now, I don't know what to charge. If I get a lot of clients, I can drop the fee down. I'm not looking to get rich, just looking for a way, at last, to make a decent living. I have a lot of expen—"

"I hear you, I hear you," Joe said. "Okay, let's go with that plan. We can work it out. Now, what else have you got?"

Brooker smiled and set to work. Shortly, he pointed to a Web site on the screen filled with a text. "This is the site of a weirdo over in Michigan—www.hillmartin.net. I don't know what that's supposed to mean, but these sites often have bizarre names. It's run by a guy named M. P. Luck, some kind of kooky patriot-militia nut. He's got quite a bit about that bombing. And look."

Brooker moved the cursor on the screen until it highlighted "Joe Service."

"What's he got to say?"

"Sit down, you can read the whole thing. But basically it says that you're a federal agent, that you provided the explosives and the whole plan, although you didn't personally attend the action."

Joe was startled anew. "I did all that?"

"Well, according to Luck, you did. He also mentions that he's being investigated, despite the fact that he was nowhere near and knew nothing about it until he saw it on television. It's all a government plot." Brooker looked at him expectantly.

"It's nuts," Joe said. He sipped his soda. It wasn't bad ginger ale. "What's the source of this guy's info? Does he say?"

"He has inside sources, he says. The official line is that the bombing was related to drugs, to the cocaine and heroin trade. Apparently, a known drug dealer was being arraigned at the time. The plot was supposed to cause a diversion, to spring this guy. Unfortunately, the explosions were too big. The drug kingpin, or whatever he was, got killed."

"No kidding? Well, it's all wrapped up, then," Joe said. "All they have to do is find me."

"Well, the Homeland Security doesn't mention you. They're still not sure that the drug stuff wasn't just a subterfuge, that it was really a terrorist act, possibly involving Islamic radicals. And there are other possibilities that the feds aren't revealing yet."

Joe nodded. "And why are they investigating this Luck?"

Brooker said that it seemed the "other possibilities" might point to a homegrown terrorist group, such as the one that blew up the Oklahoma City federal building.

"The thing about Luck's site," Brooker pointed out, "it's all in the open. Anyone can read it and he gets lots of hits, has a regular group of subscribers, and so on. His deal is he's a nut on so-called takings. Property that's confiscated by the feds, condemned, phony legal claims. Apparently, he's had property problems himself, and he's livid about the legal expense. The info about you is sort of unusual for him. Where he got his poop, I don't know, but I get the feeling that he doesn't have the inside track on these other sites, like Big John's. Someone fingered you to him."

"Can you tamper with his site?" Joe asked.

"Oh, sure, but do you want me to? This is just hearsay. It's of no value. Maybe he got it from someone on the inside at Home-land Security, maybe he just deduced it from questions he was asked, say a detective mentioned your name. Maybe he's just guessing, made it up. It's not worth changing. And I'd say that Luck is not like Lynn, that he'll notice if something is changed on his site. He'll be upset and pursue it. I've got asbestos firewalls, but he might be able to track it back to me. I don't know. I'd leave it."

"Who was questioning him?" Joe said.

"Some ex-Detroit cop, a guy named Mulheisen."

8

Dogs of War

The deputy director of operations was a stocky man who liked to dress in a kind of faux military way—tan gabardine twill suits, preferably, with dark green ties that could be mistaken for army neckwear. Recent events in American history had offered him new and improved opportunities to take a militaristic posture, but while he was the civil service equivalent of a full-bird colonel, he still wasn't entitled to wear the neat little silver eagles on the epaulets that he coveted. He had never been in the military, as it happened, but he felt like a general at times. He was frankly envious of his underling's career, that underling being Vernon Tucker (Lt. Col., USAF, ret.).

The DDO could spend minutes lost in reverie, wondering what it had been like for Tucker to drive an F-105 downtown, to bomb Hanoi. That's the way he thought about it: "drive a Thud," a fighter-bomber. "Go downtown." That was how veteran jet jockeys talked, as he understood it. *Jinking to evade SAMs.* Hot damn!

He hadn't even heard what Tucker was saying, standing before his desk. *Dodging a firecan!* He looked at Tucker, a rather small man, compared to himself, but with an unmistakable military air, albeit the casually studied manner of those kinds of officers who had done dashing things—pilots, tank commanders, cavalrymen. What did Tucker have that he didn't? Tucker was a goddamn cowboy, as best as he could figure, but of course that was valued in today's government.

The DDO longed to say, "At ease, colonel," but Tucker was at ease. Instead, he said, "Who is this guy again?"

"Joe Service," Tucker said. He didn't register any annoyance, although he'd just spent five minutes explaining about Service. Evidently, the DDO hadn't heard a word he'd said.

"I came to you," Tucker said, "because, of course, even though I'm seconded to Homeland Security, my first loyalty is always to the agency. And in the past, we've had dealings with Service."

"What's he to us?" the DDO asked. "He's not one of our agents, is he? I think I know all the agents, and I don't remember the name."

"No, sir," Tucker said. "He was just a contact. We interrogated him in Denver, a while back. He gave us some interesting background information on Echeverria."

"Ah, yes, Echeverria. That's the guy who was involved in the bombing in Detroit."

"Well, that's one theory," Tucker said. "Others think it may have been a homegrown militia outfit. Actually, the attack was in Wards Cove, a little town north of Detroit."

"What do you think?"

"It could have been Echeverria. The connection between him and the prisoner who was killed is tenuous, but real."

"Whatever happened to the al-Qaeda connection?" the DDO wanted to know.

"Not proven, sir. There could be a connection."

"That would be ideal," the DDO pointed out. "The guys upstairs would like that. Any chance of making that connection? Man, that would be great."

"That's what I was thinking," Tucker said. "That's why I wanted to enlist Joe Service. If we could recruit him . . . He's a clever fellow. He worked for organized crime for years, as a kind of in-house troubleshooter. He had some kind of falling out with the capos. He might be willing to help us make a connection between Echeverria and the Arabs. It's known that Echeverria deals with heroin internationally. The A-Q are involved in that trade. They've probably had some contact."

"Have they, by god! That's great! But didn't we do some kind of deal with Echeverria? The name's familiar."

"Oh, no, sir," Tucker assured him. "That was the DEA . . . 'War on Drugs' . . . they worked out an understanding, or something, but that's their baby, nothing to do with us."

"Well, what if we screw that up? Is that going to come back on us?" The DDO's eyes narrowed, his brow creased. "I don't want to get into a pissing match with Brown over at DEA."

"Well, sir, that's my point. Right now, this task force that I'm detached to, under Homeland, we can't touch Echeverria, because he's protected by DEA and the evidence we've got won't expose him. But if we can show Echeverria is dabbling in terrorism, that's going to take precedence, you bet. Nobody can say anything about that. Of course, the investigation is under the aegis of Homeland Security. But if the agency—you—can go to them and say, We've got a guy we think can help us break this, but we're hampered, well, the agency looks pretty good when all this works out."

The DDO's face brightened. "That would be nice. But now . . . would this Service guy be 'our' man? I thought you said he wasn't an agent."

"He was never an agent," Tucker said. "We want deniability on this, naturally. But he was an asset. He's almost ideal for the purpose."

The DDO appreciated that distinction. Deniability was important when things didn't work out, but so was credit when things did.

Tucker explained: "When I said 'recruit,' I meant simply that Service would come under the rubric, so to speak, of a contract agent. The usual thing . . . you understand. He provides the link, without him being seen as our guy, not part of the personnel."

"What can he do for us?" the DDO wanted to know.

"First of all," Tucker said, "we think he had some kind of connection with that fellow Franko, who was involved in the drug trade in Kosovo. It's a double cutout, because Franko wasn't personnel, either, he was a contract agent. He was in touch with the KLA, the Kosovo Liberation Army. The A-Q had a demonstrable contact there."

"Sounds ideal," the DDO said. "Is there anything else?"

"Well, then there is M. P. Luck, the Michigan patriot movement guy. Service seems to have some kind of connection with Luck as well."

"Wheels within wheels," the DDO said. "What's Luck's position? Didn't he give us something on Oklahoma City?"

"Ah. I wasn't sure if you were aware of that," Tucker said. "I didn't want to say anything. No offense, sir, but that was the FBI's baby and we're not supposed to know about that. Of course, we do, but we can't be seen to know, if you take my meaning."

"Hey, I don't know nothin'. But, *entre nous*, did we know?"

"It was 'in the air,' you might say. My impression was that Luck didn't exactly cooperate with the FBI, but he was a source. But now we're all in the same kennel. Right? My thinking is, we've got three or four players here, potentially: Service, Echeverria, Luck, and the A-Q." He ticked them off on the fingers of his left hand. "The trick is to make a connection with all four. The key figure could be Joe Service, sort of the wild card, if you will."

The DDO nodded, following closely.

Tucker went on, laying out the possibilities. "The DEA won't want to give up Echeverria just on the basis of Service, but if we can make a connection between Echeverria and Luck, and between Luck and Service, and between any of them and the A-Q, these other agencies will have to relinquish their options and we're well on our way to making a case."

Tucker could see from the DDO's expression that he'd lost him. "Here's how it works, sir. Echeverria's now an asset of the DEA. He's providing them with an inside angle on various narcotics organizations in Colombia and the cocaine trade. He was injured in an explosion a couple of years ago. Very painful, lots of burns. The explosion was rigged by Joe Service—that's a complicated history that we needn't explore right now. But Echeverria is known to be seeking revenge against Service. If the DEA will surrender their purchase on Echeverria, I think we could lure him back to the U.S., to get Service."

The deputy director was puzzled. "Do we want him to do that? Service is our man, sort of."

"Well, there's more," Tucker said. "Echeverria had connections with a Chicago mobster who was heavily involved in the drug traffic in Serbia and Kosovo. A guy named Zivkovic. Franko was our contract agent in Kosovo, dealing with Zivkovic. It turned out that Joe Service was involved with this Franko, back in Montana— he's actually living on Franko's old property. Franko's defunct now. Franko, through Zivkovic, had dealings with some KLA types. That's the connection with al-Qaeda, at least provisionally. It's a little sketchy, but the potential is there.

"Now we're seeing a growing connection between Service and Luck. At this point, we don't know what the connection is, but Luck at least seems to know Service. Luck is a suspect in the Detroit bombing, but it's not exactly Velcroed. We have no evidence he was there. Echeverria may have been connected, because there was a drug dealer at the scene, for a hearing, a fellow who had a demonstrable connection with Echeverria's organization. But this connection is worthless to us, since the DEA is shielding Echeverria."

The DDO's eyes had gone glassy. Where was all this going?

Tucker hastened on. "Luck has had dealings with Echeverria, we think."

"We think?"

"A few years back. He was flying stuff into Panama and Guatemala, maybe into Colombia. Perfectly legitimate, as it happens, industrial supplies. But get this, sir. It was things like money counters, trash compactors, computer equipment, stuff that could be used in the drug industry. Then he'd fly back, of course, presumably empty. Or it might be, he'd have some kind of legitimate produce. The DEA was never able to pin any of that on him, but they suspected he was also carrying drugs. Anyway, he must have had dealings with Echeverria."

"Okay, now you've got them all connected, but I still don't see the connection to the bombing. Cut to the chase, Tucker. Who was responsible?"

"Al-Qaeda," Tucker said.

The DDO was baffled. "How's that work?"

Tucker knew this was the delicate part. "The connection between Luck and Service is of my own making," he confessed. "I fed some information to Luck, who has been putting it on the Internet, that Service is a federal agent." He shrugged. "It was a pretty harmless ploy, just a little disinformation. But it was bound to interest Echeverria, as well as others, of course. It was also an incentive for Joe Service to come to us, for protection, of course. Anyway, the idea is that Luck could be an intermediary with Echeverria, get him to come to the States to attempt to revenge himself on Service. The A-Q will be interested, because Luck is a highly visible advocate for the so-called patriot cause. Depending on what happens, the A-Q will be seen to have made an attempt on Luck's life, at Wards Cove."

"But I thought you said Luck wasn't at Wards Cove!"

"He should have been," Tucker said. "He had a case pending there. There was supposed to be a hearing, about the same time as the bombing, and about the time of the hearing on Echeverria's associate. None of that implicated the A-Q, of course, because then we didn't know that Echeverria and Luck were associated, or that Luck was involved with Service, or that any of them were associated with the A-Q. But if Echeverria were to be assassinated, or if he were to assassinate someone, such as Service, then we'd have the whole bunch and a case could be made to the public."

The DDO shook his head. "I can't see you selling that to the Homeland Security people. 'Cause that's who has to buy it, you know. They'll be the ones who tell the DEA that their deal with Echeverria is off."

"The plan isn't ready to go to Homeland yet," Tucker said. "It needs fine tuning. We need to know a little more about the connection between Zivkovic and the KLA, which we can connect to the A-Q. Joe Service can do that for us. Look, sir, I know it's a little confusing, but that's one of its virtues, if you ask me. The American public is happy to believe anything of al-Qaeda. Sure, it's confusing, but that's all to the good. Arab stuff is always confusing, and Balkan stuff, the KLA connection, is even more so. It can be explained in a lot of ways and we don't have to do the explaining. The press and the rest of the media do that. They dig up connections, congratulating themselves, saying 'Ah hah!' We say 'No comment' and 'That's a security issue.'"

"I still don't get it."

"It isn't ready to 'get' . . . yet," Tucker said, a bit testily, try-ing to conceal his irritation with the DDO's obtuseness. "But it will be ready, if we can loosen the ties between Echeverria and the DEA. That's the key. That and getting Joe Service to do what he does best —find out things and, uh, clean up loose ends."

"Why can't you just find out who rigged that bomb?" the DDO said petulantly. "If it wasn't al-Qaeda, that could come out and that would blow the whole thing sky-high . . . so to speak."

"The consensus in the task force is that it was Echeverria," Tucker said. "But we don't have a shred of proof, and I don't think we'll get any, as it stands. There is no demonstrable connection with him, other than that one of his underlings was involved. The guys in the task force think it's plausible that the drug dealer's friends— let's say Echeverria himself—wanted to cause a diversion so they could spring the guy. But blow up the place? That's pretty extreme, or so the feeling goes. But these are extreme people, and maybe they just got carried away. That sort of smash and grab operation has been done in other countries—Serbia, for instance, by Zivkovic. Also in some Muslim countries, Turkey, Egypt, and so on. But we can't make a case against Echeverria if he's in Colombia."

"What about Luck?" the DDO asked. "Maybe he did it, for his buddy Echeverria."

"Service could help us with that, if I can get him close to Luck," Tucker said. "But the real deal is to associate al-Qaeda. Ser-vice could help us with that, too."

The DDO was thoughtful for a moment. "I just don't see al-Qaeda blowing up a small-town courthouse. It ain't a trade tower, or the Pentagon. It ain't even Mount Rushmore."

"It's white picket fence America," Tucker said. "And, oddly enough, there are a bunch of Middle Easterners living in the county. A surprising number, actually."

"Arabs? With connections to al-Qaeda?"

Jon A. Jackson

"They aren't Arabs, most of them," Tucker admitted. "In fact,
they're mostly Christians. But the public doesn't see that as much
of a distinction. They're Chaldeans, and some other groups. Who
knows what a Chaldean is? It's biblical-sounding. The point is:
would al-Qaeda care? They publicly claimed credit. It seemed to
demonstrate that they can hit in the heartland, in Ronald Reagan's
hometown, as it were. That's the point."

"Ronald Reagan was from Illinois," the DDO said, "not
Michigan."

"It's the same thing," Tucker said, then added, "but you're
right of course, sir. I only meant that it is Hometown, USA. That
strikes fear into the heart of the public. You're not safe in the heartland. Anyway, we can't really know what is going through the minds
of these madmen. Why the trade towers? Fifteen minutes before that
first plane hit, if you'd asked a thousand people in the streets to name
the most important symbols of America, no one would have mentioned the World Trade Center. The Statue of Liberty, sure, even
Fort Knox, but not something associated with global enterprise."

"The White House, for sure," the DDO said, obviously taking his point.

"Yes, or Mount Rushmore," Tucker said, underlining the
DDO's earlier suggestion. "Anyway, sir, you see the problem: there
are all these shadowy associations—Echeverria, Luck, Service, al-
Qaeda. We see connections, but the public doesn't. Sometimes, you
know, when the evidence is obscure, you have to shovel the ma-
nure. You know the joke about the kid whose folks promised him a
pony?"

"Yeah," the DDO laughed, recalling the joke. "All he got was
a room full of horse shit!"

Tucker smiled and nodded. Even when the DDO went on to
relate the kid's cry, " . . . there's gotta be a pony in here somewhere!"
When he was through chuckling, the DDO said, "So, what do I do?"

"If you could talk to the Homeland guys," Tucker said. "Tell them we've got this asset, you don't even have to mention his name. In fact, why not just keep it between us? Who says Echeverria was involved. Get the DEA to cut Echeverria loose. And in the meantime I'll get to work with Joe."

"That's good, that's good," the DDO said. "Nothing is really committed. We're not out on a limb. We're just saying this guy isn't clean. And, Christ! He ain't clean."

"He's very far from clean," Tucker said. "Well, I'm glad we're in agreement. I just didn't want to initiate anything without your approval."

"Quite right. Well, keep me informed."

Joe Service walked the deck of the S. S. *Badger*, looking out on the chill gray waves of Lake Michigan. Most of the passengers were inside. The ship was basically two decks over a vast hull space filled with trucks, buses, and cars. The other passengers were watching television and eating or playing the arcade games. It was only a four-hour passage and the ship barely reacted to the slight sea, but there was a brisk, cold wind following them.

Joe was glad he had thought to bring his jacket from the pickup—passengers weren't allowed on the car deck once they were under way. Being cooped up inside with all those people, the mugginess, the kids, that didn't appeal. It wasn't that he was asocial—normally, he was more than happy to chat—he just wanted to think. A sea voyage, especially a relatively brief one on a lake boat, was a good transitional phase. He was trying to figure out what to do next.

It was interesting, he thought, how easily he had abandoned what seemed like a pleasant and desirable life for one that was quite unsettled and even, apparently, aimless. It was a matter of turning right or left, it seemed. But he didn't feel at all anxious or unhappy. Quite the contrary. He felt alive.

At present, he was content to watch a gull cruising alongside the ship, seemingly within arm's reach, scarcely moving its wings. Joe leaned on the railing and watched the gull, which from time to time turned its yellow eye to look directly at him.

One gull, Joe thought, was a beautiful thing. But as soon as another showed up, and then another, and then a bunch, they began to squabble and veer at one another. But for now, this one gull just looked at Joe.

What do you think, Joe spoke silently, *turn right? Turn left?* The gull looked straight ahead, then turned its head away, toward the south. Joe looked down that way. In the distance he could see a dark helicopter, barely off the waves. It couldn't be the Colonel, he thought. Nah. The chopper sped on and was soon lost to sight. There was only one other boat on the lake, a very large container ship several miles away, headed toward Milwaukee or Chicago. Joe looked back to the gull. It bobbed its head once, then abruptly peeled away. A moment later it was gone. Joe strolled on along the deck.

Six hours later he was outside Mulheisen's house in St. Clair Flats. A car was parked in the drive. Out in the field there was a new, small house under construction. A carpenter was loading tools into a pickup. Joe drove on down the rural lane until he came to a marina. A handful of men were busy there, hoisting pleasure boats out of the water with a crane. They were being stowed for the winter. There were few cars in the large parking lot. Joe parked his pickup out of the way and set off along the canal. It soon brought him out to the channel and a well-trodden path led along that. A large ship was looming up out of Lake St. Clair and preparing to enter the channel. Joe walked along, enjoying the end of the day. Far down the lake he could see a couple of other cargo ships, downward bound, headed toward Detroit. The city was not visible, presumably hidden in a mist. The light was still strong but on the wane.

Ahead, he saw an old woman, a slight figure, moving slowly along the path. She was dressed in wool slacks and a jacket and she carried binoculars, through which she peered from time to time when she stopped. Joe quickly overtook her.

The old woman turned to look at him as he approached. She seemed unconcerned at his presence. She smiled.

"What do you see?" Joe asked.

"Not much," she confessed. "Mostly ducks—mallards. But I saw an eider not long ago. Kind of early for an eider, I'd say."

Joe had no idea what an eider was, but he nodded. "What's that bird on the post over there?" He pointed at a large bird, bigger than a crow. No duck, he was sure.

"Ah," the old woman said. She lifted the small binoculars and trained them on the bird. "It's a harrier," she reported. "A marsh hawk. You don't often see them at rest. They usually work the marsh, tirelessly looking for mice. But it's the end of the day, probably getting ready to quit." She offered the binoculars. "Care to look?"

"Sure." Joe took the glasses and fiddled with them until he could see the bird. It was really quite elegant, gray and white, with a small but wickedly hooked beak. "Very handsome," he said, handing the glasses back.

"That's the male," the woman said. "Well, that's nice. He's out late, but the days are so short. He'll soon be gone. Migrating. I guess I'd better be getting in myself. The nurse will be chasing out here to see if I'm all right."

She nodded toward a house and barn, visible a few hundred yards away. When Joe looked that way he saw, in fact, a woman in a jacket, arms folded, smoking a cigarette. She seemed unconcerned by Joe's presence.

The old lady was pretty spry, Joe thought. Up close, he could see she was really quite old, perhaps eighty. "You must be Mrs. Mulheisen," he said.

She looked at him closely. "Are you one of the Colonel's men?"

Joe tossed his head, a gesture that could be taken as yes. He expressed no surprise at her comment. He wondered if the Colonel was keeping a watch, somewhere beyond the nurse. Not likely, he thought, but he might have a man on the premises. "I was looking for your son," he explained.

"Mul is off up north," the woman said. "He called earlier. He met some fool up there, says he saw swallows hibernating! Can you imagine?"

"Birds hibernate?"

"Only in the minds of the ignorant," she said, with a wry expression. "But Mul didn't know that."

"Where is this?" Joe asked.

"Some little town up by Traverse City," Mrs. Mulheisen said. "It's called Queensleap. This fellow—Luck, his name is—claims he's seen hundreds of swallows burrowing in a hill. I told Mul the fellow's daft. He probably saw swallows shooting out of an old stream bank. Country folks, if they don't actually study the birds' behavior, can easily convince themselves the birds are burrowing to hibernate. It's an old folk belief. And Pliny the Elder may have believed it."

She started off toward the house. He walked a ways with her, out of politeness. He didn't want to encounter the nurse.

"Who lives there?" Joe asked, indicating the new little house where he'd seen the carpenter, a small cottagelike affair beyond the old barn.

Mrs. Mulheisen said that it was Mulheisen's latest project, a sort of study. "He needs a place to smoke his cigars," she said. "It's been nice for him, building it. I'm surprised how involved he's gotten in it. It started out just to be a small affair, but it's grown. He'll go out there, I suppose, and read his books and listen to music. It'll be good for him, to have a separate place."

"Interesting," Joe said, stopping. "I like the style."

Mrs. Mulheisen started on toward the older house. "Coming?" she asked. "I'll ask the nurse to get you some tea. I could use some tea."

"No, thanks," Joe called after her. "I think I'll stay out for a bit, keep an eye on the harrier."

"Well, you come up to the house when you're ready. I had a notion to call the Colonel, anyway, but maybe you could pass it on."

"What's that?" Joe said, alert.

"I remembered something," she said, "from the day at the courthouse. Colonel Tucker will know what I'm talking about. I'm sure he would be interested."

"Uh-huh," Joe said, encouragingly. He had no idea what she was talking about.

"Yes, I had some difficulty, you know, with my memory. After the bombing, I mean. I couldn't remember a thing, for quite a little while. But lately some of it has been coming back."

"I see," Joe said, eager to be off. "I'm sure the Colonel will be interested. It would be better if you called him. You have the number?"

"Oh, yes. It may not be important, probably isn't. I talked to a fellow, or rather, he talked to me, in the hall, just before the bomb went off. Quite a strange fellow, very agitated."

"That's just the sort of thing Colonel Tucker will want to know," Joe said. "You call him. I'm afraid I have to go now."

She would not let him go, it seemed. She briefly described her encounter, the tall fellow who had told her to leave. His manner had been almost rude, but clearly he was a bit deranged, so she'd ignored his rudeness, but then she'd forgotten, and only now, this morning, had she begun to recall. But she still didn't have it quite clear in her mind. She wondered if she ever would, she mused. "Recall completely, I mean."

Joe said he was sure she would.

"Well, you mean well, young man, I'm sure," the old lady said, "but you're not a doctor, are you?"

No, Joe admitted. But he knew himself, he said, that he often forgot things and then they'd come back at the oddest moments.

"Have you ever been blown up?" she asked.

"Actually, I have," Joe said. He was thinking, however, of having been shot in the head. He understood very well what her problem was. "Once things start coming back you can't stop them."

"Ah. I hope you're right. It seems unfair to endure such a horrendous experience and not even have the benefit of witnessing it."

With that she at last said good-bye. When she had gone, Joe set off for the car on a dead run.

9

Dog in the Manger

Mulheisen went for a stroll. It was a gorgeous fall day in Queensleap. The town was liberally shaded with tall oaks, maples, beech and ash trees. The shade was visibly thinning, though; every little breeze precipitated a sibilant cascade of brilliant red, yellow, and orange flakes. It was a splendid sight. A golden sunny day with a tinge of chill. A fine day to smoke a cigar while kicking your feet through the dry, rustling drifts.

He walked a few blocks off the main street and found himself on a street of old, pleasant homes. They looked, for the most part, like old farmhouses: two or even three stories, with steeply pitched roofs. They were mostly frame houses, usually with lap siding, painted white or gray, brown or yellow, with white trim. Broad, covered porches ran along the fronts and halfway around the sides. Some had swing seats on the porch. A few were built with a very warm red brick. One of these latter had a white sign on a post next to little picket fence that read: J. HUNDLY, M.D.

Mulheisen tossed his cigar aside and let himself in through the wooden gate and walked up to the front door. He rang. Shortly, a white-haired man of about seventy or older opened the door. He wore a gray wool cardigan sweater over a shirt and tie.

"Sorry," he said pleasantly, "but my wife had to run out. Did you have to wait long? I don't always hear the bell first time."

"You heard it this time," Mulheisen said. "I guess you're the doctor around here."

"Only one," Dr. Hundly said. "Come on in." He closed the door behind Mulheisen. "What's the problem?"

They stood in a little foyer. A stair ran up along one wall, with a worn carpet. It was very quiet in the house, with a pleasant smell of flowers, which stood in vases here and there. The floor was polished hardwood and there was wainscoting of a pleasing dark hue.

Before Mulheisen could respond, the doctor led him back along the hall to a room that was clearly his surgery. It was all very old-fashioned and comforting, with the addition of an air of profes- sionalism: some modern-looking furnishings of a medical nature, an examination table, a number of electronic instruments poised about.

The doctor quickly slipped on a white lab coat with a stetho- scope in one of the pockets, then turned to look at Mulheisen very keenly through his trifocals, his chin lifted slightly. "Take off your coat," he said. "You can hang it over there." He pointed to a coat stand in the corner, next to a wall of medical books.

Mulheisen hesitated. "I don't really have—"

"That's all right, that's all right," the doctor said, helping him off with his light raincoat, which he hung on the rack himself. "Just sit down on the table there and roll up your left sleeve." He snatched up a blood pressure device and, after helping Mulheisen with his sleeve, deftly wrapped it around the bared arm, securing the Velcro flap and promptly pumping the little attached bulb until the device clamped Mulheisen's bicep like a python. He inserted his stethoscope on the inner bend of the elbow and listened as he released the air pressure.

"Hmmm. That's . . . well, it's not *awful*," he said, folding up the sphygmomanometer and setting it aside. "Could be better. Unbutton your shirt." He listened to Mulheisen's chest, moving the cold metal disk of the stethoscope around. "Smoking too much," he remarked gently. "Cut back on the cigarettes. Better yet, stop."

"I don't smoke cigarettes," Mulheisen said, "never have. Cigars."

"Too many cigars," the doctor said. He lifted one of Mulheisen's eyelids. "Well, what's the complaint?"

"None," Mulheisen said. "I was just cur—"

"Open," the doctor said, cutting him off. He looked at Mulheisen's tongue. "Too many cigars. How many do you smoke a day anyway? Twenty?"

"Oh, no," Mulheisen protested. "Only two or three."

"Bosh. A dozen, more like. Too many. Okay, you can button up." He went to his desk and began to scribble on a pad. "That pressure's creeping up. This is a very mild medication. You can get it anywhere. Lane will have it uptown. One a day, in the morning, preferably just before breakfast. What's the name?" He handed Mulheisen a prescription and prodded his stomach, pointedly. "Cut back on the bacon and the french fries, son. Get some regular exercise. Walk!"

"Uh, doctor, I was wondering . . . did you know Mrs. Luck? Constance . . . ?"

The doctor looked at him sharply. "What about her?"

Mulheisen almost reached for his wallet, to show his badge, but he stopped, realizing that there was no badge, no warrant card. "I'm an investigator," he said.

"I could have guessed it," the doctor said. "You have that look. Municipal, state, or federal?"

"I worked for the Detroit Poli—"

"Down below, eh? What brings you up here?"

"I was curious about Mrs. Luck's—"

"Demise," the doctor finished for him. He sighed. "Insurance, is it? Well, I signed the certificate. Heart failure."

"Was there an autopsy?"

"What on earth for? Clear as day. Heart attack. Well, there could have been contributing factors, there always are, but what's the point? The cardiac arrest was sufficient cause. She had a congenital heart defect, you know."

"No cancer?"

"Oh, no. I'd treated her before. Elevated pressures. Not obese, not like you, but she could have stood to lose a few pounds. Rather a rich diet, I'd say. Didn't seem like much of a problem, a young woman like that. Essentially in good health."

"But she had a heart attack."

"Can happen any time," the doctor said. "Could happen to you, before you reach the street. More likely to happen to you, I'd say—she didn't smoke cigars—but these things can come on. Healthy people fall over every day."

"How recently before the death had you seen her?" Mulheisen asked.

"Oh, I don't know. I'd have to look it up. Possibly a few months earlier."

"And the circumstances didn't strike you as unusual?" Mulheisen asked the question in a matter-of-fact, pro forma way.

"No. Died in her sleep. Her husband found her dead, in the morning. He'd been out hunting, early, came home and found her still in bed."

"In the spring? Is that hunting season?"

"Well, you can always hunt something around here, if it isn't ducks and deer it's mushrooms," the doctor said. He looked at Mulheisen thoughtfully. "What's your name again?"

Mulheisen told him.

"Why are you interested in Mrs. Luck?" the doctor asked. "You've left it kind of late."

"Oh, I know," Mulheisen said, in a resigned way. He shrugged a shoulder, as if he were satisfied and probably just as glad to close the door on this apparently routine matter. But then he hesitated, asking, "Uh, you didn't by any chance consult with her previous doctor?"

Dr. Hundly brightened. "As a matter of fact I did. Come to think of it, her doctor called *me*, from down below. Where was it? Indiana, or someplace. Her husband had called her old doctor first, when he found her. The doctor then called me. So I went out to the house. I'd never treated Luck. He didn't know me. Oh, I suppose he knew who I was. He grew up around here, although I don't remember him."

"You didn't know Luck?" Mulheisen was curious about that.

"Well, you know how it is in a small community, people go to one doctor or the other. They're very loyal that way. The Lucks—Imp's folks—doctored with Pruhoff, over in Manton. They had property over that way. And then I guess Luck was away for several years, working all over the world, from what I hear. So I didn't really know him."

"But you knew her," Mulheisen said.

"Well, she came in to see me once. She had a few complaints, nothing major. Headaches. I gave her some medication."

"How long had she been dead?" Mulheisen asked.

"Possibly, six hours. No rigor mortis, or very little, but she'd been lying in a bed, covered up, warm room."

Mulheisen shook his head sorrowfully. "Young woman like that," he said. "Heart attack. We just don't know, do we?"

The doctor laughed lightly and patted Mulheisen on the back. "Don't get depressed, son. It can happen. It *will* happen. But if you watch that pressure, you'll be all right for many years, I'd guess."

He was steering Mulheisen out. Mulheisen stopped and asked, "Say, how much do I owe you?"

"Oh, forget it. I didn't do anything," Hundly said. He guided Mulheisen into the hall.

Mulheisen halted firmly. "What was that doctor's name?"

"Pruhoff? Carl. Two effs. Osteopath. That's the way of it, you know. One family insists on going to the osteopath, another won't see anybody but an M.D."

"No, the other one," Mulheisen said, not budging. "Down in Indiana. The one who called you?"

"Oh, heck, I'm darned if I could remember that. I only talked to him the once."

"Tell me, doctor, what did he say?" Mulheisen had a smile on his face but it wasn't his most pleasant smile and there was an edge to his voice.

Dr. Hundly looked a bit uncertain for a moment, then he said, "I do recall his name! I guess the memory's not so far gone as all that, even if I am seventy-five in April. Johnson. Dr. Johnson, from Indianapolis."

"Dr. Johnson," Mulheisen said with an expectant tone, the edge of his voice a little sharper.

"J. Johnson," Hundly said. "I'm not sure of the Christian name."

Mulheisen made a movement back toward the surgery, his hand on the doctor's arm now. "I'm sure you have a record of it," he said.

"James L.," Hundly said. "Ha, ha! Just popped into my head!"

"And what did he say?"

"Why, he told me he'd had a call from Luck. Constance had passed away in the night. Then he recounted a bit of the family medical history. It seems she had a congenital heart defect. Well, it wasn't the sort of thing one would notice in a simple examination. You'd need an EKG, at least. But he concurred that she also had hypertension. Migraines too."

Mulheisen relaxed. "Ah." He sighed. He shook his head again. "Well, you're sure I don't owe you anything?"

"Oh, don't push your luck," the doctor said. "I'll sock you the next time. But you watch those darn cigars. Mind, I'm not saying you have to cut them out entirely. But for your heart's sake, son, get it down to one or two. And don't give me that 'two or three' nonsense. We know better, don't we?"

Mulheisen strolled back to the motel, puffing on his cigar. He'd been unable to resist looking for the rather sizable butt he'd tossed aside. It was perfectly good, at least four inches of La Donna, lying in the grass. He'd trimmed it up and relit it.

Jimmy Marshall sighed when Mulheisen called again, but he said he'd check out this James L. Johnson in Indianapolis. Mulheisen hung up and thought about lunch, but mindful of the doctor's jab in his gut he settled for an apple. He ate it while he drove out toward Luck's. It was still a pleasant afternoon. He wished he'd thought to get a topographical survey map of the area. But he had a pretty good image in his mind of the Luck property from looking at the plat map in the county assessor's office.

Instead of turning into the lane that led to Luck's gate, he drove on down the county road. As he recollected, perhaps a mile or so beyond Luck's there was another house indicated on the plat map. But when he reached it he found it was a delapidated old farmhouse, clearly abandoned. Just beyond it, however, he saw a small boy pushing a four-wheeled ATV along the dirt road. Mulheisen pulled up behind him. The boy stopped and looked back at him.

"What's the trouble?" Mulheisen called. He got out of the car.

The kid was about twelve, a pugnacious lad in jeans and a hunting jacket. There was a rifle holster on the ATV. The kid was very open and fresh. "Ran out of gas! This dang thing, I filled 'er up yesterday!"

"I've got some gas," Mulheisen said. He opened his trunk and pulled out a five-gallon emergency can.

"Here, I can do it," the kid said. He quickly poured a gallon or so into his tank. "That'll get me home." And he yapped on about seeing a skunk and a badger. His dad and mom both worked, he said, and wouldn't be home for hours. His name was Travis. He lived about five miles down County Line Road. He had a couple of coon dogs, Tige and Mange. He and his dad went coon hunting all the time—there was a world of coons around. He was a better shot than his old man, even his grampa said so. That was a .22 in the holster, but he had a .300 Savage at home, his own. He was going bear hunting with his dad, up in the U.P., later this year, or in the spring. He was going out to Montana to hunt mulies with his grampa, who was probably the best hunter this country had ever seen. His grampa had promised him his old .303 in his will.

Mulheisen was certain that the boy had skipped school and had gone deer hunting, preseason. The kid was clearly relieved to realize that he'd be able to get home before his folks. The prospect of pushing the ATV all the way home must have been daunting, with the likelihood of discipline if he'd been caught. It could hardly have worked out better—a helpful stranger, time in hand. Mulheisen managed to break through the boy's chatter to ask if there was a road that went back into the bush other than through the Luck property.

"Hell, yes," Travis told him. "That house back there? That's the ol' Sigmiller place. They all died off, years ago. There ain't been nobody there for a coon's age. You go through the yard, there's a road winds back around the ol' barn that's all fallen in. It just goes on back there. Miles and miles. You used to could get all the way to the Manistee River on that road. But you don't want to try it in your car, mister. There's a couple trees down on it, plus some pretty deep mud holes. You need a Honda." He nodded proudly at his little red vehicle.

He was going on about it, describing it all in detail, the swamp, the pond, the jack pine flats, but Mulheisen reminded him that he ought to be getting home.

The kid was right. The car got no more than a quarter mile before Mulheisen realized that it wouldn't be wise to take it any farther. But this was close enough, he reckoned. He got out, stuffed a couple of apples in his coat pocket, along with the cell phone, and headed on down the road, enjoying the afternoon. Soon enough, he came to the pond that the boy had mentioned. If this was what he'd remembered from the plat map, Luck's house ought to be about a quarter mile to the west.

A nice, well-maintained fence was only a few yards into the woods from the road. Mulheisen was pretty sure that it marked the boundary of Luck's property, especially when he saw the NO TRES-PASSING! / PRIVATE PROPERTY! signs, metal ones hanging from the fence every twenty feet or so, or nailed to the posts. Luck had spent a small fortune on those signs if they were that numerous all the way around the perimeter.

He walked along the road a ways, looking into the woods beyond the fence. It was a mixed forest of poplars, white birch, with some slender ash and beeches, a few pines, and an occasional large tree, a cedar, a big old oak, or even a gnarled old apple tree. It was relatively sparse and open, almost parklike, with occasional deer trails and ancient logging trails that ran for a few hundred feet then disappeared in jumbled brush. The road seemed more convenient for walking, so Mulheisen didn't bother to attempt the fence.

There were small hills, boggy spots, probably old springs. Eventually, he came to a knoll from which he could see a little creek that ran along the edge of small hill. He wondered if this wasn't where the fabled silver martins were supposed to be hibernating.

He left the road and walked along the fence line a ways, inspecting it. He couldn't see any sign that it was electrified. It was barbed wire, four strands firmly and tautly strung to posts, about eight feet apart, with steel poles set in concrete at frequent intervals. A secure fence. But ultimately, of course, there was a spot where deer had evidently broken down the upper course. The wires sagged. Mulheisen pushed the wires down lower until he could awkwardly hop over. He caught the crotch of his pants and made a little tear, but he stumbled over and walked into the property, climbing up the hill. It was grassy and brambly, and fairly bare of sapling growth; he could see no sign of burrowing. Maybe this wasn't the martin hill.

There was another hill, perhaps thirty feet high, farther in. Mulheisen walked over that way. He didn't feel any need to climb up this one. It had a pretty good growth of trees on it, mostly young pines, obviously planted, looking more like Christmas trees than anything else, though grown too large for that purpose now, perhaps an old plantation allowed to grow up. He skirted the hill and came upon a road that was in more or less regular use. It wasn't graded or built up but a stable, broad road with a coarse reddish top dressing, obviously carted in. A considerable road for the middle of nowhere. He walked along it, wondering what he was doing.

And shortly he was asked just that. A man armed with a rifle stepped out from behind a tree and ordered him to halt. Mulheisen thought the rifle looked military. It had what appeared to be a banana clip.

"What are you doing here?" the man asked. He was young, about thirty, with a neatly trimmed beard. He wore a dark overall and a billed cap, lace-up boots with the trousers bloused. He carried the rifle at the ready, though not directly aimed at Mulheisen.

"I was just asking myself that," Mulheisen said. "Where am I?"

The man said, with obvious suspicion, "I guess you know that," he said.

"Actually, I don't. I'm lost," Mulheisen said. "I saw this road. It looks like it probably leads to civilization." He smiled, an ingratiating smile, he hoped.

"Where's your car?"

Mulheisen gestured back the way he'd come. "I kind of ran out of road. I was wondering if there was another road."

"The only road back that way is the old Sigmiller road," the man said.

"That's where I was. A kid told me it ran to the river."

The man frowned. Holding the rifle in one hand, with his hand on the trigger, he withdrew a cell phone from a pocket and keyed it. Into the phone, he said, "I've got an intruder. He looks like that guy from last night." Looking at Mulheisen, he said, "Are you Mulheisen?" Then into the phone he said, "It's him. All right. We'll wait. We're on the road."

Shortly, another man came jogging up. He was similarly dressed and armed. He was bearded too, and looked like he could be the first man's brother or cousin. He addressed the first man: "Whatcha got here, Darryl?"

"It's him, ain't it?" Darryl said.

"Sure as hell is," the newcomer said. "Christ! What a time for him to show up. We can't take him back to the house. You know what Hook said."

"Whatta we do?" Darryl said. Now he was aiming his rifle at Mulheisen.

"Get rid of him," the other said. "That's what Hook would say."

157

"His car's over on the Sigmiller road," Darryl said. "Plus, he says he talked to some kid, who told him he could get to the river that way."

"Who was the kid?"

Mulheisen had seen this kind of confused colloquy before, among young cops newly assigned to a beat. It was a reason that police forces generally assigned new men, cadets, to older and more seasoned officers. He sought to defuse the situation before it got too tangled.

"Hey, fellas, no need to get excited. I lost my way. If I'm trespassing, I'll just go back. I'll be out of your hair. Sorry to bother you."

"You had to of climbed the fence," the newcomer said. "There's 'no trespassing' signs all over the place. Who was the kid you talked to?"

"Just a kid," Mulheisen assured him. "I think he'd been plinking at squirrels. A teenager." For some reason he inflated Travis's age; he supposed in an attempt to obscure the kid's identity.

"Might of been one a them Goodriches," Darryl opined. "They're all dumber'n a post."

"Maybe," the other said, "but maybe it's bullshit, too. He's probably got a whole posse out there. We better call Hook."

"Oh, let's just run him off," Darryl said. "There ain't nobody out there. Hook'll be pissed. He'll lay it on us if anything goes haywire. You know he will, Earl."

Earl shook his head. "We gotta call him."

Darryl said, "Imp had this guy up to the house. He didn't say diddly about him. I reckon he's all right. Just lost, like he says."

"Yeah, that's right," Mulheisen said. "He was pouring the George Dickel like it was Coke. I was just going for a walk. I'm sure Imp won't care. I thought I'd go down to the river. But I see I'm bothering you fellas, so maybe I just better haul on out of here. I won't say anything to Imp." He started to back up.

"Hold it!" Earl snapped, raising his rifle. Mulheisen stopped. Earl said to Darryl then, "You called me on the emergency frequency. Hook might of heard it."

As if in support of this supposition, a black SUV, an older Jeep model, came flying up along the road and skidded to a halt. A slender man in a camo outfit hopped out. He was wearing a camo beret and had a sidearm in a holster on his belt. He was dark, with a thick, black mustache.

Darryl turned to him and said, "We found this guy wandering in the woods, captain. It's that guy Mulheisen, who visited the chief last night. He says he was just looking for the road to the river."

"Is that so?" Hook said. He strode forward and walked around Mulheisen, warily, inspecting him, hands on his hips. He unsnapped the flap of the holster and withdrew an automatic pistol.

Mulheisen turned to him. "Yeah, I thought maybe this was the road."

Hook ignored his comments. He asked the two others for more information and they told him what Mulheisen had said. Hook stood aside and said, "Search him."

Earl handed his rifle to Darryl and came forward. He patted Mulheisen down and took out of his pockets a wallet, the apples, and Mulheisen's cell phone, some keys, a plastic bag containing cigars, a box of wooden matches. He held them out to Hook.

Hook holstered his pistol. He waved aside the apples and the cell phone, but glanced at the package of cigars. He handed them back to Earl, then took the wallet and the keys, examining the driver's license and flipping through the other cards. Then he looked at Mulheisen thoughtfully, tapping the wallet against his thigh.

"You have come at an unfortunate moment, Mr. Mulheisen," he said. "Mr. Luck cannot see you."

Mulheisen detected a foreign accent, but the English was excellent. He thought the man could be Mediterranean, or Slavic, even Middle Eastern. He couldn't tell.

"Well, I wasn't looking for Luck," Mulheisen said. "But, as I told these fellas, I'm sorry if I trespassed. I'll just get out of your way."

"Alas, it is not so simple," Hook said. To the two men, he said, "This is the sort of thing I was warning you about. It would have been better, perhaps, if you had simply shot him. Now I must investigate. Let us go and see this car."

With Mulheisen leading the way they walked back through the woods. After they'd walked a ways, Hook asked where he had entered the property. Mulheisen didn't show him the actual place, just said he'd found a spot where the fence was partially broken down. He said he'd assumed it wasn't any big deal, he'd just stepped over hoping to find a better route down to the river. But as they walked on they didn't see any obvious place to enter, such as Mulheisen had described. Eventually, however, they did reach a point from where they could see Mulheisen's vehicle several yards beyond the fence, sitting on the old Sigmiller road near where a tree had fallen, blocking it.

"Keep him covered," Hook said. He stepped up on a strand of the wire, next to a post, then managed to vault over. He stumbled on the other side and fell. He jumped up quickly, brushing himself, evidently embarrassed to be seen in an awkward situation. But he said nothing. He strode off down to the car, still carrying the wallet and keys. He walked around it, found a key and opened the driver's door, peered inside. Then he opened the trunk. He found nothing of interest.

He walked back and climbed over the fence again, more carefully this time. He seemed perturbed. "Bring him," he said to the two men and started off.

"Hey, now, wait a minute," Mulheisen called after him. "This has gone too far. I told you I was sorry. I'm not going anywhere with you."

A rifle barrel prodded him in the back. Mulheisen lurched, but held his ground. He didn't turn to Darryl, or whoever it was, but addressed himself to Hook, who had stopped and was looking back at him. "What's your name?" he demanded.

Hook said, "You are a policeman. Why are you not armed?"

"I'm not a policeman," Mulheisen said. "I'm retired from the Detroit Police Department. I turned in my badge and gun months ago. Luck knows this. You'd better get hold of him."

"American policemen are always armed, even when off duty," Hook said, as if it were an irrefutable truth.

Mulheisen said, "You've got the phone, call Luck." He folded his arms and waited.

"No need to call," Hook said. He smiled. He had very nice white, even teeth. "I will take you to him."

"I don't think so," Mulheisen said. "You don't seem to be aware of the seriousness of your actions. If you force me to accompany you it could be construed as assault, or worse. It could even be considered kidnapping. Think what you're doing, man. This is not a serious incident . . . yet. But it could be the beginning of a day you'll regret. If I leave now, there's no harm done. But if you insist, we're venturing into very troubled waters."

Hook walked back to him and stood very close, looking him in the face. "I am serious. Are you? You have trespassed. I suggest we go to speak with the owner of this property. Do you refuse?"

Mulheisen considered. It was an equivocal situation thus far. He had hoped to head off any complications, but it didn't seem possible. He presumed that, if it came to a legal question, Hook would have the support of the two riflemen as witnesses. Almost any assertion he made would likely stand.

Hook saw the indecision. He set off again and Mulheisen, glancing back at the two men with rifles, followed.

When they reached the SUV, Hook ordered Earl to drive. He got in and turned the Jeep around. They put Mulheisen in the backseat, with Darryl. Before he got in, Hook handed him the packet of cigars, which he had retrieved from the front seat, where Earl had tossed them. Mulheisen thanked him.

Hook got in the front passenger seat and asked Earl, "What did you do with the apples?" Earl told him he'd tossed them. Hook turned to face Mulheisen and apologized. He made a gesture toward Earl with his head, as if to say, "You see what I have to deal with?"

The road circled back through the woods, up small hills and down. Within a few minutes they came in sight of Luck's house, but they pulled up behind the barn. Before they pulled in, however, Mulheisen caught a glimpse of three or four vehicles parked next to Luck's truck. Hook told Earl to get out and open the sliding doors of the barn. They waited without comment.

What was revealed was the usual drive-thru passage of an old barn, where a farmer might pull a wagonload of hay in through the front doors with his tractor for loading into the loft, and then pull out through the back. Now there was no hay in the loft. But the floor was still the old, worn wooden floor. The odor of hay lingered in the barn, along with the ancient odor of cows. Where there had been stalls, there was now new construction, a wooden wall with a metal door mounted in the plywood paneling. The front sliding doors were closed but for a narrow passage that afforded only a glimpse of the house across the yard.

Hook got out and opened the rear door for Mulheisen. "I'm sorry, but you'll have to wait here," he said, pointing at the metal door. "Mr. Luck has visitors. But he'll be with you shortly."

Mulheisen was skeptical, but what could he do? He waited while Hook unlocked the door with a key and opened it, then gestured for Mulheisen to enter. Hook stepped inside with him.

Here was, as Luck had promised the night before, a nicely fixed up little guest apartment. It was a room about fifteen feet by twelve, with a window at the end that looked out onto the pine woods a few feet distant. One couldn't see the house from this angle. And Mulheisen supposed that a guest, a genuine guest, wouldn't have paid much attention to the four stout metal bars affixed outside the window. A casual glance might have led one to believe that the bars merely prevented breakage by animals, such as cows or horses, wandering by. But to Mulheisen it was clear that they secured any exit from the room.

There was a maple frame bed with ample blankets and a white-cased pillow, all neatly made up. There were also an old wooden table, a cupboard, a counter in which were mounted a modern sink and faucet. There was a small white refrigerator. In one corner, partly shielded by a partition, was a toilet and, beyond that, a shower stall with a glass door.

Overhead was a light fixture with a frosted glass globe, another lamp stood on a table next to the bed, a little bookshelf with some paperbacks in it nearby. A couple of mission-style wooden chairs with fabric-covered cushions completed the furniture. It was rustic but as pleasant as could be.

"Make yourself at home," Hook said. "There is food and drink." He pointed to the refrigerator.

Mulheisen looked around briefly, then said, "I thought you said you were serious, Hook. You can't hold me here. Don't you understand?"

Hook shook his head. "Shall we stop fencing, Mr. Mulheisen? You have been caught spying. I don't fear to tell you that I had

instructed those men to shoot intruders. But . . ."—he shrugged—
"they are not disciplined enough yet to do this. I admit, this dis-
turbs me. When will they have the will, the discipline to act? I am
serious, I assure you. So is Mr. Luck. You have made for us a difficulty, a situation. We . . . *he* will have to decide. But he will come
to see you. It is up to him. I have returned to you your cigars and
matches. Please do not start a fire. That would be very bad. Old barns
are dry, they are . . ." he hesitated, searching for a word, then settled
on, ". . . flameable. I fear that we would not be able to escape you
. . . I am sorry, to extract you from the barn in time." He gestured
toward the cupboards. "There is coffee or tea, if you like. Also, this
place is very strong. And we will be outside. So, please, relax."

"Where's my wallet and keys?" Mulheisen asked. "This is
foolish. You're making a huge mistake."

"Ah, your property," Hook said. "I will fetch it."

Hook left. He didn't return.

It was getting dark outside, Mulheisen saw. He tried the door
handle, just for kicks. It was locked. It was a steel door in a steel
jamb, well mounted in the heavy wooden wall.

He got out a cigar but didn't light it yet. Just toyed with it
and looked around at his prison. The pictures on the wall were
mounted in old barn-wood frames, views of mountains and streams,
photographic reprints. He noticed that there was a coffee maker.
He looked in the refrigerator. As promised, there was at least a case
of Stroh's beer, packages of sandwich meat, a jar of Miracle Whip,
a package of cheese, a stick of butter. The bread was in the reefer
too. Perhaps, sturdy walls or not, they had a problem with mice. It
wasn't good bread, just some kind of white sliced loaf.

He saw there was a toaster on the counter. And in the cupboards were cups, saucers, a jar of nondairy creamer, another jar of
granulated sugar, and a couple of jars of cherry jam. This was cherry
country, he recalled. The jam appeared to be authentic, homemade

jam. Ah, well, he wasn't hungry right now. But he was glad to see a can of ground coffee and another tin of Twining's tea. Maybe later.

He sat on the bed. It was nice and firm. Double mattress. A luxurious cell. The books in the book case were mysteries: one of them by an author he liked, Michael Connelly. He was tempted to make a cup of tea and settle down to read. A guy could pass a pleasant night here, he thought, if he were truly a guest. He drank a glass of water. Good water. He lit the cigar.

Nobody came for a long time and he spent a couple of hours pondering the situation. Luck had made a big mistake. Mulheisen hadn't been idly complaining or blustering. It was a very serious thing to restrain a citizen by force of arms, then to lock him up. Of course, it was Mulheisen's blundering about that had precipitated the issue. But it was an incredibly drastic response to simple trespassing. Mulheisen reproached himself. What had he been thinking? Nothing, he had to admit, just poking around. But Luck, who obviously had something important going on, wouldn't believe that.

What the hell was Luck up to? Meeting terrorists? Something like that, he supposed. Someone Mulheisen couldn't be allowed to see, and who shouldn't be aware of him. Mulheisen considered that one reason he had leaped to that conclusion was the presence of this Hook. Who was he? An Arab? Mulheisen suspected as much, but he told himself that the evidence wasn't much. Just some foreigner, apparently, perhaps a Greek, even some fellow who had fallen in with Luck's patriot screed. Still . . .

More important, he thought, what could be the consequence of this stupid turn of events? Luck was in trouble. He'd have to do something about Mulheisen now, something drastic. Mulheisen didn't like the prospects. This wasn't something, he was sure, that could be legally excused. There wouldn't be any sheriff coming to arrest him for trespassing. Mulheisen had never, in his long police career, been in a jam like this.

The mind, he realized, resisted the obvious: these guys would have to dispose of him or face some serious consequences. And he felt helpless to do anything about it, to help them make a less than drastic decision. He'd tried, but Hook wasn't having it. Hook was the crux of the situation, he decided, a man out of his element, perhaps, who had overreacted.

Mulheisen was sure that Luck regarded him as an official, an officer of some kind of police or investigative function, despite his denials of the night before. There could be no other reason for him being here. Whatever he might have done earlier, before Hook's precipitate action, now Luck couldn't just turn him loose. He had to disappear.

He cautioned himself about sinking into desperate or depressed thinking. He had, many times, tossed a suspect into a cell to stew and fret, knowing that it would make the suspect that much easier to interrogate. The longer the wait, up to a point, the more he softened up, unless he was a hardened criminal. It was a reliable tactic. But he didn't think that was Luck's intention. Still, it didn't do to get too speculative. Something would have to happen, something that would provide him with more information. He'd have to wait for Luck. Everything would turn on how that little interview went.

He was thinking about this when Darryl brought him supper. A tray with a plate of excellent venison roast with gravy, mashed potatoes, even a bottle of wine. All Darryl said was, "Enjoy," and left. Mulheisen found that he was hungry. He ate. The bread was home-baked. Very tasty, as were the green beans with carrots. The wine was Luck's favorite, an Oregon pinot noir.

Mulheisen wondered, What kind of man serves the doomed prisoner a meal like this? Presumably, Luck wasn't planning anything immediately, else why bother with the meal? But who knew? Maybe the guy was just a nut.

Mulheisen had one last cigar. He decided to save it, for no good reason. He lay back on the bed and considered the notion of a fire, as mentioned by Hook. It might be a plan, after all. It would precipitate confusion. Anything might happen then, including escape. He eyed the ceiling. It had been paneled. That would keep the dust from the loft trickling down, but, more important, it would be extremely hard to get through. He noticed, now, that there were fire alarms installed, though no sprinklers. He sighed. Without warning, he dozed off.

10

Dog Watch

Mulheisen awoke to darkness. Someone had turned out the lights in the room while he slept. Only the diffused glow from the yard lights illuminated the room through the window. He felt groggy, at first, but his head quickly cleared. Had he been drugged? He couldn't remember falling asleep. A mild sedative might have been added to the meal. But something had roused him.

He had no idea what time it was. He had no watch, of course, and there was no clock in the room. He'd heard some kind of sound. There! He heard it again. A very slight sound. Scratching or gnawing. A mouse? He listened intently, not moving, his breath held.

Again. Scratching. From the ceiling, of all places. He stared upward, still lying on his back as he had fallen asleep. There it was again, over by the light fixture in the ceiling. Something was up there. He wondered if someone could be up there, spying on him. But that didn't make sense. If his jailers wanted to look at him, all they had to do was open the door or look in from the window.

No, it was the ceiling, all right. He stared. Then he heard a different sound, a faint, sustained creaking noise, of something in the ceiling being pried . . . like a nail. He watched and listened with great interest as this ceiling activity went on, so quietly that it was difficult to believe he was actually hearing it. Was he just imagining some miraculous rescue attempt? It was absurd. Yet from time to time the sound was just loud enough that he could be sure it was, in fact, some kind of concerted effort up there. For what purpose was another question.

This whole effort must have taken twenty minutes, but at last it stopped. Then, to his surprise, he saw the glass light fixture move, first to one side, slightly, then to the other. Suddenly, it slipped free of its metal retaining ring and he sat upright reflexively, stretching out his hands to prevent the thing from falling to the floor and noisily breaking. But it didn't fall. A hand was sticking through the ceiling, holding on to it with just fingertips.

Whoever was holding the light fixture had heard his movement. The hand did not move. Then a narrow beam of light shone down. It moved about the room, briefly, then fell on his face. It held there, for a moment, then switched off.

Then a voice called softly, so softly that he thought it must be his imagination: "Mul?"

Mulheisen couldn't imagine who that might be. The last friendly face he'd seen had been the kid's, Travis's. For a foolish second he thought it was him. Ridiculous!

He cleared his throat and said, softly, in reply, "Yeah?"

"Take the glass."

Mulheisen got to his feet on the bed and reached up. He took the glass from the hand and set it on the bed. The arm withdrew. There was just a dark hole in the ceiling. The person up there must have methodically disassembled the apparatus from above and removed most of it through the access—the junction box, the bulb, the wires. A portion of a face appeared, a pale blur.

"You all right?" the voice inquired.

"Uh, yeah," Mulheisen replied. He felt ridiculous, talking to this hole in the ceiling. "Who are you?"

"Be right with you," the voice said softly. The pale blur vanished.

Mulheisen continued to look up for a moment, then quietly got down from the bed. He stood and looked around foolishly. Now what? He could hear faint sounds of movement, then nothing. After about a minute there was a sound of a key at the door and it quietly opened.

In the dim available light from the passageway there stood Joe Service. He carried a rifle in his hand, which he leaned against the wall. The last time Mulheisen had seen Service he had been in a hospital bed in Denver, in a semicoma, draped with tubes and bandages. He recognized him immediately.

"Here, give me a hand," Service said, opening the door wider and beckoning Mulheisen toward the open bay of the drive-thru. Mulheisen stepped after him. Service hoisted a slumped guard to his feet with some difficulty. Mulheisen took an arm of the unconscious man. They dragged him into the room and flopped him on the bed. Mulheisen managed to brush the light fixture out of the way to accommodate the man. Service lifted the man's booted feet and swung them onto the bed.

"I don't suppose they left you any rope?" Service asked. "Wait here." He darted out and a moment later returned with a fistful of slender but tough-looking strands of orange plastic baling twine. He rolled the unconscious guard onto his face and swiftly bound his hands together behind his back, then did the same with his ankles. Then he rolled the man back faceup.

"A gag would be good," he said thoughtfully, looking down at his handiwork. "Well, what the hell." He yanked the man's shirt tails out of his belt and ripped his shirt up the front. With a length of this he made a dandy gag, which he bound around the man's mouth and tied behind his head. "Hope he gags," he said.

When all this was accomplished he stood up and looked at Mulheisen with a self-satisfied grin. "All right," he said. "So they caught you."

Mulheisen stared at him, marveling. "What the hell—" he started to say.

Service interrupted. "No time, Mul. This guy will be missed before too long. He won't be hollering for help, but they'll find him. Where's your car? I didn't see it in the yard. It's a Checker, right?"

"I left it back in the woods," Mulheisen said.

"How far? Well, tell me while we walk." Service snatched the guard's pistol, a Llama 9mm, out of the holster on the man's hip and took a couple of loaded clips out of a pouch on the gunbelt. "Man, these guys are ready for action," he said, approvingly. "Okay, let's roll."

Mulheisen went to the closet and removed his coat, pulling it on. Joe stood by the open door. "C'mon," he urged.

Mulheisen followed as Service flitted across to the open back door of the barn and into the darkness. When Mulheisen caught up to him they were well into the woods. It was remarkable how good it felt to be free, out in the woods. The night was cool, even chilly, and it seemed to be overcast, extremely dark. They walked rapidly, hardly a quiet progress. Sticks snapped, leaves rustled. Service was obviously not concerned. He kept moving.

"It's way the hell over there," Mulheisen pointed ahead. "Probably a quarter mile. Where's your car?"

"Clear out on the county road," Joe said. "Too far. We'd better get to your car first."

"If they haven't moved it," Mulheisen said.

Joe said, "I didn't see any sign of it Maybe they didn't get around to it yet." He set off again, then beckoned for Mulheisen to lead the way.

Mulheisen found the road. That seemed the best way to proceed. At least, in this near pitch-darkness, they were conscious of it underfoot and it was relatively smooth and much quieter. They walked quickly. Within ten minutes they reached the hill where Mulheisen had been apprehended. The road, from this approach, branched, which Mulheisen hadn't noticed when he'd been driven away earlier. One lane went to the right, around the hill, the other was the lane on which he'd been, he was sure. He stopped.

"Someone out there," he whispered.

"A guard," Joe said. They drew back. It was obvious that they couldn't slip by the guard and stay on the road, while if they tried to walk around through the woods they'd make too much noise.

"We either take him," Joe said, "or we go back a good ways."

Mulheisen turned back, Joe following. When they had gone a hundred yards, Joe cut off through the woods and Mulheisen trailed after. It took another ten minutes of careful walking before they felt that they had successfully skirted the hill. Now Mulheisen took over again and led Joe to the fence. They found the spot where the deer had gotten over, but when they arrived at the Sigmiller road there was no sign of the car.

"Uh-oh," Mulheisen said. "They've taken it. They must have a place to stash it. Well, that leaves your vehicle. We can get out to the county road along this old road."

They set off again, still not taking the time to discuss the situation. There didn't seem time for it, despite the questions bubbling in each man's mind. It was a good twenty-minute hike to the county road. By now they both felt, without discussing it, the guard was likely to have been found.

Once they reached the county road Joe set off at a jog, headed back in the direction of Luck's drive. They had not gone far, however, before Joe stopped.

"Somewhere around here," he said, not very confidently. They paced on. Shortly, he turned off the road, bounding through the shallow ditch and ducking through some brush. His Toyota pickup was sitting there, not twenty feet from the road, but invisible from it.

The little truck nimbly made it through the brush and the ditch. Within a minute or two they were passing the entry to Luck's drive, a critical point. There was no sign of activity and a short distance beyond they turned onto the paved road that led back toward Queensleap. At last, bowling along at a brisk pace, the car heater going, the two men could converse.

"What's your involvement in all this?" Mulheisen wanted to know.

"I was in the area," Service said. "I heard you were out of the cop business, so thought I'd look you up. Maybe we could have a little heart-to-heart."

"That was friendly," Mulheisen said. "But what brought you to this neck of the woods?"

"Lot of odd things going on lately," Service said. "Like rumors that I was involved in a bombing in Detroit."

"Rumors, eh? No truth to them, I suppose?"

"I haven't been near Detroit in months," Service said. "I certainly had nothing to do with any bombing. It's some kind of setup. That's what it feels like, anyway. I also stumbled on some mention of this guy Luck. He seemed to be one source of these rumors. So I had to check it out. I thought I'd come out to Detroit and talk to you, only you aren't home. When I talk to your mother, she says you're up in Queensleap, visiting the very guy who's been spreading weird rumors about me. So I drove up here."

"My mother!"

"Relax," Joe said, "it wasn't as if we went out on a date. I just bumped into her on her daily walk and chatted her up. She told me all about a hawk we saw. And a few things about her absent son. Very nice lady, but a little out of my class. I didn't even ask if I could walk her home. Anyway, I zipped up here, checked around town, and didn't see any sign of you. It's not a big place, you know. So I found out where Luck lived, went out there, and being a cautious guy I didn't feel like just walking up and knocking on the door. Besides, it's kind of late.

"But when I got within eyeball range, I saw something was going on. Cars in the yard, a couple of guys standing around, armed . . . you could almost swear they were sentries. Another guy comes out from the barn, changes with one of the yard bulls, who goes back to the barn. Something to be guarded in a barn? It looks a little weird, you know? I mean, it's two in the A.M., a little late for a quilting bee.

"So I take a little sniff around the premises. Pretty long-winded jaw jam, it looks like, some kind of camo Kiwanis meeting, guys coming out to get fresh air, discreetly discharge some methane."

"Camo? A militia meeting? How many were there?"

"Oh, I exaggerate. Probably no more than six or eight guys, the principals. With some auxiliaries, the ones packing the iron. Maybe it was more like a focus meeting, or whatever they call these things. They didn't exactly sit around beating drums and chanting, and only a few were actually in paramilitary drag, but you must have caught some of the to-do."

"I was sleeping," Mulheisen said.

"Sleeping! Whoa! That's coolness."

Mulheisen tried to explain that it wasn't like that. "My woodcraft isn't up to yours," he said. He told about being scooped up, the fact that he'd evidently been given some kind of sedative in his meal.

"Popped you in the pantry, eh? With a nice bowl of warm porridge." Joe tried to soften his amusement. "They slipped you a mickey. Crashing Luck's party had to be a jolt for him. He had some interesting visitors. I'm surprised he didn't call it off. I wonder if any of them knew you were out in the shed."

"The only guys I saw were Luck's pals," Mulheisen said. "One of them was kind of interesting, though. They called him Hook."

"Hook? What'd he look like?"

Mulheisen described him.

"Al-Huq!" Joe said. "Maybe."

"Who's he?"

"I'm not sure. Maybe it wasn't him. I'll have to look into it. But the guys at the party were interesting. Looked mostly like local clowns, businessmen dressing up to play soldier. What was interesting, though, was the guest of honor. The name Tucker mean anything to you?"

"Colonel Tucker!" Mulheisen whistled. "How did you know him?"

"An old friend," Joe said.

Mulheisen was stunned. "What is Tucker doing here? Talking to Luck?"

"Got me," Joe said, "but it doesn't look good. I don't suppose you're aware, but I'm supposed to be working for Tucker."

Mulheisen couldn't take this in. Service said he'd explain later. The point he wanted to make, he said, was that for various reasons he'd more or less decided that he wasn't working for Tucker anymore.

Mulheisen was dazed. "What time is it?"

Service said it was pushing four A.M.

Mulheisen felt alert and rested. If he'd been drugged, it had worn off, but this confusing information made his mind whirl.

"Let's go by the motel," he suggested. "I've got some gear there. It's possible they aren't aware I was staying there."

When they got to the motel, they noticed two prominent vehicles—a sheriff's car and Mulheisen's Checker. The sheriff's car was sitting off to one side; it could be perceived as being parked at the adjacent Queen's Table restaurant, which had already opened to serve the locals, farmers and hunters, presumably.

The sheriff's vehicle was occupied, probably by Corporal Dean, the deputy who had stopped Mulheisen the night before. He advised Joe to simply cruise on, as if they were just another vehicle passing through town. Dean, or whoever it was, was not facing the highway. At any rate, the windows of the Toyota were tinted and he'd have been unlikely to make Mulheisen.

A block farther on, they pulled over to discuss their next move. Luck's decision that the safest place for Mulheisen's vehicle was at the motel was a clever move. Once it was determined that Mulheisen had gone missing, the vehicle at the motel would at least suggest to any outside investigator that he'd returned from his drive the previous afternoon, wherever that might be thought to have taken him. The deputy was doubtless there to see who, if anyone, might come looking for Mulheisen. Luck would not be sure, at this point, that Mulheisen had been investigating on his own. As it had happened, an unlooked-for ally had materialized.

"By now," Service said, "Luck probably knows you've bolted. Maybe that's why the deputy is there, but I'd say it was pretty fast work if it's so. The car was probably returned hours ago and this guy has been there ever since. But what's he going to do if you just show up and go in the room? What do you need there, anyway?"

"Clothes, cigars, Dopp kit," Mulheisen said.

"You can get that stuff anywhere," Service said. "If this Luck has got the sheriff in his pocket, maybe you don't want to be apprehended."

Mulheisen didn't think that was quite the case somehow. "They might have recruited this deputy, but it's another thing to have a whole county sheriff's department in your pocket, Joe. I don't think they want me found. They screwed up snatching me. It wasn't a situation entirely of their making, but once it was done they would have had to follow through. It'll bring heat, though. Luck obviously had his hands full with his visitors. I don't have any idea what the situation is, but I'm sure I'd be better off on the loose. If this guy busts me, I don't think he's running me in. He'll be carting me back to Luck."

"They should have just dropped you on the spot," Service said.

"Yeah, well, that's what I figured was the imminent prospect," Mulheisen said, "but I'm sure Luck wanted to question me, see if he couldn't find out what I was up to, what I knew."

"I could distract the deputy," Service said, "draw him away. Hey, officer, my grammaw's on fire! Help!" He seemed keen on this kind of action. "You go in, get your stuff. You'd have your car. I could meet you somewhere else later. I'm sure I could pull it off."

Mulheisen stared at him, incredulously. "Your 'grammaw'?" He shook his head. "Anyway, I don't have my keys. They took them, and my wallet. I'm not adept at hot-wiring a car. Nah. It's probably better to just leave it."

"Hey, how about this? We snatch the deputy! We could give him what they had in mind for you. He probably has some useful info. Plus we'd have the use of his car, the radio . . ."

Mulheisen just looked straight ahead.

"All right," Service said. "I'm pretty good at getting into places. It shouldn't be too difficult to get in the back way, through the bathroom window. Off the record, I have some experience at this. If nothing else, you'll have some cigars to smoke."

Mulheisen could see he was eager. He suddenly felt weary. "Well, if you think it could be done," he said.

They doubled back on side streets and stopped some ways from the rear of the motel.

"This is a first," Service said. "I'm burglarizing a motel to get a cop some cigars!" He laughed. "All right, Dutch. Wait here. If I'm not back in—"

"Dutch?" Mulheisen had to laugh.

Five minutes later Service was back, with the cigars and the Dopp kit, with Mulheisen's draped clothes over his arm. "The suitcase wouldn't fit through the window," Joe explained. "Oh, and I thought you'd like these." He tossed Mulheisen his wallet and car keys. "They must have figured it would make the mystery of your vanishing act even more mysterious."

Mulheisen looked through the wallet. Everything was there, even the money. "It's a mystery, all right," he said. "Glad to see the cigars. Hope you don't mind?" He gestured with a cigar.

"Just keep the window cracked." Joe started the engine. "Where to, Dutch?"

"Let's find a motel, or a hotel. Traverse City is a big enough town."

"Traverse City it is," Joe said. And a few minutes later, driving out of town, he spoke into the silence, "Thank you, Joe."

"Joe," Mulheisen said, "I always knew you were a remarkable fellow. In my estimation you're the finest burglar I've ever encountered. Plus, you do a great take on the U.S. cavalry. I never knew how thrilled I'd be to see you again."

"That sufficeth," Joe said cheerfully. "I'm relieved myself."

"How's that?"

"I was afraid, back there, that you might have some cop plan," Joe said. "Call in the SWAT team, stage a big raid on Chez Luck, and sweep up the whole mob."

"We're into extra innings here," Mulheisen said. "You don't want to make them longer."

"Yeah," Service said. "These night games are exhausting. Too many wheels within wheels."

"Exactly. I've got to think this out."

"We've got to think it out," Joe amended.

As it worked out, they settled on a hotel. A huge hotel north of the city, towering over a fancy golf course. Very luxurious. They checked into a couple of rooms on the eighth floor.

11

Hark, Hark, the Dogs Do Bark

Straight talk is still just talk," Tucker said.

The men seated around the big dinner table set up in Luck's back room listened politely. They'd just had an excellent meal, cooked by Luck himself, with some help from his assistants. There were no women present. The men were drinking beer now, comfortable and seemingly willing to hear out this man who had blithely informed them that he was a federal agent. They were ordinary-looking men, some of them apparently farmers, others small businessmen or skilled workers. They were between the ages of twenty-five and fifty-five, it appeared. There were ten of them, dressed casually, in a country way, for the most part—jeans and flannel shirts. They were all avid members of Luck's informal group.

"It's actions that count," Tucker said. "But even there, actions can be ambiguous. It turns out that the actions have to be viewed in the context of what is avowed. And even then, one man's freedom fighter is another man's terrorist." He paused to let that sink in, glancing around the table for a reaction. There was none. The men seemed interested, but not stirred in any sense. They sipped their beer, puffed on their cigarettes or cigars, and looked up at him expectantly.

Tucker went on: "For instance, we have this bombing in Detroit a few months back. Different groups claimed responsibility, ranging from fundamentalist Muslim groups to a couple of so-called militia groups."

Tucker's eyes flickered across these generally benign-looking faces. Nobody reacted. He'd have thought the mention of militia groups would raise the temperature a bit, but they were as cool as their beers.

"Well, why do people do that?" he asked. "Take credit for an action that killed one innocent man, another who was a felon being arraigned, and injured dozens of others? This didn't used to happen. These kinds of actions were considered heinous. What kind of fool—or monster—takes *credit* for doing what is clearly evil? Once upon a time, different groups might be accused, but they'd protest, 'No! It wasn't us!' Even when everybody knew it was, say, the IRA, or some radical revolutionary group. There was a kind of public wink.

"Then, somewhere back in the sixties, I believe it was, groups began to claim *credit!* They wanted people to know that they were serious, that they meant business, even if they hadn't, in fact, been responsible. Maybe that's progress. I don't know. It hasn't helped us in trying to find out 'whodunit.' It's like those headline murders: the police are resigned to the fact that once a couple of murders are deemed sensational enough to make the evening news, and especially if the media can come up with a nickname for the latest celebrity killer, all kinds of wackos will show up at the precinct declaring, 'I'm the Triple-X slayer, arrest me!'"

Tucker paused to get a good look at these stolid men. None of them even blinked, not even when he had labeled some actions as evil. But, finally, he got a couple of laughs when he cracked, "I'm glad to see that the Holy American Flag and Farm, Fishing and Hunting Society has not aspired to the status of celebrity terrorists." He laughed with them at that play on their name. At least he'd gotten some response.

"Okay, I know it's just 'American Flag and Farm,'" he said. "But I am glad you aren't claiming to be terrorists. I doubt I'd be here if you were. Imp Luck was kind enough to let me come here and speak my piece," he went on. "Imp and I go back a long way, to a war that a lot of decent Americans bitterly opposed. I don't know if he has told you, but this man saved my butt." He pointed to Luck, who shrugged diffidently at his place at the end of the table.

"I was standing on a hilltop in Vietnam and about a thousand militia and VC troops were beating the bushes, carrying torches and flashlights, looking for me after my F-105 augered in. I figured I was about done for, headed for the Hanoi Hilton, when Imp Luck showed up with his chopper and yanked me out of there."

The men, Tucker was pleased to see, ate this up. They turned to stare with genuine regard at the man whom, perhaps, they had heretofore regarded as a thinker, a kind of professor, old and wise but not a man of heroic proportions. They were clearly thrilled.

"I know Imp's a little embarrassed," Tucker said, "but it's true. The thing is, to a lot of good, reasonable folks back home the U.S. looked like it was being a bully over there, in that distant, strange, and tiny country. But Imp and I know that one of the things we were doing was protecting and defending a whole slew of folks who were being overrun by a vast and well-supplied army of radical leftists, communists, who were hell-bent on imposing their vision of society on a bunch of peaceful farmers and peasants in South Vietnam and in the neighboring countries of Laos and Cambodia. These folks didn't want a totalitarian socialist state imposed on them. They were happy to be out from under the thumb of a colonial power, the French, but they sure as hell didn't want the French replaced with Mao and Ho Chi Minh's Red Army. But I guess it didn't look that way to the folks back home in the U.S."

Tucker was gratified to see the men nodding now. "A lot of people feel that we lost that war, and it's true that we didn't exactly win anything. We didn't defeat Ho, but I think we did make Mao think twice about moving in. But that was yesterday's war. A lot of time has passed and I'm not going to fight that one again. I'm not in uniform, but I still represent the federal government."

"Who elected you?" one man broke in. He was about thirty, an open-faced fellow in a jeans jacket, who looked like he could be a high school basketball coach. His tone wasn't exactly unfriendly, but challenging.

"I'm not an elected official," Tucker said agreeably. "Nowadays, I'm just one of those damn bureaucrats. But I take my responsibilities to the American people seriously. As a federal officer, I've taken an oath to uphold the laws of this country. I have been delegated to my task by people who are themselves directly responsible to elected officials." He looked around. No one offered any comment.

"Here's what I'm authorized to say. We understand that you folks are concerned Americans, patriots."

"You got that right," said another man. He glanced around, acknowledging the nods of his friends.

"I want you to know that your government accepts that, as long as you don't break the law of the land." Tucker held up a hand to forestall what appeared to be some comments. "I'm not going to debate the law with you. I just want to say that this administration is prepared to hear your arguments. Not me, personally, but others who are qualified to hear them. This is not the usual kind of administration, as I'm sure you're aware. This is a patriotic administration. It's an idealistic administration, and it means to change what the government has become. It welcomes patriotic organizations. We need your help. There will be no more Ruby Ridges or Wacos."

That got a pretty good response, not applause but a notice-able smoothing of brows. Tucker thought he could leave it at that. Better get back to the straight talk.

"Frankly, I have the feeling that if this administration had been in power when I was in uniform, we wouldn't have left Viet-nam without winning. But"—he held up his hands to forestall com-ment, which, after all, wasn't coming— "I said I wouldn't try to refight that war and I won't. The problem now is, before we can reshape this government, we have to deal with a new and powerful enemy—foreign terrorism. In case you hadn't noticed, there are people out there who don't like America." That usually got a chuckle, but these men were silent. Tucker wasn't sure what that meant. He had to soldier on.

"We need your cooperation, your help. Specifically, if any-one has any information about who was behind the bombing in Detroit, I'd love to hear it. Not right now, but I'll be around for a while and I'll be in touch with Imp, so you can pass it on to him. We'd appreciate it. What I'd hate to see is for the press to keep pushing some of the rumors we've heard that it was some home-grown patriot organization like this one that was behind it. I don't buy that. I have my own ideas on who was responsible, but I won't dwell on them here. Let me assure you that when I ask if anyone has information, it in no way implies that we think any of you might be associated with those who would do something like that. But others might think that, because they assume that anyone who calls himself a patriot is likely to be a man who is in favor of blowing up government installations, or even worse things. We don't think that. We think patriots are what most Americans are, naturally and in-nocently. But there are those who wrap themselves in the flag in order to attack that flag. I'm sure you understand that."

He went on in this vein for somewhat longer, carefully tread-ing a line that suggested he approved of them, but not some other, perhaps similar groups. It was at once ingratiating and warning. When it looked like they'd had enough, he finished with, "Anyway, thanks for coming and thanks for letting me speak to you. Enjoy the evening."

The applause was light and soon ended. They adjourned to the living room, where there was a fire in the hearth, plenty more beer, and, of course, Luck's ample supply of George Dickel. Tucker talked to each of the men, spreading himself around the room, being amiable and, while not offering contrary views, staying firm and noncommittal. By and large, they did not converse about the bombing but about hunting and fishing, plus some issues of interest to them like taxes, government interference, or obnoxious programs like the Endangered Species Act—familiar topics in almost any social gathering. Occasionally, one would get onto Oklahoma City, or Ruby Ridge, or the FBI attack on the Branch Davidians at Waco. Arguments were presented and listened to sympathetically. A few made some approving remarks about his and Luck's heroism in Vietnam. Tucker was happy to see that these men were taking his "patriotic" pitch seriously. They seemed encouraged by the tone of the present administration.

"Well, that was pretty tame," Luck said, much later, when they were alone. "Although, you could have left out some of that Vietnam stuff."

Tucker shrugged. "Speech making is not my forte," he said. "But what the hell . . . maybe somebody knows something. It doesn't hurt."

"They don't know anything," Luck said.

"How do you know, Imp?"

"I know these guys," Luck said. "They're guys with a conservative bent, happy to horse around in a tame militant way, flirting with an authoritarian style. They think they're Minutemen or something. They don't quite go for that skinhead shtick, because it looks trashy. They drive American-made pickup trucks and think it's making a statement, for crissake."

Tucker laughed. "You're kidding."

"I'm not kidding. You know what I think is the primary motivating factor in them joining this outfit? I mean, besides getting them out for an evening where they can drink beer and have a good feed and hang out with the guys?"

Tucker smiled. "Don't be so loud, some of your guards might hear."

"The guards? Well, they're the genuine ones. They don't have much respect for the guys you were talking to. They're true believers. But they're a little loony and they get paid. They can't find work. They're not too sharp. No, these other guys, the members, what it is . . . they look back on the three years or so that they spent in the army, or the navy, and they realize that was about the best time they had in their lives. That was before they got plugged into making a living, raising a family, paying a mortgage, or trying to keep a business or a farm going."

"That's it?" Tucker was surprised. "I thought they were more . . . I don't know . . . ideological."

"They wouldn't know ideological from idiotical," Luck said.

"Well, hell, Imp. I thought you were going to be the magnet for all the wacko right-wing nuts in this part of the country. Now you tell me all you've got are Republicans."

"It's always gonna be that way, Vern. You know that. They're mostly gonna be wannabes. I mean, aside from these semiliterate, semicriminal scumbags who I've put into uniform and made into guards. But it's early days. You should see the hate stuff I get from the Web site. There are some wackos out there, but they haven't shown up yet, not here. There's a guy in the U.P., a guy in Wisconsin, before you know it we'll have a couple sniffing around. They'll see the layout and they'll buy into it. But so far all I've got is these Kiwanians."

Tucker shook his head. "Maybe it's a waste of time. Still, you never know. There might be a sleeper among them."

"I don't think so," Luck said. "I'm positive there isn't a guy in that crew who even knows anyone who would dream of tossing a cherry bomb into a Parks and Recreation outhouse. Besides, we know who did the bombing, and it wasn't any Arabs or militia groups, and it damn sure wasn't some pissant Flag and Farm outfit. I liked that gag about the Holy American Flag, though."

"Who do you think did it?" Tucker asked.

"Echeverria."

Tucker smiled. "Could be."

Luck frowned. "Why, you all but told me so yourself."

"That's what I thought yesterday," Tucker said. "Maybe I still do, but I'm not positive. I'm keeping an open mind."

"All right, then," Luck said, "who the hell else is there?"

"I haven't eliminated anybody," Tucker said. "But there's also the Mafia. And there are other, rival drug organizations, such as the one we almost got in Kosovo—Zivkovic's group. They're capable of it. They'd stick it on anyone. They seem to be interested in pushing aside Echeverria. You notice they don't claim credit, by the way."

He mentioned some other possibilities, even suggesting some left-wing groups, some neocommunists. He thought that would get a laugh from Luck, but he realized now that the man was a little preoccupied. He had noticed it earlier, in fact, but he'd attributed it to the stress of getting this whole meeting up, cooking, acting the host.

"So what's bothering you?" he asked finally.

Luck grimaced. "I've been wondering whether to tell you," he said. "I've got some trouble."

"Uh-oh. One of your 'patriots' got a little too exuberant? He did throw a cherry bomb into a park toilet. Or . . . don't say it: one of them *was* involved in the bombing!"

Luck shook his head gloomily. "I wish it were that simple. I'd shoot the idiot myself. No, the trouble is, your little project has gone awry. I've got Mulheisen locked up in the barn."

"Mulheisen!" Tucker sat up. "Tell me all about it."

Luck explained what had happened. "But now what do we do?"

Tucker thought for a minute. He didn't seem all that concerned, oddly enough. But at last he said, "You'll have to figure out some way for him to escape."

It was Luck's turn to be shocked. "We can't do that! He'll blow the whistle! We'll be crawling with cops. This whole plan, this whole setup that we've worked at so hard, it'll be blown. And we could end up in prison!"

"Don't panic," Tucker said. "I think I can handle it. He'll have to come to me. He won't go running to the cops. Besides, I am the cops. No, he'll come to me. But, man, that was a close thing. What if he'd seen me!"

It took more discussion, of course, but soon enough Tucker was able to calm Luck down. It could be worked out. In fact, Tucker thought it might make his work easier, that it would be a piece of cake now to recruit Mulheisen.

Luck wasn't so sure. He had a feeling, he said, that

Mulheisen wasn't the kind of guy who would ever buy into the Lucani.

"Oh, not the Lucani," Tucker said, "but into my new and top-secret 'research group.'"

"You mean the Homeland Security thing," Luck said.

"Well, that, of course. But you see, Imp, the Lucani are not the only group of its type that I envision."

Luck was interested. Tucker explained that while he'd had some success with the Lucani, the concept needed to be expanded, he felt. There could be several such groups, with different constituencies. The Lucani had been started by disaffected agents, upset with the way the government had often thwarted their investigations for political and bureaucratic reasons. Tucker had gotten interested in the concept, generally. Why shouldn't there be a whole range of such organizations, loose affiliations of like-minded people, designed to further the cause of justice and even, yes, patriotism? He wasn't thinking of radical groups like Luck's, he said.

"Remember," he said, "I was the one who got you going on this. I thought, why shouldn't *we* have our own patriot group? We could channel some of that anger and vitality and also get some of these guys under observation and control. It's a good plan. But I'm thinking there could be more such groups, with a broad variety of interests and functions. Homeland Security is the government. It's political. I don't think it's going anywhere. I could be wrong, but I don't have much confidence in it. What I was thinking was a quiet, shadow Homeland Security."

Luck was not sure he saw how that would work, especially with a man like Mulheisen.

"A guy like Mulheisen," Tucker said. "I don't know . . . he doesn't seem very enthusiastic about working for the feds. Maybe he's skeptical, like me. He might be interested in a more secret organization, a small, elite group. He doesn't have to know that it doesn't have official status, or even recognition. I'll call it a task force. It's so secret the government can't even acknowledge it. He won't be paid through regular channels, won't have to be vetted, won't have to even talk to federal authorities. That might appeal to him. I'll see."

"But, in fact, the feds won't know anything about it," Luck said. He smiled and nodded. "It'll be interesting to see if he goes for it."

"But first," Tucker said, "we've got to 'escape' him. So let's put our heads together, Imp, and figure it out. What have you done so far?"

Luck explained about moving Mulheisen's vehicle back to the motel.

"What were you thinking?" Tucker said, shaking his head. "Don't tell me. You were thinking you might have to 'disappear' him. No, no, Imp. You've got to put those kind of ideas out of your mind. You're dealing with Mulheisen. This guy is some kind of legend, you know. You can't imagine how they talk about him in the department, in Detroit. They'd never stop looking for him. No, we'll have to get that car back from the motel. Leave it where it was."

They were working on that and their subsequent plan when the news was brought to them by Earl that Mulheisen had, in fact, already escaped.

"Oh, hell," Tucker said. "All right. Everybody calm down. Let's not get people overreacting. Have you got radio contact with all your men? Good. Keep them hunting for now, but alert them not to do anything stupid if they find him. No shooting, no rough stuff. In a way, this doesn't change anything. We were going to spring him anyway."

Luck immediately dispatched one of the two men who had brought the news. "Get on it, Earl. Make sure these guys don't get trigger happy."

Tucker turned to the remaining man, Darryl. "How long has he been gone? Not more than a half hour? Okay, it may still be all right." He turned to Luck. "Is there any reason to believe that he's aware that I'm here? No? Good. It's important that he doesn't know I'm here. That will blow everything. The second thing, we've got to make contact with him before he calls in the authorities. As for the car, well, at least it'll take him some time to get to town. Find out if he's been there. Most of all, find out where he is. How can I get out of here without him seeing me?"

Luck explained about the deputy at the motel.

Jon A. Jackson

"Pull him out of there, right away," Tucker said. He got up and started to pace, then realized that the windows were unguarded. "Don't you have curtains?" he snapped. "Let me think. How can I get out of here? Man, this is a mess."

Within a few moments, he said, "All right. I *am* here. That's the point. And the reason I'm here is . . . I heard you had picked Mulheisen up. I'm here to get him out and explain the situation. So we need to find him so I can explain. If he has already called somebody, that's too bad, but it can be worked out. I hope. But it'll be a lot simpler if I can find him and talk to him. It's kind of pushing things, but that's the way of it."

Luck said he'd go talk to the men to make sure they understood what had to be done.

"Good," Tucker said. "I've got to make some phone calls."

Outside, Luck called his men together. The first thing, he warned them, was to make sure they didn't say anything about Hook in the Colonel's presence. "Tell him to keep out of sight, in the bunker. I've got a job for him later." He went back inside.

Tucker was on the phone to his task force office in Detroit. He explained to the duty man there that he was expecting a call from Mulheisen, or possibly from some police authority regarding Mulheisen. "The man has gotten himself into some kind of jam," he said. "I learned about it from other sources. Alert the following agents." He rattled off a list. "Have them contact me as soon as they hear anything about this." He gave his personal cell phone number. "And have Agent Schwind call me immediately."

When that was accomplished he said to Luck, "Okay, that ought to do it. Maybe we can head this thing off."

A few moments later, Schwind called. She was one of Tucker's most reliable associates, a fellow member of the Lucani. "Ah, Dinah," he said. "I'm glad you're available. Thanks for responding so quickly. Listen, this guy Mulheisen, you remember him? Good. He's stumbled

190

into a bit of a mess. I'm hoping it can be ironed out without any trouble. The thing is, I'm up here talking to Luck. I should have discussed this with you beforehand, but the opportunity didn't come up. Well, Luck is cooperating with us on this investigation. That's right. The trouble is . . ."

He went on to explain about Mulheisen's accidental stumbling into the situation, his unfortunate detention, then escape. She caught the drift of the situation immediately, he was pleased to note. He went on to explain the importance of keeping this situation quiet. She should use whatever means she had to intercept any official reaction, if Mulheisen should contact police authorities. "You can use the Homeland Security authority to override their objections," he said. "And keep me posted. I'll try to locate him and iron all this out. I don't think it's a big issue, but I don't want it to go any further. Understand?"

He clicked off. "All right," he said to Luck, "I think we've got it in hand, for now. Let's go see if we can find him."

"You want me to come?" Luck said.

"Why not? The fat's in the fire. We can deal with it."

Twenty minutes later they were in Queensleap. The deputy was gone, but Mulheisen's car was still there. "Well, what are we waiting for?" Tucker said. "Let's go in."

It took them only a minute to realize that Mulheisen had been there and gone.

Tucker stood in the room. He noticed, of course, that the bathroom window was wide open. He stood on the edge of the bathtub and peered out into the alley. The little screen had been removed and was lying on the ground. He tried to imagine Mulheisen clambering through this window, then back out, while the deputy stood watch in the parking lot.

"I smell a rat," he said to Luck. He clambered down.

"Did you talk to the guard in the barn?" he asked.

Luck had. The assumption was that Mulheisen had somehow managed to open the door. It had been dark. All the guard could remember was being "sucker punched," then he'd been dragged into the room and trussed up.

"I think Mulheisen had help," Tucker said. "He didn't get out by himself. That changes things."

He paced around the room, thinking. "The guy I need is Joe Service."

"The mob guy you told me to mention on the Web site?"

Tucker nodded. "Ex-mob," Tucker said. "He's a contract guy, been doing a little work for us. Trouble is, he's got some kind of wild hair up his ass. He's not being cooperative lately. That's why I wanted you to put his name out there, put a little pressure on him." He shrugged. "It's just a little gamesmanship. It looks like it didn't work. But he's just the guy to help us with this."

Luck looked resentful. "It might help if you didn't keep everything so close to your vest. Maybe he's the guy who sprang Mulheisen."

"Some things have to be kept close," Tucker said. "Sorry, but that's the way it has to be. Need to know. But one thing you can count on, Joe Service isn't ever going to be helping Mulheisen. These guys go back a long way, to mob days. Mulheisen almost had him in the slammer once or twice. Oh, I had some notion, I guess, that they both might work for me, in a way, but not together, you see. No, that wouldn't work. These old mob guys, they don't forget. You and me, we go back a long way too, Imp, but we always worked on the same side. It'd be like us working for Charlie."

Luck nodded. "That's something that'd never happen."

Tucker looked at him. "You yanked me out of that crash zone, Imp. I'll never forget that."

Luck laughed. "I guess not. Those VC were coming up the hill when I spotted you and dropped the ladder."

"The wildest ride of my life," Tucker said. They both laughed, recalling the chopper ride through the Vietnam night, with Tucker clinging to the rope ladder, rifle shots whizzing through the tree-tops. A hair-rasing escape, it created a bond that would never break.

"What do we do now?" Luck said.

"Now we've got a manhunt. I'll get some of my people up here. I'm wondering if we can get some local cop help, scour the motels and hotels, see if we can't locate Mulheisen. He must be with his pal, whoever it is. They could be halfway to Detroit by now, but somehow I don't think so. Mulheisen had some reason to be out there, snooping around. What do you suppose it was?"

Luck gave it some thought while they drove back to the house. Colonel Tucker was busy on the cell phone, talking to various agents, arranging for them to fly in to Traverse City.

"I think he was curious about the Hill," Luck told Tucker when the phone was quiet for a moment or two.

"And what's the Hill?" Tucker wanted to know.

"Well, that's where the boys nabbed him. He was nosing around back there in the woods. It's just a little . . . um, I guess you could call it a dump."

"A dump?" Tucker eyed him shrewdly. "An ammo dump, I take it?"

At the gate, Luck got out to talk to the guard while Tucker waited in the truck.

"I'm taking the Colonel to the Hill," he told Earl. "He has to see it. Call ahead and get Hook out of there. We won't be long."

Luck drove directly to the Hill. There was a door, a discreet metal one. Luck opened it. He flicked on the lights. It resembled a barracks, with the addition of its own kitchen, plus the usual bunks, some desks, and other apparatus like computers. It obviously doubled as a classroom, where Luck could conduct lectures, complete with a blackboard.

"Interesting," Tucker said. He gestured toward a door in the back. "What's back there?"

Luck showed him. There, in a largish room with slatted wooden floors, were piles of arms. RPGs, boxes of automatic rifles, ammo. Explosives of various kinds, from Plastique to cans of black powder. Boxes of grenades.

Tucker didn't say anything. He looked around.

"Well," Luck said defensively, "you gave me the money. I thought I should equip the guys as well as I could. It's well ventilated, has good drainage. You don't need heat, really, but I've got some generators for power."

"Jesus, Imp, you took this pretty seriously," Tucker said. He glanced back out into the barracks portion, nodded at the cots, the blankets, the cans marked with a red cross indicating medical gear. "You could fight a war. All you need is the army, eh?"

Luck didn't say anything.

"I suppose the men are well trained, know how to use all this stuff?"

"Sure," Luck said. "It's what we do. You can't just have them come over for cookouts and talk about what we'll do when the big day comes."

"The big day?"

"You know . . . invasion, whatever. Look, we've got lots of supplies, staples, got a well that provides twelve gallons a minute. We're pretty well prepared here. There's filters, in case of a nuclear attack . . ."

"Imp . . . nuclear attack?"

"What?"

"There isn't going to be an attack," Tucker said. "Nuclear, or otherwise. Unless, you mean . . ." He let it hang.

"Our own government, you mean," Imp finished. "Well, that could happen too, you know."

"They'd take this place out with one bunker buster," Tucker said, "on the first pass."

"If they can see it," Luck countered. "There's pretty good camouflage, grown trees, mostly pine. It's not visible from the air, Vern."

Tucker picked up an RPG launcher. "You could take out a bank with this," he said. "Or a courthouse."

"Don't look at it that way, Colonel. These guys aren't thinking of doing any such thing."

"Are you sure? The truck that slammed into that courthouse—or would have, if that bus hadn't been in the way—was packing a mass of nitrate, a kind of homemade bomb like they used at Oklahoma City. Where's your nitrates?"

"Over here," Luck said. He showed him the barrels. "But it's all here, Colonel. None of my guys used this stuff, they weren't involved in that."

"You're sure?"

Luck said, "I'm positive."

"I've got to have your files on these guys," Tucker said. "We've got to check them all out. You might have some sleepers here."

Luck looked pensive. "I vetted them all," he said. "I'm confident."

"All right," Tucker said, "for now. But give me a list of names."

"I can do that."

Tucker looked around for a few minutes, then said, "All right, let's go." In the car, he said, "Mulheisen didn't get a gander at any of that?"

"No way," Luck said. "They stopped him two hundred yards away. He probably saw a hill, a wooded hill. That's all."

"And that nice road," Tucker said. He sighed.

When they were alone in the house, Tucker said, "You've got to get rid of that stuff, Imp. It won't do. You can explain to the guys something about security. Get some heavy equipment in here and bury it. Deep."

Luck nodded. "Will do, Colonel. But what about Mulheisen?"

"The people will be showing up in Traverse City before long. I've already made arrangements for them to requisition a government facility at the Coast Guard base. We'd better get out there, organize a quiet little manhunt. Although . . ." —he paused, thinking— "maybe you'd better stay here. Get cracking on that disposal project. I'll drive up there myself. Let me have a jolt of that Dickel, eh?"

12

Running Dogs

Mulheisen was no tourist. He'd spent a couple of hours in Traverse City the day before and hadn't even noticed its main attraction, the bay. Actually, there were two bays, separated by a long, narrow peninsula; on the map it was the space that created the little finger on the mitten of Michigan. From his eighth-floor room in the hotel the view in the morning was spectacular, if one had a taste for shining lakes, rolling hills, and gorgeous fall foliage. He could see the east bay below, beyond it the Old Peninsula, and beyond that the west bay. Mulheisen wasn't in the mood for it, but he could hardly ignore the glorious scenery.

His main concern was getting free of Joe Service, not a prospect he'd ever envisioned. He had sometimes imagined that he would be happy to see the man safely tucked away in prison. All that was changed, of course. What he felt was that he needed to be free of Joe Service, free to do some things that Service's presence seemed to inhibit. But he had a feeling that it wouldn't be so easy to shake him. For one thing, he was dependent on Service for transportation.

They were at breakfast, not in the huge and too-fancy resort hotel but at a pleasant little country restaurant several miles from Traverse City. Service had the idea that the city was not the safest place for them. Colonel Tucker and his crew would be looking for them and Traverse City was the obvious place to look, with its airport and bus terminals. It wasn't a big enough city to hide in. A few hardworking agents had a good chance of spotting them. They would, for instance, almost certainly discover that they'd stayed at the high-rise hotel, although it might be pretty low down the list of hotels to check. Just a telephone check would reveal that Mulheisen had registered, though not Joe Service—he'd used an alias.

Once one drove out of the city a considerable array of convenient options presented themselves—motels, restaurants, resorts, dozens of small lakes with cabins. This was prime tourist country and the fall color tour was on. Joe had driven to a little place up in the highlands, among blazing hardwoods under a beautiful blue sky. Mulheisen would have preferred rain, but Joe was upbeat. He was a blue-sky boy.

Mulheisen wanted to know what was going on and to get his car back. Independence was a burning need. He was not, after all, a dog who ran with the pack. He was grateful for the rescue, but that was last night.

Joe suggested that they find an obscure little resort cabin to use as a base of operations. Joe offered to register for them, with a name that Tucker would never identify with either of them. Mulheisen rejected that.

"We're like two guys in a horse costume," Mulheisen said.

Joe laughed. "Sounds like fun."

"That depends on whether you're the horse's ass," Mulheisen rejoined. "Either way, you can't run with the field."

Mulheisen's mood improved as he hungrily dug into breakfast: pancakes with dried cherries drenched in local maple syrup. After two forkfuls he decided it was his favorite breakfast ever.

Especially with local country sausage. With every bite he remembered the warnings of Dr. Hundly. But he felt that diet was something he'd have to worry about later. He had too many other problems to think about for now.

Joe was giving him a highly edited version of his employment with Tucker. Mulheisen understood that the account was necessarily short on details; he was, after all, a cop, even if a retired one. Joe Service wasn't about to provide complete information; who knew what Mulheisen's next role might be? The account was interesting, nonetheless.

"Tucker is some kind of empire builder," Joe said. "Maybe it's the natural way of spies. He's got angles, little groups he's formed over the years. What do they call it . . . networking? Something like that. Well, we all do stuff like that. I suppose when you were on the force you had your own little groups—allies, snitches, resources. I do a little of that myself."

Mulheisen nodded. But, as he told Service, he'd pretty much put that kind of stuff behind him. Tucker sounded like a guy who reveled in it. "Tell me more about this Lucani outfit," he said.

Joe explained what he had learned about it. "The essence of it, of course," he said, "is that no one knows but the Colonel who all is involved. Maybe he has other groups too. But this one seems to be special. I'm not sure how much of it is known to his bosses. Maybe none of it, maybe all of it. But I'd be surprised if they knew about his association with guys like this Luck character. Still, what do I know? Maybe it's all part of his program."

"But I thought you said that it was a group of disaffected agents," Mulheisen said.

"That's the way it was presented to me," Service said. "But for all I know that's just what he, and they, want me to know. The point is, the Lucani got me out of that hospital."

"Why?"

"Obviously, to help them infiltrate Humphrey's outfit. I helped them. In the long run, though, Humphrey slipped through their fingers."

"Slipped through everyone's fingers," Mulheisen grunted. "Except for the Reaper's." He finished up his pancakes. He knew that someone had gotten to Humphrey ahead of him. He supposed that had been Joe's work. Obviously, Joe wasn't going to tell him about that, so he didn't bother to ask. It was a dead issue, dead as Humphrey. "And now he wants you to help find these bombers. What do you know about that?"

"Nothing," Service said. "But he wants me involved. He's put out the word, with the help of Luck, that I was tied in. He must think that will bring me in. That's the way he works, always from an angle, always some kind of misdirection. If all he wanted is my investigative help, why not just ask for it? But, no, that's not his way."

He shook his head at Tucker's deviousness. "You know, Mul, I've made it my business to find things—information, people, money. I'm good at it. I have my own contacts in the so-called underworld. If there's a connection there, I could find it."

"So why aren't you helping him?"

Service shrugged. "Tucker's a manipulater. He thinks he's some kind of genius psychologist, maybe, but if he was he ought to know that I hate that kind of screwing around. I'm not against helping him, I just don't like the way he goes about it. Wheels within wheels, little plots and subplots that you don't know about. I need clarity," Joe declared, "a view of the terrain. Otherwise, I feel like the guy in the hind end of the horse. I can't operate that way. Carmine was like that, you never knew what was going on. But Humphrey, he'd level with you. Still, I have to admit, if Tucker had asked straight out, I'd have told him to get lost. 'Sorry, not interested.' I helped him with his other stuff—I felt obligated. So I paid him back for his help. But I've had enough of his games."

"But now he's pulled you in anyway," Mulheisen said. "Well, I'm in a different situation. I'm interested in getting to the bottom of this but I'm like you, I don't like being manipulated. And now it's gone too far. There are other angles, too, that puzzle me."

"Like what?" Service wanted to know.

"Why is he involved with Luck? What is Luck up to? And what does it have to do with the bombing?"

"So, what do we do?" Joe asked.

"We?" Mulheisen smiled.

Joe smiled back. "I'd like to help."

"Joe, I'm out of my depth," Mulheisen said. "I don't even know what's going on. I'm no longer a sworn officer. I should be calling the sheriff, except that I don't trust the sheriff. I should be talking to some old pals at the DPD, but I'm not sure of that either. I'm not used to operating like this. I feel lost."

"Who don't?" Joe shrugged. "Look at it this way: we're not officials, but we've got resources. And the thing is, you know and I know that the Colonel and his friends are looking for us and as long as we don't know what they intend, it's probably best if they don't find us, at least until we get a clearer idea of what the game is."

Mulheisen sighed, at least internally. Service was right. "What I'd like to do is get my car," he said. "I feel too hampered without it."

"We could do that," Joe said. He went on to explain that as long as Luck and Tucker didn't know that they were allied, he had a considerable latitude to act. "For instance, I could steal your car."

Mulheisen had to laugh. "And then what?"

"Well, it's a pretty obvious vehicle. You shouldn't be driving it around. But if you're worried about it, I could get it, I'm sure. Then we could park it somewhere and rent another vehicle to use. What do you need it for anyway?"

Mulheisen didn't feel he could explain. He was sure that Joe hadn't been fully forthcoming with him about his own activities. Mulheisen didn't want to be too frank about his plans. "But," he said, "there are some things about Luck that I'd like to find out. Maybe the most important thing is, I need to feel that my mother is all right, that she's not going to be harassed."

"We can work that out," Joe said.

Mulheisen supposed it was so, but he felt impotent. For all his independent attitude, he realized now that he'd always been deeply dependent on being in an official position, with authority, with an official legal apparatus at his fingertips. Now what did he have? A disaffected outlaw who wanted to be his sidekick. It didn't encourage him.

"You have to take stock," Joe advised. "Who do you know who would help you? What kinds of friends do you have? Do you know anyone in these parts?"

Mulheisen told him about the mechanic, Charlie. He'd been helpful.

"Well, that's one," Joe said. "Who else?"

Mulheisen thought. Suddenly, for no reason that he could think of, it flashed into his mind that he'd met some friendly folks up this way several years ago, when he was investigating an earlier case. This case had involved a man who was the chief counsel for an insurance company and been involved in a massive insurance swindle. The man had run into unexpected trouble when his wife discovered his involvement. He'd had his wife killed. Mulheisen had tracked the man to his summer home in the middle of a brutal cold snap following an incredible blizzard that had nearly paralyzed the state of Michigan for days. The summer home had been near a well-known resort some miles south of here, Jasper Lake.

In the event, Mulheisen had caught his man and his hired killer. But the stolen money, in the form of bearer bonds, had disappeared.

Mulheisen remembered what had happened to the money. A private investigator had taken it. Somehow, this clever fellow, in the employ of then mob boss Carmine Busoni, had slipped into the midst of an altercation between the disgruntled killer and the maddened executive, and while they were distracted with their own dispute he'd absconded with the loot. This clever fellow was Joe Service.

It had been Mulheisen's first contact with Service. He hadn't known much about him then. Later, he'd gotten to know too much about him. It wasn't at all clear if Joe Service was aware that Mulheisen knew of his involvement in this case; they'd had very little, if any, direct contact on it. In fact, it was only later, after he'd questioned the two principals, that Mulheisen tumbled to the fact that it was Service who had been the mysterious interloper.

Mulheisen shook his head. "I can't think of anybody else," he said.

Service said, "Well, you know Charlie. You think he'd hide you out?"

"Do I need to hide out?"

"What do you think?" Service said. "Those guys were holding you, probably for Tucker to show up and tell them how to dispose of you. I'd say they were going to relocate you permanently, underground, in some undisclosed location. Your cop connection isn't worth much now, you're on your own. You're on the street, Mul. You have to fall back on friends, take stock, figure out your next move."

Mulheisen sipped his coffee and thought about it.

"I'm happy to help," Joe Service said. "We've got a common purpose."

"Really? How's that?" Mulheisen asked.

Service sighed. "I told you: my whole world is at stake with the Colonel, and with his buddy Luck. I can't afford to just walk away. Pretty soon, they'll figure out it was me who sprung you. Now, I know a lot of useful people, Mul. It's my life. Networking. I could disappear, I'm sure, but I don't want to do that. But you? Can you hide out for the rest of your life? No way. You've got your mother to think about."

"I was thinking about Luck," Mulheisen said. "He's the key. And a part of the key is his late wife, I suspect."

Joe Service perked up. Mulheisen spelled out some of his suspicions: the wife's odd disappearance, but possibly her presence in Luck's life to start with.

"I could help with that," Service said. "I told you, that was my business, finding out things like that. I've still got lots of contacts."

"Do you think you can find out who she was?" Mulheisen said.

"It's possible. Even probable," Service said. "Want me to try?"

"Sure. But first I need to liberate my vehicle."

"Let's check with Charlie," Service said.

On the drive to Queensleap, Mulheisen said, "You said something last night about Hook. What was that all about?"

Joe related what he'd heard from Fedima—he didn't go into details about her history, except to say that she had been in Kosovo. "It's a stretch," Joe said, "but it could be the same guy. I thought I'd mention it to Tucker, if the occasion ever came up, see what he thinks of it. Just a coincidence of names, probably."

"There are no coincidences," Mulheisen said.

In Queensleap, they simply pulled into Charlie's gas station. When Charlie came out to pump the gas, wiping his hands on an oily rag, Joe rolled down the tinted window and Mulheisen said, "Hi."

"I'll be damned," Charlie said. "Hey, there's some revenooers lookin' for you."

"I know," Mulheisen said. "I need a little help. This is my associate. He'll tell you his name, but it'll be a lie."

"Uh-huh," Charlie said, stuffing his rag in his hip pocket and leaning on the door. "What kind of help you need?"

"It's about your old school chum, Imp," Mulheisen said.

"Is Imp after you? Or are you after Imp?" Charlie asked.

"Both. What I need is to get my car. It's up at the motel."

"I could have it towed," Charlie said. "Johnny Dobbs's boy, Lester, does all my towing. He could bring it to Dobbs's Garage, or he'll bring it here. But do you want to be driving around in that car? It sticks out like Johnny's pecker when he sees a woman."

"Just bring it here, if it can be done without bringing the revenooers with it," Mulheisen said. "When I went by to get it before, the sheriff was up there, keeping an eye on it."

"They ain't now, as far as I can tell," Charlie said, "but it could be someone is watching. Lemme think." He stood and audibly scratched his chin. "Maybe I oughta just take a run up there and have a look. Pull your truck into that open bay." He pointed toward his garage. "I'll be back in a sec."

The two men waited while Charlie jumped in his truck and drove the four blocks or so up the hill to the Queen's Castle Motel. He was back before any customers deigned to stop.

"I think it'll be all right," he said. "Trudy Morehouse is running the front desk. Lester knows her. I didn't see nobody else around." He went to the phone and dialed. "Hey, Johnny! Yeah. I need Lester to go pick up a car for a customer, haul her down to me. It's at the motel. If Trudy's up there, which I think she is, and she asks, it's for the sheriff. Thanks."

He hung up and said, "Anything else you need, Mul?"

Mulheisen shook his head. "Just like that, eh?"

"Wal, a feller buys you a drink, you got to reciprocate." He grinned. "I like that word. Especially if it means piss in Imp's boot. What's Imp done to you, if you don't mind me asking?"

"He pissed in my boot," Mulheisen said. "What did he ever do to you?"

"'Bout the same," Charlie said. "You ever run into a guy that just rubbed you the wrong way? That's Imp. That sumbitch all's had everything his way, ever since we was kids. I never liked him. His ol' man, Eb, was all right, I thought, what I knew of him, but Imp was a pain in the butt. Anything else I can do for you? How 'bout you, Phantom?" he said to Joe.

Service just laughed. "Actually, Mul's too polite to ask, but he needs a place to stay. Someplace quiet and private, if you know what I mean."

Charlie thought he might have something in that line. It wasn't too fancy, he said, but it had a phone. He could also provide an old pickup truck. "It runs good," he said. "Four-wheel drive and everything. Got a good radio. It'll get in and out of the cabin."

The cabin was back in the woods, at the end of a long road, next to the Manistee River. Good brown trout water there, Charlie said. The cabin had been built by a friend of Charlie's, Old Tom Adams—"his grandfather invented the Adams fly, for Tom! One of the greatest fishermen ever." Adams had built the cabin himself, as a fishing retreat, and when he died he left the cabin to Charlie, having no heirs. Charlie didn't use it much. "Only trouble was," Charlie said, "he built it on some land belonged to Eb Luck. Tom claimed Eb give him the property, and I think he did, but we ain't never found a deed. Still, Eb never contested it. I used go out there with Tom and fish and drink. But with him gone it wasn't the same. Made me lonely. Fish were gone, too."

Nowadays, he rented it for hunting—"For a ton of bucks to some guys from down below. Imp wants it back, but he ain't getting it." The hunters wouldn't be up for a couple of weeks; until then it was just lying empty. Mulheisen was welcome to it. Charlie refused any payment, and ditto for the truck.

Mulheisen was amazed. The cabin was ideal. As Charlie had warned, "it wasn't too fancy." It also needed some cleaning. It was a log building, but built with vertical half-logs in a clever system that alternated the interior half-logs in such a way that they covered the joints of the exterior logs and permitted a layer of insulation; it was very tight and snug. There was a single room for kitchen and living, with a so-called cathedral ceiling. A bedroom, bath, and utility room took up the rear and above that was a large loft that overlooked the living area, obviously where the hunters slept.

The cabin had electricity, running water, an indoor toilet with a shower, and a woodstove. The hunters brought cots, Charlie had said, and slept five or six there. Refrigerator—Mulheisen had stocked up at a store out on the highway, well east of Queensleap— no television, but plenty of privacy. No other buildings seemed to be within miles.

It was positioned on the side of a hill, at the edge of a mixed forest of hardwood and pine, with the river flowing by in a great bend, some thirty feet below the cabin, no more than fifty feet away. The river was quiet, sliding smoothly past. Beyond it lay a great marsh, with dense cedar. One could see for miles to a distant wooded ridge.

The property abutted Luck's property, according to a large U.S. Forest Service topo map that was pinned to the kitchen wall. The map had numerous ballpoint markings, obviously drawn in by hunters to indicate good hunting sites, or routes to get to them. Between this property and Luck's house was a considerable forest, an entire section on the map. By road, it was easily five miles, a long, awkward route.

Joe had driven out with Mulheisen to the site, although it was understood that he wasn't staying. He had plenty to do in town, he said. But he was clearly charmed by the cabin and the setting. "I've got to get myself something like this. I tell you, Mul, you fell into it here." He walked about admiring the handiwork, explaining that he had become something of a carpenter himself lately.

Mulheisen was surprised. He began to relate his recent experiences in building his study. "It's turned into a cottage," he said. "I was thinking, eventually I'll be moving back into the old homestead, but once the study is finished it'll be a good retreat. Nothing as fancy as this, no Manistee River at my door, but I do have the lake, the St. Clair River . . ."

Joe said he'd seen the place, when he had visited Mul's mother. He complimented him on the style and appearance. They fell into a discussion of building problems, flooring, insulation, the cost of plumbing and wiring.

"I like this post-and-beam style," Joe said. He admired the huge, double-glazed windows that looked out over the river, some thirty feet below, winding in a great bend before turning west and disappearing into a vast cedar forest. The view was impressive— one could see nothing but trees for miles, until the horizon loomed in the blue distance.

"Not a sound," Joe said, "just the river gurgling by. You fish?"

"Oh, I've tried it, when I was out looking for you, in Montana," Mulheisen said. "I didn't get the hang of it."

Joe smiled at the reference to that old episode. "I've taken it up," he said. "It gets under your skin. This guy was supposed to be a great fisherman. I've used those Adams flies. Great all-purpose fly pattern. You can use it just about year-round. I'll bet he left some gear." He began to poke around until, sure enough, he found the rods and reels in the utility-room closet. One rod was already strung, with a fly tied on the leader.

Joe brought it out. "Here you go! All set. You ought to go down and cast a bit. I'll get out of your hair."

Before he left they settled their plans for contact. Joe warned Mulheisen against using the phone.

"Tucker will have your mother's phone tapped, I'll bet," he said. "Use a pay phone when you're in Traverse," he recommended, "or wherever else you get to, as long as it isn't too close by. I can call you on this phone—I'll ring twice, then call back. You can figure out some way your mother can reach you, if you're careful and she doesn't use her home phone."

"I think I can figure it out," Mulheisen said patiently.

Joe caught the tone of exasperation. "I know, I know, I'm the horse's butt and you're a hardened ol' copper. But the thing is, I know how not to get caught by making dumb mistakes. It's a street thing."

Mulheisen sighed. "I could use the cell phone." He'd recovered it, along with his other stuff from the Checker, which was now stashed in Charlie's garage, out of casual sight.

Joe shook his head in mock despair. "Forget the cell. I don't know how it works, but they can track those things. Satellites, maybe."

Mulheisen walked out to the pickup with Joe. They settled that Joe would see what he could find out about Luck's late wife, Constance. Mulheisen would drive to Cadillac tomorrow, a city to the south about twenty miles, actually somewhat closer than Traverse City but in another county. He'd contact friends at the Detroit Police Department to see if he could gather anymore information from that source.

"I'll call you when I get a motel," Joe said, "and we can figure out how to communicate from there." He stopped at the door of the pickup and said, "You're not armed, are you? Let me leave a couple of pieces with you."

Mulheisen refused, but not vehemently. He was shocked to see the arsenal Service revealed. He ended up accepting a Llama 9mm automatic pistol.

"A beautiful piece," Mulheisen said, turning the elegant handgun over in his hand. "Where did you get it? Or should I ask?"

"A friend of mine left it with me," Joe said. "It's a Model XI. Here's some clips." He prevailed upon Mulheisen to also accept a Stoner .223 automatic carbine—"Just in case one of Luck's guys comes snooping around. This will put out a lot of lead without making a big mess. Just leave it in the cabin."

Mulheisen was relieved when Joe left. He felt like he was on vacation. He spent spent some time sweeping out, washing dishes, and straightening out the bedroom. He even found a clean set of sheets and made the bed. He still had time to walk down to the river with the fly rod Joe had found. He'd had a little practice with casting when he was in Montana, more than a year ago, but he found it difficult at first; the fly wouldn't turn over and the bushes kept snagging his backcast. Eventually he got the hang of it.

The water was nothing like the mountain streams he'd seen in Montana. This water was opaque, it seemed, not broken into riffles by rocks and gravel bars. He had no idea where to cast, no sense of where the fish might be lying. And after a half hour of erratic casting and untangling the fly from brush, he became discouraged. Like every novice fisherman, he became convinced that there were no fish in this stream. Still, if Old Tom Adams had built his cabin here, he supposed that it was for the obvious reason.

It was getting toward dusk anyway. Time to quit. Suddenly, he noticed that there were quite a few small insects hovering over the water. This must be the famous "hatch," he thought. And shortly, a fish leaped out of the water, not far off, falling back heavily with a great splash. A trout! He made several casts, each one an improvement. The fly line hardly made a single *splat*. And with the very next cast, he hooked something!

It was astounding. The fish leaped into the air, almost three feet—to his eyes—and with a terrific contortion snapped the leader. The trout disappeared.

Mulheisen stood on the edge of the water, his mouth open in awe. So that was it! He was amazed. He'd actually hooked a trout. He thought, That son of a gun must have been . . . oh, two feet long! He suddenly realized his feet were getting wet. He scrambled back to the bank.

He was thrilled. But it was too dark to go on. He knew he'd never be able to tie on another fly. In fact, he hadn't one with him. He went back to the cabin and prepared a sandwich and drank some water. He felt very good.

Thoughts of his mother intruded. He drove out in the old truck along the two-track road and eventually got on the highway. He went to the place where he'd bought his groceries and made a call. He wanted to tell her about the trout, but as it happened she had already gone to bed. He told the nurse not to wake her. He asked if anyone had been around, asking for him, but the nurse said no, not that she knew, but she hadn't been there earlier, of course.

Mulheisen thought quickly. Then he said, "Tell her I may be home tomorrow, but if I'm not, I'll call. I may ask a friend to stop by, possibly later this evening, just to sort of check up. He's a policeman, Captain Marshall. Let's see, you go off duty in a couple of hours, don't you? He'll stop by before that, if he can, but don't worry if he can't make it."

The nurse said that would be fine, and if Captain Marshall didn't show up before her relief, she'd leave a message.

He called Jimmy Marshall at home.

Marshall was excited. "People looking for you, man," he said. "What's up?"

Mulheisen asked him to go to his mother's house. "I know it's a long way, clear across town, but I need your help," he said. What he wanted, he explained, was for someone he could trust to check out the situation there. His mother had met Jimmy and liked him. Then he explained in some detail about his detention, but for some reason he left Joe Service out of the account.

He gave the phone number at the cabin. "You can call me there, but not from Ma's," Mulheisen said. "She's already in bed, there's no need to wake her. Just make sure there's no one snooping around and everything's all right. There will be a nurse there. You can leave a message with her. She, or my mother, can call me at the cabin, in case of an emergency. By the way, did you check out that Dr. Johnson, in Indiana?"

"Yeah. He's deceased," Jimmy said. "Died two years ago."

"Damn," Mulheisen said. "That would be not long after Constance Luck died. How'd he die?"

"He was killed, Mul. Got blown up in his car."

Mulheisen was silent. "No other details?" he said, after a moment.

"I talked to a guy on the Indianapolis squad. They didn't have a clue. And now, guess what? The files are impounded. Homeland Security."

"What does your friend say, in Indianapolis?" Mulheisen wanted to know.

"They were working on the theory it was drug-related," Jimmy said. "The trouble was, Dr. Johnson wasn't ever suspected of that kind of activity. He was just a GP, in family practice. He'd never been implicated in any drug dealings."

"Could you check on Constance Luck, or Constance Malachi, as far as where, when, or if she was buried in those parts? How far does this Homeland Security thing go? Would it prevent you from finding out if she ever lived in Indianapolis?"

Jimmy didn't grumble at any of these requests. He just said he'd call back after he'd been out to St. Clair Flats.

Mulheisen thought about all this on his way back to the cabin. It was another pitch-black night. He'd noticed while he was fishing that clouds were moving in; it looked like they had arrived. It began to sprinkle while he was slowly pushing the old truck up the long lane. By the time he got to the house it was raining, a good steady rain.

He settled down to study the topo map, particularly Luck's property. Jimmy would be a while, he knew. But it was very odd: sitting in this lighted house, with huge front windows, surrounded by utter darkness. He felt like a target. He couldn't concentrate. Soon, he turned out the lights and sat in the dark, listening to the rain drum on the metal roof. It was coming down pretty steadily. He thought it was the most soothing and relaxing sound he'd ever heard.

13

The Dogs of Helen

It did not occur to Helen that Joe had left her until she retrieved her Durango from the hotel parking lot in Helena. The vehicle was completely cleaned out, not even a note from Joe. She was driving back to the ranch when the dangerous idea struck her: maybe he's gone for good. She swerved, almost losing control. She'd been unprepared for that.

Unprepared, but she quickly realized she'd had a premonition. Nothing conscious, hence the reaction. But an uneasy feeling had been lurking, like a tiny black cloud just beyond the corner of her eye. She thought it might have been implanted when she received the message from his answering service, telling her not to speak to Colonel Tucker, informing her of the whereabouts of the car . . . and nothing else. No personal message at all.

They had made love the day he'd left. According to him, he was just going to "straighten the Colonel out," after which their life could continue on its increasingly domestic arc. They were rich, they had the place they wanted, they were secure from the authorities.

Well, perhaps not secure, that was the point of settling the deal with Colonel Tucker: to make sure that they were secure. Legally, Helen was sure that could never really be accomplished short of a presidential pardon. But she didn't see why it shouldn't be so in practice.

Nearly a year had passed since their last work for the Colonel. They had built their house. It wasn't finished, but it was livable and, to be honest, they were in no hurry to finish it. She had even begun to think, in a remote and theoretical way, about having a child. She hadn't mentioned a word, not even a hint, of this to Joe. She had hardly permitted herself to think about it seriously. But what was left for the absolute fulfillment of their lives? She was over thirty, as was Joe. It was getting late to be starting a family. Not too late, of course, not by any means.

Could she have unconsciously given him a hint of that? And if she had, was it something that would cause him to panic and flee? Because the feeling that he had gone, not planning to return, was strong . . . so strong, in fact, that she knew it.

When she got back to the house she checked the crucial indicators: the money cache, the guns. She saw right away that he had taken a substantial amount of cash, more than two or three hundred thousand dollars. She knew that he had other sources of cash, money hidden in numerous banks around the country. He had also taken all of the guns that he really liked—mostly handguns, but also some automatic weapons, such as a Bushmaster, a Heckler & Koch MP5A3, an Uzi, as well as a few other, less exotic guns.

None of this was conclusive, of course. He could walk in this afternoon and say, "Hi, babe. Well, it's all settled." But somehow she just knew that he wasn't going to.

She thought of calling the Colonel, but she didn't know how to get in touch with him. She supposed she could find him—he was a government employee, after all. Still, Joe had warned her not to talk to the Colonel. In her present mood she was inclined to ignore Joe's advice, but she didn't call.

Her next impulse was to go see Fedima. And do what? she thought derisively. Cry on her shoulder? Seek comfort? She rejected the idea. She wasn't so fond of Fedima lately. Then she thought of calling her mother. Instead, she called Roman Yakovich, her late father's retired bodyguard.

Roman was not home.

That gave her pause. She sat down in a chair by the great windows that looked out on the valley, toward the river, the bluffs, and the mountains beyond. It was a golden day. But she didn't see it. She just sat and gazed and thought.

Her feelings for Joe were intense. Some time ago, they had gotten into the habit of wrestling. They were of a size, small, muscular, lithe, like young panthers. The wrestling could get dangerous, at times, with chokeholds. At one point, when they had approached very near a desperate moment, from which they had both backed away, she recalled telling him that she would never allow him to leave. He had sworn in return never to do it. Hadn't he? She was sure he had.

Now he was gone. She had no choice: she had to go find him. This was a breach, a fatal gesture. She would find him, confront him, and if he did not give her satisfaction . . . she would kill him. Or he would kill her. It would be that kind of a confrontation, she was sure.

She remembered that she had a contact number for Roman, an emergency number. She found it and called. A man answered. He said he didn't know any Roman Yakovich. Who was she? She told him. The man said he would ask around. He'd call back. She started to tell him her number when he hung up.

Roman called in fifteen minutes. "I was gonna call you," he said. "You okay?"

"I'm fine," she said. Then she remembered that she wasn't all right. "I'm upset."

"What's wrong?" Now Roman was upset. She could hear the anxiety in his voice.

"Joe's gone." There, it was out. She almost burst into tears.

"He's gone, sure," Roman said, in his gruff voice, still with a faint Balkan accent, rather like her mother's. "But he ain't gone gone."

"What's that supposed to mean?"

"I mean, he ain't, you know—*gone*. He's okay. I think."

Helen was puzzled. "What? Where is he? Have you heard from him?"

"That's the problem," Roman said. He actually said "Dat." "He's 'posta be in Detroit, but he ain't."

"He called you? What did he want?"

"He din't say, just meet me in Detroit. But he ain't here. He tol' me not to tell you—don't worry the Liddle Angel."

That was Roman's pet name for her, Helen was aware. Joe would not have used that phrase—doubtless, it was Roman's unconscious attribution—but the usage momentarily softened her anger. But only momentarily. "Don't *tell* me! Why didn't you call, you oaf?"

"I'm sorry, I shoulda. I was gonna, and then you called Denny, down in Miami."

"That was Denny? Denny Spinodi? Itchy's brother? He never said a word. What a bunch of fu—. What the hell is going on?"

"Baby, baby, sweetie," he crooned, as he used to when she'd had a fall, when he picked her up and petted her. "Slow down. I'm sorry. I swear I was gonna call you. I t'ought he just meant, don't bother you. I was 'posta meet him, but he never showed."

At her demand he told her that he knew nothing about Joe's plans, but Joe had said he needed some help, and as he had some free time he'd flown to Detroit, but Joe was now at least a day overdue and no word. He, Roman, was staying at the house, by which he meant her mother's house, on the east side. No, he had no hint of what Joe was up to. He swore.

"I'll be there in a few hours," Helen yelled. "Don't you move. I mean freeze!" She slammed down the phone.

For five minutes she raced around in a frenzy, yanking out suitcases, opening dresser drawers, flinging open the closet doors, until she found herself standing there, staring at dresses and wondering what she was doing. She calmed down. She paged through the phone book, found a private air service in Helena, and called. The best they could offer was a Beechcraft, a twin-engined airplane that could, possibly, get her to Detroit around midnight. It wasn't even noon yet.

She concentrated. It took three more calls. Mel, a friend who was in the Business—who had, in fact, succeeded to the top of the Detroit syndicate with her help—was very happy to be of service. Some associates, Mel said, had flown out to Seattle, to take care of a few things. They had taken the Gulfstream, a very nice, speedy executive jet. They would be in Seattle for another day or two. The pilot and crew were being paid to sit around and wait, so why didn't they fly over to Montana—it was just a state away, wasn't it—and pick her up and carry her to Detroit? They could land at the City Airport, handy to her mother's house. He'd make sure that Roman was there to meet her.

"Fine, thanks Mel."

Mel was grateful for the opportunity to help. He hoped her mother wasn't in ill health or anything. She said it wasn't like that, but a personal emergency that she'd rather not go into. Mel understood. She'd almost screwed Mel once. She wondered what he'd have done for her if she had.

Mel called back in ten minutes. She would have the plane all to herself; it would be at the Helena airport in about an hour and a half. She'd probably be in Detroit by six. He hoped they could have dinner while she was in town. Which reminded him, there would be food and drink on the plane. And don't even think of trying to pay for this, he was just happy to be of service.

She asked, "I don't have to go through any kind of check-in, or anything, do I?"

"Aw, no. You go to the general aviation place. It should be a small airport, you'll find it. It won't be the commercial terminal. They'll have a place you can park and everything. You can bring anything you want on board—a pet, whatever. It'll just be you, right?"

She said she'd be alone. She didn't have much luggage. But it reminded her to call Fedima and arrange to have the dogs taken care of. She packed clothes, grabbed a pile of money, her favorite gun—a nifty Browning 9mm automatic pistol—and especially a cut-down Remington Model 870 .20-gauge shotgun. These weapons fit nicely into a duffel bag. Then she drove to Helena. She wasn't familiar with the town; she and Joe normally did their shopping in Butte, sixty-some miles in the other direction. But she got there in plenty of time and found the general aviation hangar. The airplane arrived fifteen minutes later, a half hour later than Mel had promised. They'd had to call around to get the crew together.

It was a beautiful plane, a white G500. It had a cabin for fourteen, with large, plush leather chairs, a divan, a galley. There was a pleasant young attendant named Virna, who immediately opened a bottle of champagne, compliments of "the boss." There were also bunches of flowers, again specially ordered by the boss—huge bouquets of roses and even some orchids. She would provide a meal, which the boss had ordered put aboard from an excellent Seattle restaurant called Campagne. It involved pâtés, cheeses, fresh fruit, and an already prepared fish of the day in a wine sauce with shallots. Virna apologized for the fact that they'd had to keep the fish warm, and thus it was not at its peak, but it was very good. Salad, of course, with a walnut vinaigrette.

Helen couldn't remember having flown on this plane. It belonged ostensibly to the Krispee Chips Corporation, one of the mob's long-standing fronts. It must have been purchased since her departure. Her mentor, the late Humphrey DiEbola, would have enjoyed something like this, although the cuisine, she was sure, would not have been French, but something spicier, something with chilis.

"What's our ETA?" she asked Virna.

Virna had to ask the pilot, who responded that it would be 7:30, local time. They would cruise at fifty thousand feet.

It was dark when they landed. Roman was there. He looked scared, as scared as a burly man in his sixties could look. Helen put him at ease: she apologized for calling him an oaf. "I was furious," she said, "but I'm feeling calmer. Still mad, though . . . so don't say anything. Any word from that bastard?"

No, and Roman was a little worried. "This ain't like Joe," he said. He had no idea where Joe was, he hadn't given a hint as to what the problem was for which he'd needed help. "Mel wants you to call," he said.

"Screw Mel," Helen said.

They went to the house, where she spent all of fifteen minutes hugging her mother, a dumpy little Serbian woman of Roman's age. She had a number of medical problems, which had to be discussed. Helen listened for a few minutes, but when it was clear that nothing serious was wrong with her mother, she said she was exhausted and had to rest, and they could talk later. She went to her father's study and called Mel, to thank him for the ride and promise to have dinner before she left town. She also asked if he'd heard anything from Joe, or about Joe.

"Baby, the less I hear about Joe the better I like it," Mel told her. "I know he was Humphrey's buddy and he helped Humphrey to the end, but the man is poison. Forget about him." He went on in this vein for a minute and then Helen finally was free of him.

Who could help? She sat at her father's old desk, drumming her fingers. Suddenly, it occurred to her that Joe might be in a hospital. Perhaps he'd had a relapse, as had happened in Colorado, on the train, a recurrence or complication of his head injury. Thinking of that, which she didn't really believe in, given Joe's good health of late, she thought of Mulheisen, the cop who had investigated her father's murder and later pursued both Joe and her. Mulheisen might have him!

Why hadn't she thought of that? A man was crazy to come back to Detroit as long as Mulheisen was here. For that matter, maybe she was crazy as well. But Roman, who kept up on all such matters, naturally, informed her of Mulheisen's retirement.

That was something of a relief, but then it occurred to her that if Mulheisen was a civilian now, maybe he could be of assistance. As a matter of fact, she was on pretty good terms with Mulheisen, she felt, despite a fairly stormy past. She'd once punched him in anger. And he'd tried to pin a murder rap on her, but all that was history. More important, she knew that he continued to order cigars from a small firm she owned. The cigar factory was closed at this hour, but she had access to the files from her home computer. She looked up his address and phone number.

A woman answered who said she was a nurse. Mr. Mulheisen was not at home and Mrs. Mulheisen was in bed. Helen thought at first that the nurse meant Mulheisen's wife, but she seemed to recall that Mulheisen was not married. It must be the mother. It was like Mulheisen to be living with his mother, she thought. She declined to leave a message.

Roman couldn't enlighten her. He wasn't aware that Mulheisen's mother had been injured in the bombing. He knew only that Mulheisen had retired. Helen supposed that his mother, who must be fairly old, was ill. It seemed odd that he would go off and leave her with a nurse, especially if the illness was such that he had retired early, as she suspected.

Helen was frustrated. She felt compelled to do something. She hadn't flown all the way out here just to sit and stew. She could have done that at home. Once again, she was tempted to call Colonel Tucker. But, again, she couldn't bring herself to do it. She had a feeling that Joe's warning not to call him was intended to protect her. But good god, she didn't need protecting from the Colonel. On the other hand, she recalled some hints she'd received that Joe and one of the Colonel's agents had a little thing going.

Yes, she thought, that was probably it. He was with that woman, that Dinah Schwind. This had nothing to do with the Colonel at all.

This was no help. She had no way of finding Dinah Schwind. She felt like driving to Mulheisen's house and demanding to know where Mulheisen was—an absurd notion. Very likely, Mulheisen knew nothing at all about Joe, and could care less. Besides, if the old lady was ill . . . She couldn't bring herself to do it.

Resigned, she went in to talk to her mother, who was herself getting ready for bed. Her mother, of course, had seen immediately that her daughter was distraught, but she'd tried to ignore it, in case it was not serious. Now the old lady drew her out. When she learned what the matter was, she commiserated, but in a deprecating way. Helen's father had been a notorious philanderer. Soke Sedlacek had suffered mightily. But in the end she had resigned herself.

"It's how men are," Soke told her daughter. "They see some pretty girl, always someone younger, and they can't help themselves. A stiff prick has no conscience."

Helen was not having that. She wasn't old, and she didn't think Dinah Schwind, the Lucani agent, was any younger, and certainly not more good-looking. She'd merely thrown that notion out as a possibility; she didn't really believe it . . . not really. Did she? No, she thought there must be some other reason. "I even called Mulheisen," she said. "You remember him, Mama, the police detective . . . he was in charge of the investigation when Papa . . . died. I thought he might know something. But he's gone off somewhere too."

Mrs. Sedlacek remembered Mulheisen. "The poor man," she said. "His mother was almost killed in that bombing, out in some awful suburb. I don't know where it was—Ann Arbor?"

Soke knew nothing much about it, only what she'd read in the newspaper. But Helen felt it might be important. She went off to call an old friend of hers from school, Christi Rose. Christi's mother had worked for Humphrey at one time. Christi was a very bright young woman who had married a bright young man when they were both in law school. Christi did the family law in the firm and Ron did criminal and personal injury law. If anyone had any useful knowledge about this bombing, Christi would.

She did. After they got past the greetings and "let's have lunch, soon," Christi told Helen what she knew about Cora Mulheisen, the investigation, Homeland Security. Yes, a Vernon Tucker was part of the investigation. Christi had lots of information, including the scuttlebutt in the legal world. Insiders speculated that the bombing was all about the case of a young drug dealer, named Calona, who was at the Wards Cove Municipal Building for a preliminary hearing. Presumably, the bombing was intended to provide cover for springing Calona. Unfortunately, Calona had died in the bombing; the hearing had been held in a judge's chambers that was located all too close to the point where the bomb-laden truck had crashed.

This information wasn't very enlightening to Helen, but she was a thorough person. She listened to the other theories, the ones that presumably had interested the Homeland Security people, about rival Arab factions. There were a few Arabs in that county, but nothing like the thousands of expatriate Syrians, Lebanese, Chaldeans, Iraqis, and others in nearby Wayne County (where Detroit was located). There were no hearings or any other activities involving them going on, although there were some citizenship processes in train. The Arab angle was a no-go. The only other activity scheduled, besides the hearing on the environmental issues that had attracted Cora Mulheisen's group, was a routine matter concerning the disposition of the property of a deceased woman named Constance Malachi.

"My ears perked up when I heard that," Christi said. "You remember Jerry Malachi, don't you?"

"Oh, sure," Helen said. "Jerry was at Michigan State when we were. Tall, good-looking . . . a golfer, wasn't he?"

"Tennis," Christi said. "He was a psych major. I dated him pretty seriously, when we were seniors, don't you remember? For a while, he thought I'd marry him, but no way. Then I went off to law school and met Ron."

That wasn't exactly how Helen remembered Christi's brief fling with Jerry, but she didn't say anything. "Was he involved in this . . . what was it, a hearing?" she asked.

"Oh, no. It was just the name. No connection," Christi said. "Jerry turned out to be gay, you know."

"You're kidding!"

"I'm not sure he even knew he was gay, at the time. But I had my suspicions. Not that he and I ever, uh, did anything. Which made the switch to Ron a lot easier, believe me."

Helen had known Jerry Malachi rather more intimately. One thing she knew for sure: he wasn't gay. No point in mentioning it now, of course. They went on to discuss a number of things about school, about Ron, the kids, Detroit. After a few more "Let's have lunch" suggestions, that was it.

Helen was still frustrated, still seething. She went downstairs to the elaborate workout area her father had installed in the basement. She took a swim, and then a sauna. She'd had some adventures with Joe in this room. The thought of it vanquished the momentary feeling of relaxation. She went upstairs and called the number for Jerry Malachi. He still lived in Grosse Pointe, not far away.

"I ran into a friend of yours," she said when he came to the phone. "Christi Rose. Your name came up."

Jerry was delighted to hear it. "How's Chrissy doing these days?"

They chatted for a bit and then Helen mentioned the Malachi connection, the hearing in Wards Cove. "Christi said it caught her eye, but it turned out that it was a different Malachi."

"I wonder where Christi gets her gossip?" Malachi said. "Actually, there is a connection, but it's pretty distant."

"That's Christi," Helen said. "Always jumping to conclusions on insufficient evidence. She told me you were gay. I guess you weren't lying when you swore to me you never touched her."

Malachi laughed. "I never lied to you, sweetie. Now you know."

"So what is the connection?"

Malachi explained that Constance was a cousin, somewhat distant. Her father was an uncle of Jerry's father. "I met her, once or twice, a long time ago," he said. "They weren't from Detroit. Most of that side of the family are in Indianapolis."

"What was the hearing about?" Helen asked.

"A dispute about property," Jerry said. "I wouldn't have noticed, except there was a hideous bombing the same day, some kind of terrorist thing. Connie had married a guy from up north somewhere. Then she died. There was some kind of disagreement about her inheritance. So . . . what are you doing these days?"

Jon A. Jackson

Helen wasn't sure if Christi had been aware that Helen had also dated Jerry, although she was pretty sure it was one of the reasons Jerry had broken off with Christi. She wasn't in the least surprised, in fact, when Malachi said, "What are you doing tonight?"

"Tonight? It's kind of late, isn't it?" Helen said.

"Gee, what time do you usually go to bed?" Jerry asked. "I mean, to sleep? It's only ten o'clock."

Helen was amused. She was also restless. She agreed to meet in an hour, at a bar they knew on Kercheval, Pierre's.

Jerry was as handsome as ever, she was glad to see. It turned out he was divorced. He was in marketing now, obviously doing fairly well. He knew about her late father; perhaps it added some glamour, another attraction. Helen felt hard-pressed to keep the conversation in the direction she preferred. The Jerry she had known in college was still a wolf.

Malachi wasn't interested in his remote cousin, but as it seemed that Helen was, he was happy to tell her what he knew. Constance Malachi was a little older than them, probably in her late thirties when she died. He remembered seeing her when he was a kid and she was a rather sexy teenager. She'd gone into the law, he said, working for the government.

"I think she was doing pretty well, actually," Malachi said. "A prosecutor or something. Worked for the U.S. Attorney's office. Then, I guess she married this Luckenbach guy, who was some kind of big farmer, or developer—I don't know what the deal was. She dropped out of sight. They had some kind of property settlement deal, part of the marriage, or maybe his business. Then— *boom!*—she dropped dead. Heart attack. Amazing, isn't it? She was so young. I have this image of her, the bold, vivacious older girl. Very bright, too."

It was sad, Helen said. Too young. "But what was the issue? Why the hearing?"

"The family was upset, I heard," Malachi said, "because some property that belonged to the family, her dad, I guess, was claimed by the husband, this Luckenbach guy. Pretty nice chunk of property, too. Upstate, somewhere, I heard. Probably lake property. There might have been some development scheme."

"So what happened?"

"What happened? To the property, you mean? Well, nothing. The hearing was disrupted, of course. It was a thing with lawyers. Nobody was injured. I think it's still in contention. These things can go on for ages, you know."

Jerry really wanted to talk about Helen. She, however, had heard enough. And she was tired, a little hungover, from the champagne on the plane, or a bit of jet lag. It ended with a brief tussle in the parking lot. Jerry insisted on a kiss, for old time's sake. Helen finally gave in to the kiss, and then solemnly agreed to meet him the next night for dinner.

Helen drove home thinking the whole thing had been a bore, a waste of time. Talking to Jerry had reminded her of why she preferred Joe. The kiss had awakened no passion. But she had gotten from Malachi the name of the town where Luckenbach lived. He had dredged it up from his memory, only because of the oddity of the name: Queensleap.

Was it anything? she wondered as she drove. She looked up the town on a map when she got home. It was way up north, probably a four-hour drive. Well, she thought, she didn't have anything else. Maybe that was the connection. But to what? How could it involve Joe? Mulheisen, maybe . . . but it did seem to concern Colonel Tucker. By now, of course, she had half-convinced herself that Joe's meeting with Tucker was just a cover for a renewal of his affair with Dinah Schwind. Oh, she was reaching for straws. She went to bed, exhausted.

14

Mutt and Joe

Mulheisen woke up. The rain had slowed a bit but it was still coming down steadily. It was almost midnight. The phone rang. Had it rung before? He wasn't sure.

It was Jimmy Marshall, calling from home. "Your mother was fine," he said, "sleeping peacefully. I didn't disturb her. I talked to the nurse. She said no one had come by, although she'd had a call from some woman, looking for you. There was no message and she didn't identify herself. Your mother had been out bird-watching in the afternoon, according to the day nurse. She's fine, Mul. I looked around, didn't see any sign of the Homeland people or anyone else."

Mulheisen thanked him. "Did you leave a message, how to contact me?"

"Yeah," Jimmy said. "I wasn't quite sure what to do. What if the nurse gives it to this Tucker guy? I put it in a sealed envelope. Maybe that'll keep her from opening it. In the message I said call the cabin in an emergency only."

"Great, thanks, Jimmy," Mulheisen said. "What about Constance Malachi?"

"She's not buried in Indianapolis, looks like," Jimmy said.

"I don't know what to tell you, man. I didn't do too well for you. Sorry."

Mulheisen assured him he'd done fine. The nurse, he explained, was hired by him. He was sure she'd simply pass the message to his mother.

"You all right, man?" Jimmy asked. "If you need anything, give me a call. There's a lotta guys around here who'd help out, too, you know."

Mulheisen thanked him. "What about Wunney? Do you know him? What's his home number?"

It took Jimmy a little while to find it, but he delivered it without comment. Mulheisen pondered for a moment whether it was too late to call Wunney, but he quickly decided that it was not a time for social niceties, and it ought to be safe enough to call a man on the task force from this number.

Wunney answered on the first ring. It was that same old flat voice. "Yeah?"

"Sorry to call so late—" Mulheisen began, before Wunney cut him off.

"You're in Queensleap." It was spoken flatly, without any recrimination.

"You've got caller ID," Mulheisen said.

"Doesn't everybody? Charles McVey a friend of yours?"

"Something like that," Mulheisen said.

"Some people want to talk to you," Wunney said.

Mulheisen heard the sound of a match, an intake of breath.

"What's your suggestion?" Mulheisen asked.

Wunney said, "Never hurts to talk."

"That's what you tell a suspect, or used to, before Miranda," Mulheisen said. "Anymore, we tell 'em to save it for the witness stand."

He sat in the darkness, listening to the rain and Wunney's periodic inhalation on a cigarette. He thought about lighting up a cigar himself, then decided against it. He still felt like a target in this windowed room.

"So don't talk," Wunney said. "Good night."

But he didn't hang up. Mulheisen explained briefly what had happened.

Wunney said, "I see what you mean about talking. It's touchy. Still . . ."

After a bit, Mulheisen said, "Who's Tucker's boss?"

"You don't want to talk to him," Wunney said. "He's some kind of idiot, a chair-warmer. Let me think . . ."

They sat in silence.

"Raining there?" Wunney said.

"Not quite Niagara. You can hear it?"

"Sounds nice," Wunney said.

"A tin roof," Mulheisen said. "You think it's important to talk to Tucker?"

"Yeah. But I see your concern, you'd want a secure situation. I don't know how these guys think, but there could be a good reason for him being at Luck's. You can't just sit there and hope that the whole thing goes away."

"How do I get hold of him?"

"I'm thinking. Okay, how 'bout if I come up there? He asked me to anyway. I said I would if he absolutely needed it, but I had stuff to do."

"You think I need backup?" Mulheisen asked.

"We all need backup," Wunney said, "but I was thinking more of an intermediary. I could get hold of him up there . . . kind of suss out the situation."

"Have you talked to him? What does he think happened?"

"He didn't lay it out, but my impression is that he thinks you're a loose cannon. You're in over your head in something you don't know anything about. He wants you . . ."—Wunney hesitated—"to shut up. I think he'd be happy if you came into the circle."

"Get with the program?"

"Yeah."

"I'm not sure what his program is," Mulheisen said. "I can't very well join up until I do."

"I didn't think so. Should I come up? Or is there something you want me to do down here?"

"Can you come without telling him you're coming?"

"Sure. We can always contact him from there—if you want to. How long will it take me?"

"Four hours."

"I'll be there. Any hurry?"

"No," Mulheisen said. "Get here in the morning. Ten, all right? I'll meet you in Cadillac. I'm within an hour of there. As I recall, there's a little park by the lake, right in town."

"See you," Wunney said.

"Wait. What do you know about Constance Malachi?"

There was a long silence, then Wunney said, "Luck's wife? She died a couple of years ago."

"They've put her on some kind of security list," Mulheisen said. "No outside inquiries. Why?"

"Where'd you hear that?" Wunney asked.

"Marshall told me. He was trying to look up some leads for me. Says it's blocked. Homeland Security."

Wunney digested that, then said, "I didn't know that. Probably something to do with Luck. You know how these guys are—everything about a suspect is a matter of national security. Is it important? I could check it out."

"That'd be useful maybe," Mulheisen said. "Tell me: how did Luck become a suspect anyway?"

"I'm not sure," Wunney said. "It was before I came on board.

I just assumed it was a matter of 'the usual suspects.' He had a connection with patriot groups, questioned in the Oklahoma City bombing, that sort of thing. Kind of a shady history. He knew some of the principals."

"And that was the connection to Luck?"

"It's enough."

"Okay." Mulheisen sighed. "See you in Cadillac. Oh, one more thing. While you're checking out Malachi, see what you can dig up on a character named al-Huq. He's supposed to be al-Qaeda."

"What's this all about?" Wunney asked.

"There's a foreigner here working for Luck, it seems. They call him 'Hook.' Probably no connection, but. . . . A description, maybe a picture, would be good. I think he's supposed to be a Saudi."

"I'll check it out," Wunney said.

Joe Service wasn't listening to the rain. He'd checked into the fanciest hotel in Traverse City, the old Park Place, a huge, square edifice close to the main drag. He had taken one of the most, if not *the* most luxurious room. Very spacious. He'd spent some time in the spa, exercising, and then a swim, a sauna. Now he was cleaning guns and idly watching television. There was a knock at the door.

"Who is it?" Joe called. He'd gone to the door in a hotel dressing gown, embroidered with a crest on the terry-cloth. He had a snub-nosed Smith and Wesson .38 in the large pocket.

"It's me," the Colonel said.

Joe peered through the peephole. He saw a somewhat forlorn-looking Tucker in a wet raincoat, slapping his khaki bucket hat against his leg.

"You alone?" Joe called.

"I've got some guys downstairs," the Colonel said, looking at the peephole.

"Just a minute," Joe said.

He went to the window and opened the drapes. The lights of the city below were obscured by the rain. Joe thought about the foolishness of taking a room on the sixth floor. He supposed he could get out, but he'd have to get dressed. He'd want to take his weapons, but he couldn't climb down the face of a hotel with a bag of guns, even going down from his balcony to the one below, then the next one. It was stupid. He supposed it was the mistake of using the "Joe Humann" credit card. Lax. He was still in his stupid "straight life" mode. He sighed and went back to the door. The Colonel stood there, hat in hand.

"Back across the hall," Joe said. "I'll unlock the door."

He unlatched the chain and went to stand next to the table, where an Uzi lay close to hand. He called, "Come in," and the Colonel entered.

"Hello, Joe," he said.

"It was the credit card," Joe said.

"Yeah, I spotted it. Or, actually, Dinah did."

"Is she with you?"

"Downstairs. Shall I ask her up?"

"No," Joe said. "Well, what's up?"

The Colonel looked around. "Mind if I sit?" He took a chair. "I missed you out in Dakota," he said.

"I saw you," Joe said.

"I figured you had. Ah, well. So, Joe, what's the problem? Why so . . . so aloof?"

Joe shrugged. "What can I do for you?"

"Where's Mulheisen?"

"How would I know?"

"C'mon, Joe. I had a look at that room. Mulheisen didn't get out of there by himself. I thought of you immediately. Although I wouldn't have thought you and Mulheisen were such good buddies."

Joe shrugged. "He's an old acquaintance. As for strange partners, what's with you and Luck?"

The Colonel looked around again. "You haven't offered me a drink. Got any scotch?"

There was a mini-bar. Joe nodded at it and said, "Help yourself." He stood next to the table. He felt dumb in the dressing gown.

The Colonel went over and rummaged in the mini-bar. He found a couple of small bottles of Johnny Walker. He wrinkled his nose, but he located a glass and poured one of the bottles into it. "Join me?" he asked, half-turning.

"No, I don't drink much," Joe said. "Help yourself."

The Colonel drank down the scotch, shuddered, then poured the other bottle into the glass. He brought it back to the easy chair and sat down, holding it.

"You aren't really up to speed on the intelligence community, are you, Joe? It's a strange world."

"Tell me about it," Joe said.

"People think——. There's the FBI, the CIA. They're official agencies, they have a director, a chain of command. They think that's what the intelligence system is. But you used to work for the mob, Joe. The FBI used to occasionally put out little reports, maybe it'd be in a national magazine—J. Edgar Hoover, talking to some reporter. They had a chart of the 'families,' who was the capo di capo, who was an 'enforcer,' who ran this or that. It looked very organized, interlocking functions, just like a big business. But it wasn't like that, was it?"

"You tell me," Joe said.

"Well, you knew them. Didn't you?"

"I knew a lot of them. I worked for quite a few, when they had a problem." Joe was seemingly relaxed, but he was thinking about who was downstairs. He strolled over to the door, carrying the Uzi, and relatched it. He came back to the table. "What are you driving at?"

"The families were actually factions, working against one another. Cooperating when they had to, but mostly with their own agendas, their own goals," the Colonel said. "Am I right?" He sipped at the whisky, made a face, but went on. "The world of intelligence is rather like that," he said. "It looks like a well-ordered organization, but it's riddled with factions. You know about the Lucani. Let me tell you," he leaned forward, elbows on knees, both hands on the whisky glass, "there are dozens of groups like the Lucani, with different objectives, different loyalties. I'm into a lot of them. They aren't recognized, mostly the organization doesn't know about them, or tolerate them when they find out, if they become too . . . too 'known.' But that's how intelligence is done. Small groups of people, working with and against one another. It's like any other large organization. The mob knew this about themselves. It's why they needed you, to be a kind of all-purpose in-house cop."

"And Luck?"

"Luck is something of an 'informer,'" the Colonel said. "He's not an employee of any government agency, not technically. But he's involved in some intelligence activities. He's also on his own, has his own program. He's sometimes employed, as a contractor. Sort of like you. I don't think anyone in the community really approves of his other activities, but they're tolerated, because he's useful. He's a conduit, a contact within. We have to work with guys like him. Otherwise, we'd never know anything about what's going on. That's all."

He sat back.

Joe could see it. "So how do you know him?" he asked.

"I knew him in Vietnam," the Colonel said. "He had a contract, flying helicopters for the CIA. They operated out of places like Burma, or other peripheral locations. He was a useful guy. He's still useful. We keep an eye on him, and he's our eyes and ears in the patriot movement."

"All right, but who watches you?"

"Who watches the watchers?" The Colonel smiled. "We all watch each other. Sounds crazy, doesn't it? You should see what it's like in Russia, what it was like in the old Soviet Union. Talk about factions. Everybody *had* to belong to some group, had to have some allegiance to those who would protect them when they screwed up, who would further their career, or some project they might have, save them from a purge when a superior got canned. We're not that bad. Most of our informal groups, the ones I know about, have relatively limited objectives. The Lucani are very secret, Joe. Not many know about them. You know our objective: we want to see justice done. We don't want to see criminals being allowed to function even after they've been caught, because of corruption, or political maneuvering, or just plain bureaucratic fumbling. I have a hand in some other groups. I'm not disposed to say too much about them. But they have objectives too."

"Like what?"

"Well, let me put it this way," the Colonel said. "There is a political shift going on in the country. Not everybody is thrilled about it. Some people feel it's a significant threat to what we have traditionally thought of as our American freedoms, our democracy. I'm being very simplistic, of course. It's more complex than that. But it's real. It'll pass, I think. American political life is always in flux. One administration comes in, with its particular agenda, then it's soon replaced by another with a different 'vision.' Mostly, though, they aren't so different. They're just variations on the basic, familiar American system or style. But some folks, lately, think that a real sea change has occurred. Some folks are very, very pissed off. They think this new mob needs to be . . . regulated, let's say. Slowed down a bit, even diverted."

He tossed off the remainder of his scotch and set the glass on the carpet next to the chair. "Well," he said, more briskly, "sorry for the civics lesson. I'm sure I haven't told you much that you weren't at least a little aware of. Every government in history faces this same problem. They typically have a leader, a president, a national figure, a dictator maybe, who has a publicly avowed program. It's sold to the public. But there's always a secret agenda, a political philosophy that isn't made public. The politicians don't trust the public.

"Anyway, the regime intends to implement its program. But there are naturally opponents. That's party politics, right? Nothing unusual, the public expects that. They even count on that to keep the regime 'honest.' What's interesting is that some of those opponents are actually within that regime, often deep within it—there are contesting views. Depending on the strength of the leader, of the regime, these views don't get much opportunity to be expressed, or they get too much. But they're all working to thwart the ostensibly prevailing notion. Even in Hitler's Germany, in the Nazi party, there were contesting factions. It's natural."

"Okay, so you're working with a few different groups," Joe said. "You're telling me not to take your chumminess with Luck at face value. Okay, I won't. So what happened to Echeverria?"

"Ah, so that's it," the Colonel said. "What have you learned?"

"You're the one who needs to answer," Joe said.

"I hate to tell you this, Joe, but Echeverria wasn't in that ambulance you blew up. Sorry about that. You did good work, though."

"Did you know he wasn't in that ambulance? Was I being set up?"

"No, I didn't know. But someone did. Someone knew that there might be an attempt on his life. He had left earlier, on another plane. I didn't find out until, oh, maybe a month later.

Someone thought that Echeverria, as bad a guy as he was, and is, was still useful to the U.S. in our war on drugs. They got to him, turned him. He agreed to cooperate, and they got him out. They should have let me in on it. It would have saved a lot of trouble. But they couldn't risk it. Or maybe they even liked to create the impression that he was dead. Anyway, from your point of view, what difference does it make? You did your job, you got out of that jail rap.

"It turns out that Echeverria was worth the trouble. He's been a help. We got some more lethal guys with his help. And, maybe, we'll get more. But Echeverria, he went free. He's still mad at you, though, Joe. You almost killed him, twice. You ruined his handsome face. He's had a number of transplants, he has a lot of pain. I think he might be a drug addict himself by now. He doesn't like you, Joe. That's one of the things I wanted to warn you about, but you were too leery."

Joe sat down. "Okay, you've warned me. Now what?"

The Colonel got up and went to the mini-bar for a refill. All he could find was some J&B scotch. He frowned but poured it into his glass. He came back and sat down across from Joe.

"Now we've got to iron out this problem with Mulheisen. He's complicated things. I was trying to recruit him, but he went off snooping around on his own. I guess he was just trying to check out the terrain, but he screwed up. Now, Luck is out of his mind—he thinks Mulheisen is going to blow the whistle on him. We need Luck. He's got some good contacts. We've spent a lot of time and money setting his program up. And we need very much to resolve this bombing case. Mulheisen is making a mess of it. I'm hoping that you can help us figure out how to straighten it out."

"What can I do?" Joe said. "Mulheisen's his own guy. I don't know who he gets along with. I mean, he gets along, he's an agreeable guy, but he has his own mind about things."

"Where's he at?" Tucker asked.

"Who knows? He couldn't get away from me fast enough," Joe said. "Actually, the feeling was mutual. I tried to give him some advice and he basically flipped me off. I'd guess he was on his way back to Detroit."

"How about you?" Tucker asked. "What do you want? Have I answered your questions?" ·

"Well, I'd kind of like to know what was the idea setting me up? I mean, Luck's saying all kinds of things about me online. I'm sure he's not doing all that on his own."

Tucker smiled. "I knew you'd be difficult, Joe. I needed to encourage you. That's all."

"Well, if that's all . . . ," Joe said. "Then so long. I won't stand in your way. I've got other things to do."

"Oh, now, Joe, don't be that way. I need your help. You're the best at finding out what everybody else can't. I need to find this bomber."

"What do I know about Arabs?" Joe said. "Or was it something to do with drugs? I don't know anything about that either. I'm out of the loop. The mob won't give me the time of day. Besides, you say Echeverria's looking for me. Maybe I should look for him. You're from Montana. You know you've got to put out those little fires before they become big ones."

"Speaking of that," the Colonel said, "you're sitting out there on French Forque in plain view. A house, a dog, a wife . . ."

"I don't have a wife," Joe snapped. "Anyway, you can leave Helen out of this. I made a mistake bringing her into that deal with you. Whatever happens to me, happens to me. Helen and I are history. She has nothing to do with Echeverria. Neither does the house, neither does the dog, for that matter. I'm out of there."

The Colonel was taken aback. "It's like that, is it? You're a tough man, Joe. You give up a lot."

Joe shrugged. "Sometimes that's what you've got to do. I enjoyed it, but it's over. Kaput. I'm on my own. That's the way I like it."

"I admire you," the Colonel said. "But I'm not sure it'll make much difference to Echeverria and his goons when they get to French Forque, which I'm sure they will eventually."

Joe's eyes narrowed. "I hope that is just a surmise, Colonel, and not a threat."

"It's almost a certainty. It doesn't have anything to do with me. I never said anything to Echeverria. I've never even spoken to the man. I'm just assuming that he'll do what anyone else would do in his position. He's got a lot of pain, a lot of anger, and he's out of a culture that believes in the vendetta. He thinks he'll be less of a man, in the eyes of others and in his own heart, if he doesn't pay you back. If that involves Helen, I'd guess that he'd like that even better."

"You just convinced me that I don't have any more time to sit around talking to you," Joe said. "Sorry to be inhospitable, Colonel, but I've got work to do."

"Does that mean you won't work for me? For us?"

Joe laughed. "Who's this 'us'? The Lucani? Homeland Security? America?"

"It's all pretty much the same," Tucker said. He got to his feet.

"So you're the good guys," Joe said.

The Colonel shrugged modestly. "We're not the bad guys."

"How could anyone tell?" Joe said.

"Joe—" the Colonel began.

But Joe waved him off. "Good night, Colonel. Hope you catch the bad guys. Say hi to Dinah for me."

The Colonel looked down at his wet shoes. They were well-burnished cordovan penny loafers. He seemed to be debating something internally. Finally, he looked up and said, "Joe, I always liked you, even when you were a bit . . . um, a bit of a smart-ass. I can't let this go like this. There are some agents downstairs. They expect me to come down with you. If I don't, they'll come up here. In fact, I wouldn't be surprised if they were already on the floor."

Joe didn't react. His hand was in his pocket, lightly fingering the .38. The Uzi was within reach on the table. He didn't like being in a dressing gown, but what the heck. He felt ready for whatever was going to happen.

The Colonel could see the resolve in his eyes. "It's not like that, Joe, believe me. I was just thinking . . . you're concerned about Echeverria, for yourself and—whatever you say—for Helen, too. I can give you Echeverria."

Joe couldn't restrain a smile. "That's more like the Colonel I have learned to expect. Why didn't you say so before?"

The Colonel smiled too. "He's protected, Joe, by people higher up than me. I can't *give* him to you, literally. But I can tell you where to find him. You've got to promise me that you won't let it out."

"You mean, 'scout's honor' and all that?" Joe said, smiling.

"Scout's honor," Tucker said.

Joe held up his left forefinger, then two fingers, then the one. "Is it one or two?" he asked.

"Just don't blab."

"You got it, Colonel."

"All right," the Colonel said. "But first things first. I've got to get this bomber."

"It's probably Luck, isn't it?" Joe said.

"Why do you say that?"

"Just a stab in the dark," Joe said.

"And how about Mulheisen?"

"Ah. I'm sorry, I can't give you Mulheisen," Joe said. "I don't have him. I told you, the guy is . . . what's the phrase . . . a dog who hunts by himself. Shouldn't be that hard to find, though. Where's he gonna go? He's not a street person. He's got a house, an invalid mother."

"She's a problem all by herself," the Colonel said.

"How so?"

"She was there, at Wards Cove. If she saw anything, she doesn't remember it. That doesn't mean she won't remember something. And when she does, she'll tell her son."

"And you think he'll tell you?" Joe smiled.

"It's more likely, if he's on the team," the Colonel said. "Anyway, this situation is more pressing. We need him fast, before this gets out of control," the Colonel said. "You could find him."

Joe thought for a moment, then grinned. "Done," he said.

"And quickly. I need to resolve this issue with Luck. I don't want this guy going off half-cocked. If this hits the news, it's too late."

"Actually, Colonel, if you'll wait until I get dressed we can go see him right now."

The Colonel had started toward the door. He stopped and looked at Joe, then uttered a short laugh. "You're something, Joe. Where is he?"

"I'll take you to him," Joe said, "but just you. Not the others."

"Um . . . I don't know about that."

"Oh, sure you do," Joe said. "Just have another drink and sit while I dress." He tossed his robe onto the bed.

The Colonel glanced away from Joe's nakedness, then started toward the door again. "I'll just go down and tell the fellas," he said.

Joe was pulling on his briefs. They were cut very low, muscleman style, in black. "Don't," he said. When the Colonel hesitated, Joe added, "Just pour yourself a drink. I won't be a minute."

Tucker shrugged, went to the mini-bar, and rummaged about. He found another J&B, grimaced, and poured it into a glass, then stood sipping while Joe finished dressing in slacks, a navy blue turtleneck sweater, and a pair of light hiking boots.

"Does the name al-Huq mean anything to you?" Joe asked as he slipped on a harness and fitted the Llama automatic into the holster.

Tucker frowned. "Not offhand," he said, "unless . . . you mean the al-Qaeda guy? Where'd you hear about him?"

"Private sources," Joe said. He packed a small nylon bag with some clothing and the Uzi, along with some loaded clips. "What does he look like?"

Tucker searched his memory, sipping his drink. "Kind of slim, dark. Speaks very good English, I'm told. I never met him. I think he studied in the U.S., law or something. He's Saudi. Very well connected with bin Laden. What do you know about him?"

"Nothing," Joe said. "One of my contacts mentioned him. Does he have any connection with Echeverria?"

"Not that I know of, but he could," Tucker said. "He was active in Kosovo. I think he had some interest in the drug business there. Yeah, there could be a connection. If you know anything, Joe, it could be very valuable."

"Valuable? I like the sound of that," Joe said, zipping up his bag. "I'll inquire further. How much would it be worth? Just theoretically?"

"By all means, inquire further," Tucker said. "If you can make a connection between him and Echeverria, that would be worth . . . oh, how does a hundred thousand sound?"

"Sounds like a start," Joe said. He picked up the bag, hefted it. It clanked a bit. He set it aside and looked about for something. "But just a start."

The Colonel asked, "Is it true, you and Helen split?"

"It wasn't a mutual decision," Joe said, shrugging on a dark blue nylon windbreaker. "I'm not sure she knows yet. It's one of those things, Colonel. Sometimes you have to change your habits. I'm sure she had a different view of the future."

"She's a hell of a woman," the Colonel said. "You could do worse."

"With Helen, you don't get to choose," Joe said, picking up the bag again. "It's not like you can sit down and discuss it. She has her notion. If it coincides with yours, life couldn't be better. If it doesn't, you better find another country."

"Dinah will be interested to hear this," the Colonel said with a sly smile as he unhooked the chain on the door.

Joe shook his head. "Let's leave Dinah out of this. Now, before you open that door," he said, fumbling the .38 out of the pocket of the robe and stuffing it into his jacket pocket, "let's get the details clear. Okay?"

"What details?"

"We'll walk out together. I'll be very close to you. Whoever is out there, you explain to them that you and I are going for a ride. It's all very friendly. Right? They can go on back to . . . well, wherever they have to go. You'll contact them later. Is that all right?"

The Colonel nodded.

"Fine," Joe said. "Let's go. And remember, I'm very close, and this is a friendly departure. I'm not pulling anything funny. I just don't want anyone to get excited and do something foolish."

They walked out. The Colonel called to a man at the end of the hall. "It's okay, Allen. Joe and I are just going for a drive. Go on back to the others and explain. I'll give you a call later."

The man vanished down the stairs. "Follow him," Joe said, prodding the Colonel with the gun in his back. They could hear the man descending, but no one stopped them. There was a door on the ground floor that led to the parking lot. Joe gestured and they went out into the rain. "Let's take your car," Joe said.

15

Bad Dog

Mulheisen was still sitting in the dark and listening to the rain, but now he was smoking a cigar. The phone rang. It was Joe.

"Mul, sorry to bug you, man. Were you sleeping? No, I didn't think you would be. Listen, I'm at the pay phone at the convenience store on the highway. I've got someone who wants to talk to you—Tucker. Yeah. We'll be along in fifteen minutes or so. Maybe we can work the good cop, bad cop routine. I'll be the bad cop."

Mulheisen laughed. "I'm sure he knows all about that. But sometimes it works anyway. One thing: does he know about Hook?"

"I don't know," Joe said. "I didn't mention it."

"Good. Let's keep that between us. It might be worth something."

In fact, it was twenty minutes before Mulheisen saw headlights moving slowly up the drive, bobbing with the undulations of the dirt road. He put down the cigar and picked up the Stoner rifle Joe had left with him. When the car stopped, he flicked on the yard light.

The two men walked through the rain to the cabin.

"Very nice," the Colonel said as he entered, looking about. "But kind of dark, isn't it?"

"There's plenty of light from the yard," Mulheisen said. "Sit down, Colonel."

"Plenty of light," Joe said. "Leave the yard light on. I'll make some coffee."

"There's some whisky," Mulheisen said. "You prefer that, Colonel?"

"Sure," the Colonel said.

Joe set about making coffee in the automatic machine. "The Colonel's got a little story to tell," he said over his shoulder. "Go ahead, Colonel, tell Mul about the intricacies of intelligence work."

"I'm sure Sergeant Mulheisen is familiar with it," the Colonel said sourly. He accepted the whisky. It was Johnny Walker Black Label. "You're a better host than Joe," he said.

Joe outlined the Colonel's association with Luck while he finished putting the coffee in motion. "Turns out it was all a misunderstanding, Luck grabbing you like that," Joe said.

"I'm sorry you were, ah, discommoded," Tucker said. "His men did what they thought was right, but it wasn't right. And then, the damage was done."

Mulheisen puffed his cigar. "Did you talk to the men?" he asked.

"Not directly," Tucker said. "Luck explained it to me. I guess it was a couple of the Huley boys. They're kind of . . . naive, I guess you could say. Not the brightest bulbs on the tree."

Mulheisen nodded. "Now what?"

"Well, that's up to you," Tucker said. He glanced at the phone. "I should call and tell my people to stand down."

"Let's wait on that," Mulheisen said. He looked to Joe, who was leaning on the kitchen counter, waiting for the coffee to finish. "You weren't followed?"

"I don't think so," Joe said. "It's not easy to keep up a tail in this weather, on these lonely roads. It didn't look like anyone was behind us. But . . . " He shrugged. "They have access to planes, choppers, that sort of thing. For all I know, the Colonel had some kind of locator device on his car."

"Nonsense," the Colonel said. He looked tired. Obviously, it had been a long day, a lot of tension. He poured himself another shot of the Johnny Walker. He looked across the kitchen table at Mulheisen and said, "Mul, I am sorry about all this. I really have only one mission here, and that's to find the bomber who injured your mother and killed those innocent people. There's still a spot for you on the team, if you're willing to help us, after this . . . this screwup." He sounded sincere, but he managed to insert a tone of disgust at the end, in reference to the "screwup."

Mulheisen eyed him. "You don't think the bomber was Luck?"

"No. No, I don't. I've known Imp for a long time," Tucker said. "He's a bit rash, at times, and he has, ah, a radical outlook, but I don't think he'd do anything like that. What would be the motive?"

Mulheisen shrugged. "Who knows? That's what I'm checking out. What do you know about his wife?"

"His wife? Connie? What does she have to do with it? She died a long time ago."

"Not so long ago," Mulheisen said. "It's not real clear just what happened. The records have all been hushed up."

"Oh, that was my doing," Tucker said. "I used the law, the new laws, to keep that out of the press. I was convinced, from my own investigations, that it was not germane."

"Who was she?" Mulheisen asked. He accepted the cup of coffee that Joe placed before him. He sipped it gratefully. The smoke from his cigar drifted across the table.

"Just between us?" the Colonel said, absently waving away the smoke. "She was one of my agents. Luck didn't know that. She'd worked for us before, and when she met Luck . . . well, as odd as it sounds, she fell for him. When she moved up here, with Luck, she wanted out. But I asked her to keep an eye on him. She agreed. That's all there was to it."

"So it was just coincidental that she hooked up with him?" Mulheisen said. He was noncommittal about it. He drew on his cigar, then looked at it thoughtfully. "She hadn't been assigned beforehand, to keep an eye on him?"

"No. It was just, as you say, coincidence. But it seemed like too good an opportunity to pass up. The fact is, she never had anything significant to report. I trusted her. She was reliable. I think if she'd found out anything, she'd have told me. But, of course, you can't be sure. When a woman falls in love, gets married . . . her loyalties can change."

"Did they change? Did you have a chance to talk to her about it?"

"Yes, I talked to her. I don't think anything changed. She was a loyal woman, a patriotic American."

"Was she still on the payroll?" Mulheisen asked.

"Um, yes, she was. It wasn't much. But she continued to make reports."

"Written reports?"

"Mostly verbal, to me. But, yes, there were some written reports," Tucker said.

"What about this Lucani group?" Mulheisen asked.

The Colonel seemed startled. He glanced at Joe, who didn't reveal anything in his expression. "I don't know what Joe has told you," Tucker said to Mulheisen, "but it's just an informal group of agents, with like minds about some things. I'm sure you're familiar with the kind of rapport that some law enforcement people develop with one another." He glanced at Joe again, then added, "Joe might have gotten a mistaken view of it . . ."

He said to Joe then, "I'm sorry, Joe. I probably misled you a bit. But you are, essentially, an outsider on this issue. Sometimes

it's necessary, a need-to-know sort of thing. Mulheisen, I'm sure"—
he glanced at Mulheisen—"understands how that works. It's a necessary evil, a way of doing what needs to be done."

Mulheisen asked, "Was Constance Malachi a member of the
Lucani?"

"Not really," Tucker said. "She might have thought she was. I
may have given her that impression. Once again, it's just a way—"

"Of doing business," Mulheisen finished for him, with a wry
tone. "And you're confident that Luck never knew she was an agent?"

"Well, you can't ever be sure," Tucker said. "But, yes, I'm
fairly confident. I never had any indication otherwise, from her or
from him."

"All right, then. What's all this stuff about this Echeverria?
Did you set Joe up to assassinate him?"

"Echeverria is a complicated issue," the Colonel said. "I'm
really not at liberty to discuss—. All right"—he noticed Mulheisen's
impatient expression, and went on, hastily—"all right, he's another
of those snafus that crop up in bureaucratic situations, one group
trying to carry out a mission, an official mission, and then another
group intervenes with a superior mandate. You know the sort of
thing. I never agreed with the disposition of that case, but what
could I do! My hands were tied. And then it seems he had a connection with the bombing. One of his men was being heard that
day, making a deposition. I thought we might be able to make a
connection. Plus, Joe here had reason to be interested. Echeverria
held a grudge against him. But let me say, there was no assassination plot."

"No?" Mulheisen raised an eyebrow toward Joe.

The Colonel shrugged, sipped his whisky, poured some more.
"We needed Joe's help. It had to look like Echeverria was hit. That
was the cover. Then, when I needed his help again, on this investigation, he was being a bit cute with me. I applied a little pressure.

Joe can be difficult, you know." He smiled wryly at Mulheisen, then said, "Sorry, Joe."

Joe was looking out the window. He didn't acknowledge the remark. Mulheisen was thoughtful, gazing quietly at Tucker, puffing gently on his cigar.

"What do you know about Constance Malachi's death?" Mulheisen asked finally.

"Not much," Tucker said. "Why? Is there a problem?"

"I don't know," Mulheisen said. "Is there?"

"Not that I know of," Tucker said.

Mulheisen sat quietly, drawing on the cigar and looking at Tucker. It was a long silence. Joe turned from the window, waiting. The silence was accentuated by the rain drumming steadily on the metal roof.

Finally, Tucker said, "She had some kind of congenital heart problem. Tragic. She was so young . . ."

"She was a federal agent, you said," Mulheisen noted. "I guess she must have had some training? Yes? And a physical. You usually have to pass a physical. That'll be on record. It must not have been detected. Eh?"

"I don't know," Tucker said. "I guess not. Her doctor said—"

"I know what her doctor said," Mulheisen said, "or at least what someone who was supposed to be her doctor said to the doctor who actually examined her, postmortem. I suppose one could have her remains exhumed, just to clarify the cause of death. If one knew where she was buried. Do you know where she's buried?"

But Tucker had heard enough. He pushed back from the table. "Gentlemen, I'm tired," he said. "I've had a long day. This is absurd. I'm not in the mood for sitting around discussing the death, by natural causes, of a woman who obviously has no bearing on my mission."

"Ah," Mulheisen said calmly, "what do you want to discuss?"

"I'd be happy to discuss the bombing. That's my task. If we're through here—"

"Relax, Colonel," Mulheisen said. "Have another drink." He pushed the bottle. Tucker hesitated, then poured himself a shot. While he drank, Mulheisen asked, "What do you know about Luck's operation? You had an agent there. What's the point of the armed guards? What's he hiding?"

Tucker shook his head wearily. "It's just some pseudo-militaristic patriot group," he said. "It's nothing. A bunch of lard-ass conservative flag-wavers. But really, fellas, I'm not here to be interrogated by a man who isn't even an official pol—"

"Tucker, listen up," Mulheisen said calmly, drawing on the stub of his nearly depleted cigar. "People don't die unattended without the body being autopsied. And when the body disappears—"

"Bodies can disappear," Joe interjected. "Especially out here. Float away in the river. Sometimes they aren't found." There was no menace in Service's tone, just a flat, almost careless assertion that sounded fairly reasonable.

Tucker's eyes flickered from Mulheisen to Service, then back. He finished his drink, then reached for the bottle. Mulheisen moved it away, casually, before he could touch it. The Colonel sat back, watching.

"What is this," he said, looking at Joe, "good cop, bad cop?" He snorted contemptuously.

"I'm not a cop," Joe said, "and neither is Mul." He was leaning his butt against the counter, fiddling with the .38, flicking the cylinder open, spinning it, then snapping it shut. "I thought about shooting you more than once, Tucker," he said, without emotion. "You tried to set me up once before, with that idiot agent of yours. What was his name? Pollak. The guy who never came back. I'll tell you what . . ." He set the .38 on the table next to Tucker's hand. Then he opened his jacket to reveal the Llama automatic in his shoulder holster.

Tucker smiled derisorily. "Am I supposed to throw down on you? Joe, you've been living in Montana too long." He waved his hand toward the pistol.

The Llama flashed out, into Joe's hand.

Tucker was visibly taken aback. His chair scraped as he reeled back from the table, his hands up, his eyes wide. He wasn't tired anymore.

Joe said, his voice low and tight, "Pick it up. I'll blast your ass through that window. Pick it up."

Tucker stared at him. Suddenly, Joe leaped. He seized Tucker by the collar. Tucker fell back, tipping over the chair and landing on the floor. Joe was on him, twisting his collar, the Llama thrust into his face. Joe's eyes were wild.

"Joe! Don't," Mulheisen cried, scrambling to his feet.

"Get away, Mul," Joe snarled. "I'm gonna blast this asshole!"

"Joe! I can't let you do it," Mulheisen shouted. "I swear, I'll hunt you down. Let him up."

Joe didn't move. His and the Colonel's eyes were locked. Then, abruptly, Joe released the man and stood up. He slipped the Llama into the holster and then picked up the .38. He stepped back casually.

Tucker got to his feet, awkwardly, straightening his clothes.

Mulheisen helped Tucker pick up the overturned chair and got him seated. He poured him a jolt of whisky and waited until he'd drunk it. Then he sat down. "Sorry about that, Tucker," he said. "Are you all right?" He glanced at Joe warningly, but Joe was nonchalantly leaning against the counter again, as if nothing had happened.

"I'm all right," Tucker said. He didn't look at Joe.

Abruptly, Mulheisen asked, "You were Constance Malachi's superior. You have access to her files. Her medical file, her reports. It would be interesting to see them. Let's say that you had no reason to suspect any problem with her demise. But now a question has arisen. It wouldn't be much of a problem for you to obtain the records and review them."

"No," Tucker said, responding to Mulheisen with alacrity, eagerly seizing on a different topic. "No, it wouldn't. I could get them. That's a good idea. Just to clear things up. Would that satisfy you, sergeant?" He glanced at Joe, who was toying with the chamber of the .38, idly spinning it.

Mulheisen drew on his cigar and found it was dead. He laid it in the ashtray at his elbow. "Yes, it would be helpful. If there was no problem, as you say. But, if there was a problem, then I suppose the next step—"

"We'd have to talk to Imp. Luck." Tucker seemed eager to pursue that. "There might be questions he'd have to answer."

"But would Luck cooperate?" Mulheisen asked rhetorically. "Mightn't he say too much, about other questionable issues? If he felt threatened, I mean?"

"Ah. I see what you mean," Tucker said. He seemed more composed now, collaborative. "Well, that's something we can face when and if it arises. But he'll have to answer for Connie, won't he? That's really, after all, a separate matter. Yes, I think it could be managed."

He gestured toward the bottle and Mulheisen nodded. Tucker poured himself a sizable jolt, then drank. "Ah, that's not such bad stuff," he said, "though a little commercial. I prefer the single malts. You don't drink, sergeant?"

"Where was Luck when the bomb went off?" Mulheisen asked.

"Fishing," Tucker said. "He had an alibi."

"Who attested to it? One of his men?"

Tucker shrugged. "It seemed to be substantiated. It would be hard to dispute."

"I wonder," Mulheisen said. "There must have been some kind of trail associated with the explosive, the truck that was used, the other men involved."

"Oh, we've gone over that meticulously," Tucker said. "No witnesses could identify the accomplices. The truck was stolen, no fingerprints. It was a well-planned job. No, we've found that to be a dead end." The Colonel spoke confidently now, recounting the details of the incident. "The explosives were common materials, nothing that could be traced. No pattern that could be associated with known bombers, particularly. We've been all through that." He nodded at Mulheisen. "That's something you might be able to help us with, though, if you came on board, Mul. You might see something that we missed, as thorough as we have been."

"What's this group that Luck runs?" Mulheisen asked.

"Well, again, it's . . ." Tucker hesitated. "Well, it's just a local patriot group. They're just conservative types, like a lot of good, ordinary, staunch citizens. He calls it the Holy American Flag and Farm, Hunting and Fishing Society, or something like that." He laughed lightly. "It's a kind of joke, I think. A bunch of guys get together and drink beer. A night away from the wives. The government doesn't pay much attention to it: it's harmless, releases some tension, some crankiness about government. Hell, it's an American tradition to complain about government."

"It's not a mask for something more serious?" Mulheisen asked.

"No. I don't think so," Tucker said confidently. "Hey, I've known Imp for years. He's got some beefs, some of them legitimate. But he's been a loyal citizen."

Mulheisen looked up at Joe. "Do you have anything?"

"Me? No," Joe said. "I've heard enough. What do you want to do with this guy?" He gestured at the Colonel. "Lose him?" Then he laughed. "Just kidding, Colonel. Well," he said to Mulheisen, "have you got room? I don't think this guy is fit to drive, and I'm tired."

"Yeah, there's room," Mulheisen said. "That all right with you, Tucker?"

"I'd like to call my people," Tucker said. "Get them to stand down. I'm sure they've been anxious."

"Oh, I'm sure they're used to it," Mulheisen said. "You can call them in the morning. Is that all right?"

"Ah, yes. Sure. So, where do we . . . ?"

Mulheisen pointed to the loft. "There's beds up there. Bedding. It's comfortable enough for hunters, I guess."

"Well, since we're not going anywhere," Tucker said, reaching for the bottle again, "join me in a nightcap?"

"No, thanks," Mulheisen said. "Well, get a good night's sleep. Tomorrow we'll go get those records on Constance Malachi. Okay?"

"All right," the Colonel said agreeably. He drank, standing by the table. "Well, I'm glad we had this talk. You've given us a good direction here, Mul. Maybe something will come of it. It'll clear the air, at least. See, I knew you'd be a good guy to bring in."

16

Dogged

Helen drove out to the Mulheisen place first thing in the morning. She got there early, a little after eight. She'd been prepared to have to wait, but she saw that the household was up and moving about. Mrs. Mulheisen was quite perky and friendly. She was just finishing her breakfast and invited Helen to have some tea and toast with her before she went on her morning walk. Helen had introduced herself as a friend of Mulheisen's, which both the nurse and the mother accepted without question, although Mrs. Mulheisen soon began to probe the nature of this association.

"You're very young," Mrs. Mulheisen said. "How long have you known Mul?"

"Oh, not long," Helen said. "I met him a couple of years ago when he was investigating a case about a colleague, a man named Grootka."

"Oh, I remember Grootka," Cora Mulheisen said. "Rather a formidable fellow, don't you think?"

"I didn't know him," Helen said. "I was just administering a foundation. One of our grantees was researching a history of the police department, and she got interested in Grootka's career. Which was how your son came into it."

"Ah. Well, tell me, dear, are you married?"

Helen smiled. "No."

"Goodness, why not? You're very pretty."

"Well, I guess I've just been busy," Helen said.

"Mul isn't married either," Cora said. "I've given up nagging him about it. In fact, I despair of him ever getting married. Probably too late for grandchildren now."

"Well, he's a fine fellow," Helen said. "I wouldn't despair, if I were you."

"Do you think so?" The old woman sized Helen up out of the corner of her eye. She seemed to like what she saw. "Well, we've finished the tea," she said, "and it's a fine day. Not too late to see a few birds. Why don't you join me?"

Helen agreed. The nurse said she would accompany them, but she soon fell back, obviously happy for Helen to walk with her charge while she herself had a cigarette.

Mrs. Mulheisen carried a set of small binoculars. She seemed quite agile for a woman of her age who had recently suffered a serious accident. She walked slowly. She explained that when looking for birds one always walked slowly, often stopping. "They'll come out, if you just wander," she said.

"Does Mul enjoy the birds?" Helen asked.

"I think he likes the idea of bird-watching, but he's never really gotten into it. I don't push it. If you try to get a child to like something they're sure to hate it. Maybe when he gets a little older. He's gone off, up north, to some little town called Queensleap."

"What an odd name," Helen said.

"The people there are even odder, it seems," Mrs. Mulheisen said. She paused on the path and focused her glasses, scanning across the waist-high marsh grass. More to herself than to Helen, she muttered, "Birds hibernating! What nonsense!"

"What's that?" Helen said.

Mrs. Mulheisen explained the cockamamie theory of the fellow up north, as it had been told to Mulheisen. "It's absurd," she said.

"Why on earth is Mul up there?" Helen asked.

"Oh, it's something to do with terrorists," Cora said. She lowered the glasses and moved on, alongside Helen, toward the channel. "He's wondering whether to get involved in this investigation the government is doing. A fellow named Tucker is heading it up. Nothing will come of it, I daresay. But it's good for Mul to get out of the house. It's ridiculous for him to retire at his age. He's really not very old . . . in his prime, one might say . . . the child of my old age. A man can go to seed without something to occupy his time and energies. Well, he does spend a good deal of time on his study."

Helen seemed puzzled, so Cora explained. "You doubtless saw the little cottage that's going up out near the barn."

Helen looked where she pointed. She had noticed it, a small building, hardly large enough to be more than a single-bedroom house, with a four-sided roof. She hadn't realized, she said, that it was on their property.

"Oh, yes. We have several acres here," Mrs. Mulheisen said. "It was supposed to be just a kind of glorified hut. Mul needed some place to go smoke his cigars. The poor boy won't smoke in the house, although I don't mind, as long as he doesn't smoke too many. He used to smoke one or two in the evening, when he was living here. Well, he got involved, as one will, with the project. He's over there at all times, bothering the contractor. The project has grown. I'm amazed at how quickly it went up, but now of course the contractor is doing the interior, and that takes forever. I hope I'm not dead before it's finished."

Helen hastened to assure her that it was obvious that she would be around for many years to come. But Mrs. Mulheisen waved that away with a careless gesture.

"If I linger too long, the hut will be a mansion," she said. "I think Mul's planning to live there once it's done, now that I'm so much better. Well, it's a good project for a man. It would serve as a honeymoon cottage."

Helen didn't rise to this bait. "Still, I'd think bird-watching would interest him, with an expert at hand to point out the various species," she said. "Wasn't he interested as a boy?"

"Why, I don't know that he was," Mrs. Mulheisen said. "Perhaps he might have been, but I only took it up late in life myself. The poor boy doesn't know a hawk from a handsaw. Now this young fellow who came by the other evening, one of Colonel Tucker's young men, he immediately fell into it. We were fortunate enough to chance upon a marsh hawk. A very handsome and dramatic bird, a male—"

"What was his name?"

"Well, the American Ornithological Union now prefers the term 'northern harrier,'" Mrs. Mulheisen said, "but it's the same old *Circus cyaneus*, of course. The A.O.U. keep messing with these names. They even tried to change the Baltimore oriole to the northern oriole, but that didn't go over. They claimed it was the same as the Bullock's, but that's nonsense."

Helen was momentarily baffled. She had no idea what the woman was talking about. Then she caught on. She laughed. "I'm sorry, I meant the young man."

"What about him?" It was Mrs. Mulheisen's turn to be baffled. "He didn't seem to know much about birds either, but at least he was interested, I could tell. He even borrowed my binoculars to look at the hawk. It was sitting on a post along the river channel. Maybe he'll be there again today. They'll do that, you know, come back to the same perch, although most of the time these marsh hawks are tireless fliers, working over the fields, looking for a mouse . . ."

"He didn't tell you his name? The young man? Was he sort of small and dark?"

"Why, yes. Very handsome, very lively little fellow," Cora agreed. "Actually, he rather resembled you, my dear. You could pass for brother and sister." She looked at Helen appraisingly. "No, I didn't catch his name. But Colonel Tucker is always sending his fellows around, to sort of keep an eye on me. You'd think *I* was a terrorist."

They both smiled at that notion. They walked on and Helen told her that she'd read about the bombing. "Were you very badly injured?" she asked.

They had reached the channel and began to walk along it, toward the lake. "Yes, it was quite harrowing," Cora said. "By rights, I should have perished, but I survived. Poor Mr. Larribee was killed. Some others, too, although I'm not sure who all. None of my group was even hurt. We were there protesting the planned disruption of the habitat of the Nelson's sharp-tailed sparrow, you know— *Ammodramus nelsoni.* At least, that's been put off for some time, one hopes for good. But you know how these developers are: you think you've stopped them but they just start up again."

"I don't believe I've ever seen a Nelson's," Helen said.

"Few have. They're quite . . . well, I don't suppose I should say 'rare.' They're certainly not widespread, or common. Uncommon, is the word, occurring in isolated breeding groups. I always hoped to see one around here—they like these kinds of grassy marshes—but, alas, no. Plenty of grasshopper sparrows, though. Nelson's is a small, rather orangish sparrow. So you see how important it is to preserve the locations where they do appear."

"Yes, I can see that," Helen said. "I'm so glad you didn't suffer any lasting effects from the bombing."

Cora had stopped and was thoroughly scanning the marsh, as if intent on discovering the Nelson's. "Oh, I lost my memory," she remarked, over her shoulder, not lowering the glasses. "It's a little late for the sparrows, I'm afraid. They've migrated south, I expect. Unless," she said, with a snort of amusement, "they're hibernating."

"But that's horrible," Helen said. "I mean, your memory."

"Oh, I'm recovering it, as I'm sure you've noticed," Cora said. "Why, just the other night, I remembered a very odd person." She lowered the glasses and turned. "He was at the hearing. Well, outside, in the hall. Very agitated. Nice-looking gentleman, though. He told me . . ." She hesitated a moment, her brow furrowed in concentration. "Why," she said, as if it had just struck her, "he told me to 'get out'! He was quite vociferous about it. 'Get out of this,' he said. Do you suppose he knew what was going to happen?"

Helen caught her excitement. "It certainly sounds like it. What did he look like? Did you recognize him?"

"No, he wasn't with our group. Although he looked like he could be a bird-watcher. He wore rather rustic clothing. He had on one of those canvas field hats. One of our gentlemen, Chad Parsons, wears one. It's called a Filson, I believe. Rather rakish, with a brim around it. Waterproof, Mr. Parsons says. Quite useful, I'm sure. We often meet with inclement weather."

"If he was with the bombers," Helen said thoughtfully, "I imagine that right now he's hoping that you won't remember him. What else do you recall about him?"

"He was tall," Cora said, "about fifty, or older. And, as I say, agitated. Rather a long face. Strong nose, blue eyes. Oh, I'd recognize him, all right, if I saw him again. I told that young man of Colonel Tucker's about it, but he didn't seem very interested. Of course, at that time I hadn't recalled as much as I subsequently have. I've pieced it all together now, though. The young man suggested I tell the Colonel about it, but I haven't had the opportunity. And, after all, I'm not sure it would actually be pertinent. Do you suppose it's something I should tell Colonel Tucker?"

"It might be a good idea," Helen said. "It might be important. So, the Colonel's young man wasn't interested?"

"No. Well, as I say, it was pretty sketchy at that juncture. I'll mention it to Mul when he gets home. He can decide."

"When will he be back?" Helen asked.

"He was supposed to return last night, but he got involved with something up in that town, Queensleap. A friend of his came by last night and left a note about it. I was asleep, but the nurse gave it to me this morning, a little while before you came by. I'm to call him at a number, in an emergency. But I'm not to call from home. He said to go to a phone booth. That seems odd. There's one down by the marina." She pointed up the channel. "I could walk there. But I don't think this is pressing news. It can wait until Mul gets home."

"I could call him," Helen said. "Do you have the number with you?"

The old woman looked at her for a moment, then said, "Oh, that's all right, my dear. Thank you for volunteering. But I think I'd better wait." She made a humorous grimace. "Police business, no doubt. Mul is funny that way, rather like the Colonel. All very hush-hush. He'd be upset, I'm sure, if you called him."

Helen smiled. She suddenly thought: *I could get that message from her right now. I'll bet it's in her pocket.* But she didn't do anything. Instead, she said, "You ought to have some protection. Doesn't the Colonel—"

Cora interrupted her. "The note said, come to think of it, that I shouldn't communicate this number to the Colonel. I thought that was especially odd. What do you think?"

"More hush-hush," Helen said.

"That's what I think. Oh! There's the harrier." She pointed as a large and elegant hawk swept past them and alit on a post.

"That's the very same post where I saw it the other evening, when that young man came by. What did I tell you? They often come back to the same perch." She held out the glasses to Helen, inviting her to look.

It's an agonizing thing to delay when you are dying to be going. But Helen controlled her impatience admirably while the old woman dawdled, looking at birds, chattering away. But eventually they drifted back to the house, with Helen silently urging the woman to get a move on. There, Mrs. Mulheisen invited her to stay for a cup of tea, but Helen demurred. She reiterated that she'd just stopped by on the chance of catching Mulheisen in. She had an appointment in nearby Mount Clemens, she lied.

However, she said, she had a need to use the bathroom, if Mrs. Mulheisen didn't mind.

"Oh, by all means," Cora said, "freshen up. You want to look your best. Use the bath in my room, dear." She pointed the way.

Helen hurried to the bathroom. She had to go, desperately. But afterward she lingered to look about the old woman's room. As she'd hoped, there was the envelope with Mrs. Mulheisen's name scribbled on it in ballpoint, lying on her dresser. Helen took the chance and opened it. She instantly memorized the number and replaced the note.

Mrs. Mulheisen watched her leave and remarked to the nurse, "She's very pretty, but she hasn't a chance with Mul, I'm afraid. Much too small, I think. And probably too young."

An hour later, Helen had Roman behind the wheel of her father's elegant Cadillac, headed upcountry. Ten minutes of that time had been spent online, locating the address of that phone number on a Yahoo! Web site. Unfortunately, the map on the site had not been able to pinpoint the location, just indicating the road and the presence of the Manistee River nearby. But she felt confident she could find the place. It was apparently the home of a

Charles McVey. Just for reference she'd also looked up Luckenbach, but all she could find was an M. P. Luck. Still, that address seemed to be close to the McVey house, where Mulheisen was presumably staying. She supposed that, if necessary, she could stop and visit with this Luck. He ought to be able to tell her how to get to McVey's. After all, they were neighbors.

17

Friendly Dog

Wunney stood staring at the lake, fists buried in the pockets of an old twill tanker jacket. The lake was empty and gray, rimmed in dark green pines on the far shore. A couple of lonely rays shot through the low gray clouds, spotlights searching an empty stage. Where the light struck the water it glowed emerald green and the luminescent patches wandered across the lake toward the shore but never quite reached it before being blotted up by the leaden chop. Wunney's eyes glistened in the chill breeze.

Wunney turned at the sound of truck tires on the gravel of the parking lot. Mulheisen spotted him immediately: he looked like a merchant seaman. His hair was cut in a brush, as ever—no hat. His face blank, noncommittal. He looked neither comfortable nor ill at ease, just ready for whatever presented itself.

Mulheisen's heart unexpectedly warmed. He knew this man. Reliable, honest, intelligent, if not overly imaginative, or one might say not incapable of imagination but distrustful of it. A man who knew what he knew, and no bullshit. Mulheisen realized that he missed men like this. Wunney was nothing like the man riding with him, the subtle Colonel Tucker, to say nothing of the mercurial Joe Service, whom they'd left behind.

They got out and went to meet Wunney, who stopped short when he saw Tucker. When they came up he nodded to Mul and said, with hardly a glance to his boss, "Tucker." Wunney looked to Mulheisen for enlightenment.

Mulheisen turned to Tucker, "Excuse us for a minute, Colonel."

"Sure," Tucker said. He walked away toward the lake, hoisting the collar of his trench coat against the breeze. He trudged through the sand toward an empty wooden jetty.

Wunney looked after him, then he and Mulheisen strolled back toward the old truck. Wunney said, "I thought you and he weren't communicating."

"The Colonel dropped by last night." Mulheisen explained about Joe Service. "Joe stayed behind at the cabin. He's trying to keep his buddy list down to one cop, I guess. He was planning to take Tucker's car back to Traverse City, to exchange it for his truck. The midnight visit was a spur of the moment thing, it seems, inspired by Joe with a little input from Smith and Wesson. Anyway, Tucker and I had a little heart-to-heart. About Miss Malachi. He agreed that her case might bear looking into."

Wunney nodded. "That's what I thought after you called. I picked up some files. Tucker's involved. You want to discuss this with him present?"

"Let's be open," Mulheisen said. "He seems prepared to let it all come out. Do you mind?"

Wunney shrugged. "Okay."

"Oh, what about Hook? Anything?"

"I couldn't get much on short notice," Wunney said, "but it appears that he's on the list of al-Qaeda operatives that the FBI and others want. Some kind of specialist in military organization. No pictures of al-Huq, I'm afraid. But the description sounds likely: mid-

thirties or early forties, slim, medium height, dark-complected, usually a mustache. Whatever that's worth. Homeland Security says
he's important, and they want him. Do you want to discuss it with
Tucker?"

"Let's see how the talk with him goes," Mulheisen said.

They went back to the beach. Tucker was standing right out
on the end of the wooden jetty, hunched and staring across the
lake. They started after him, but he turned, saw them, and came
back. He appeared refreshed by the changeable weather. He'd been
hungover, then talking nervously driving in, but now he was cheer-
ful, calm, and self-possessed.

"I was telling Mul," he said to Wunney, "that it seemed ad-
visable to take a look at the records of Malachi. It appears we were
a little hasty in dismissing her role, her potential impact on case.
It's possible there could be an enlightening element here, in regard
to M. P. Luck's involvement. What do you think, lieutenant?"

"Could be," Wunney said. "As a matter of fact, I brought some
material along about Malachi." He nodded toward his car, a black
Ford parked nearby. "You want to go someplace to discuss it? Or do
you want to chat out here?"

Mulheisen said, "There's a café back on the main street. We
can walk, if you'd rather."

"Yeah," Wunney said. "It's good to get out in the fresh air.
It's nice up here. The rain must have cleared the air."

He went to his car and got out a briefcase, then the three of
them walked without comment to the café. They ordered coffee and,
after it was served, Wunney opened the case and brought out some
files. He looked at Tucker to see if there were any objections, but
Tucker seemed unconcerned, so he began.

"This is a report on Malachi, from the FBI. She was hired as
an attorney by the Justice Department, as you can see, about ten
years ago. Appointed finally a U.S. attorney. Then she was recruited

by the CIA." He hauled out another file. "Her case officer was Colonel Tucker. She was investigating some so-called patriot groups. Not really CIA business, but . . ." He glanced at Tucker, who didn't react.

Wunney went on: "One of her objectives was Luck. As it happened, she'd already met Luck. Which was . . . lucky, I guess." Wunney didn't smile.

"That was the point of recruiting her," Tucker said.

"It doesn't look like you got much from her," Wunney said, tapping the papers.

"No, it was disappointing. I explained all that to the sergeant," Tucker said. "I'd say she fell under his thrall. It happens, as you know."

Wunney nodded. He sipped his coffee, then said, "She inherited some property from her father, downstate. It's near that town Wards Cove. For some reason, the investigation of the bombing never touched on this."

"I never heard anything about it, until the bombing," Tucker said. "When I looked into it I couldn't see anything relevant. Just an issue with her family, not connected to Luck, really. As she was an undercover operative, the powers that be decided it was just as well to sit on it."

Wunney looked at Mulheisen, who said, "I'd have thought that any issue in which Luck played any part at all would be relevant in an investigation. No?"

"The Wards Cove property was an old farmstead, just sixty acres," Tucker said. "The old man had acquired it back in the thirties. Evidently, he bought it from a couple of relatives, presumably as a way of helping them out during the depression. Those folks stayed on the property for several years, but eventually they moved on and he leased it to another farmer, who used it for agricultural purposes—he didn't live there. The house and other buildings were allowed to fall into dilapidation. He signed it over to his daughter before he died, in the seventies. It might have been a tax thing, or maybe it provided her with an income, or collateral, but that's just speculation. I didn't see any substantive connection to Luck. It seemed like sheer coincidence that a deceased agent's family was wrangling over her estate."

"That's all I have about it," Wunney said. "Not much of an issue, as you say. But when Constance died, apparently intestate—which is a little odd for a lawyer, don't you think?—other members of the family sought to recover the property. A couple of cousins, children of the original owners. They claimed that it was supposed to come back to their parents, if they survived Constance's father, which their mother did, barely. For some reason, they didn't contest it as long as Constance was alive, but since she had died . . . They felt it belonged in the family, shouldn't pass to Luck. He naturally dismissed their claim. But somehow they came up with this notion that he'd never actually married Malachi. And so far, he hasn't provided any evidence of a marriage. He could claim a common-law marriage, I'm told. But the question of the promised reversion might override that anyway.

"Now, we have the bombing. Most of the original papers and documents in the case were destroyed, along with some people. There are copies, of course. Quite a bit of fuss for a piece of not very valuable property."

"Are you sure it isn't valuable?" Mulheisen asked.

Wunney shook his head. "Just an old farm, leased out for hay. The state has built a campground nearby. The farm has no great commercial value. It's not related to that industrial developement in Wards Cove that was, coincidentally, the subject of a hearing that day, which your mother attended. This property is way on the other side of town, out in the country. I suppose, in some unforeseeble future, if Wards Cove continues to grow, it will become more valuable. But for now its value is still just as more or less ordinary agricultural property."

Tucker observed, "It didn't look like a meaningful connection to Luck. It wasn't enough of a link, and anyway he didn't bother to come and contest it. Didn't even send a lawyer. It looked like he had decided to let it go."

"It could be an issue, of sorts," Mulheisen mused. "If Luck thought he'd have trouble proving a marriage it might be problematical when it came to other property of Malachi's."

"What other property?" the Colonel asked.

"All that property along the Manistee River, before you get to McVey's cabin, where we were last night," Mulheisen said. "I noticed it on the plat map when I was looking in Traverse City to see how much and where Luck owned property. Just a coincidence . . . sort of. But it's a similar situation: Luck's grandfather seems to have given it to a faithful servant, who built that cabin. Subsequently, the servant left it to McVey. When I talked to Luck, a couple days ago, he displayed some interest in regaining property he felt belonged to his grandfather, presumably that property. There's also some adjoining property that, for some reason, was in Constance Malachi's name. A different issue, but it suggests he's very keen on his property rights. It's a fundamental part of his antigovernment philosophy, in fact. This might be part of the same problem, in his eyes. I got the impression from McVey that Luck wasn't likely to recover the cabin property. But if this Wards Cove suit by Malachi's family goes through, he could also lose that other property."

"That's a bit far-fetched," Tucker said. "A lot of what-ifs."

Mulheisen shrugged, then gestured at Wunney's briefcase. "You wouldn't happen to have a copy of Malachi's employment records with the CIA?"

Wunney dug them out. Mulheisen riffled through some official forms until he came to a medical record. He scanned that while the other two looked on. Finally, he said, "Looks like she had a clean bill of health. No mention of any congenital heart defect. She evidently went through the agency's training program—that should have revealed any serious condition. Still," he tossed the forms back, "it's inconclusive, isn't it? Pretty hard to demonstrate the absence of something, especially if you don't have the body. No autopsy, of course. You could ask the family doctor, but it seems he's deceased. Might not be easy to locate his records, if they still exist. I talked to the doctor who saw her. He's an old country doctor, I don't think he'd ever seen her before. He admits that he based his diagnosis on information from the family doctor. I'd say we need the body. Question is, where is it?"

"When she died," Wunney said, "the doctor up here signed the death certificate and that was that. No record of a funeral, no indication of where she's buried. Any ideas on that?"

Tucker shrugged. "I was out of the country. When I heard about it, I sent condolences. I assumed it was taken care of in the normal way. It didn't ring any alarm bells."

"Where would you guess she's buried?" Wunney asked Mulheisen.

"Same place you would," Mulheisen said. "So now, what we need is a search warrant."

"I can get a warrant," Tucker spoke up eagerly. "It shouldn't be a problem, with the authority of the Homeland Security. I'll have to go back to Detroit, probably even Washington. We'll need to clear this on the highest level, get the best pathologists, the latest postmortem equipment. They've got some terrific techniques now. If there's a body, they'll find out how she died." He sounded enthused.

Mulheisen had visions of a massive operation forming up. Squads of federal marshals, maybe even troops, a mobile lab, helicopters, infrared sensing equipment to locate possible burial sites, earth-moving equipment. He wondered if there weren't satellite infrared mapping technologies available.

"I think we could get a warrant from a local judge," he suggested. "It would save time. There could be an easily identifiable gravesite on the property. Luck might even take us to it."

"No, no," Tucker said. "That wouldn't do. This will have to be a federal operation. We're talking about the murder of a federal agent! This has, besides, immense security implications. No, I'll have to get back, right away."

"I can drive you," Mulheisen said.

"Thanks, but that's not necessary," Tucker said, "besides, it's too slow." He glanced at his watch. "My crew should be here, *tout á l'heure.*"

Wunney frowned. "Toodle-loo?"

"Sorry," Tucker said, smiling. "ASAP. I called them a little bit ago, from the beach, while you boys were chatting. They'll have a chopper. You're both welcome to ride back with me, but you have your vehicles, don't you? Well, I better get down to the beach."

Fifteen minutes later, Mulheisen and Wunney stood by while the chopper lifted up and whirled away. The Colonel had been explicit: they were not to approach Luck or his property. One thing he hadn't mentioned was Mulheisen's employment with the task force. Evidently, that was a dead issue. As for Wunney, he expected him to be back in Detroit, "toodle-loo." He'd added that with a sly smile.

"Well, I guess I blew that," Mulheisen said. "I thought I had the man in a corner, but it looks like it was my foot in the crack. And I didn't even get a chance to ask him about Hook."

Wunney said, "He kind of blindsided you."

"The man's a whiz at stonewalling," Mulheisen said. "I wouldn't be surprised if, somehow, that body wasn't found. Well, it's out of our hands."

Wunney nodded reluctantly. "What are you going to do now?"

"I guess I'll return this old beater of a truck, get my car, and go home. I'm out of cigars anyway."

"Just like that, eh?" Wunney said. "You don't want to take a look, see if Luck doesn't have a pretty little shrine out back, with plastic flowers and a headstone?"

"Let's leave it to the Colonel," Mulheisen said. "If this Malachi angle works out, he'll have the case all wrapped up. I feel bad about dragging you all the way up here. My guess is you'll be back in Homicide next week."

Wunney nodded. "Ah well, it got me out of the city for a day. Give me a call, if you're not doing anything."

Mulheisen said he would and watched while the man ambled off to his car. There was no point in driving back to the cabin. Joe had taken the Colonel's car back to Traverse City. Mulheisen wasn't sure what to do about Joe now that events had taken such an abrupt turn. They had anticipated that Mulheisen might have to go back to Detroit with the Colonel, to look into Malachi's files, after they met with Wunney. Mulheisen had put his gear in the back of the truck, just in case. Joe had told him he'd be in touch, not to worry.

Mulheisen wasn't looking forward to explaining to Joe how he'd let the situation get away from him. For that matter, he wasn't quite sure how it had happened. Hell, he thought, let the Colonel explain it.

He drove back to Queensleap to return the truck to McVey.

"You ain't staying?" McVey said. "A little too lonely out there?"

"On the contrary," Mulheisen said, "it was great. I'd like to come back some time. I kind of liked that fishing out there." He told about losing the trout.

"There's some big ones in there," McVey said, "but they're hard as hell to get out. You're welcome anytime."

"I'd like that," Mulheisen said. "By the way, you said something about Luck wanting that cabin property back. I take it he's tried in the courts?"

McVey smiled sourly. "More than once," he said. "He's been gonna take me to court from the day he heard Tom left it to me. He claims that his old man only left it to Tom on a life lease, which it should of reverted to him, when Tom died. To hear him tell it, ol' Tom didn't have no right to leave it to nobody, much less me. But so far, the courts haven't paid him no mind. There's something called a common deed, or something. The old man had to of done it. Too late now. But don't it burn ol' Imp's ass!"

"Did he ever offer to buy it?" Mulheisen asked.

"Oh, yeah, but he didn't offer anything like the going price, and anyway I wasn't gonna sell. That's when he began talking about going to court."

This had all the earmarks of a country feud, to Mulheisen's ears. It fit with what he had told the Colonel and what he had heard from Luck. Still, he told himself, it was none of his business anymore. To Charlie, he said, "Well, they tell me possession is nine-tenths of the law. Hold on tight."

McVey seemed surprised. "Ain't you gonna arrest him?"

"What for?"

McVey cracked a knowing grin. "Well he must of done something, or you wouldn't of come up here pokin' around."

Mulheisen shook his head. "I don't have any authority. I'm just a retired cop."

"Oh sure," McVey said. He winked. "Wal, I won't blow your cover, Mul. You can count on me. But just between us . . . what is it? FBI? CIA? Or one a them new outfits that nobody knows about? Never mind." He waved an understanding hand. "Better if I don't know. Well, you come back, maybe in the spring, and we'll go catch us a mess a trout."

Mulheisen put his stuff in the Checker, thanked Charlie again, and waved good-bye. He stopped in Manton for a leisurely lunch at a friendly country-style restaurant. The cherry pie was exceptionally good. He took the opportunity to call home.

His mother was out bird-watching, the nurse said. "I can see her, she's out in the field. Shall I call her?"

"No," Mulheisen said. "Just tell her I'll be back, probably about dinnertime, but don't wait for me."

18

Northern Spy

Joe felt that Mulheisen had made a mistake, but he didn't feel that he could say anything. Mulheisen should never have let Tucker breathe once he had him running. *Don't give the man air*, he'd said to himself when Mulheisen had Tucker babbling. But Mulheisen had eased up once he got the concession on Malachi. Still, Joe had to admit, it was a delicate thing. You get the guy talking and admitting stuff, eagerly filling you in, justifying himself . . . it's not so easy to tell when enough is enough, or too much, or maybe the tension can go up another notch.

Mulheisen had gotten what he wanted: the key to Malachi's data, which was probably the key to the whole business. That had been finessed, Joe had to admit. He hadn't quite seen it coming himself. He wondered if he would have taken Malachi as the point of entry.

In the morning, with Tucker hungover and morose, Mulheisen had played it coolly. He revealed that he had earlier arranged to meet a cop who was temporarily assigned to assist Tucker's task force. This Wunney apparently had some inside information for Mulheisen. Joe and Mulheisen hadn't discussed it; Joe didn't know what it was all about. The opportunity for Mulheisen to explain hadn't arisen, and anyway he'd claimed that he didn't know what Wunney had.

Joe admired that. Going behind the Colonel's back to one of his trusted assistants was a good ploy. Joe wondered, though, if Mulheisen couldn't have used it to effect while questioning Tucker. By the same token, he wondered if they shouldn't have used the al-Huq/Hook angle to some advantage. But in the few minutes that he and Mulheisen had found to discuss the night's work, Mulheisen had said that they didn't have enough information.

"Let's just sit on it," Mulheisen said. "It could still be useful. The thing is, we really don't know if it's the same guy. But I asked Wunney to check it out. Maybe he'll have something."

"Oh, I'll bet it's al-Huq," Joe said. "Incidentally, did you know that one reason Tucker was looking to recruit you was that he felt it would give him an inside track on any revelations about Wards Cove that your mother might recollect?"

Mulheisen smiled at that notion. "I don't think there's much to hope for from that quarter," he said.

Tucker had seemed quite indifferent about meeting with Wunney. To Joe's mind, it meant just delaying whatever revelations there might be about Malachi. Maybe good, maybe not. The plan was that Tucker and Mulheisen would go on to Detroit, after meeting Wunney, to retrieve Malachi's files and see if they could turn up something that would expose Luck, depending of course on what transpired in the meeting with Wunney.

Joe could see the logic of all this. He would hang out here, shuttle the Colonel's car to Traverse City, retrieve his own vehicle. Yet he couldn't help feeling that Tucker had held out on them. A little pressure last night might have revealed something more, something useful. But he thought, all in all, Mulheisen had played it well.

Joe felt . . . how did he feel? Like a man halfway to town and unable to shake the feeling that he'd forgotten something. He missed

Helen. If he'd brought her along, he thought, they might have been able to work something better. He felt he needed to be in two places at once. Roman would also have been useful, but Joe had felt that he couldn't linger in Detroit once he'd learned that Mulheisen was up north, talking to Luck. Where was Roman now? Probably hanging out at the Sedlacek place, Joe thought. One thing Joe wasn't going to do was call there. Old lady Sedlacek didn't like him, Joe was sure: she didn't feel he was good enough for her brilliant daughter, had led her astray, taken her off to remote Montana—Siberia. It would be his luck to have to talk to her if he called the house. She might have heard from Helen, who probably by now was pissed at Joe's leaving her. No, he'd have to forget about Roman.

The Echeverria factor still nagged. Call it the Itcheverria, he thought; it demanded a Scratcheverria. He wished Helen were here, she'd appreciate that gag. Thinking about it, Joe called his service and found that he had a message from Caspar. His return number was in Chicago.

"Kinda early ain't it, Joe?" Caspar said when he answered. He was obviously awakened from sleep.

"You're getting used to civilian life, Caspar," Joe said. "In the joint you'd have been up for a couple of hours. So what's up?"

"I met a guy," Caspar said. "He says Echeverria might be in the States. He's got some deal with the government, some kind of protection. But nobody knows where he is for sure."

They discussed the reliability of Caspar's contact—so-so, Caspar thought. It just added to Joe's discomfort. Caspar would try to find out more.

Joe called Brooker Moos to see if he had any new information. Moos didn't have anything, but he was antsy. His paranoia was on the boil. He'd been getting more indications that someone was trying to get to him, monitoring his lines, he thought. But when asked to describe how he knew, it just added up to funny clicks, slow transmissions, missed connections. Joe wasn't sure how to interpret this, just paranoia, maybe. Brooker, however, had noticed that references to Joe had declined. He wasn't getting any responses on his filtering system. Of course, he admitted, he'd pretty much cleaned up the info on the Web, so it was bound to decline, theoretically. "I mean, that was the idea," he said.

Joe decided it was time to head for Traverse City. Exchanging vehicles could be tricky, he thought. He expected that Tucker's crew would be watching his vehicle. They'd probably tagged it, stashing a tracking device. He'd have to go over it pretty carefully. One thing he didn't want was to have to deal with any of those agents, Dinah Schwind among them. They might try to pick him up, although he expected that Tucker would have contacted them, maybe by now, and cleared him from interference. But then it had already occurred to him that Tucker's vehicle might be similarly bugged; maybe the Lucani knew all along where the vehicle was. Joe kind of wished he'd not taken the Colonel's car last night, but it had been a judgment call: if they'd tracked him to the Park Place Hotel, they'd have had plenty of time to bug his pickup and he'd wanted to get clear of Traverse City without interference.

He decided to sweep the Colonel's car before leaving. He didn't find anything. It was now midmorning. Presumably, by now Mulheisen and Tucker would have met with Wunney, in Cadillac. Joe decided to take a chance on the exchange. He drove to Traverse City. Just to give himself time, he left the car in a parking lot by the bay and hiked over to the hotel. There was no one around. Evidently, the Colonel had called off his people. Joe swept his own vehicle without finding anything, then cleared out his room and checked out of the hotel. No one approached him.

What now? Joe felt at loose ends. Go back to the cabin? He could do that. But for what? Sit around and wait for Mulheisen to call? He didn't think so. Then he got an idea: why not visit Luck?

It was still early, not quite noon. Mulheisen would have met with Wunney by now and was probably on his way back to Detroit.

He found Luck conferring with a group of his guards. They were gathered in a clearing surrounded by tall pines, from which a great camouflage netting was suspended—doubtless, from above, it looked like forest. There were a half-dozen men, all in the black military outfits, armed with assault rifles. Luck was haranguing them, with Hook standing by looking like a trusted lieutenant, but Joe wasn't close enough to hear. Evidently, it was heat about security. Joe lingered in the trees, watching to see who went where, then he slipped away to the house. As he'd expected, Luck came back to the house alone. He was naturally surprised to find Joe sitting in a chair in the living room with a Llama 9mm automatic in his lap.

"How did you get in here?" Luck asked.

"Trade secret," Joe said. He introduced himself without getting up, although he could see that Luck already knew who he was.

Luck recovered his usual affability quickly. "Can I get you some coffee?" he asked. "A drink?"

"No thanks," Joe said. "I just stopped by to get acquainted. You've been splashing my name all across the Internet. What's that about?"

Luck shrugged. "Just trying to keep my fans posted on your activities."

"Yeah, well it's not polite," Joe said. "I don't appreciate the publicity."

Luck didn't seem bothered by that. "I'm happy to remove any of that stuff," he said. "I take it you've been conferring with Colonel Tucker. Are you now 'on board'?"

Joe nodded. "To a degree. First, I thought I'd check out the operation, see if it was something I wanted to be associated with."

Luck relaxed, sat down across from him. "What do you think?"

"I don't know," Joe said. "I haven't seen much."

"I could give you a little tour. When did you see the Colonel?"

"Last night," Joe said. "He says that you're part of the team."

"Come to think of it," Luck said, "I probably ought to get confirmation from Tucker before we take the tour. Just a matter of security."

"According to the Colonel, you guys go back a long way," Joe said. "Vietnam. He didn't say much about later activities. But it looks like we're fellow Lucani. We ought to have some kind of secret handshake, or a password."

"Shibboleth, you mean," Luck said, with a smile.

"Shibboleth," Joe said. "Maybe we could get special rings, or whistle the opening bars of a Dixie Chicks tune."

"Except I don't know any Dixie Chicks tunes," Luck said.

Joe confessed he didn't either.

"By the way," Luck said, as if the thought had just struck him, "you didn't have something to do with Mulheisen's abrupt departure a couple of nights ago?"

"Mulheisen! He was here? Well, I guess he would be. He's the kind of guy who keeps poking around. Hard to keep anything from Mulheisen, although he never seems all that intrusive, does he? Just always around. I'm not usually happy to see Mulheisen. So what is this operation of yours? The Colonel says it's just a bunch of patriotic yokels. What's the story on that?"

Luck seemed disposed to explain, in a general way. He talked about the patriotic movement. According to him it was just ordinary citizens with reasonable concerns about the federal government, its interference in personal lives and activities. It was all about law and private rights.

Joe was interested. He talked about his place out west, the problems with privacy. Luck responded. They traded comments about private land, taxation, the interference of agencies that had no business interfering. Luck was impressed with Joe's description of the extent of his property in Montana, the fortunate disposition of national forests and Bureau of Land Management holdings as borders. The idea of a couple of thousand acres, nicely sequestered, seemed enviable.

"It's different here," Luck said, "the available acreage is limited. It's all owned by someone, been in the family for ages, that sort of thing. You can't buy them out, even if it's worthless marshland. That farm next to me, for instance, it hasn't been used or even visited by the owners for decades. But will they sell? Never. It's owned by people who live in Illinois. They inherited. I don't think any of them have even seen the property in a generation."

"You remind me of my neighbor," Joe said. "He says he doesn't want to own everything, just the land next to his."

Luck chuckled. "Well, it makes things easier, doesn't it?"

"How much do you have here?" Joe asked.

"By rights, it should be close to a thousand acres," Luck said, "but there are some legal disputes. My grandfather had quite a bit more, but through some legal chicanery I'm down to just a few hundred. I've been working on that. I think I'll win out, eventually, but it takes up too much of my time, it's expensive, and, hell, it's just plain not right!"

"I hear you," Joe said. "I thought I had a good deal with my neighbor, but now he wants to run cattle. That'll mean brand inspectors coming around. They can walk right onto your land, without a warrant, no warning. And if you want to divert a little stream, you have to file a plan with Fish and Game. That has to be inspected and approved, and approval doesn't come easy. You practically have to file an environmental impact statement to bury your garbage. More agencies. The Forest Service wants to survey, take a census of your trees, your riparian rights, whether you're complying with best forest practices. It goes on and on."

Luck was nodding his head eagerly. "It's probably worse here in Michigan," he said. The problem was the long tenure of settlement, compared to a state like Montana, where there were sizable tracts of privately owned land.

"Other than privacy," Joe said, "what do you need with all this land?"

"Isn't that enough?" Luck said. When Service smiled at him, he smiled back. "All right . . . you're Lucani. I accept that. The Colonel told me as much. The plan was a little different, in the beginning. I got interested in the patriot movement. It wasn't difficult to drum up interest, but the people you get, they're just bumper-sticker conservatives. No fire in the belly. Then I got online. There are thousands of guys out there who are truly pissed. Most of them are pretty much like the locals. Their idea of activism is to join a group like the one I started. They get together, spout off some antigovernment sentiments, plaster a flag on their SUV, maybe go to a liberal gathering and shout some angry words. But there's always a few willing to throw a bomb."

"Literally?" Joe said.

"Oh, sure," Luck said. "It's like the old anarchists in Russia, back in the days of the czar. But we don't want that."

"You don't?"

"No. It's too helter-skelter," Luck said. "What you want to do is get them into a more organized environment. It's the age-old process: identify the true radicals, divert them into a program with an actual philosophy. The irony is, the buffoons, the bumper-sticker flag-wavers, they make a good cover. You get investigated, the feds, or whoever, see the buffoons and they report that. You're just a group of harmless cranks. I had a different notion entirely."

Basically, as he explained it, Luck had gotten interested in the security business. Guards, equipment, protection for wealthy clients. He'd worked in that for a while and then he saw that the people who were really making the money were offering not just rent-a-cops but actual troops.

"You thought you'd put together a private army?" Joe didn't conceal his skepticism.

"Well, others have done it. You get outfits like this Vinnell Corporation, working all over the Mid East and other places. They actually started out in the construction business. They got into oil, building sites and then protecting them. They hired ex-Rangers, guys like that. Pretty soon they had an army. They get contracts in the hundred-million range. I had good contacts in the government—my ol' buddy Vern Tucker, for instance. But you know what? There's just not enough room here to do the soldier training. Besides, it was too much like being in the army. So I scaled back."

"Ah," Joe said. "No army, but . . ."

"Key men," Luck said. "That's where it's at." He leaned forward, his eyes intense. "What's the biggest problem going? Terrorism, right? The public forgot all about guys like McVeigh and Nichols the minute those planes drove into the World Trade Center towers. All they could think about was Osama bin Laden. They eagerly supported a war against sovereign nations, thinking they were destroying Osama. But they can't destroy Osama. Not that way."

Joe attended to Luck's argument, but he was also keeping his ears open for other noises. Was this guy for real? Who else was around here? He stayed alert. "So what's the answer?" he said.

"Osama provided a good answer himself. Everybody looked at the camps he had, the actual layouts. They thought, 'We destroy that and we've destroyed this terrorist threat.' But there was more to it. I don't know how much of Osama's interest was, or is, vested in the camps, but I don't think it's training camps. His real business is a clearinghouse for guerrilla projects and in providing a host of core agents. The would-be saboteurs flock to him. He takes a few in, trains them, discusses philosophy with them, and sends them back out to the rest of the world where they get together the people they need to carry out the terrorist activities."

"Kind of like a finishing school for agents," Joe said.

"Exactly," Luck said, sitting back with an air of satisfaction. "Grad school. There's no shortage of young men in the world full of fury and rage, boiling over with testosterone. Not just Arab kids who want to blow up Americans and other infidels, but American kids who want to blow up . . . well, just about anything. What you need is someone to focus these guys. In the Mid East, they go in for martyrs. Americans don't like the idea of martyrs. To us, it's sick. But if we want to fight these guys we've got to use Osama's tactics: create the guys who will go out and organize counterterrorists."

"And you don't need a big camp for that," Joe said.

"No, nothing huge. But you have to have *some* space, a facility, and a lot of security. You're just training a small cadre. You provide a philosophy, study the history of the terrorist movements, and work on field craft."

Joe nodded. It was an interesting concept. "So, have you had much success?"

"A little," Luck said modestly. "We're just getting going. My guys are in the early stages. The thing is, with the Internet you reach the whole world. You wouldn't believe the inquiries I get, from all over the country, Australia, Europe, even the Middle East."

"The Middle East?"

"Hell, yes," Luck said. "You think there aren't guys in the Middle East who want to defeat Osama and his gang? Of course, you have to vet them to make sure they aren't just spies. That's a problem. But Tucker helps with that, of course. That's useful, and it's a quid pro quo thing: he can keep an eye on attempts of terrorists to infiltrate. Works out well."

"How about contracts?" Joe said. "Are you on your way to competing with Vinnell?"

"No firm contracts yet," Luck said. "I'm working on it. I need a couple of demonstrations."

"Exercises?" Joe said. "With live ammo . . . real-life situations?"

"Exactly," Luck said. He eyed Service shrewdly. "What do you think? Would something like this interest you?"

"Me?" Joe said. "Hey, don't look at me. I'm the original stray dog. All this stuff sounds too military."

"It is military, Joe. It has to be. If you're training guys to lead men you have to have discipline. You don't think the al-Qaeda is run like the Mafia, do you? There's too much at stake."

"The outfits I knew relied totally on family. That was how they built loyalty. You didn't have to be a blood brother, but if you wanted to succeed in the family you had to at least be adopted. That's why I didn't like it. But they needed a dog who wouldn't come to every master who waved a bone. My impression is the terrorists use religion for family."

"They do," Luck said, "but we have religion too. And it's allied to an intense nationalism. There's a conventional myth about the great American Christian nation. There are elements of racism involved. You want to avoid that. It's divisive. It's all about God's chosen nation, the City on the Hill. Onward Christian soldiers. Osama recognizes it and calls us crusaders. That's good. That's useful. We don't mind that."

"I don't know diddly about terrorism," Joe said. "Not my game. And the last thing I want is to march and make my bed so tight you can bounce a quarter off it. I didn't go into the army—it didn't sound like any kind of fun."

"I spent a lot of time around the military, Joe, but I didn't join up either. I went another way. I had the same feeling as you. I didn't like the regimentation concept. But I ended up working with these guys. Plus, I've spent a lifetime studying military history and tactics. So I'm kind of into it, without being *in* it, if you know what

I mean. But I wasn't trying to recruit you . . . I mean, not as a *recruit*! I meant, would you be interested in being one of the instructors? You wouldn't be subject to the discipline. What we need is guys who know what these kids need to know.

"One thing I noticed about the military, Joe: they know how to educate young men. The soldiering part is one thing—discipline is essential. But when the military wants a kid to know something about, say, jet engines, they don't leave that up to some sergeant who read a textbook. They go out and get guys who wrote the textbooks, guys who know all about the latest engines, who have worked on them, built them, and so on."

"I don't know anything about that," Joe said.

"Yeah, but you know a lot of other stuff," Luck said. He was enthusiastic. "The fact that you walked in here without anyone detecting your presence . . . man, that's what these kids need to learn. Right now, that's my main job, recruiting the kind of men who can provide the expertise."

"Any luck?"

"A little," Luck said. "A start. I've got one guy, he came to me through the Web site. He's had hands-on experience building cadres, and in the Middle East. Military specialist. That's the kind of thing you need. No substitute for practical experience in the field."

"Mercenaries," Joe said.

"I get some of those guys applying too. I'm vetting them, or the Colonel is. They're in the pipeline. But you need all kinds of experts. Explosives, surveillance, electronics, even finance. Once we get some contracts, I'll be open for business."

"Speaking of finance, who's bankrolling all this?" Joe said.

"Ah, I can't reveal too much on that score. It takes a lot of money to start up, but I have sources."

"Tucker, huh?"

"Mmmm, maybe a little," Luck conceded, "but there's also private sources. Lot of money out there, looking for a cause to spend it on. More money than you would believe."

"Count me out," Joe said. "I've got my work to do. I don't have time to do yours."

"What do you have to do? Tucker told me you were taking up carpentry, and fly-fishing!"

"That was just a vacation. That's over," Joe said. "Right now, I've got to find a guy. Before he finds me."

"Who's this?" Luck inquired.

"I don't think you know him. Hell, I don't know him. The Colonel does, though: a drug dealer named Echeverria. I call him Itcheverria. I need to Scratcheverria." Joe was disappointed that Luck wasn't amused.

"I've met him," Luck said. "The Colonel needed a backup when he went to see him, down in Panama. I drove the plane and carried an Uzi. Weird guy, wears a veil."

"A veil?"

"Some kind of gauze mask thing," Luck said. "It has a face painted on it, kind of . . . eyes, lips. He got burnt. It's very eerie to be around. He's talking through this mask, you can see his lips moving, and this painted face is grinning at you like Mr. Pumpkin. What's he got against you?"

"Just between us, he thinks I hung the mask on him."

Luck was impressed. "Did you, by god? Playing with fire, were you?"

It was Joe's turn not to laugh.

"You know, maybe I could help you get to him," Luck said. "Would that interest you? Maybe we could work out some quid pro quo ourselves."

"It sounds possible," Joe said. "We could discuss it, but not here." He glanced around. "It's too much like Nixon's office."

"Let's go for a walk then. I want you to see the grounds anyway."

Joe was agreeable. The two of them strolled out among the trees. Joe explained about the occasions when he'd booby-trapped his house, which had led to Echeverria's getting all but burned to a crisp, and the subsequent occasion, when he'd thought he was making a hit for the Colonel. Echeverria had survived, but now he was, as Joe put it, "prejudiced" against him. "Just to make life more relaxing, it looks like I've got to take him out," he said.

Luck thought he could help. He had contacts. Echeverria could be set up. Panama would be a good place, but Guatemala was also a possibility. Luck had done some work down there.

"No," Joe said. "I'm not going out of the country. He'd be more at home there than I would. It would have to be here, in the States."

Luck said that would be more difficult. Echeverria didn't like coming to the States. Tucker might be able to help, though.

They had walked along a pleasant wooded path, kicking up leaves. They came to the edge of the woods and a high, stout fence. Luck unlocked a gate and let them out. They continued out into a broad field and along an old, sandy two-track that led up to a ridge. The field had long lain fallow, obviously, now overgrown with sumac and various brambly bushes. At the top of the ridge there was an old ironwork gate that opened into an enclosure surrounded by a low fence. It was an old cemetery.

Luck paused. "All my people are buried up here," he said. He pushed the gate open and they entered. "I'll be buried here someday." There were perhaps twenty tombstones. An old apple tree shaded one corner, very gnarled. It was festooned with greenish apples with a red patina. Luck reached up and plucked one. "Try it," he said, handing the apple to Joe. "They're not bad. The

deer eat most of them. They're an old variety, the Northern Spy."
He picked another for himself and polished it on his wool field
jacket.

Joe tasted it. "Very good," he said. He stood among the scattered graves, munching and gazing off into the fields below. In the
distance, he could see a farm, several other houses. A red fuel truck
rolled along a distant county road. The wind ruffled his hair. Shafts
of sunlight broke through the heavy overcast and played across the
largely yellow and brown fields.

"You should have built up here," Joe said. "It's a nice view.
Airy."

"Yes, the old homestead was nearby," Luck said. "But 'the
woods are lovely, deep and dark,' to quote the poet. And they're
more secure. Down there"—he gestured—"were pastures and corn-
fields, gardens."

Joe peered at the stones. They were well worn, some kind of
soft, white stone, but he could read most of the faded inscriptions:
Alois Luckenbach, 1824–1901; Johanna Siegmuller Luckenbach,
1841–1875; and many of the stones, small ones, bore the names of
children, none of whom had lived longer than a year or two. There
were other, only slightly newer stones. The names were all Luckenbach. The site was well cared for, mowed, with a few pruned rose-
bushes, a couple of dark evergreens, not very large. A rather new
site was in one corner. It had no stone, but there were some flowers
planted at the head, not in bloom, just greenish shoots, now with-
ering in the fall.

"Who's this?" Joe said.

"Ah, my father," Luck said. "He wasn't buried here. I relo-
cated his grave a couple of years ago. I've been meaning to get a
stone up, but I've been remiss."

Joe glanced around. He'd seen a stone, a little ways off,
marked "Martin Parvis Luck, II." He had assumed it was the father.

Which would make Luck the third, presumably. He didn't say anything about it.

Luck seemed eager to leave now. Joe followed him out and they proceeded on down the sandy road, toward a little pond that lay below. There was an old foundation, overgrown with weeds and brush off to one side. Luck pointed it out. "The old homestead," he said. "It burned down, ages ago."

They walked past the old pond and, shortly, the road entered the woods again. Luck opened another gate and closed it behind them, locking it.

"So what do you think? Can we work out something? The pay is pretty good for this kind of stuff. Say, seventy-five a year?"

Joe laughed. "I don't think so."

Luck smiled. "A hundred? I'm sure we can work something out."

"I don't need money," Service said. "I've got things to do."

It had been breezy up on the hill. In the woods it was well protected, but the treetops were tossing and leaves constantly rattled down. Their stroll brought them to another hill, this one covered with young pines. A well-kept road skirted it. Luck led Joe along the new road without comment.

Soon they returned to the house, without passing the area where Joe had seen the men gathered. In fact, he didn't see any other people during the tour.

It was still just midday, or a little after. Luck suggested they have lunch. Or Joe could stay for dinner. He was planning to prepare a roast, he said.

"Hey, stay the night," he suggested. "I have some nice quarters. Or have you seen them? They're in the barn, but very comfortable."

Joe couldn't stay. "Where do the men stay?" he asked. "I didn't see any barracks."

Jon A. Jackson

"I guess I forgot to show you," Luck said. "There are some sleeping quarters for the men back in the woods. I could show you, if you've got some time."

"Oh, that's all right," Joe said. "I've got some business in town."

"Well, I'd better take you to your car," Luck said. "Where is it?"

"Oh, I can walk," Joe said.

Luck insisted. He said the men were likely to confront him. They were armed and had instructions. The fences were not easy to get past.

Joe said, "Let's just take it as a demonstration. I won't have any problems getting out."

"If you like," Luck said.

They went out on the porch and Joe said his good-byes, thanked Luck for the brief tour, and said he'd consider his offer. He sauntered up the road toward the gate. Once out of sight of the house he slipped into the woods. He saw one of the men, a fellow in woodland camo, watching the gate. The guard didn't see Joe. He thought of approaching the fellow, but decided against it. Ten minutes later he was at his truck, parked in the usual place, well hidden off the county road. He got in and drove away without any problem. All in all, he thought, it had been easier than getting into Brooker Moos's house.

19

Missing Dogs

It was mid-afternoon by the time they got to Queensleap. It had been a lovely drive, although it began to cloud up as the day wore on. The sun was still out, mostly, but Helen had been distracted by her thoughts and her incessant perusal of the road map. She hardly noticed the spectacular foliage. She was darned if she could find any road to McVey's place. But in their rambling around the backcountry outside of Queensleap, they suddenly came upon the Luck mailbox.

"Stop," Helen said. "Let's go down there."

"This ain't really the car for it," Roman said, eyeing the bushes crowding the road, thinking of the scratches. "What if I can't turn around?"

Helen waved that objection off. Sure enough, they came to a locked gate and no place to turn. Roman groaned. But Helen got out. Within twenty seconds, however, a rough-looking fellow wearing a vaguely military uniform appeared. He wore a holstered side-arm on his hip and carried a cell phone. He stood on the other side of the gate and asked Helen what she wanted.

"Are you Mr. Luck?" she inquired.

"No," the man said. "He ain't around."

Helen didn't think he was being uncivil, merely a bit bumpkinish. She wondered momentarily if M. P. Luck was some kind of reclusive tycoon; who employed armed guards out in these sticks? She had more pressing interests, though, and inquired if he knew where McVey's place was.

"McVey? McVey don't live around here," the man said.

"Well, is there a place in there where we could turn around?" Helen asked. "This car is so big. It's too far to back up."

The man looked at the vehicle, recognizing the problem. "Lemme see," he said. He snapped the cell phone open. Apparently, it had a walkie-talkie function, because he immediately began talking, explaining the problem. After a brief discussion with whoever was on the other end, he said to Helen, "Gotta wait."

He just stared at Helen, and at Roman behind the wheel, silently, until the phone buzzed. He lifted it to his ear. "Yeah," he said into it. "There's a guy, too, a driver." To Helen he said abruptly, "What's your name?" When Helen told him, and he'd relayed that information, he said, "Who's he?" nodding toward Roman.

"He works for me," Helen said. "He's the driver. Hey, what's the big deal? I just want to turn—"

The guard held the phone to his ear and waved her to be quiet. Then he said, "All right, he says you can come down."

"Okay!" Helen scrambled back into the car while the man unlocked the gate.

He stopped them as the vehicle pulled forward. "Just go on down there to the house. It's a little ways, but keep going. You can turn around there. Don't get out, don't stop. And come right back."

When they got to the clearing around the house, a tall, handsome man was standing there, smiling. He wore an elegant plaid wool shirt under a sheepskin vest. His hair was full and dark, with gray at the temples. He came to Helen's side of the car when they pulled up and stuck out his hand when she lowered the window.

"Hi, I'm Imp Luck," he said. "You must be Miss Sedlacek."

While Helen shook his hand, Luck stooped and looked through to Roman. He nodded to him.

He stepped back from the car. "Sorry about the gate," he said. "What can I do for you?"

"I was looking for the McVey place," Helen said.

"Well, you know . . ."—Luck rubbed his chin and looked around thoughtfully, as if trying to figure out how to describe where this might be— "McVey . . . if you're looking for Charlie McVey, he lives back toward town, on the Summit City road. Is that—?"

"No, no," Helen said, opening the door and getting out. She looked up at Luck. He was a big man and he projected an attractive aura, familiar to her, like certain football players she had known—very masculine, protective. Her father, Big Sid, had been like that. Helen responded to that. She couldn't resist looking him up and down, flirting a bit.

"Maybe it's some other McVey," Helen said, her hands on her hips, squinting up at him, smiling. She had set her legs apart, in her short skirt, and twisted back and forth slightly, as if stretching. "Ohhh, I'm stiff," she said.

Luck stepped back slightly to get the full view. He seemed flattered by her vivacity, as well as appreciating her lithe legs. He grinned broadly. "Why don't you come in and we could look in the phone book? I could offer you a drink."

"Oh. That would be great."

"What about your friend?" Luck said, gesturing toward Roman.

"Oh, he'll be all right," Helen said, stepping toward the house. She couldn't resist taking Luck's arm.

"I could send out a beer for him," Luck said. He helped her up the short step onto the porch.

Helen assured him it wasn't necessary. Inside, standing in the kitchen, she said, "What a terrific place!" She glanced about. "It's so neat. So . . . masculine."

"Thanks," Luck said, pleased. "Well, it's a little early for a drink, actually, but what the heck! Eh? Join me in a taste of scotch? Or can I get you something milder? There's a pinot gris chilling."

"The pinot sounds great," Helen said, "but so does the scotch, frankly. We've been driving all morning and I'm frustrated at not finding this McVey."

"By all means, scotch. I have an excellent, smooth single malt. It comes from a distiller in the hills up by Strathmore." He disappeared into a pantry and returned immediately, holding a dusty bottle. "Look at this label," Luck said smiling.

The two of them stood close to each other, peering at the brown paper label, handwritten in faded black ink and pasted on the dark green bottle slightly askew. It attested to the fifteen years of aging and was signed by Robbie Robertson. The label had been printed with what one might presume was Mr. Robertson's coat of arms, but it wasn't quite clear what it was—a shield with a stag, a beaver, and an acorn, perhaps. In a fine but not too legible flowing script, it was declared to be "Robertson's Choice."

"Robbie makes only a few barrels at a time," Luck said. "You can't buy this stuff, except from him personally."

Helen laughed delightedly and dared to squeeze Luck's arm. "I'll have that!"

When they were seated in the living room, Luck inquired, "Who is this McVey you're looking for?"

"I'm not sure," Helen said. She sipped the scotch. "This is *so* smooth. It's like . . . I don't know what, some kind of golden elixir.

It goes down so smoothly, and yet it has that glow. I can feel it all the way down."

"Yes, you feel you can taste the peat smoke. You can't, of course, but . . ."

"Oh, you can! *I* can, anyway. Well, some kind of smoky taste."

Luck smiled at her, pleased with her. "Hey," he said, "I forgot the phone book." He jumped up. When he returned holding it, he said, stooping to look out the windows toward the yard, "Your friend seems a little anxious."

Helen bounded up and looked. Roman had gotten out of the car and was pacing a few steps this way and then that, looking at the house but undecided whether to approach, rather like a puzzled bear. Helen went to the door and opened it, calling out to him: "I'll be right there, Roman! Just wait in the car."

She returned to her seat. "He worries about me," she said. "Well?" She looked to Luck, who was seated, paging through the slender rural telephone book.

"Don't you have a first name for this McVey?" he asked, looking up. "The only ones I see are Charlie and Verna, his wife."

"Well, actually, I'm looking for a piece of property," Helen said. "It's supposed to be on the river, not too far from here. But I didn't see any road down that way."

"You know what I think?" Luck closed the phone book and set it aside. "I'll bet it's that old hunting cabin of Tom Adams's. My father left it to Tom, along with some land—gratitude for long service. Then, of all things, when Tom died he left it to Charlie." Luck's expression darkened momentarily, as if recollecting an annoying circumstance. He smiled and added, "It's not occupied. McVey never uses it, but he rents it out in deer season to hunters from down below. There won't be anyone over there. Deer season isn't for a couple, three weeks anyway."

"That must be it. But how do you get to it?" Helen asked.

"I could draw you a map," Luck said. "Or heck, I could take you over there. It's just beyond my property. There's an old logging road, but I don't think your car . . . Were you supposed to meet someone?"

Helen could almost swear he winked, or came close to it. Abruptly, her warm feelings toward Luck faded. He seemed to be implying some faintly disreputable behavior on her part, perhaps a lovers' tryst or something equally absurd.

"A friend of mine is staying there, taking a little vacation, I guess," she said. "I have a message for him." Spoken like that, she realized that it sounded lame. She compounded the false impression by compulsively adding, "It's from his mother."

"His mother?" Luck nodded, knowingly, his brows arched.

Helen hated him for that look. "It's *about* his mother. She's ill or, rather, she was ill."

"Ah. And now . . . she's better?" Luck sipped his scotch, almost audibly relishing the taste.

"Yes, she's better," Helen said, with an edge in her voice. Almost against her will, she babbled on: "She'd been having trouble with her memory, you know, a 'senior moment.'" That sounded spiteful, she knew, but she rushed on: "She's remembered something . . . something important. She wanted me to tell her son."

"It must have been very important for you to drive so far. All morning, you said. From Detroit?" Luck tried to ease her apparent embarrassment by sounding detached.

"Yes, Detroit." Helen wanted to get up and leave, but somehow she couldn't. She was transfixed by Luck's intense gaze. She tugged at the hem of her skirt, but it wouldn't cover her knees.

"What's your rusticating friend's name?" he asked.

Helen wondered if he was patronizing her. "Muh—" she started to say, then finished with "—ullin."

"Mullin? I don't know him, I'm afraid." Luck shook his head. "I haven't seen anyone about, no strangers. Has he been up here long? Fishing, is he?"

"I guess so," Helen said. "He's been up here for a few days, I think."

"The Manistee is famous fishing," Luck said. "Mr. Mullin must be a fly fisherman. Guys come from all over—New York, Pennsylvania—to fish the Manistee. But usually it's more over toward Kalkaska, for those big summer hatches—the ephemera, gray drakes."

"I don't know anything about that," Helen said. "Well, I guess we better get going," she said. She managed to get to her feet. "Thanks for the drink. I'm sure Roman is getting antsy."

"Hey, I'll tell you what," Luck said, rising. He was his old, warm self. "We could just walk back there. It isn't that far . . . a pleasant walk. Your friend, Roman, could wait here." He reached for her glass. "Sure you won't have another?"

Helen let him take the glass. She flinched when their fingers touched. "No, no, it's too much to ask," Helen said. "We'll drive around, if you'll just point out the way."

Luck followed her into the kitchen and set the glasses on the counter. "You know, I'm intrigued by this memory loss, this 'senior moment,'" he said. "What is it, Alzheimer's or something? You know, I'm getting to that point . . ." He laughed, a bit wildly.

Helen stared at him. "No, nothing like that. She'd had an accident."

"Ah, yes. You said. I forgot. A 'senior moment' of my own. And you know what? I had another one. Maybe I'm the one with Alzheimer's." He offered another laugh, in which Helen did not join. "There is, or used to be, a phone in that old cabin. But I'll bet it's under Tom Adams's name still. Want me to get it? You could call your friend Mullin."

There was something about the way he said "Mullin" that seemed almost derisive, as if he didn't believe there was a man named Mullin.

Somehow, Luck had gotten between Helen and the door. He gestured at a telephone on the counter.

Helen looked wary. "No, I think I'd rather surprise him," she said.

"Ah. He doesn't know you're coming?" Luck said. He leaned back against the door. "That'll be a nice surprise. It's not often a pretty girl comes knocking at the cabin in the woods. Sort of like Little Red Riding Hood."

He was making some kind of joke, Helen realized, but she wondered suddenly if he wasn't a little crazy, just babbling, as she had been a moment earlier. He didn't look crazy, but . . . the association of the fairy tale and the woods, the two of them alone . . . For a confused moment his smile seemed fixed, even wolfish.

She laughed cheerfully. "Yes, that's . . . kind of *primal*, isn't it? Well," she said, in a more practical tone, "do I just go on down this road, the one we turned off at your mailbox?"

Luck's smile shifted to wry. He folded his arms and looked thoughtful, as if pondering how to explain the terribly complicated route through the forest to Grandmother's house. He said, "Well, you could go that way, but it's so far around. You have to go clear back out to the highway, then south toward Cadillac. The road to the cabin is not marked, no sign or anything. You'd miss it, sure as shootin'. And heck, through the woods it's . . . oh, not more than a fifteen-minute walk."

"Oh, I'm really not dressed for it," Helen said, glancing down at her skirt, her white sneakers. "And besides, there'd I be and Roman would still be here, with the car. No, we'd better drive and take our chances on finding that road. After you turn on the highway, how far would it be to the road?"

"Well, suit yourself," Luck said. "You go about, oh, a mile on the highway, something like that. It won't be the first road—there's a bunch of more or less unused roads in these woods. Only the hunters use them. You might have to try one or two. But you'll have the same problem with that Cadillac. No room to turn around, places where the car might get high-centered. You could lose a muffler, if you don't go slow! Hey! Why am I fooling around? By now I could have driven over there and shown you the way! How would that be?"

"Oh, I couldn't put you out," Helen said. "I'm sure we'll find it."

"Nonsense! Just give me a sec. I'll have to let the guys know I'm going out. Well, heck, I can call them on the radio. Come on!" He grabbed a field jacket off a peg next to the door and clapped a Filson hat on his head at a rakish angle.

He opened the door and gallantly waved her outside. Luck leaned on the driver's door of the Cadillac with both hands and explained to Roman that he'd lead them over to the cabin.

"Go ahead and turn around, I'll be right with you," Luck said. "Hey, you could ride with me, if you want," he called across the front seat to Helen. But it seemed that she preferred to ride with Roman. He shrugged and jogged quickly to a large black pickup, pulled it out, and led them out of the yard.

Helen could see him talking on one of the walkie-talkie phones as he drove slowly through the woods toward the gate. "Roman, that guy is really creepy," she said.

Roman looked at her with narrowed eyes. "He didn't try nothin'? You shoulda said somethin'."

"No, he didn't try anything," Helen reassured him. "He was just . . . creepy. At first he seemed really friendly, then I think he figured out I was looking for Mulheisen."

"How'd he figure that?" Roman said.

"I almost gave it away," she admitted. She related the conversation.

"He's sure takin' his time," Roman said, "jabberin' away a mile a minute. But so what if he knows you're lookin' for Mulheisen? I don't get it."

Helen didn't get it either. What was Mulheisen to Luck? They came to the gate and waited while he unlocked it, drove through, then waited again while he locked it.

"This guy is into security," Roman said.

Luck stopped as he passed by them to say, "Just follow me. It's not that far, but you'll miss the road if you don't tag along."

They nodded and followed him out. Ten minutes later they were on the highway. Again they drove along quite slowly, causing a few cars to pull out and pass them, although this was hardly a high traffic area, through a rather extensively forested countryside. The trees came right to the edge of the road, making it almost dark already, although it wasn't that late in the afternoon. But the clouds had moved in again after a pleasant morning and early afternoon of mostly sun. The trees were brilliant in their fall foliage, despite the rain of the previous night, and despite having lost many leaves in the wind. It was clear that fall was coming to its end with a quickened pace.

After about two miles, they crested a long hill and there was a large iron bridge below, painted silver. Luck slowed the pickup and turned at a road just before the bridge.

"Oh, for heaven's sake," Helen groused, "he could have told us it was the road just before the bridge."

Indeed, it was the river road, obviously, although it soon moved away from the stream to take a easier route around some knobs and gullies. They lost sight of the river through the trees. And very soon they lost sight of Luck, who had sped on. Roman did not dare to match his speed, the big old Cadillac already

bounding alarmingly on the undulating rough road, with its de-
clivities and rises. It went on for at least a mile. Soon enough, they
pulled up short of the rustic cabin, perched on a rise looking out
over the river and the forest beyond. Luck was standing next to
his truck.

"Doesn't look like anyone's here," he said, when they drove
up and parked.

He looked around at the forest behind them.

"Did you knock?" Helen said, getting out.

"No," Luck said. "Try it. Looks like someone has been here,
but whoever it was is gone now. Sorry."

Helen went up to the door and pounded, looking in through
the large windows from the spacious deck. There was no response
and in general there was that utter absence of sound and life that
tells one that no one is at home. She strolled out on the deck and
stood there, hands on hips, gazing out over the broad expanse of
forest that reached off to the west.

"I'll be darned," she said, returning to the vehicles.

Luck looked at her amiably. "Now what? Maybe he's gone
back to Detroit."

Helen was stymied. "Maybe," she said, "but he might have
just gone into town, for groceries or something."

Roman got out and stretched. "Jeez, I'm hungry," he said.

"Well, why don't you folks come on back to the house?" Luck
said. "I'll fix you some dinner. Hate to think of you sitting out here
waiting, not knowing if Mullin is returning."

"No, I don't think so," Helen said firmly. "We'll go on into
town and get a motel. How far is it to Traverse City?"

"Cadillac's closer," Luck said. "About eighteen, twenty miles.
It's kind of a toss-up, but Cadillac's easier to get to."

"Well, I guess we'll go to Cadillac then," she said. She
thanked Luck for all his help.

Jon A. Jackson

He assured her it was no problem. He waited for them to drive off, then turned around and followed. He soon fell back and they lost sight of him.

Helen looked back. "He was in a hurry to get here," she said, "now he's dawdling."

Roman drove on. When they got to the highway he turned south, toward Cadillac, but once they were beyond the bridge and out of sight of the river Helen told him to pull over.

"What's up?" he said, easing the Cadillac onto the narrow shoulder. There was a little house a ways ahead.

"Let's just wait a bit," Helen said. "Mulheisen had been there. I saw his cigars—*my* cigars—the butts anyway, in the ashtray. La Donnas. He'll be coming back. A guy doesn't leave them for someone to clean up. I'll tell you something else: Joe was there."

"He was?" Roman was surprised. "You mean, just now?"

"Maybe. I think so."

"There wasn't no car," Roman pointed out.

"No, there wasn't," Helen conceded. "Maybe he went somewhere with Mulheisen. Although . . . that doesn't seem too likely. Does it?"

"I don't t'ink so," Roman said, shaking his head slowly.

They sat silently for a while, then Roman said, "You wanna go back?"

"In a minute," she said.

"I'm starvin'," Roman said. "You? We ain't had nothin' since breakfast."

"All right," Helen said. She nodded forward.

They drove to a small town up the road a few miles and ate a country-style meal of chicken with mashed potatoes and gravy at a family restaurant. Roman ate with great gusto, but Helen wasn't so keen on the cuisine. It was way too starchy, she said. Roman shrugged and ordered the cherry pie with ice cream. "Good pie,"

304

he said as they left. "I remember that pie. I come up here with your dad once."

Helen was astonished. "Up here?"

"Somewheres around here," Roman said.

"I can't imagine Pop up here, in the woods. What were you doing here?"

"Nothin'," Roman said. "I can't remember. Your old man hated it. We hung out for a few days and went back. Almost drove him nuts."

There was a log cabin bar on the highway a few miles from Luck's place. It was currently named the Dog House, but Joe thought it could just as easily be called the Road House. A spacious barroom, a low ceiling, suitably gloomy, with a tiny bandstand toward the rear and space for patrons to dance. No one was dancing there now, of course—it was only a little after midday. They had large jars of pickled eggs on the bar, pickled pigs' feet, too. Joe had a couple of each. They were a bit alarming to look at but tasty. He ordered a draft beer and sat chatting with the busty blond woman who was tending bar. They were the only people in the bar. She said her name was Jerri. She had a sad look but a lovely smile. She asked Joe if he was from around here.

"I'm not," Joe said, "but I'm looking at property. I'd like a little cabin in the woods."

Jerri thought that was a good idea. Was he a fisherman? A hunter?

Neither, Joe told her, he just liked the idea of a cabin in the woods. But why, he wondered aloud, was a pretty woman like herself so sad? Was it because it was a nice day and she had to work?

Jerri's smile got even brighter. She seemed to be about thirty-five, a little older than Joe. "It doesn't look like that nice a day," she said. She glanced in the mirror behind her. "Oh, I don't

know, maybe I didn't sleep right or something." She frowned, recollecting something, but added, "It's just my nature, I guess."

She wore a wedding ring and Joe wondered if it had something to do with her apparent sadness. She was married to the owner,
it turned out. She freely admitted that he could be the source of
her sadness. He was very jealous, but then he didn't pay her much
attention either. She, too, she told him, was attracted to the idea
of cabins in the woods. She liked flowers, and birds too.

Joe suggested that if he could find some property and build a
cabin she could visit him sometime. Jerri seemed to like that notion.
Joe had another beer and mused aloud on what he would do in the
woods. Bird-watch, perhaps, he suggested. He'd recently met an elderly lady who had made it seem interesting. He'd never thought
about them much, but now he wanted to know more about birds.

"And the bees?" Jerri suggested, arching a brow.

Joe smiled and said that was also a good idea. This seemed a
promising gambit, one that Joe was happy to pursue. But now a string
of customers came in, some from off the highway, others local farmers who also flirted with Jerri and she with them. Joe sat quietly,
thinking about Luck.

Luck had been the second person in twenty-four hours to
suggest that Echeverria could be lured to the States so that Joe could
settle their accounts. It occurred to Joe that, after all, he had no
beef with Echeverria; it was all one-way. Or was it? Maybe it was
another of the Colonel's fictions, facilitated by Luck. Joe thought
it would be smart to discuss it with Echeverria himself; maybe they
could settle this peacefully. All Joe wanted was to be left alone. He
had more of a beef with Luck, if it came to that. He was the one
spreading malicious rumors about Joe and telling people where he
lived—not that Joe lived there anymore. Or did he?

The sexual interplay with Jerri had aroused him, but mostly
it reminded him of Helen. He had to admit, he missed her. Right

now. Not just sexually, although that was always present in his thoughts of her, but also in terms of comradeship, for want of a better word. He appreciated her help. She expanded his reach, he felt. Without her, he realized, he was less versatile.

Joe thought it would be a good idea to contact Echeverria. But how? Well, Luck could do that for him. He'd said as much. As soon as he thought it, though, he knew it was bullshit. Any contact would go through the Colonel, and who knew what the Colonel's agenda was? Luck couldn't contact Echeverria.

Luck, Joe realized clearly, was an inveterate loser. He was a plausible-looking guy, impressive for a while, but the longer you were around him the more you realized that he was a loser. Losers are dangerous people, Joe thought, especially when they're oblivious to their inferiority. So . . . what to do about Luck?

The momentary rush of custom had just as suddenly abated. There was again no one in the bar, Joe realized. Jerri drifted back to him, looking lonely. Joe liked her, although he couldn't help thinking that she, too, was a loser. Joe asked her if she knew Luck.

"Imp?" Jerri's face clouded. "Yeah, I know him. He comes in here just about every day, or used to. He doesn't come in much lately. Why you interested in him? He doesn't have any property to sell."

"He doesn't? I thought he was a big property owner around here. Doesn't he own some river property?"

"He might have, at one time," Jerri said, "or his grampa did. Seems like Imp has pretty much pissed all that away." Her tone said clearly that she was not fond of Imp Luck.

Joe said, "Well, he's got a cabin in the woods, hasn't he? Have you ever been there?" That was pointed enough, Joe felt. And Jerri rose to the bait.

"I'll never go again, that's for sure."

So she'd had an affair with Luck, and it had not turned out well. Oddly, knowing it made Joe think less of both of them. Her wistful loneliness suddenly seemed pathetic. He knew it was unfair. Minutes earlier, he'd been contemplating making a play for her himself, but now he knew he couldn't do it. Joe felt sorry. As for Luck, it seemed that he was the sort of man who . . . well, like Joe, putatively . . . fooled around with roadhouse barmaids.

"I heard he was a big man around here," Joe said.

Jerri looked contemptuous. "Imp always thinks he's a big man," she said. "That's his problem. He thought he was somebody, but it was his grampa. He steps all over people, but what is he? A big man in the barnyard. He has all them fool Huleys following him around, wearing camo, waving the flag, marching in the woods, toting guns, and scaring folks."

"Huleys?"

"The Huleys are from over near Beckley. No-account hicks. Well, there's always a few ornery pups in a litter. There's good Huleys and bad Huleys, like anybody else. Most of them are all right, but there's a few could do with a little more time in the pen, not that they haven't already spent more than they should have."

Joe asked about the sins of the bad Huleys and was treated to a long list: robberies, petty crime, bullying, ignorant shiftlessness, multiple bastardies . . . she could go on, but what was the point? Luck had always gotten along with them, though. Indeed, he'd urged them on, kept them going with small loans, jobs. Luck was a facilitator of backwoods skullduggery. According to Jerri, he did it because it flattered his ego to have a bunch of worthless followers. Although, lately, she conceded, he seemed to be attracting a more middle-class kind of supporter: outsiders, in her opinion, folks from down below, newcomers who didn't know who they were dealing with.

Joe could see it. Luck was one of those guys who gave a meaning to the concept of "rabble-rouser." Although Joe had never thought in these terms before, Luck was a man who ought to be shot. He couldn't recall anyone about whom he'd had such feelings. Most of those he'd shot had been bad enough, but Joe's reasons for shooting them had never been based on the men's character, but rather the necessity of shooting them before they shot him.

This man was so self-involved, so oblivious of everyone else, that he was simply too dangerous. Even petty concerns were likely, Joe felt, to be the premise for disastrous actions.

The notion actually gave him a bit of a shock. Was he himself guilty of Luck's kind of thinking? Was he being petty, self-obsessed, in even thinking casually that Luck should be erased because he was causing some minor discomfort to him? Joe didn't think so. Luck was bad news. Also, he was too tall. And Joe wasn't in a good mood.

"What about this guy Hook?" Joe asked. "I talked to him on the phone. He didn't sound like a Huley-type."

"Hook? I never heard of any Hook," Jerri said. "He must be a new one, from down below."

Joe smiled at Jerri as she drew another beer. She caught his glance and smiled at him, the same sweet, lost smile. Joe almost winced. She was still thinking about the birds and the bees, he saw. He took a sip of the beer and pushed it away. "I've got to run," he said. "See you later," and he left. He didn't look back for her reaction.

He drove along the highway, thinking at first that he'd go back to Luck's. He'd ask him to contact Echeverria, set up a meet. Luck, he was sure, would agree. But it would go through Tucker, and who knew what would ensue.

Just at that moment he came to a lonely-looking dirt road that led back into the forest. He followed it for a mile or so, bumping along slowly. It hadn't been used much lately. That was good. And he'd passed no dwellings. He pulled off into a little clearing and immediately set to work, inventorying his arms. He'd already done this, of course. He knew exactly what he had. But it was well to make certain.

He had an AK-47, a Remington .12-gauge, a Stoner rifle, a Heckler & Koch MP5A3, a Llama 9mm automatic, a Smith and Wesson Model 59 9mm auto (he liked the fourteen-round magazine). There were others, but that ought to be enough for something. He checked over each piece carefully. The Remington shotgun was a Model 870 that he had cut down to a fourteen-inch barrel and added an A&W converter for a flattened horizontal shot pattern. He decided on #4 buckshot for this gun, preferring the .27-caliber pellets; at least a third of each shell's thirty-four pellets were likely to strike a target fifty yards distant. It also had a recoil pad, an extended magazine for eight shells, and rifle-type sights.

A neighbor of his out in Montana used to remark, wryly, "The people you bump into when you ain't armed." It had been amusing. He wasn't sure why it had occurred to him. The context was different.

Now all he had to do, he thought, was wait for dark and go back for a more serious conversation with Mr. Luck. He'd had that old familiar feeling, after he'd left Luck, that somehow he had not covered the points he'd meant to. Maybe a revisit would be more productive. But he knew that a revisit would be unlikely to be appreciated. Luck wouldn't be so happy to see him and would likely react differently.

He decided to take a little nap, here in the woods with the wind rattling the leaves. The beer had made him sleepy. Or maybe it was the pickled pigs' feet. He spread his ground tarp and sleeping bag out on the leaves and lay back, staring up into the trees. They swayed in the wind with a fine rushing noise; the leaves came spinning down, the clouds rolled over . . . it was a hypnotic feeling. He could hear a distant woodpecker, hammering away. He wondered what kind of woodpecker it was. That in itself added to the odd, displaced feeling he had: he couldn't recall ever wondering what

kind of bird this one was, or that one. He supposed it had something to do with his conversation with the barmaid. Then he knew
it was the effect of meeting Mrs. Mulheisen. She knew all the birds.
He was sure she would have been able to tell him the name—the
species? is that what they say?—of this woodpecker, hacking away
so industriously, mindlessly, in this lonely, drafty woods.

He was dozing off, thinking about the little bird woman . . .
she was like a bird herself, a sparrow . . . when he recalled something that Cora Mulheisen had let drop. He couldn't quite recall
it, something about remembering. Then it struck him. She had remembered a man who had been at the bombing, a very strange man.
She hadn't been able to recall much about him, it seemed, except
that he was agitated. And he was tall.

Suddenly, Joe sat up. It had been Luck. He knew it. It was
like Luck to have been there. And if he'd been there, he was involved in the bombing. Joe also recalled the Colonel's remark about
Mulheisen and his mother's memory problems. Did the Colonel
know that Luck had been there?

Joe then thought that if Mulheisen heard this he'd say Joe
was jumping to conclusions. Mulheisen would withhold judgment,
he'd weigh everything he'd heard, he'd dig deeper, he'd refuse to
pin it on Luck until he had more conclusive evidence. But Joe knew.
That was the difference between him and Mulheisen. Mulheisen
pondered; Joe *knew*. Call it intuition, whatever, he knew.

The question was, did Luck know that Mrs. Mulheisen knew?
Well, how could he? She hadn't known it herself until the day Joe
had met her. And he had stupidly ignored it. Well, it didn't concern him. He hadn't known much if anything about Luck. Now he
did. Which led to the next question: what to do about Luck? The
answer seemed to lie in the same direction as he'd earlier surmised.

*   *   *

Roman and Helen drove back to the cabin. When they were perhaps a quarter mile from it, Helen told Roman to find a place to pull off. That wasn't so simple, but ultimately he managed to get the hulking Cadillac off to one side. The ground was rough, but they were shielded from the road by the brush.

Helen jumped in the spacious backseat. "We could sleep back here, if we have to," she remarked. She rummaged in her bags and got out some jeans and a sweater for herself. It had turned cool now that night was coming on. She had thrown in some clever-looking rubberized low-cut boots when she had packed that morning. They were bright blue. She couldn't remember where she'd gotten them, but they were perfect for what she had in mind.

From another bag she took the Remington shotgun that Joe had modified for her. He'd shortened the barrel a couple of inches. She loaded it with shells while Roman looked on. He had brought his overcoat, naturally. He wore his usual businessman's hat, with the brim turned up all the way around. He looked like a cartoon bear.

"Are you armed?" Helen said.

Roman patted his breast.

"Okay, let's walk," she said. They went forward along the edge of the road, cautiously. At length they came to a spot where they could just make out the dark roof of the cabin jutting up against the barely lighter sky. There were no lights. No one had returned. They could see no sign of Luck's vehicle, so evidently he hadn't lingered either.

Helen was tempted to go on to the cabin, but something held her back. She couldn't have said what it was. The silence, perhaps. It was now quite dark. They had to walk on the road, which had a light, sandy base, in order to find their way. The clouds had moved in and the wind had picked up. The hardwood trees rattled their leaves, and the pines—which seemed to predominate along here—

swayed and soughed gently. The inevitable owl hooted distantly. Off to their left they could hear the vague sound of the river, or so they imagined. It was there, they knew, but it wasn't making a truly identifiable noise, except that infrequently something splashed, presumably a leaping trout.

Roman clearly had no taste for this. The woods spooked him, it seemed. He urged her quietly, "Le's go back to the car. If Joe's around, we'll see him comin'."

"You go back," Helen suggested. Roman stayed. But in fact Helen didn't know what to do. She didn't want to go forward, or go back, and that left her just standing on the edge of the woods. It seemed dumb. It was too damp to sit. So what did one do? Just stand next to a tree all night? And to what end?

Then Roman murmured, "There's somebuddy." He pointed down toward the cabin.

Helen strained her eyes. She saw nothing. But eventually a dark form detached itself from the bulk of the cabin, then merged into the general darkness again. Someone was on the deck, or had been. Helen instinctively stepped back into the edge of the woods. Roman joined her. Unfortunately, she realized, there were so many leaves down that one couldn't walk here without creating what seemed to her like a tidal wave of rustling. She considered that the sound of the wind was high enough and the cabin distant enough that whoever was out there could not hear them . . . if they kept quiet.

And then, from behind them, well back in the woods—how far neither could estimate—there came a persistent machine noise. Not a vehicle. It came no nearer. It was an engine of some sort, though well muffled. Also a clicking, grinding sound. It came from the direction of Luck's place. Neither of them had any idea how far or near that could be. This noise seemed hundreds of yards away, perhaps a thousand. It was muffled by the intervening trees, obviously. It may have been a quarter mile, for all they knew, or more. And then it stopped.

Now they could hear an occasional voice, although they could make out no words. Helen peered into the woods, ignoring the man at the cabin for now. She was strongly tempted to go in there, see what was going on. It sounded like more than a couple of people, talking or calling to one another.

There followed a long silence, during which both Helen and Roman turned their attention back to the cabin. Whatever was happening in the woods was over. Shortly, they were startled to realize that someone was walking through the woods not far from them. They guessed it was the man they'd spotted earlier. He passed quite near. They could hear his breathing. And then he spoke, evidently into a walkie-talkie phone.

"I'm comin'," he said. "No. Not a sign." He swished on.

Obviously, with the noise he was making, they could follow unheard. Helen murmured to Roman, "You stay. Wait for Joe. I'll be back." She set off after the man.

Roman was set to go after her, but the woods deterred him. He was from the old country. There, the woods were not a place a sensible man went at night. He had childhood memories of tales of witches, ogres, wolves, and bears. They were just tales but not so easily effaced from the psychic memory. Besides, he told himself, someone had to stay in case Joe returned.

The man in the woods was walking a path that he knew, Helen discerned. She stayed back. He soon must have determined that it was safe to make a light, because now she could see a powerful beam racing ahead of the man, flicking back and forth, sometimes directed at the ground, as if he were picking his way. In the beam she noticed that there were small reflectors mounted on the larger trees, rather high up, above eye height, say ten feet. They marked a definite route. One would scarcely notice them during the day, unless one were a bird-watcher, perhaps. Even so, they were tiny red lights. At night, a stranger in the forest might take them for the eyes of arboreal beasts. Perhaps even owls.

Eventually the man came to a road, and Helen shortly thereafter. Now both could make quicker passage. She stopped when she was perhaps a half mile from the river. The man she was following had not stopped. She could easily see him striding on toward a remarkable, well-lighted area. Huge floodlights bathed a large clearing. What she saw astonished her.

She appeared to be looking directly into a large hill that had opened up. Inside, or rather just outside the hill, a black helicopter sat on a ramp that had projected out from the interior. Several men were walking about, talking. The man she'd followed approached and engaged a couple of the others in conversation.

Luck strode out from the interior, dressed in a dark jumpsuit. He carried a pilot's helmet. He spoke to the men. The one who had returned trotted off while Luck climbed into the helicopter. The man returned quickly, carrying an odd-shaped weapon, some kind of rifle with an assortment of attachments. The man was also wearing a helmet now, and he lugged a satchel bulging with what Helen supposed was equipment. He tossed that into the chopper and climbed in beside Luck.

A few minutes later there was a whirring, whining noise and the rotors began to slowly revolve. The engine coughed and roared, then settled down to a steady drone. The rotors whirled faster, and abruptly the chopper rose off its ramp, straight up into the sky, then banked and sped off to the south.

Helen slipped back into the woods. The last view she had of the scene was the ramp retreating into the interior of the hill and two vast doors rumbling and grinding, the sound they'd heard from the river. The doors closed, the lights were gone, and all that one could make out as they pinched together was the impression of a hill re-forming itself.

When Helen got back to the river she found Roman, pretty much where she'd left him. "What the hell was that?" he said. "A chopper? Out here?"

She told him what she'd seen while they walked back to where they'd left the car.

"I wonder where he's off to in such a hurry?" Roman wondered.

Helen had a bad feeling, but she didn't voice it.

20

Wag a Dog

It was perfect driving weather, cloudy but with occasional sunniness. Mulheisen decided to stay off the interstate and make his way home leisurely on the smaller highways that carried him across state over toward Lake Huron. He enjoyed driving through the small towns with names like Sugar Rapids, crossing rivers named Titabawassee. He'd angle home from Bay City, through the base of the thumb.

This was thoroughly domesticated agricultural land, but still with considerable forests. He tried to imagine the country as it had been in Pontiac's time, heavily forested, with established trails for the tribes to move back and forth to their various seasonal villages. And he found himself thinking about the Colonel.

On their way to Cadillac, the Colonel had been silent at first, recovering from the heavy drinking of the night before. Mulheisen was familiar with that state, although he had not experienced it for a while now. Eventually Tucker had begun to feel more lively and talk. He'd talked about the "spy biz," as he called it.

"I came to it late," he said, "after the air force. But, heck, it's been over twenty years now, and I've learned that it's something other than I'd expected. You think of agencies like the CIA and all kinds of images occur, mostly what you get from novels and movies, television. It's not like that, Mul."

Mul had muttered something like, "I suppose not."

"No, it's not a single agency," the Colonel went on. "It's all these little groups and subgroups." He reiterated some of what he'd told Joe, but in a different vein. "Joe doesn't quite get it," he said. "You're a professional. I'm sure it was similar in the force."

Mulheisen didn't recall now what he'd replied, but thinking of it, he realized why the scene in Cadillac had left him out of sorts. He'd been in Homicide for a while, but left to go back to the precinct for approximately the reason that Tucker's actions had disgruntled him. You could rarely follow a case through to a conclusion, working in a large bureau, working downtown. At least in the precinct you were left alone to follow up your cases. You didn't always "solve" them, but you tended to find out pretty much what had happened. That was gratifying, to a degree.

He passed along next to yet another small, unidentified lake, noticing the masses of ducks sitting near some reed beds. His mind wandered to Constance Malachi. He knew almost nothing about her, hadn't even seen a picture, but he recalled that Charlie McVey had been impressed with her beauty, her cooking. She'd been a lawyer, obviously a bright, ambitious woman. Then she'd fallen for Luck. He was a fairly dashing man, handsome, presumably a man of property and substance. A bit of a con man. Mulheisen had seen lawyers, bright women, fall for their clients. It was often hard to account for. Even harder were the rare cases he'd heard of where a prosecutor had fallen for someone she'd been after. Which was Malachi? It might be interesting to find out, but it wasn't going to happen now, he thought. The crucial issue was whether Malachi had been murdered. Did anyone really care? Would it all be revealed?

Tucker, in his conversation this morning, had mentioned an agency. Mulheisen thought he had called it the Office of Special

Projects, or something like that. "Did you ever hear of it?" Tucker had asked him. Mulheisen hadn't. Tucker said it was more powerful than the CIA. "It isn't secret," Tucker said. "It's been written about in the *New York Times*. It's mentioned on Sunday talk shows. 'Everybody' knows about it, but the public doesn't pay attention. It's very powerful. It wags the dog. And then there are the groups that people don't know about, not even in the agencies themselves. I know about a lot of them. They're very important. They work for, and against, the administration, depending on who's in them. Quite often, what gets done is because of these informal groups . . . and what doesn't get done."

Mulheisen wondered if a group like that would determine whether Malachi had been murdered or not. And if that would determine whether or not Imp Luck was brought to justice, assuming he had been responsible for the death of Malachi. Mulheisen hated that kind of thing. What kind of country were they living in where the rule of law had been so . . . so what? Corrupted? Subverted? Or was it how things had always been, and he hadn't noticed?

He recalled how, after Pontiac's conspiracy and war, evidence had come out concerning the Ottawa leader's role in the casual murder of little girl, a captive whose parents had been murdered. Pontiac had never had to answer for that bit of brutality. Indeed, because of his usefulness to the British, it had been decided by "higher powers" to allow him to go free. That is, until another cabal had plotted and successfully murdered him in Illinois. Of course, those were lawless times, but were times less lawless now? Presumably. That's what the U.S. Constitution was all about.

The question now was what he would do about Luck. He didn't know. Probably nothing. It was out of his hands.

Joe got up and stashed his gear away. It would soon be dark. He drove out to the highway, then doubled back toward Luck's. He decided that an approach from Charlie's cabin was not the best idea. He would go in the way he'd come out. In the event, he got into the Luck property approximately where Mulheisen and he had come out. It was quite dark by this time. There was some kind of activity going on over near the mound, or the hill, whatever that site was. He counted at least four vehicles, including Luck's pickup. Joe skirted the area and made for the house. What he needed was to confront Luck, but alone. He could wait for him to return to the house. If things went well, he could promote the Echeverria meeting.

As expected, Luck was not in the house. Joe looked around. In the rear of the house there was a computer room. Nothing as extensive as Brooker Moos's layout but still quite up to date. Unfortunately, Joe had almost no computer skills. He supposed that on that computer, currently running a screen saver that was like an electronic Persian rug being woven and rewoven, he would have been able to find addresses, phone numbers, documents, who knew what all? In a way, he was just as happy; he didn't like sitting and looking at screens. For one thing, you never knew who was sneaking up behind you.

Instead he looked for other stuff: address books, letters, lists. But that kind of thing didn't exist. What did exist, however, was a telephone. Having been reminded of Brooker Moos, he called him.

"Hello?" Brooker said tentatively. When he learned it was Joe, he exclaimed, "Jeeziss! You're calling me from M. P. Luck's phone!"

"How'd you know that?" Joe asked. He was walking about, checking the approaches to the house.

"For some reason he hasn't blocked his number, and it's registering on my caller ID," Moos said.

"Ah. Well, he's not here at the moment," Joe said. "I may have to hang up suddenly, in fact. So let's talk fast. He's got all this computer gear here. How do I get into it?"

"If he's got any sense, you can't," Moos said.

"It's running a screen saver," Joe said.

"You're kidding. Okay, he's got a mouse there. What is it, a standard type with two oval discs on either side, or does it have a wheel?"

Joe found what Moos was talking about. "It has two oval things and a ball."

"Roll that ball. That controls the cursor on the screen, but it also activates the screen. The screen saver will disappear."

Joe did as told and got a simple screen, apparently some kind of home location, with lots of information about news, temperature, time, and so on. "Now what?" he said.

Moos explained that the screen saver was an automatic thing that came on when the screen hadn't been used for a while. Luck, he said, would know if he came in that someone had been on the screen if the screen saver wasn't activated.

Joe took a little tour of the windows. No sign of Luck. "How do I activate the screen saver?"

Moos led him through the process, but he warned that it would take precious seconds if Luck suddenly appeared. Joe managed it in about ten seconds.

"Just hit preview and don't touch the mouse afterward," Moos said. "The next time he touches it, it'll just disappear, as usual. So what is it you're looking for?"

Joe explained. Moos pondered for a moment, then said, "Go back to the screen and look in that row at the bottom for an icon that looks like a letter." He led Joe through the process, explaining that there should be a row of functions running across the top of the mail server, one of which would be the address book. Alternatively, there might be a list running down the side of names. If he left-clicked on one of them he would, possibly, find messages Luck had received from that person, if he'd saved it to a folder. It didn't seem likely, but . . .

Under "Contacts," Joe found the abbreviation "Etch." He clicked on it and *lo!* There were messages from Echeverria.

Moos was surprised. "This guy has no security at all. Well, there you are. Read anything interesting?"

Joe said, "I'll say. Echeverria is flying into Traverse City this evening. It looks like he's expecting Luck to pick him up. How do I find out when and where? He doesn't mention it."

Moos told him how to find "Sent," where there might be a message from Luck to Echeverria.

Joe got to that quickly. And there was the message. "He's meeting him with a helicopter! Now, where's he going to get a chopper? Oops, I'm out of here."

Luck's, or somebody's, footfalls were heard from the porch. Joe clicked off the phone. He desperately fiddled with the mouse, trying to activate the screen saver, but he got screwed up. He abandoned the effort in a panic and slipped into a closet. Under his breath, he cursed all computers. The screen blandly displayed the last message Luck had sent, to Echeverria.

He waited tensely, Llama in hand, while he could hear Luck moving about in the house. He seemed to be in a room immediately adjacent, probably a bedroom. He was opening what sounded like a folding closet door, similar to the one Joe was standing behind. Then he went into the bathroom. Water ran. Joe was still holding the telephone. He darted out and replaced it on the hook in the kitchen, then ducked back into the closet. The toilet flushed. Luck went into the kitchen. Various noises, cupboards opening and closing. Back to the bedroom. A sound that Joe felt must be the changing of clothes. Then out the front door.

Joe peeked out. The screen saver was running. He was about to slip out himself when Luck returned. Joe barely got back in his closet. Luck came in, glanced at the computer, then switched it off, apparently not noticing anything problematical.

He turned off the lights in the room and went back out to the living room.

Some other men came in and he spoke to them, but Joe couldn't catch much of the conversation, only that Luck would be back later. Then they all left.

Joe went to the computer again, hoping to gain further information about Luck's plans, but he couldn't figure out how to turn on the machine. He called Moos again, using his cell phone this time, as he now realized he should have in the first place. Moos said that Luck must have locked the computer.

"That's his idea of security," Moos said scornfully. "Oh well, there's no point in trying to break in. And since he's turned it off, I doubt that I could crack into his setup and read the e-mail."

"Can you do that?" Joe was shocked.

Moos said he could, sometimes. But if the computer was locked and off, well, forget it.

Outside, Joe got as close as he could to the hill. He was in plenty of time to witness the opening of the hangar doors, the emersion of the helicopter, and the takeoff. It surprised him, beyond the actual circumstance of the elaborate concealment device, since it was far too early for Luck to be flying to Traverse City. Echeverria wasn't due for hours. He watched the buttoning-up process after the departure with some bemusement.

By now it was dark. Mulheisen had passed through Bay City and was arcing down toward Mount Clemens, and home. It was late. He hoped they hadn't waited supper for him. He saw, as he passed the marina, that the guys were still working—the floodlights were on over there. This was their busy time, of course. They would have been hauling boats out for the winter, he was sure, and getting them ready for storage.

The lights were on in the house, as he'd expected. The nurse would have been relieved, and the new one settling in for the evening. As he parked in the drive, he glanced over at the new building, the study. It looked unchanged, except that the roof was shingled, gleaming with new shakes. Just as he turned off his headlights, he glimpsed a man run around the corner of the building.

He sat there, surprised. Had he seen that? Had that man actually been wearing some kind of headgear and binoculars, or some kind of night-vision apparatus? Had he been carrying a rifle of some sort?

A second later Mulheisen was out of the car, on his knees, and scrambling toward the protection of the old oak tree. He made it and stood up carefully. He had one of Joe Service's Llamas in his hand. He'd meant to give it back before they'd parted that morning, but he'd forgotten it. He'd snatched it off the seat as he'd bailed out. He couldn't remember if there was a round in the chamber. He presumed not, and he feared making the noise of racking the slide back to make sure. But it was useless if it wasn't cocked and ready.

He slipped off toward the opposite edge of the old barn, racking the slide as he ran. He made it without making too much noise, he thought. But he had to assume that if the intruder was still around he must know where he was. Why was the man here? And who was he? One of Tucker's men? Had Tucker decided to provide a guard? Mulheisen didn't think so. Tucker would have said something. You didn't put an armed man on a property without the knowledge of the people being protected. But there were a dozen exceptions, of course. Maybe he'd only put the man out since Mulheisen had gone, but he'd had ample opportunity to inform him last night or this morning. Maybe his mother knew about it, or the nurse.

He could see the nurse in the kitchen, standing at the kitchen window, peering outside. Obviously, she could see Mulheisen's car, must have noticed him pulling up, his lights being doused. He willed her away from that window. *For god's sake, don't come out on the back porch and call.* But she merely disappeared—to call the police, he hoped, or even Tucker's office. She didn't seem concerned about anyone she expected to be outside.

Mulheisen slipped away from the barn, in a crouch, intending to reach an old apple tree, halfway between the barn and the new study.

Almost immediately his fears were answered. A splinter flew from the corner of the barn, at about chest height. Mulheisen had heard no shot. This man had a silenced gun.

Mulheisen lay flat on the ground in the darkness. The ground was damp, but he barely noticed. He eased toward the tree on his forearms and toes. A neighbor's car drove by, went on up the street, and turned in.

Mulheisen could see, though not well. This was a rural or, at least, a suburban setting. There were no streetlights on the road, for instance. It was dark, but there was more light than one might expect; not just from houses, including his own, or the not too distant floodlights at the marina, but a general glow from the low base of the clouds, the reflection from the lights of roads and businesses, civilization not so very remote as one imagined.

Mulheisen's mind buzzed with questions, most of which he scarcely acknowledged. Where had this man come from? The lake? It was dark out there, and the field was dark.

Then he saw his assailant. He was creeping along the edge of the study. Perhaps he thought that he'd hit Mulheisen and he was checking. He was a slim fellow, all in black. He seemed to be carrying a heavy pack on his back and the silhouette of his head was distorted by some kind of apparatus he wore. Night glasses, apparently.

Mulheisen wasn't very familiar with this equipment, but he had the impression that, while it employed available light, too much light could have the countereffect of somewhat occluding vision. He wondered, uncertainly, if that was what was happening, because he could see the man all right: night glasses might be more of an hindrance than a help.

Another question intruded. Was the man alone? Did he have a backup shooter stationed nearby? Mulheisen peered about from the brush near the base of the apple tree. He couldn't see anyone else. But he was reluctant to expose himself, to rush the man, who was now no more than fifty feet away. He was looking toward the barn, obviously focused on that corner, scanning it for the body of his presumed victim. He edged away from the side of the new structure, evidently considering the apple tree as a halfway point from which he could reach the barn.

The moment of decision was fast approaching. The man stood erect, moving away from the study, and raised his weapon, an awkwardly shaped contraption with a heavy barrel and some kind of fancy scope mounted on it. When he began to move toward the tree, Mulheisen got to his knees. The man hesitated then, perhaps reconsidering. He turned away, as if to head toward the field beyond.

Mulheisen cried out, "Drop it! Now!"

The man whirled toward Mulheisen, the gun at hip level, and fired. The rifle made a plopping sound.

The bullet struck near Mulheisen and a splinter of the apple tree hit Mulheisen's cheek. He cried out and in the same instant squeezed the trigger of the Llama.

Mulheisen had never been an outstanding shooter, usually avoiding his scheduled mandatory qualifying sessions at the range until he couldn't put it off any longer. This shot, however, accompanied by a bright flash and a terrific crack, hit the target.

The man cried out. The weird weapon was thrown high and to the side and landed in the grass. The man struck his back against the study, then recovered. He turned and fled into the dark field, shouting into a handheld device, "I'm hit!" Then he changed course and headed for the marina.

Mulheisen rose to a half-crouch. He looked about intently, in the event that there was another shooter at hand. He saw no one, heard no associated noises. He waited, indecisively. It may have been what saved him.

In the next instant, the back side of the study erupted with a shattering *boom*! The windows blew out of the little structure and fire could be seen inside. Mulheisen swiveled away, taking cover behind the apple tree.

There were no further reports. Smoke billowed up. The structure was on fire. Mulheisen gawked, then raced toward the house. He was arrested by the sound of a helicopter approaching from off the lake, very low. The engine grew louder, seemingly determined to come in for a landing. Then it veered toward the lights of the marina. There, it hovered for a long moment, quite close to landing, although Mulheisen could not adequately see it through the billowing smoke of the study. Then the helicopter rose up and fled away.

Mulheisen ran to the house. The frightened nurse peeked out of the archway to the dining room.

"It's all right," he said. "You okay? My mother?"

She stared at him. "You're bleeding," she said. Then she nodded. "We're all right. Your mother's in bed."

Mulheisen's hands were full. He slipped the Llama into his coat pocket. He went to his mother's room. She appeared to be sleeping soundly, unawakened by any noise like a gunshot or an explosion. He bent closely to be sure she was all right. She was breathing quietly.

He returned to the kitchen. The nurse was filling a kettle, presumably for tea. She stared at him. Mulheisen snatched up the phone and called the fire department. While he explained the location he caught a glimpse of himself in the dark window that looked out on the drive. There was blood all down the left side of his face. The splinter from the intruder's wild shot had opened a small gash. He hadn't even noticed it, but now it stung.

He hung up and went to the sink. He tore a section of paper towel off the roll under the cabinet, wetting it at the faucet and mopping his face clean with the aid of the dim reflection in the glass.

He told the nurse that he'd seen an intruder. "He must have set a bomb," he said. "I don't think there's any danger of it spreading, but I have to check. I'll be right back."

"Should I call the police?" she said.

"No, I'll be right back."

He could see there was no way to save the structure. Flames had already engulfed the roof. The heat was intense and he could not approach very closely. The grass around the construction site was dry, but because of the construction there was only packed dirt. He stamped out a small fire. By now, several neighbors had arrived and they helped him. He could tell them little, except that there had been an explosion, which of course they already knew. One of them, an elderly fellow that Mulheisen didn't know well, declared that it must have been from the propane. There was no propane, of course, but Mulheisen didn't bother to correct that impression. He left the neighbors to deal with the small spots of fire and ran to the marina.

It wasn't that far to the marina, a couple of hundred yards to the parking lot. There was only one person there, a local kid not long out of high school named Jason. Mulheisen knew him vaguely. He was one of those boat-crazy kids who had been hanging around the marina since he was eight until, finally, they'd had to employ him.

Mulheisen asked him about the helicopter.

Jason seemed to think it was pretty cool. "He just swung in here and scooped his guy up like nothing."

"Did you get the identification number on the chopper?" Mulheisen asked.

Jason hadn't, but he knew who it was: "Homeland Security," he said. "They called about twenty minutes before the chopper came in and told me to turn on the lights in the parking lot."

"Were you here alone?"

"Yeah. The other guys went home about seven. I was just finishing up the caulking on Dr. Hubbard's cruiser."

"Did you talk to anybody from the chopper?"

"No. He just dropped in and this guy comes running up and dives in and they bailed."

Jason had seen no markings of any kind on the chopper, which was painted black. He seemed to think that was cool, too.

Mulheisen went back to the construction site. The fire engines had arrived along with a pumper truck. There was a hydrant, but it was too distant. By the time they got water on the burning structure the roof had caved in. They pulled back and shut off the hoses. It was as well to let it burn. The fire chief told Mulheisen that there was nothing to be done. They had soaked the area around the structure to prevent any spread.

"It's lucky there's not much wind," the chief said. He wanted to know, of course, how it had started. Mulheisen told him that there had been some kind of explosion, but other than that he really didn't know. He said nothing about the intruder.

The chief opined that the explosion was probably the windows blowing out. The fire most likely had smoldered inside, stifled by lack of oxygen, but perhaps finally had penetrated a wall. Once it got oxygen, it had simply blown. That was his guess. They'd investigate in the morning. In the meantime, they'd keep the pumper handy to make sure there were no further problems.

Mulheisen thanked him and headed back to the house. He had gone only a few steps when he kicked the rifle, lying in the dark grass. He looked around; no one seemed to be paying attention. He bent down, picked up the rifle, and carried it to the house, setting it inside the back porch.

"You're still bleeding," the nurse said. "I'll fix it."

"It'll be all right," Mulheisen said. He got another piece of paper towel and dabbed at it while he called Wunney at home. He was recounting what had happened when his mother appeared in her dressing gown. Evidently, she'd heard Mulheisen's voice.

"What happened?" she said. "What's wrong with your cheek? Why are all those lights out there?"

Mulheisen asked Wunney to hang on. He covered the mouthpiece of the phone and asked if she was all right.

"Of course I'm all right," she said. "You're the one who sounds upset. Did you hurt yourself?" She reached out a hand toward his cheek, but hesitated.

He explained that he'd encountered a suspicious man outside, but he'd run away. He said he'd fallen, chasing him. Then the fire had started. Presumably, the man had set it.

"Why on earth would he want to burn down your study?" she asked. She didn't seem alarmed, just shook her head at Mul's clumsiness. "Running around in the dark," she said. "You're bound to stumble on something." She offered the opinion that his "suspicious fellow" had probably been one of the Colonel's young men.

"They come by, at odd times," she said. "What did he look like? Was he a small, dark man?"

Mulheisen said no. He realized that she was thinking of Joe Service. "It wasn't one of Tucker's guys. Just some character, snooping around."

She thought it was absurd. Obviously one of Tucker's fellows wouldn't have set a fire. Probably it was a cigarette or something that the carpenters had tossed aside. "They worked until dark, you know," she said. "It might take a while for the fire to get started. You really can't blame Colonel Tucker."

He could see she'd been a little rattled, but she seemed quite composed now. He suggested she have some tea. She said that she didn't want tea. "It'll keep me up. Well, I wanted to talk to you anyway. I remembered something. I wasn't sure it was important enough to call that number. I didn't want to go traipsing down to the marina. They've been busy all day, and into the evening. Horrible racket."

"What was it?" Mulheisen asked. "I'm calling one of the guys who works with Tucker right now." He gestured with the phone.

"Well, go ahead, don't let me bother you," she said.

"No, what was it?" he asked.

She said it was just that she'd remembered about a man she'd seen at the Wards Cove courthouse just before the bombing. She described him briefly and related his warning to her to get out. Mulheisen said that might be important. He urged her to go on into the kitchen and have some tea.

When she'd gone, he told Wunney what she'd said. "It sounds like it could have been Luck," Mulheisen said.

"So, he *was* at the courthouse," Wunney said. "That might have been one of his men at your place, too. The guy's an old chopper pilot, you know, from Vietnam. He must have flown a sniper in—a sniper with a bomb, just in case. He must have got the wrong house!" He laughed.

Mulheisen wondered if they weren't leaping to conclusions. But who else could it have been? The question was: how had Luck learned that Cora had remembered him?

Wunney said, "Who knows? He probably put two and two together and figured that was why you were up there snooping around. He must have figured that you being up there meant your mother was alone. If he was gonna eliminate a witness, now was the time to do it."

Mulheisen wasn't so sure. "He's taking a hell of a chance, flying into that parking lot. If his shooter had been successful he's almost bound to be identified."

"Well, he wasn't," Wunney pointed out. "The Homeland Security gag seems to have worked. It was bold, all right, but he'd probably sussed out this possibility well ahead of time, he just hadn't felt enough pressure to do it. But he didn't scout it out properly, or his man'd never have hit the wrong building. Not too bright, I'd say. The thing is, Mul, you don't know what was going through his mind. A guy who goes to the trouble of blowing up a courthouse to forestall a minor property claim . . . who the hell knows how that kind of mind works? He's compulsive, and impulsive. But the fact that your mother can place him at Wards Cove is pretty much all we need."

Mulheisen could see the point.

Wunney raced on, "Now listen, Tucker has gone to Washington. I got back in time to see him before he left. He's gonna be screwing this whole thing up, wait and see. By the time he gets through conferring with the nobs back there Luck could be in South America. We got a little window here. We have to use it."

"What do you want to do?" Mulheisen asked.

"I'll get some guys out to your place," Wunney said. "They ought to be able to secure the place, no sweat." He paused for a moment, then said, "This is an opportunity, Mul. I'll make a good faith attempt to get hold of Tucker, but I don't expect to locate him tonight. I've still got some authority around here. I'm thinking we oughta haul ass up to Traverse City and bust Luck. I've been around these guys long enough to know that a fait accompli is what's needed. You get the guy in the can, then you let them try to explain everything. We'll grab that chopper. It's bound to have some evidence on board, blood from the guy you popped, that sort of thing. You up for that?"

Mulheisen told him about the rifle he'd retrieved. Wunney agreed that it would be valuable evidence if there were any useful prints.

Mulheisen was cautious about Wunney's enthusiastic plans. "What's my position in all this?"

Wunney laughed. "I'll deputize you, or whatever. I can always say that Tucker told me he wanted you on board, and he did, too. No need to say that he changed his mind. He didn't say anything about that when we met anyway. You're in it because this guy took a shot at you, at your house. This is an emergency . . . Tucker's unavailable . . . time is of the essence. I can get a plane. We can be up there in an hour."

"You can do all that?" Mulheisen said. Evidently, Wunney could. "We'll need a warrant," Mulheisen reminded him.

"No problem. I can have one waiting for us. I know Tucker's crew, where they're staying. No need to let on to them that Tucker doesn't know, or might not go along. Hell, I can get a warrant before we lift off. How quick can you get into town?"

Mulheisen explained that he didn't want to leave before Wunney's men showed up. Wunney agreed to that. "I'll come out there with them. You say the chopper took off from the marina? We'll land there, then. What's that kid's name? I'll call him."

While he waited, Mulheisen had ample opportunity to get the full story from his mother. He told her he'd have to go back out, but he wouldn't leave until some officers arrived to make sure she wasn't bothered further. He got her to go to bed. She was quite tired anyway, and he could tell she had already adopted the attitude that he was making too much of this snooper.

"Don't tell me," she said, "it's police business. Hush-hush. Which reminds me, one of your girlfriends came by to visit this morning. And now that I think of it, I've forgotten her name!" She told him about Helen. Mulheisen couldn't for the life of him figure out who it might have been. The notion of a woman who had been connected with Grootka just left him confused. All he could recall was a young African-American woman—the name Allyson came to mind—but that didn't seem to be connected with the visitor. At the moment he had other concerns and put the whole issue out of his mind.

Joe returned to his vehicle and drove around to the cabin. He needed someplace to hang out while he figured out how to proceed. He was shocked to see Helen and Roman suddenly loom out of the darkness into his headlights.

He skidded to a halt and leaped out, his arms wide. "Honey, am I glad to see—" he started to say, but Helen already had her shotgun leveled at him.

"You son of a bitch!" she shouted. "What the hell was the big idea running out on me?"

"Honey, honey," Joe said, trying to calm her. He looked over her shoulder at Roman, but he was no help. Roman drew back from this impossible situation.

"I didn't run out on you," Joe said. "I was just trying to protect you. I'm sorry, babe, it was a mistake," he pleaded. "I've missed you." He went on with his pleadings until the gun wavered.

There is some kind of strange connection between certain couples, perhaps triggered by familiar gestures or appearances. It may even be an odor. It was kicking in furiously now.

"Honey, I'm so glad to see you," Joe said. "I need your help. Something weird is going on."

"You've got a leaf on your sleeve," she said. "What have you been doing, sleeping in the woods?" She reached out and brushed his shirt.

They fell into each other's arms, both of them nearly sobbing with relief.

Once they got to the cabin, they quickly exchanged notes. Joe was appalled to learn that Helen had inadvertently revealed Mrs. Mulheisen's recovery of her memory, especially since it confirmed what he'd suspected: Luck had been at the Wards Cove site.

It was clear now why Luck had flown so early: he was going to silence Cora Mulheisen. Obviously, they had to warn her.

Joe immediately called Mulheisen's home, but only the nurse was available. She said that Mulheisen was expected at any time, he was on his way. Joe didn't feel that it was useful, for now, to explain the situation to her. He stressed that Mulheisen must call the cabin the minute he got in. It was crucial.

Now all they could do was wait. Joe was at great pains to tell Helen how much he'd missed her, how much he needed her. He explained as fully as he could about why he had kept her out of the loop, to thwart the Colonel. He hadn't felt that she was in any danger from Echeverria, he explained, but he admitted that he'd probably been wrong about that. And he had really missed her help, he assured her. That went a long way toward healing things.

In the meantime, Roman was keeping watch. After a while, when Helen had calmed down, Joe went out to him.

Roman looked at him cautiously. Joe apologized for not meeting him and thanked him for helping Helen. "She's getting something ready to eat," he explained. "Mulheisen should be calling soon. Why don't you go on in? Let me know when Mul calls." After that he began to patrol, without getting too far from the house, in the event that Mulheisen called. There didn't seem to be any interlopers.

The hours ticked by. Joe debated how to proceed. Go to Traverse City and meet Echeverria there? Or wait until Luck returned with him? He felt that it would be best to wait here. Luck was supposed to meet Echeverria about 12:30. If all went well, he could be back by one A.M., easily. But it could well take longer. He didn't know their plans. Possibly, Echeverria wasn't even planning to return with

Luck; maybe he was only meeting him for some unknown purpose, a brief conference, perhaps. As the hours went by and Mulheisen didn't call, Joe began to think that going to Traverse was a better idea. He discussed it with Helen when she brought some food out to him.

Helen thought it was almost certain that Luck would return with Echeverria. But "almost" was not a good plan, she conceded.

Finally, at 11:30, they felt they had to move. Joe gathered his firepower and doled out what he couldn't use. He would drive to Traverse City while Helen and Roman would remain. He was about to leave when Mulheisen called.

"Man, you left it kind of late," Joe said. "I'm almost positive that Luck is on his way to your place. Somehow, he's tumbled to the fact that your mother now remembers seeing him at Wards Cove."

"He's been here," Mulheisen said. "I wonder how he knew?"

"Who knows? Maybe Tucker tipped him off. It looks to me like that was why he was so eager to rope you in. He wanted an inside track on whatever she remembered." Joe rapidly sketched out what he'd learned. He made no mention of Helen or Roman.

Mulheisen listened patiently, then said, "I didn't say anything to him. I didn't know myself until a short while ago. But maybe he had some other source." He went on to explain what had happened on his end. He told Joe that he and Wunney would be leaving for Traverse City as quickly as they could manage. He wasn't sure if they'd be in time to intercept Echeverria, but it was possible, he thought. "Hell," he said, "if we're in time, maybe we can snap them all up on the spot." He explained that federal agents would be on hand. If Mulheisen and Wunney couldn't get there, maybe the agents could do it. This operation was looking better.

Joe hung up. Helen saw the look on his face. "What's up?" she asked.

Joe lifted his hands, a gesture of carelessness. "That's it," he said. "We can go home."

21

Cur Tale

Joe's infor-
mation had removed any remaining doubt about what the purpose
of the intruder's visit had been. Particularly interesting was Joe's speculation that Tucker might have known about Luck's presence at Wards
Cove. Mulheisen wasn't so sure of that, but he hadn't debated the
point with Joe. The conversation wasn't quite satisfactory for Joe, he
knew, but there didn't seem any help for it. There didn't appear to be
a role in this operation for him. The only suggestion Mulheisen had
been able to offer was that it might be a good thing if he was able to
monitor Luck's home base, just in case the Traverse City situation
didn't succeed. Joe hadn't asked for any clarification of what "monitor" might mean and Mulheisen hadn't volunteered any.

Not so pleasant, however, was the ambiguous nature of Joe's
status in the presence of federal agents. Obviously, Mulheisen had
no notion. Nor could he speak for how Wunney might react to Joe's
presence.

The problem was clear enough, but neither Joe nor Mulheisen
had been willing to discuss it. What was the point? It wasn't up to
them. He'd left Joe with the implication that, if he were prudent,
he might want to disappear now. Let the feds handle this.

When he hung up there was nothing for Mulheisen to do but wait for Wunney. In the event, Wunney and his men didn't arrive for almost an hour. It was close to 12:30 before he heard the chopper come in. Shortly, Wunney appeared at the back door, accompanied by a couple of youthful officers. He looked uncharacteristically animated, almost enthused. The young agents made themselves at home and Mulheisen accompanied Wunney back to the marina. On the way, he related Joe Service's news.

Wunney glanced at his watch and swore. "Hell, we've missed them, probably. But we can call ahead. Maybe they're still there."

They called from the chopper as soon as it lifted off. "They're on their way to the airport," Wunney told Mulheisen once he'd gotten through. He turned back to the cell phone and Mulheisen listened while Wunney yelled over the noise of the engine, exhorting the agents to "bust their asses" to intercept the meeting of Echeverria and Luck. "Approach with extreme caution," he bellowed. "Luck is armed to the teeth and he's got a killer in the jump seat."

"All right!" he said when he hung up. "If those mopes get their butts in gear, this could be simpler than we hoped."

Wunney explained to Mulheisen what he'd laid on. "We'll go to Selfridge," he said. This was a nearby air national guard base. Wunney had arranged for a jet to stand by. It would fly them to the Traverse City airport. The Homeland Security agents would be waiting there—with Luck and Echeverria, if all went well. If not, if the intercept failed, they could drive to Queensleap, which would take them about a half hour.

"It might be just as well if Tucker's crew misses them," Wunney said. "There could be some fireworks. Luck's place is probably a safer place for that."

Mulheisen had to agree. He was impressed with Wunney's sense of authority and organization. For the operation Wunney had acquired a couple of blue jackets that had HOMELAND SECURITY/ SPECIAL AGENT boldly emblazoned on them, as well as a couple of baseball caps similarly marked. He also had official government forms, identifying Mulheisen as an employee, a special agent. They were signed by some figure that Mulheisen had never heard of, but Wunney assured him that they'd hold up. They authorized Mulheisen as a federal officer, empowered to make arrests, to carry out official functions, and so on. He was even authorized to carry arms— Wunney handed him a Colt .45 automatic. Others were enjoined not to interfere with the performance of his official duty.

"And here's the signed warrant for the arrest of one Martin Parvis Luck, aka M. P. Luckenbach," Wunney said. "It's all properly authorized."

The aircraft waiting for them at Selfridge was a C-20, a rather fancy administrative jet, built by Gulfstream, and peacefully quiet after the racket of the chopper.

Mulheisen said, "Wunney, you're a wonder boy."

"This Homeland outfit has anything they want," Wunney explained. "This plane was flown in for us from some base in Ohio."

"I can't help thinking the crap is going to hit the fan when Tucker finds out," Mulheisen said, settling into a plush seat and strapping in. The aircraft started to roll almost immediately.

"You can't think like that," Wunney said. "That's tomorrow. This is tonight. By tomorrow, if what your pal Service says proves out, Tucker's gonna have to figure out some way to say it was all his idea. Otherwise, his ass is in a sling. This will be a real test of his bureaucratic survival skills."

"I get the feeling that Tucker's right at home in the bureaucratic jungle," Mulheisen said. "I won't be surprised if he comes out smelling like a rose."

Wunney nodded. "Maybe. But it could be more than a career at stake this time. It could be his personal freedom."

As soon as they had climbed to cruising altitude, Wunney got on the phone to the agents in Traverse City. This time, when he hung up, he shrugged philosophically. "They missed him," he said. "They've seized Echeverria's plane, but apparently Luck was waiting and as soon as the plane parked, Echeverria got in the chopper and split. Just as well, I think."

The flight to Traverse City wasn't long, but Wunney got the flight attendant to serve them coffee and sandwiches. He discussed how they'd deal with the agents up there. "It shouldn't be a big problem," he said. "Just let me do the talking. The important thing is not to let them assert themselves. They'll try to take over. Technically, I suppose one of them would outrank me, but since I'm coming in with you and all the info, the impetus will be with us. Just back me up, and don't defer to these clowns. They're used to taking orders. The idea is we sweep into the place, snatch Luck and Echeverria and whoever else we can find, and bring them all back. An important thing will be to grab that chopper and impound it."

"Don't forget Hook," Mulheisen said. "He'd be the grand prize."

Wunney nodded. "Probably worth the op all by himself," he said. "Well, might as well sit back and enjoy the ride." He called to the attendant for more coffee. "Bring me up to date on the layout up there, will you, Mul?"

"So that's it," Joe said to Helen and Roman. "We're in the way. Worse, we could get swept up with the rest of these clowns." He tried to toss it off as a joke: "Imagine, getting busted for trying to do your duty. That's what comes of messing around with the Home Guard."

Helen wasn't amused, but she shrugged. "We're here. I feel like an idiot for tipping off that creep. I think we ought to reconnoiter. Who knows how these guys will react if Luck gets nabbed?

It might be a good idea to stop them from destroying evidence, files and that kind of stuff. Besides, anything could go wrong at the airport, you know."

Joe was looking at his Remington, the H&K. He felt the anticlimax deeply. Not given to depression, however, he bucked up and said, "Sure. Why not? Let's take a look."

Roman didn't quite roll his eyes but he did sigh. He heaved himself up out of his chair and said, "Gimme the Stoner rifle, eh? How many rounds you got?" He filled the cavernous pockets of his overcoat with extra clips and walked out with them.

It took them all of fifteen minutes of careful walking in the dry leaves to get to the area near the hill. They had seen no one. The wind was kicking up a bit, tossing the tops of the trees, filling the air with tumbling leaves. It was quite dark, an overcast night. They gathered on a small rise, well back from the clearing where the chopper would have to land.

Helen pointed out the large lights that would flood the area when the hill opened and the chopper came in. "If it comes in," she said. "If the federales don't sweep them up in town."

"That's the thing," Joe agreed. "If the bird comes home, if they weren't intercepted, they might still be feeling the heat of pursuit." He peered through the darkness at the hill. It was as quiet as any other part of the forest; the only sound, apart from the occasional hoot of an owl, was the rushing of the wind in the treetops.

"We could get closer," he suggested. "It might be possible, in fact, to get inside." There was a single pickup truck parked on the road near the hill. The entry to the hill was blind, they knew, but they hadn't seen anyone go in or out. Joe thought that there must be some guys patrolling. It made sense. "But maybe," he said, "these Huleys don't have any sense." He explained briefly who the Huleys were, leaving out any mention of barmaids.

Helen didn't see any point to getting inside. "If Luck comes, the whole face of that hill will open."

"But there'll be too much light, too much activity," Joe said. "I'd like to know what they've got in there, besides a retractable launchpad for a chopper. These guys could have tons of explosives, rockets maybe. Hell, they could have a tank in there. If the feds are in hot pursuit, it could be a slaughter."

"Are you sure you aren't just spoiling for some action?" Helen said. "The feeling I get is that all three of us might more wisely be heading down the road toward Cadillac."

She was not wrong, Joe knew. "If both of you agree," he said, "we can leave right now. Sometime down the road I'll have to deal with Echeverria. This may be the chance."

Helen didn't bother to look at him. It was dark, anyway. What could be learned from a face in shadow? She listened to his voice. She knew that, Echeverria or no Echeverria, Joe was excited by the prospect of some action.

"There's no reason not to stay and at least see if Luck returns," she said. She felt excited as well.

Neither of them concerned themselves with Roman. Apparently, they were confident that he would do as they did. Roman didn't comment.

"If I'm going in," Joe said, "now's the time. I think it might be a good idea." When the other two didn't respond, he said, "Just don't shoot me when the balloon goes up."

Helen said, "When, and if, the balloon goes up, what are we supposed to do? Watch?"

Joe said it was impossible to say. They would have to simply be patient and calculate their actions according to events. The important thing, obviously, would be to prevent Luck and/or Echeverria from leaving before the feds arrived. At some point, assuming that the feds arrived and he hadn't reappeared, they would have to with-

draw to some safe location and wait. In other words, leave it all to
the feds.

With that, he departed. Five minutes later he was inside the
hill. It proved to be simple. One of the Huleys came out for a smoke
break. Joe dropped him with a chop. A few seconds later he entered.

The interior was essentially a large Quonset hut with earth
mounded over it. The entry was a narrow passage that descended
by concrete stairs, six steps down, to a spacious dayroom with a low
ceiling. It was furnished with cots, shelves, worktables, desks, display boards, a couple of computers, a television set, refrigerators,
cooking facilities, plumbing, and so on. The larger area, which had
been revealed by the opened hangar doors, was not apparent from
this location. Presumably, if a visitor were brought in here, he would
likely be permitted to see only this aspect of the interior. There
would be no reason to suspect that beyond the dayroom and an
adjoining storage room, no doubt an armory and ammo magazine,
there was a much larger area.

There was no one in the dayroom. Joe retreated and hauled
in the unconscious form of the man he'd dropped. He tumbled him
into one of the cots, with some effort, and trussed him with his own
belts and gear, then covered him with a blanket. Then he went to
the steel door that led into the hangar. The other men—there were
a half dozen—were lounging about the plywood-sheathed platform,
mounted on a track. They were talking among themselves, not so
much arguing or disputing as spiritedly discussing some familiar
sports topic—evidently, a high school basketball team, from the
sound of it. One of them, a rangy fellow leaning against a tool bench
along the far wall, was loudly expounding and demonstrating certain moves. The others occasionally asserted their opinions. They
seemed in good spirits.

Mounted above the long workbench, a bank of radio receivers
uttered occasional remarks, obviously from normal aircraft traffic.

The Huleys mainly ignored it, although Joe noticed that whenever a voice initiated a comment with a call sign, a couple of the men would momentarily turn toward it. When it proved not to be addressed to them, or to concern them, they immediately ignored the message. Clearly, the men were waiting for a call from Luck.

Joe returned to the dayroom, checked his still comatose victim, and then went into the armory/magazine. This room, he saw, was basically a poured-concrete vault, complete with a reinforced concrete roof. The wiring for lights was all metal conduit stuff, secured to wooden members embedded in the concrete itself, obviously cast in. There were also ventilation tubes cast into the ceiling, white six-inch PVC tubes, which presumably extended up through the soil above. Probably, the whole room had been cast in a single unit and moved into place with a crane, then covered over with several feet of soil.

Much more interesting was what was stored inside. There was stuff here he was unable to identify. Besides rifles and ammo there were some rocket-propelled grenade launchers. He'd used these before, specifically to attack the aircraft of Echeverria. There were also metal containers of hand grenades. And in one corner there was an array of tall, slender rockets. It was likely that the launchers for these were mounted on vehicles, but he hadn't seen them on his earlier reconnoiter. They looked like they had a considerable range. Joe was unfamiliar with most of the armament here. Possibly some of it could be mounted on the chopper.

Suddenly, Joe heard someone enter the dayroom. He hid.

"What the hell?" the man said. Then he went back out. Joe raced to the door in time to hear the man call to the others, "That fuckin' Harley is sacked out!"

The others hooted. Someone shouted, "Don't wake him! Let Imp find him!" There was laughter. The man went on across the hangar to join his comrades.

Joe returned to the storeroom. He filled his pockets with grenades and, slinging his H&K across one shoulder and the shotgun across the other, he lugged three RPG launchers outside. He laid them down in the brush, then made a quick tour around the exterior of the hill. On the far side there was an open Jeep with a .50-caliber machine gun mounted on a stand in the back. Two Huleys were sitting in the front seats, smoking cigarettes and talking.

He doubled back to recover his RPG launchers. He was almost there when every light in the place went on. Huge floodlights lit up a cleared area. Machinery began to grind and whine and the massive doors of the face of the hill began to part and roll back, obviously running on heavy tracks buried in the earth. The lights created virtual daylight before the vast maw of the opening hillside. Joe raced for cover.

In the end, he decided to simply scramble up the grassy hill itself, until he was perched, breathless, among some pine saplings near the top. He'd had to drop one of the RPGs, but he still had two. This spot, at the very crest of the hill, provided an excellent view. He could see inside the now opened hangar, where the men were busily running out the mechanically driven telescoping track that bore the plywood-sheathed landing platform. On the other side, he could see the Jeep start up, someone standing in the back to man the cannon and another pulling forward to a position from which the gunner could cover the landing zone.

Overhead, he could hear the approaching *whomp, whomp, whomp* of the chopper. Then its landing lights went on, and the bird came whirling down out of night sky. The ground crew walked forward, one of the men brandishing the twin red-light torches of a wing walker, gesturing toward the landing platform. Another had pushed out a small cart on which was mounted a tall, flexible pole bearing a wind sock, positioning it to one side but well illuminated for the benefit of the pilot.

The chopper came in very fast, very adroitly, and settled onto the platform. The pilot cut the power and the rotors began to slow. The men rushed forward to apply hand clamps to the skids of the chopper. Almost immediately the doors of the chopper flew open and Luck dropped to the platform. Two other men, one of them clutching an arm, hopped out the other side. The third man was wearing a suit. Joe assumed that was Echeverria. He held a white hat down on his head and stooped, skipping nimbly off the platform to the ground. One of the Huleys helped him dismount. Another helped the wounded man down. Echeverria and the wounded man—Joe assumed from his stature that it was Hook—walked together into the shelter of the hangar.

Luck was bellowing, "Get 'er inside, quick! Quick! On the double! Get those doors closed!"

Everybody ran to comply. The huge doors began to grind shut even as the track bearing the chopper on its platform started to retreat. The blades had stopped. A man was clambering up to restrain them.

Joe thought, This won't do. He squatted on his perch, armed his weapon, took aim at the track, and fired. The angle wasn't good, too steep, but he'd corrected for it. The rocket whooshed through the night, struck the front of the platform, and exploded. The blast dislodged the helicopter, which tumbled sideways, off the platform, despite the restraints. Joe tossed the launcher over the side and it tumbled down inside the hangar.

He snatched up the other. The doors were continuing to close but, of course, now they wouldn't be able to close, because the retractable launchpad was stopped. One side of his brain considered what would happen when the powerful motors driving the doors ground up against the pad. The other side of his mind was concerned with the Jeep and its heavy machine gun.

They knew he was on the roof, of course. The Jeep swung out into the clearing, slewed around, and faced the opening of the hill. The man on the gun was peering up into the darkness of the top of the hill, where Joe was. Joe gave him something to aim at: he fired his second RPG at the Jeep. It didn't hit it but it did not miss by much. The cannon thundered, spraying bullets wildly, as the driver tried to evade any further RPGs. Joe unslung the H&K, racked it, and began to descend.

The back of the hill was quite dark and covered with saplings. Joe slipped down rapidly. He could hear a lot of shooting going on from out front. By the time he was halfway down, he'd decided that he was outgunned here. Now was a very good time to take to the woods. Still, a notion struck him. He recalled the PVC ventilator tubes he'd noticed in the vault ceiling. He began to search about for the point where they would exit in the hillside.

It took too long to find. The Huleys were rapidly moving about the perimeter of the hill, trying to trap him. But then they began to take fire from Helen and Roman, who had separated and were firing from the woods. The Huleys were forced to respond. In the respite that provided, Joe finally stumbled on a weathered wooden box with louvered panels. This must be the covering for the ventilator tubes. Joe tried to figure out how to remove it, to get at the tubes, but it was securely anchored. At last, he simply kicked in the louvers. The framework gave way and he kicked the whole thing aside.

He pulled the pins on three hand grenades and dropped them, one after the other, down the pipe. Then he scrambled down the hill, tumbling in his haste and tearing his clothes, even his cheek, on the branches of saplings, in order to get the hell off that mini-mountain before it blew. In the event, he got to the ground and reached the perimeter road before it went.

He didn't hear the grenades themselves, or at least he didn't think he did. But whatever blew up inside there was pretty impressive. The hillside bulged, chunks of dirt flew, finally a crack opened in the earth, more explosions rocked and reverberated, and finally a spectacular ball of fire spewed out of the side of the hill, caught the trees on fire, and was followed by a thunderous, growling, crackling, rumbling blast that knocked Joe down.

He was on his feet in a flash and began running. He had no idea of the direction at first. Then he began to arc through the woods, his way lit by the flames behind him, headed toward the river. He caught up to Helen and Roman before they reached the cabin.

They could hear sirens somewhere beyond the trees behind them. They ran through the woods to their vehicles. "Follow me," Joe yelled, leaping into his truck. The other two pushed the old Cadillac at a lunging pace along the river road, following the leaping and bounding pickup truck. When they got to the highway they still didn't stop, driving on to Manton. There was a bar open there.

Over a cold beer, Joe advised his companions, "Let Mul sort it out. Who's dead and who's not. I don't care. For now."

Mulheisen was describing the layout of Luck's place to Wunney—the guards, the gate. They had no idea how many guards Luck might have, or if they'd put up any resistance.

Wunney didn't think they would. "From what I've seen of the reports on Luck's activities, most of his supporters are local sympathizers, not 'soldiers.' Obviously, if we're right and the operation at your house was engineered by Luck, he's got some guys who are willing to trade fire, some kind of trained grunts, but not overly bright from the looks of it. Those aren't the ones who are listed as members of his patriot group. He's probably got no more than a dozen grunts, is my guess, and at any time he might have only half of those around him. But he'll be on his toes. He knows we're bound to react to this strike at your house. He's got to figure we're on to him. So there could be resistance. I just don't think a bunch of backwoods guys playing soldier will offer much. I could be wrong, though. We sure as hell don't want another Ruby Ridge or Waco."

Mulheisen pointed out that there was a major difference here: Luck had initiated the violence with his strike. Still, it was obviously important to minimize the potential for explosive reaction.

Mulheisen wondered if it didn't make sense to come in the back way, from McVey's cabin. They debated these and other possibilities as the plane rushed through the night, high above the clouds. It seemed the plane had hardly leveled off at cruising altitude before they felt it tilt to descend.

Wunney remarked, "It musta been kinda weird hanging out with Joe Service, eh?"

Mulheisen had tried to put Service out of mind, not very successfully. He thought about him now, wondering what he was up to. Joe could take care of himself, he thought, and he'd have to, because there wasn't anything Mulheisen could do for him.

"Joe's got his own agenda," he said.

"We'll have to do something about Service when this is over," Wunney said.

Mulheisen didn't think that likely, but he didn't say so.

"I'm sorry about your study, Mul. But you'll be able to rebuild. You had insurance, didn't you?"

Mulheisen thought it would be covered under his existing home insurance.

"It was lucky you hadn't moved anything in it," Wunney observed.

"You know, I'm thinking," Mulheisen said. "Maybe I ought to get a place up north. A fishing cabin."

"That's the spirit," Wunney said. "All right, buckle up. We're going in."

"I can't help feeling there's more to it," Mulheisen said, as the aircraft turned on final.

"What do you mean?" Wunney asked.

"From what I've learned about Tucker, he's a devious, complicated man. This operation has the earmarks of that kind of thinking. I have a feeling he was after something bigger, all along. He protected Luck, but he may have just been using Luck to get to somebody else."

"Now you're thinking like Tucker," Wunney said. It wasn't clear if he meant that approvingly. "Anyway, we'll soon find out."

A half hour later they were standing on a county road, watching the combined volunteer fire departments of eight townships battle a small forest fire with the help of the Forest Service. They seemed to have it well under control. No buildings had been burned; even the tinderbox barn had been saved. But ground zero could not be approached yet. There were still occasional explosions and isolated rounds of ammunition were firing off.

Wunney conferred with one of the agents, Dinah Schwind. When she left, he said to Mulheisen, "We've got what's left of the hill cordoned off, and the buildings. Special forensic crews are coming in. They'll start sifting the ashes as soon as the embers cool. But it doesn't look like anybody got out of the bunker, or whatever it was, that blew."

Mulheisen left Wunney to coordinate with these details and he wandered off into the woods, where firefighters were still dousing small fires. He wore his "Homeland Security" jacket and hat for identification. When he had the opportunity, he'd question a firefighter about the possible presence of individuals whom they couldn't identify. The men working—felling trees, directing equipment, clearing fire lanes—were mostly young and exuberant. They didn't get much of this kind of action and they enjoyed demonstrating their techniques, which they had learned and practiced for years.

But no one could recall seeing any odd personnel wandering about, or fleeing.

A first-aid station had been set up at Luck's house to deal with injuries to the firefighters. They hadn't seen any survivors of the horrendous explosion and subsequent fire. Old doctor Hundly was there, bandaging burns and sprained ankles. He nodded to Mulheisen but they didn't converse.

Mulheisen skirted the ground-zero site and wandered toward the river. As he'd expected, there were plenty of cops at the river road and near Charlie McVey's cabin, which was unharmed. McVey himself was standing on the deck, surveying all the activity.

"By golly, Mul," Charlie exclaimed, "looks like ol' Imp has bought it this time! I wouldn't of wished it, but damn, he went out with a bang! C'mon in and have a drink. I seen you left some good stuff for me."

He admired Mulheisen's jacket. "I knew you was somebody," he said.

Mulheisen stood with him in the kitchen, sipping scotch. He affirmed McVey's supposition that no one had apparently survived. He asked if McVey had been aware that Luck had been flying a helicopter out of the area.

"Well, you know, folks talked about hearing a chopper," Charlie said, "but no one took it seriously. The Forest Service and the Fish and Game use 'em, and the Coast Guard comes in and out of the area all the time from the station in Traverse City. Their route takes 'em over this way if they're headed for Frankfort or Lake Michigan. So no one paid it too much mind."

"Did you imagine that Luck might have all those explosives in there?"

"Well, he was all's doing something with Cats and stuff, working on his place. I never paid no mind. I don't think anyone did. But lord, he must have had a regular ammo dump in there!"

"He did, apparently," Mulheisen said. "Some of the agents who know about these things said he must have stockpiled tons of explosives. They estimate the blast was bigger than Oklahoma City. But tell me, have you searched this property?"

McVey hadn't. He'd been at home when he heard the blast, as far away as Summit City. He had tuned in his scanner and heard the fire departments responding, so he'd hustled straight over to the cabin. "They was cops here when I came in," he said. "State police and the sheriff's. They let me on in. No one's been in the house. No damage a'tall. I was afraid a window might of been broke on the woods side, from the blast, but they was all okay. The door was unlocked," he added accusingly, "but no harm done. Tell you the truth, I was more worried about them big windows in the front. Them puppies run a purty penny."

"Let's take a tour," Mulheisen said.

A quick tour of the interior didn't reveal anything. Charlie picked up the bottle of scotch and led him outside. They walked around the house. There were three windows on that side, all of them intact and locked, except for the bathroom window, near the back.

"The bathroom window was open," Charlie said. "But you know how it is, a feller goes in there and sometimes the fan don't quite clear it out, so he opens the window. Must of forgot to close it when you left."

"I confess I didn't close up the place," Mulheisen said. "Joe, my, ah, associate, did. I should have stopped and checked it. Sorry." It occurred to him that Joe had reentered the cabin, at least following the takeoff of the helicopter—he'd talked to him on the phone from there. Presumably, he'd left too abruptly to bother closing up again, probably following the blast. Mulheisen didn't say anything about that to Charlie.

They stood outside in the dark for a moment, sniffing the smell of burning wood and leaves. Mulheisen noticed a low structure to the rear, some sixty feet away. "What's that?" he asked.

"That's the ol' pump house," Charlie said. "Ol' Tom Adams put that in. It sits over the well. Sumbitch used to freeze up ever' winter. When I took over, I put in a submersible pump. That was the end of that problem. I should of just jerked that ol' mess out of there but it didn't seem worth it."

Mulheisen wandered over toward the little house. Basically, only the roof stood above the ground. The door was down in a shallow well with steps. Mulheisen looked at it. It appeared to have been jimmied; the hasp where a padlock hung looked broken to Mulheisen. He called back to Charlie, clearly, "Well, it looks all right. Let's go."

They reentered the cabin through the rear door. Mulheisen stopped there and looked back toward the pump house. He said to Charlie, "I think someone's in there."

Charlie peered over his shoulder out the window of the door. The pump house entrance was dimly visible in the dark. "Who do you think? Imp?"

"Could be," Mulheisen said, "but I doubt it. More likely Joe. Whoever it is, he'll want to get the hell out of there while it's still dark, if he's not injured."

"I'll get the troopers," Charlie said, excited.

"No, no," Mulheisen said, stopping him. "Relax. What you don't want is a bunch of armed men in the dark, ready to shoot. Let's just wait."

He took the bottle of scotch and uncapped it, then took a quick swig. He handed it back to Charlie. "You wait here," he said.

He opened the door quietly and stepped out. He pulled out a cigar and clipped it, then lit it. When it was well lit, he walked softly back toward the pump house, but angling off to the right. About thirty feet away and well to the right of the door well, he took up a position next to a mature pine tree. It gave him excellent cover. He stood and waited, puffing occasionally on the cigar. He hoped this wouldn't take long. Charlie was almost bound to alert the troopers out front if Mulheisen didn't return soon. He was counting on the hidden fugitive realizing that a quick move was in order.

As he'd expected, he hadn't long to wait. First there was a soft scrape as the door was opened. Mulheisen cupped the cigar to hide the glow of the lit tip and drew out the .45 that Wunney had given him. In a moment, the head of a man appeared above the rim of the door well. In the darkness, Mulheisen could not identify him, but he appeared to have a full head of black or dark hair. If it was Joe, Mulheisen hoped he wasn't foolish enough to shoot first.

The man crept up the stairs. He didn't appear to be armed, or at least no weapon was evident. At the top of the stairs, the man moved around the pump house in a crouch, toward the river—away from Mulheisen.

Mulheisen stepped quickly toward him, using the roof of the pump house for cover. The roof was low enough that Mulheisen was able to look over it when he got close.

Captain Hook was crouched beyond, his back to Mulheisen, peering intently toward the house. Mulheisen leaned on the roof of the pump house, resting his hand on the ridge and holding the .45 in plain sight.

"Stay still," Mulheisen said quietly.

Hook spun around. His face was smeared with soot. When he realized who it was, he straightened up and lifted his arms slowly.

"I am unarmed," Hook said. He smiled wryly. "So I was right. You are not a retired policeman."

"You have the right to remain silent," Mulheisen said.

Fifteen minutes later, Wunney arrived.

When Hook had been bundled away in a trooper's car, Wunney and Mulheisen stood in the yard, talking. Mulheisen said, "I wonder if these warrants will work on Tucker."

"What an interesting idea," Wunney said. He sniffed the night air. "Love the smell of pines, even when they're a little scorched. When I got the call, I figured you had run your faithful hound to ground. But Hook's better. I guess Joey tucked his tail between his legs and ran, probably as soon as you said you were on your way."

"Think so?" Mulheisen looked around. "He's a wary pup, for sure. But he's no man's dog."